Kathryn started her working life as a retail pharmacist but soon realised trying to decipher doctors' handwriting wasn't for her. In 2011, backed by her family, she left the world of pharmaceutical science to begin life as a self-employed writer.

She lives with two teenage boys and a husband who asks every Valentine's Day whether he has to bother buying a card again this year (yes, he does) so the romance in her life is all in her head.

@KathrynFreeman1
@kathrynfreeman
kathrynfreeman.co.uk

Also by Kathryn Freeman

The New Guy
Strictly Come Dating

Up Close and Personal

Kathryn Freeman

OneMoreChapter

One More Chapter
a division of HarperCollins*Publishers*
The News Building
1 London Bridge Street
London SE1 9GF

www.harpercollins.co.uk

This paperback edition 2020

First published in Great Britain in ebook format by
HarperCollins*Publishers* 2020

A catalogue record for this book
is available from the British Library

Ebook ISBN: 978-0-00-836583-7
Paperback ISBN: 978-0-00-836584-4

Set in Birka by Palimpsest Book Production Ltd, Falkirk
Stirlingshire

Printed and bound in Great Britain

Chapter 1

Zac straightened his already straight silk tie, checked his cufflinks were still in position and brushed the non-existent fluff off his Hardy Amies Saville Row suit. Slotting his smile into place, he accepted the proffered glass of champagne and stepped into the impressive ballroom of Heatherden Hall, the nineteenth-century, Grade II-listed mansion at the heart of Pinewood Studios.

As his eyes skimmed the room, noting the faces he knew, he raised the glass to his lips. Dutch courage. His job title might read *actor*, his online profile might say *film star*, but he wasn't the gregarious type and never felt entirely comfortable in film industry crowds. Today's rather ostentatious gathering had been put on by Vision Films to celebrate thirty years in the business. As it was the film company he was currently contracted to, he'd felt obliged to show his face. Now all he had to do was find the key people to show his face to, and he could be out of here . . .

What the hell?

Someone careered into him from behind, and champagne that should have been fizzing delicately in his glass now began to run down the front of his white Turnbull & Asser tailored shirt.

'Shit.'

A pair of hands flew out to grab his arms, presumably for support, and the resulting jolt knocked the remaining contents of his glass down his jacket.

'Oh, my flaming God, I'm so sorry.' Two horrified brown eyes locked onto his. 'I knew I shouldn't have worn heels, but my niece was adamant I couldn't wear my boots with this dress. They wouldn't have got caught in the flipping carpet though, would they.'

'Err, no?'

Perhaps he should have been more annoyed – champagne was a treat when swallowed, but plastered against his skin, not so much. Yet it was hard to muster any anger when the person he should be directing it against was so apologetic. So amusing. And so . . . striking.

Her hand flew to her face. 'Holy moly, listen to me carping on about my shoes while you've got champagne dripping down . . . well, dripping where I'm sure you don't want it dripping. Hang on a sec.'

Bemused, and yes, dripping, though perhaps a more accurate description would be *sticking*, he watched as she shuffled off to one of the grandly set tables and snatched a few of the carefully folded napkins.

'Here.' She started to wipe the napkin down his sodden chest, then paused and gave him a wry smile. 'I'm guessing you'd be better doing this yourself.'

'Maybe.' Fighting a smile, he nodded down to the napkin. 'But you seem to be making an excellent job of it.'

'You think so?'

Chocolate-brown eyes sparked back at him, amusement in their depths, and he found he was unable to drag his own eyes away. Short dark hair framed a face that wasn't beautiful – it was far too interesting to have such a mundane label attached to it. Sharp edges, yet softened with an easy, unaffected smile.

Abruptly she withdrew her hand. 'You know what, I have a far better idea. Wait here.'

As if he could do anything else. Enthralled, he waited, waving away those who approached him, explaining he'd see them later, he was waiting for someone. She returned a few minutes later, brandishing a T-shirt.

'Instead of Turnbull & Asser I get to wear,' he peered at the logo, 'Pinewood Studios?'

'It'll be a good look on you. Everyone will be after one by the end of the evening.' A soft sigh escaped her. 'I really am sorry, though. Can I get your shirt dry-cleaned?' She winced as she saw the splashes on his jacket. 'Err, all of you dry-cleaned?'

'No, it's fine.' He could see she was about to leave and realised with a start that he wasn't ready to say goodbye. Talking to her seemed infinitely more preferable than polite conversation with studio bosses and fellow actors. 'You could help me find somewhere to change, though.'

She gave him a wary look. 'This isn't some sort of trick, is it?'

'Trick?'

'You know, we head off to find a quiet room and when I'm not looking you produce a bottle of wine and pour it all over me to get your own back.'

He searched her eyes, trying to get a read on whether she was joking or not. He couldn't. They were seemingly bottomless pools of rich, smooth brown. 'I can think of far better things to do to you in a quiet room than douse you in alcohol.'

Surprise flickered before her guard came down. 'Oh no, that's not . . . we're not.' She huffed. 'Look, I'll show you to the gents'.'

Great. Now she had him down as some entitled, pervy actor – that's if she even recognised him. 'I was hoping for somewhere a little more salubrious,' he ventured.

'Salubrious?' She wrinkled her nose; slim and attractive, like the rest of her. 'Is that a fancy way of saying a room without urinals?'

'It's my way of saying I'd rather not strip off in front of urinating males, yes.'

'Okay.' Her face relaxed a little. 'I guess that makes sense. And my role in this shirt changing exercise would be what, exactly?'

'Help me find a room. Be on the lookout while I change.' Keep talking to me, he added silently. And flash me another of those amazing smiles.

'Fine.'

They began to walk towards the grand wooden archway he'd entered from. 'Which way, left or right?'

'Wow, you're entrusting me with this huge decision?' Her gaze came back to his. 'You realise if I get it wrong, you'll be wearing champagne all evening?'

'That's true,' he agreed soberly. 'Yet you're the one who's got me into this pickle. It seems only right you're the one to get me out of it.'

'This pickle?' She burst out laughing. 'I guess that's one way to describe it. Alcohol is a good preservative, after all. And if we don't get you out of that shirt soon, you might literally be pickled.'

Her laughter fluttered across his skin, leaving tingles in its wake. God, there was nothing sexier than a woman who liked to laugh. 'I like the *we* in that sentence,' he murmured, unable to help himself. His third attempt at flirting. And this time, he couldn't have been more obvious.

For the second time that evening, Kat stumbled over her feet. The first had launched her headlong into the one man she'd come here to see. Yet not be seen by.

Not only had she failed spectacularly at that, he was – unbelievably – flirting with her. The comment about the quiet room had been shocking enough. The last statement, delivered with a low, sexy murmur, had been hot enough to weaken her knees and make her lose her footing.

Awkward did not begin to describe it.

Heavens above, he was gorgeous, though. Some actors, and in her line of work she'd met a few, disappointed in the flesh. They were less; diminished somehow from how they appeared on the big screen.

Zac Edwards was more. Much, much more. Those green eyes of his didn't just captivate, they snared a woman, making her want to keep on looking at him. Then there was the quirky smile, a sort of tilt of his lips, that had her unwittingly not only smiling back at him but, honest to God, melting.

Yet this man was off limits, out of bounds. Someone she

could not afford to flirt with, no matter how much her hormones demanded her to.

He was also someone she could not afford to piss off.

'I meant *we* as in me on lookout and you on stripping.' Hot damn, that wasn't how she'd meant to phrase it. And the sexy raised eyebrow thing he was doing now, together with the flash of heat in his eyes, didn't help stop the showreel that had begun in her head.

'When I'm doing this stripping,' his gaze drifted across her face before zeroing in on her eyes, 'where will you be, exactly?'

She'd never felt so flushed, so flustered. Kat Parker, tough as nails, except, apparently, when it came to Zac Edwards. 'I'll be outside the door. The firmly shut door.'

'How . . . disappointing.'

Was he aware of the effect he was having on her? He had to be. The amusement dancing in his eyes suggested this must happen to him all the time. The realisation was enough to cool her heated skin. Forcing her gaze away, she hurried forward as fast as the annoying heels would carry her. 'Let's try in here.' She didn't know the building all that well, but she'd visited enough to know this was the smaller of the two boardrooms.

It was empty inside, bar the table and chairs and the stunning wood-panelling. 'Okay, then. You go and . . . do your thing—'

'Strip, you mean?'

That humour again, and the small smile that was possibly a smirk. Yes, he knew exactly what he was doing. 'Swap shirts, yes.' Moving towards the antique sideboard, she grabbed one of the bottles of water. 'You might want to use this to stop yourself getting sticky.' Damn him, now his eyes weren't just amused, they were laughing. 'Oh God, just go and change, please.'

She marched out hurriedly, very aware of the soft, low chuckles that followed her.

Standing guard outside, it was impossible to not think about what was happening behind the big wooden door. She'd seen his last film, the one that had catapulted him into stardom. So she knew what he looked like without his shirt on.

Not helping, not helping.

Shaking the images away, she drew in a breath. Was she right to keep quiet and not tell him who she was? Jerry Collier had been very definite when he'd dished out his instructions. She was here to make polite small talk to a few of the bigwigs from the production company and to watch out for Edwards. From a distance.

Not crash into him.

Certainly not flirt with him.

She inhaled another lungful of air. Okay then, this was fine. She'd walk back with Edwards to the ballroom, and when he was surrounded by the people she'd seen reluctantly hang back while they'd been talking, she'd quietly slip away.

He'd barely remember her when they met again. The odd woman with the short hair who'd barged into him.

The door opened and Zac Edwards appeared, charcoal-grey suit in place, but now with a black T-shirt with the word Pine – part of the Pinewood logo – peeking between the jacket lapels. He slipped the cufflinks and tie he was holding into his jacket pocket, his other hand gripping the abandoned white shirt.

'You should look ridiculous,' she commented.

He grimaced, glancing down. 'If it helps, I feel ridiculous. I suspect Hardy Amies will be turning in his grave.'

'Hardy Amies?' God, the man had a weird way of talking. She needed to remember that the next time he flashed her a smile.

'The founder of the label who made the suit.'

'Oh.' She suspected Mr Amies was more likely to be doing cartwheels at the sight of one of his suits looking so . . . hot. 'Not Marks and Spencer then?'

Another small grimace. 'No, not M&S.'

'I take it you're not a fan of high street fashion?' She was deliberately trying to wind him up, because it was safer that way.

'I like clothes to fit my body. Not perch haphazardly on top of it.' His eyes dropped to the knee length fitted black dress she was wearing and back up to her face. 'I'm a fan of clothes that enhance a body's shape.'

The flutter in her belly was all the warning she needed that it was time to escape. It hardly seemed possible that he was attracted to her. She might be glammed up today, had even managed lipstick and eyeliner, but no way on God's earth would anyone describe her as beautiful. And a face like his surely demanded beautiful in return.

He was probably just enjoying the distraction. A moment away from an event he'd likely been heavily persuaded into attending. Production company anniversaries might be thrilling for those on the board, but for everyone else, not so much.

'Time to return to the party.' She was poised to walk back when she heard him sigh. 'You don't want to go back?'

'I'm not a big admirer of these types of events, no.' He gave her a sideways glance. 'I'd far rather acquire a couple of drinks and take them somewhere quiet.'

She tried to ignore the dip in her stomach. 'Two drinks? That's a bit greedy.'

'They aren't both for me.'

Kat's heart jolted. 'You, me and two glasses of champagne. That sounds dangerous.' *In many ways.*

His mouth curved, the result looking so, so sexy on him. 'I'm willing to risk it.'

God help her, she was massively out of her depth here. He was a master at flirting, and she wasn't just rusty, she wasn't supposed to be flirting back. Yet she couldn't stop the response of her body. The flush she knew was on her cheeks, the breath she knew he'd heard catch in her throat.

'As tempting as that sounds, Mr Edwards, I'm afraid I have to pass.' She began walking again, relieved to hear the sound of the music coming out from the ballroom. A few more seconds and he'd be engulfed, and she'd be able to breathe again.

'Wait.' Two long strides and he was beside her, his hand briefly touching her arm. 'You know who I am then?'

'Sure I do.' Electric sparks seemed to shoot over her skin where his hand had been. 'My sister's a huge fan. She dragged me to see *The Good Guy?* twice last year.'

He laughed softly, and the sound seemed to reach inside her, tingling parts that hadn't tingled for years. 'Dragged? My ego feels crushed.' His eyes searched her face and Kat felt her pulse start to race. How long since anyone had looked at her quite so intensely? Especially with eyes that were such a pretty green. 'It seems unfair that you know my name, yet I don't know yours.'

'It's Kat.' She paused at the entrance of the ballroom. 'Kat Parker.'

She saw him open his mouth to speak, but then a tall, elderly man walked up to greet him, slapping him on the back, and soon he was swallowed up.

Relieved, yet also utterly unbalanced, Kat slipped away, but not before casting a final glance in his direction.

As if aware of her, he looked over, and when their eyes met, he flashed her that small, sexy smile.

A smile that promised they'd meet again.

Of course, they would, but Kat knew when they did, he wouldn't feel quite so amiable towards her.

Chapter 2

Zac swung his classic Aston Martin into the Vision Films entrance. For classic, read *second hand* – though when the car in question was a Vanquish, who cared if it was fifteen years old? After waving his ID at the security guard he scanned the packed car park. Spotting a space, he eased his foot onto the accelerator and headed towards it. He wasn't late – he never was – but his fear of being late ensured he planned for every eventuality. It meant zeroing in on the first available space he saw, just in case it was the only one left.

As he headed towards it, he became dimly aware of a car hurtling towards him in the opposite direction. 'What on earth?'

He slammed his foot on the brake just as the Jeep Wrangler slipped neatly into the space. Into *his* space. Taking a deep breath, Zac slowly, calmly – he refused to rush over anything – levered himself out of the car and slid his sunglasses onto his head so he could get a better look at the driver who'd just jumped down from the Jeep. As the slim, dark-haired female turned to face him, the smile on her face faltered.

'Oh, it's you.'

'Yes, Kat Parker, it's me.' Any annoyance he'd felt immediately vanished at the sight of the woman he'd spent a tantalising twenty minutes with last night, before she'd disappeared. 'Do you have something against me?'

'Of course not, why?'

'First you drown me in champagne, now you pinch my parking space. I wondered if this was part of some sort of vendetta.'

She tipped her head back and laughed. A spontaneous sound, as natural as breathing yet startlingly attractive. 'The champagne I can blame on my shoes. The car park space was entirely your doing. You should have been quicker.'

'Or perhaps you should have been more considerate,' he countered mildly.

She shook her head, slamming the Jeep door shut. 'I saw an empty space and I went for it. If you'd wanted it, you should have put your foot down.' Her eyes flicked over his car. 'You've got a, what, six-litre engine?'

He was ashamed to realise he had no clue what engine size the Aston had. He only knew it was elegant, and he loved elegant things. 'Probably.'

A grin settled across the face he'd spent an embarrassing amount of time searching for last night. 'You don't even know the engine size, do you? Well, whatever it is, it's wasted if you don't use it.'

'I thought I was in a car park,' he felt compelled to point out. 'Not a race circuit.'

She laughed again, this time adding a small shake of her head. 'I remember that about you from last night. You're funny.'

'Thank you. I think.'

She moved away from the Jeep and now he could see her trim figure, dressed today in black leggings, black boots and a plain black T-shirt.

'I see you've got your boots on today. Does that mean the public are safe from flying beverages?'

Another husky laugh. 'I'm not sure about safe, but I'm certainly a lot steadier on my feet. Look, I'd love to stay and chat, but I've got to leg it, I'm late. Good luck finding a place for the Aston.' Her face lit up with another smile. 'Fancy cars are a dime a dozen round here, but she's a beauty.'

Intrigued by her, he watched as she marched quickly towards the Vision Films entrance. What connection did she have to the production company? The fact that she was at the party last night and here again today suggested she worked for them. Film editor? Set designer? She was confident enough to be a director, but he didn't recognise her. Maybe she was in admin, though it was hard to see her in anything so ordinary. Even dressed as she was, all in black, she was far too . . . vivid.

Whatever she did, she didn't have to walk far to it. He, on the other hand, was probably going to end up in the overflow car park. Not that he was against a walk, but preferably not on a hot June morning when he was wearing a lightweight wool suit. Yes, he knew he hadn't needed the suit. He also knew that linen would have been a more sensible choice. But linen creased, and when Zac didn't know the person he was meeting, he preferred the armour of a smart suit.

Muttering under his breath, he climbed back into the Aston and blasted the air-conditioning up as he drove slowly around the car park looking for another space.

Five minutes later he strolled through the entrance. Despite the car park altercation, he was still early for his meeting because punctuality was one of his – obsessions was too severe a word – he preferred idiosyncrasies. It was manners not to keep people waiting, just as it was manners to dress well for them and be polite. It was also manners not to tear into someone else's car park space, but Kat Parker didn't seem to observe the usual conventions.

Maybe he'd check with reception after his appointment and see if she worked here.

The thought of potentially seeing her again gave his mood a brief, but very welcome lift. Considering everything else that was going on in his life, he could do with another dose of the vital, attractive woman he'd enjoyed verbally sparring with last night.

First though, he had a rather more pressing matter to attend to. Shoulders set, he strode through the swanky marble reception area of Vision Films, trying to ignore the insecurity that pricked, like needles, whenever he was faced with the enormity of the world he was currently inhabiting. His star was on the rise, he was working with a major film production company, yet the doubts and worries continued to plague him. How long would it all last? And when the bubble burst, how damaging would the fallout be?

Christ. He was piling paranoia on top of paranoia. Brushing the negative thoughts aside, he slid a hand into the pocket of his suit trousers and pasted on a smile for the pretty blonde on the reception desk. 'Good morning, Cassie.'

'Hey there, Zac.' Her expression, warm, admiring, was a

long, luxurious stroke to his ego. 'You're here to see Jerry Collier?'

'Correct.' Exactly why the Head of Security had asked to see him, Zac wasn't sure, though he hoped it had something to do with the note he'd found taped to the door of his apartment yesterday afternoon. *Lucky me,* it had said. *I know where you live. But will it be lucky for you?* All neatly signed off with a vivid pink, lipstick kiss. It had been the fifth such note he'd received, each slightly creepier than the last.

Likely it was nothing, of course. By starring in the shock success of last year – the relatively low-budget action film, *The Good Guy?* – he'd probably simply acquired that miserable celebrity curse: a stalker.

Even so, the idea of someone watching his every move made his stomach turn. He was only just getting to grips with the concept of being famous, and the restrictions that placed on his life. The dread when he noticed he'd been spotted. The interruptions to sign autographs, to take his photo. The worry about the photos he *wasn't* aware of. He was a private man, catapulted into a celebrity world where privacy was a luxury. Still, if that's all this was, a celebrity stalker, he could deal with it. A small price to pay for the joy of being able to make a living from his passion, from immersing himself in another personality. Becoming someone else.

A skill he'd practised for most of his life.

But what if he wasn't being stalked because he was a celebrity? What if there was another reason behind the notes? That's what had woken him up in a cold sweat last night.

'Jerry says to go straight up.' Cassie's voice was a welcome interruption to his spiralling thoughts. 'He's on the second floor, first door on the right.' She gave him a coy smile. 'Would you like me to show you up?'

'Thank you,' he answered smoothly. 'But I'm sure I can find it.'

With a nod and a further flash of his perfect smile, he strode over to the lifts.

Son of a bitch, now she was really late. Kat dashed out of the ladies' where she'd spent the last few minutes sitting on the loo – yes, she could multi-task but no, in this case she'd put the lid down – trying to talk her sister out of a total meltdown. Mandy, who she'd just dropped off at rehab, had totally freaked out on being told she needed to stay there for sixty days.

'Two fucking months, Kat,' she'd screamed down the phone. 'I can't do that long. Debs will go nuts.'

Kat had already warned her niece that her mum would need to stay longer this time. 'Debs will be cool with it,' she'd reassured her sister, though having spent the second part of the crappy morning taking her truculent fourteen-year-old niece to school, she'd said it with her fingers crossed. 'I'll be there for her, and we'll come and visit you. Chill.'

'I can't chill. Come and get me, please. I don't want to be here.'

Kat's heart had ached for her, but she'd lived with Mandy's addictions for too long. Softening her voice, she'd told her the truth. 'You've tried outpatient therapy and shorter stays, and they didn't work. If you want your daughter to remember you as the strong, vibrant woman I know you are, then you need to work through this.'

It had done the trick, and her sister had promised she'd stick it out.

But damn it, now she was running so far behind even she was embarrassed by it. Collier, the guy in charge of security for the production company, would likely go apeshit. He'd asked her, via Mark, her boss, to turn up half an hour before their meeting with Zac Edwards, so he could brief her. Now she was just hoping she could get to Collier's office before Edwards did. Why the hell had the man arrived early? Didn't he realise celebrities were allowed to be late?

Dashing towards the lifts, she jammed her hand on the button just as the doors were about to close. As they slowly opened again, she stared at the man inside and sighed.

Looking as cool and laid back as he had in the car park in his immaculately fitting suit, designer shades now slotted into the top pocket, Zac Edwards gave her a sexy smirk of a smile. 'Not content with pinching my car park space, I see you now want to encroach on my lift.'

'I'm joining you in *the* lift.' Ignoring the flutter in her chest, she went to press the second floor, but it had already been pressed. Of course, it had. Because the man she appeared to be having an embarrassing hormonal reaction to, was her new client.

'Apparently you are.' With a languid grace she'd never aspire to, he leant back against the wall of the lift and crossed his ankles. 'Are you always so . . . impatient?'

She hiccupped out a laugh. 'I'm not impatient. I'm late.

And please don't give me the speech about setting off earlier, because I know that now. Trust me when I say I've had the sort of morning it would be hard to predict.'

He gave a lazy shrug of broad shoulders that were showcased by his perfectly fitted jacket. 'Expect the unexpected.'

She rolled her eyes. 'Hey, you're preaching to the converted. That's totally the motto I live my professional life by.'

'But?'

'Let's just say my private life is way too chaotic to call.' Suddenly the lift came to a shuddering stop. 'You've got to be kidding me.'

He eased off the wall. 'Not claustrophobic, I hope.'

'No. Just frustrated that I'm now going to be even later.' She jabbed at the emergency button. 'Come on, come on.'

'There's that impatience again.' His lips curved into the smile that had made him a household name. 'Relax. It'll just be a temporary blip.'

Sighing, she turned to face him. 'I suppose there are worse things than being stuck in a lift with, you know.' She waved a hand in his direction. 'You. I could have been stuck here by myself, or with a sweaty, overweight bloke who smelt of BO.'

'I'm glad I was here to save you from that purgatory.'

Kat had to bite into her cheek to stop an unprofessional giggle. This man with his fancy suits and fancy looks sure used a lot of really funny, fancy words.

The lift gave another shudder before moving again, smoothly coming to a stop a few seconds later.

As she stepped out and turned down the corridor, she was acutely aware of him walking beside her. The warmth of his body through that ridiculously smart suit – who wore a suit during the hottest June on record? Then there was his expensive aftershave. She was almost hyperventilating with the desire to keep inhaling it.

'I see we're going in the same direction.' He gave her a quizzical look. 'What is it you do for Vision Films?'

They both came to a stop outside Jerry Collier's door and she sucked in a deep breath. 'You're about to find out.'

At his bewildered expression, she felt the first jangle of nerves. This wasn't how it had been planned. Mark was already worried about assigning her to such a high-profile case, a fact that had both touched and really frigging annoyed her. Despite assuring him she was totally up to it though, here she was, ballsing it up before she'd even properly started. She wasn't supposed to have met Edwards yet. She also wasn't supposed to be so late this morning that she was arriving with the guy. And they certainly shouldn't have been flirting with each other, no matter how mildly.

The door swung open and Jerry, a big, imposing guy in his mid-fifties you wouldn't want to piss off, stared at her before reaching out to shake the actor by the hand. 'Good to meet you, Zac. I see you and Kat have already been introduced.'

'Err, not exactly.' Usually Kat had no problem talking herself out of a situation, but this was a bit tricky. 'We sort of bumped into each other last night.'

'Literally.' Zac narrowed his eyes. 'What's going on here?'

Jerry looked between her and Edwards, and sighed. 'When I heard about the note stuck on your front door yesterday, I asked Kat to discreetly keep an eye out for you last night.

Today she was supposed to have arrived before you, so I could make the introductions properly, but it seems she's jumped the gun.'

'Keep an eye out for me?' Zac was clearly confused, and Kat felt a knot of tension tighten in her stomach. Her gut told her he wasn't going to like what he heard next.

'Yes. That's what she's here for.' Jerry nodded in her direction. 'Zac Edwards, meet Kat Parker. Your bodyguard.'

As she watched the news sink in, Kat noticed the differing emotions flicker across her new client's handsome face. The bewilderment and disbelief, she was used to. All part of the joy of being a woman in a man's world. She didn't mind the annoyance either, because God knows she wouldn't like to have someone foisted on her. No, it was the interlaced horror that alarmed her.

Was he horrified Vision Films were so worried about his safety they'd assigned him a bodyguard? Or horrified his bodyguard was a woman?

Worse still, was the horror because his bodyguard was *her*?

Kat unconsciously squared her shoulders. She couldn't do much about her job, or her gender, but she could make sure he only saw Kat the professional from now on.

Chapter 3

Zac didn't know which of the mind-blowing pieces of information to focus on first. That the production company had hired him a bodyguard who looked so inexperienced, and appeared so chaotic. Or that said bodyguard was the woman he'd been flirting with last night and just now in the lift.

Five minutes ago, he'd been anticipating tracking her down so he could ask her out for a drink, hopefully get to know her. Now he didn't need to do that. Because from now on she was going to be sticking to him like glue.

'Pardon?' It seemed the safest response. He'd long ago curbed his natural instinct to say what he thought, which was something along the lines of *Are you shitting me?*, with a heavy dose of *What the fuck?*

Jerry let out another long exhale – he'd clearly been expecting this to go more smoothly – before pointing to the seating area in the corner of his office. 'Why don't you take a seat and I can go over a few things.' He narrowed his eyes at Kat. '*With both of you.*'

Kat winced, and Zac felt a smidgen of sympathy for her.

Then again, she'd known about this . . . arrangement all along, and hadn't had the decency to tell him. Not even after she'd upended champagne all over him.

Not even after he'd tried to flirt with her.

Steering clear of the sofa, he headed for the armchair, figuring he needed the small amount of space it provided. Space to remind himself that Jerry didn't know the things Zac did. Jerry had no reason to believe the stalker wasn't just a crazy fan, and likely, make that extremely likely, that's all he or she was. It's just, in those moments between sleep and wake, when doubts and worries were hugely exaggerated . . . in *those* moments, Zac had begun to think of other, far more terrifying possibilities. None of which he could voice, because in the world of Zac Edwards, actor, the part of his life that lent itself to those dark thoughts, had been scrubbed clean.

Jerry hunkered down on the sofa, but Kat shook her head and walked over to the desk, resting against it with her arms crossed. Her face, the one he'd enjoyed seeing smile, was now serious, those dark eyes watching him. Under different circumstances he'd have enjoyed her eyes on him, but not as his bodyguard. Not when he was riddled with fear over who might be trying to frighten him.

Deciding his best play was to feign nonchalance, Zac leant forward on the chair, loosely clasping his hands. 'Who decided that I need a bodyguard?'

'I did.' Jerry twisted to face him. 'We're used to actors getting weird mail, but when the sender sticks the letter to the actor's front door, it's time to worry.'

'Really?' Zac felt his pulse kick up a gear. 'You don't think it's just a deranged fan? Notes signed in pink lipstick don't exactly scream menacing.'

'And you'd know menacing when you saw it?' Kat asked, her tone detached now. No longer the warm, chatty woman he'd talked to in the lift.

You have no idea what I know. Words he couldn't say. 'I know I don't need a bodyguard if this is simply a crazy female fan,' he settled for.

'So because the stalker might be a female, you think you're safe?' Kat's eyes narrowed. 'If I decided to attack you, you could, what, just swat me away?'

She was offended, he realised. 'Of course not. You're a professional. You'd wipe the floor with me.'

At last, a return of her smile. 'Good answer.'

'All I'm saying is that if it's just a crazy fan, then I don't see the need for a bodyguard.' He could do without intrusion in his life, thank you very much. 'But if you believe the stalker might be more dangerous than that . . .' Or if my fears turn out to be correct, he thought grimly. 'If you really believe I'm at risk, then I'm happy to concede that I need protection.' *In fact I'll need the most experienced, most professional bodyguard you can put your hands on.* He doubted that was Kat.

'It's less about how dangerous the stalker might be,' Jerry interjected. 'And more about anticipating and preventing an attack in the first place. That's where Kat comes in.'

Zac avoided looking at Kat as he spoke his next words to Jerry. 'Do you mind if we discuss this privately?'

Jerry heaved out a sigh and with that, and the way Kat's back turned ramrod straight, Zac knew exactly how unimpressed they were with his request. 'There's nothing you can say in front of Kat that she won't have heard already.'

Okay, so this was going to remain at Awkward Level 10. And if he couldn't get Collier to change his mind, Zac knew he'd just pissed off the one person he'd be relying on to keep him safe.

'Jerry.' He spread his hands out in a show of geniality. 'I'm sure Kat is excellent at identifying risky situations, as you say.'

'I am.'

'She is.'

Don't be put off by the steely glares. This is your life they're discussing, not a part in a film. 'However, she's not as experienced as I imagined a bodyguard should be for this particular situation.'

'First you say you don't need a bodyguard, now you're saying you want one with more experience.' Jerry leant forward, his eyes piercing Zac's. 'Are you usually this contrary or is there something you're not telling us?'

Inside Zac squirmed like a worm on the end of the hook, but outside he knew he looked cool, calm and collected. That was acting for you. 'You know as much as I do, Jerry. I'm simply asking questions to identify if I really am at risk, and if I am, if you're going to be able to protect me.'

Jerry's voice hardened and Zac felt the power behind the *Don't mess with me* tone. 'Vision Films takes the safety of our actors very seriously. Kat works for our preferred provider, UK Security. She's had twelve years with the army, and another three doing exactly this, so she's got plenty of experience under her belt. Listen to her and do what she asks. She knows what she's talking about. Even if she can't always turn up on time.'

'And it was going so well,' Kat muttered. 'Thanks, Jerry.'

The pair of them exchanged a look and Zac realised he'd been wrong in his initial impression that Jerry was annoyed with her. They clearly shared a bond. Respect, certainly, but he guessed something more, too. Affection, maybe. It explained why Jerry hadn't liked him questioning Kat's ability. It also told Zac any further push to change her would be viewed in a distinctly unfavourable, and possibly suspicious, light.

Jerry's attention was back on Zac. 'I realise you're going to find this all very inconvenient, but while you're under contract with Vision Films you're going to have to suck it up. If Kat determines something is necessary for your safety, you do it or the studio lawyers will be onto you for breach of contract.' He gave Zac the faintest of smiles. 'Is there anything else you need to ask me, before I leave you in Kat's very capable hands?'

'Have you seen this approach before? Are there any suspects?' Probably he was worrying about nothing, and lipstick notes had been delivered to other celebrities with no harm done.

'Stalkers sending notes to celebrities isn't new, but I've not heard of any being signed in pink lipstick before.' Jerry stood, clearly signalling the meeting was over. 'We're working closely with the police on it, though. Kat will keep you in the loop.'

Reluctantly Zac rose to his feet. Reluctantly, because when he walked out of the door, he was going to have a bodyguard trailing around with him. Not only would that bodyguard be a constant reminder of the danger he could be in, she was also a woman he'd been flirting with. And one he'd just thoroughly pissed off.

Kat's assignment was quiet as they walked into the lift.

'Which was the biggest shock,' she asked as the doors closed. 'Being told you were being assigned a bodyguard, or finding out the bodyguard was me?'

A wry smile crossed his handsome face. It sure wasn't going to be a hardship looking at him for the next however long. 'Would it offend if I said the latter?'

'That depends. The part about me not being experienced enough. Was that your way of saying I wasn't male enough? That you'd feel better if I was a big, muscle-bound dude?'

He smiled again, the very smile that had helped make *The Good Guy?* such a big hit. Actors with beaming white grins, the public were used to, but the little sexy smirk Zac Edwards had going on? That was both unusual and, even to a cynic like herself, rather charming. 'I bet you get that all the time, but actually, no, it wasn't.' He shifted his hands into his trouser pockets. 'It was a reference to your age. Size, I'm given to understand, isn't important.'

She snorted. 'Are you seriously going to tell me it's what you do with it, that counts?'

'Actually, I was going to say it's how you're trained to use it, that counts.' Before she had a chance to shake her head at his innuendo, he added, 'You, I imagine, can be lethal.'

Despite her irritation at him, laughter burst out of her. 'Neat catch.' As soon as it had come, though, the laughter died and the anger, the disappointment, returned. 'Okay, say I buy that, and you really weren't going to ask Jerry for a male bodyguard in that private little chat you wanted, why the look of horror when Jerry told you I was your bodyguard?'

'You know why.'

'Err, if I did, I wouldn't be asking.'

His shoulders rose and fell as he sighed. 'I was annoyed you didn't tell me who you were last night.' The lift came to a stop and as they walked out into the reception area, he slid her a glance. 'You had me at a disadvantage. I would have reacted differently if I'd known.'

She figured he had a point. 'Yeah, sorry about that. I did consider telling you, but Jerry's got this real bee in his bonnet about doing the introductions.' She cleared her throat. 'It sets the boundaries, Kat,' she said, imitating Jerry's gruff voice. 'Makes it clear I'm the one in charge and you both need to take instructions from me.'

'I see.' A glimmer of a smile. 'Though I find it hard to imagine the rather intimidating Mr Collier in a bonnet, bee or not.' Zac paused, glancing down at his highly polished black shoes before raising his eyes back to hers. 'And you? Would you have reacted differently if you'd met me by accident, with no hidden agenda?'

I'm pretty sure I'd have flirted right back at you. No, no, no. For their relationship to work, she couldn't admit it. 'We'll never know.' Before he could say anything more, she threw out a question of her own. 'So you're unhappy I didn't warn you who I was when I dumped champagne all over you, and you think I'm inexperienced. Is that it, or is there more?'

Zac's eyes drifted away from her and through the window to the car park. 'If we believe the stalker is simply a fan with a screw loose, having a bodyguard, aside from the obvious intrusion, feels a little . . . emasculating.'

There he was with his fancy words again. 'Will your balls feel safer if I tell you just because the letters appear to have come from a woman, doesn't mean they have? But say yours have, you're assuming a mere female couldn't hurt you. Tell that to the male victims of "Monster" Aileen Wuornos, and to the husband of Katherine Knight whose body parts ended up in a stew. Or to the men who visited Belle Gunness and ended up being fed to the pigs.' She paused. 'Do you want me to go on?'

'I'm not sure my stomach can take any more.' He ghosted her a smile. 'I suppose I should be grateful that at least my balls feel safer now, even if I don't.'

She winced. 'Sorry, I usually employ more of a filter when I'm working.'

'Please don't, not with me.' He raked a hand restlessly through his hair. 'This situation is going to be intolerable enough. I'd rather you were . . . you.'

Well, she'd hadn't expected that. Then again, she'd not quite got the measure of the man yet. Most actors she'd met wouldn't put on a suit to meet the head of security. Nor would they have taken her spilling drink over them, or pinching a car park space from under their noses, quite so calmly. They certainly wouldn't have flirted with her, because actors went for beautiful willowy types, and she was more of a, well, a holly bush. Short but could do some serious damage if provoked.

'You don't realise what you're letting yourself in for,' she felt duty bound to warn him. 'In unfiltered mode I can be pretty full-on. Just ask my sister, or my niece. They've been trying to gag me for years.'

'Oh, I think I know.' Those obscenely pretty green eyes met hers. 'At the very least it will be a welcome diversion from . . .' His shoulders rose and fell as he exhaled. 'All this.'

His unhappiness with the situation was clear, and she felt a dart of sympathy for him. Knowing the threat was real enough to convince a film company he needed a bodyguard had to be a pretty scary prospect.

Almost as scary as being assigned to be that bodyguard.

Kat forced her mind away from the dark alley. She needed this. Three years of protecting film company bigwigs and minor stars who were no more at risk than she was just wasn't enough. It was time to prove to Mark, prove to *herself*, that she could step up. Zac Edwards, a high-profile celebrity currently being stalked, would give her that chance.

And damn it, she was ready for it.

Nodding towards the exit, Kat started to walk. 'Okay then, you get the real me. But no moaning later when your ears are complaining. Now, what's your filming schedule like today, because at some point we need to head to your place and work out if it's secure enough for you to stay there.'

He came to a halt just before the revolving door. Well, more of a slow, gliding stop because, like his speech, everything about this man was elegant and controlled. 'I might have to move?'

There was no *might* about it. The nut job knew where he lived. No way was she, or the film company, going to be happy with him staying in his own home from now on. Not with the implied threat in the note. Still, he'd had enough shocks for now. 'I'll decide once I've taken a look.'

He ran a hand across his face in a gesture that looked both weary and frustrated. 'I wish I'd kept quiet about the blasted note.'

'Better that, than staring into the maniacal eyes of a knife-wielding psycho, and wishing you'd told someone.'

The blood drained from his face. 'An eloquently made point.' He paused, clearly trying to find his balance. 'In answer to your question, I'm due on set at midday. But I have lines to go through.'

'You've not learnt them already?' It didn't seem to fit with the man who'd turned up freakishly early to his appointment with Jerry.

'Of course, I have.' He glanced away, and she thought he looked embarrassed. 'But a person can never be overprepared.'

She had to fight a smile. God, he was definitely on the obsessive side of the spectrum. 'Is that the same way a person can't be overly early for an appointment? Or overdressed?'

'Exactly.'

If he knew she was taking the mickey, it didn't show. 'How about, just this once, you stick to being simply *prepared*, and we head over to yours now. That way, I can check out alternative places for you to stay while you're filming.'

His right brow shot up. 'What happened to deciding once you'd taken a look?'

Busted. 'It's still the plan.' Oh, stuff it. He'd asked her to be herself. And that person said things how they were. 'Look, don't get your hopes up. Now this stalker knows where you live, your place would have to have more security than Fort Knox for me to agree to you staying there. Better that we move you to a hotel.'

His shoulders slumped. 'Great.'

'It could be kind of great. Just think, room service 24/7, laundry done for you. All those tempting miniatures with the studio picking up the minibar tab.' When his expression remained bleak, she added, 'Fresh towels every day. Bed turned down for you every night. Chocolate on your pillow?'

'Please tell me you're not always this . . . upbeat?'

'You wanted to say irritating, didn't you?'

He blinked, eyes darting away from hers, though his mouth twitched. 'I wouldn't be so rude.'

No, she thought. Yet all those manners, those careful words, weren't going to help the situation. 'Look, you asked for the real me, but that works both ways. We're going to be pretty much glued to eachother for a while, so I need to know what you're thinking, too. If I'm being annoying, tell me. Ditto if you're worried about something. My job is to keep you safe but if we don't get on, or if you keep things from me, it'll make life difficult.'

He nodded, though she noticed his eyes avoided hers. 'Understood.'

'Okay then. We'll take the Jeep to your place.'

She started towards the door, but stopped when she realised he wasn't following her. Instead he remained where he was, hand loosely in his trouser pocket. Whoever had made that suit, the image of him now would make one hell of an advert for it. 'Is this one of those occasions I can say you're being annoying?'

'Because?'

He glanced out of the door and towards the car park. 'I have a perfectly good car. A beauty, I believe you called it.'

'So I did. And because it's a beauty, it's also highly recognisable.'

'But you'll be following me.'

'No, I'll be driving you.' She watched as his expression turned pained. 'Not a fan of female drivers?'

'It's not that.' His chest heaved with a sigh. 'I bought the car because I like to drive it. You know, one of life's luxuries?' He shook his head. 'Sorry, that sounded crass.'

Her respect for him went up a notch. They were clearly polar opposites; personality, background, earnings. You name it, she had a hunch sometime soon they were going to clash because of it. Yet so far he seemed quieter, more thoughtful, and less arrogant than she'd expected. 'Hey, for me luxury is a plate of nachos, heavy on the cheese, and a bottle of beer while watching the Grand Prix on the TV, but I can relate.'

He regarded her soberly for a moment before the edge of his mouth curved, ever so slightly, upwards. 'So, you're a motorsport fan. Why doesn't that surprise me.' With that he started towards the door, leaving Kat to hurry after him so she could ensure she walked out ahead.

This assignment looked like it was going to test her in more ways than she'd bargained for when she'd first pleaded with Mark to let her take it.

Chapter 4

He hadn't planned on anyone seeing inside his place today. Script open on his knee – yes, he caught her smirking at him, no it wasn't going to stop him – Zac tried to focus on his lines while she drove. And not on how intrusive it felt to have a stranger come and inspect his home. At least it would be tidy. Unlike the inside of Kat's Jeep. He glanced again at the centre console. There was a half-eaten bag of Starburst, surrounded by a rainbow of discarded wrappers, an open pack of Polo mints, an empty take-out coffee cup and a pen with a chewed end.

It made him wonder again about her professionalism. Turning up late, untidy . . . call him old school, but they hinted at a sloppiness that wasn't a trait he wanted in someone responsible for his safety. Especially now she'd convinced him even a crazy female fan could be more dangerous than he'd bargained for.

To take his mind off things, he started to pick up the discarded wrappers.

'I thought you were overpreparing.'

He dragged his eyes back to the script. 'I am.'

'Really? It looks like you're tidying up for me.'

'No,' he corrected. 'I'm doing it for me.'

'I bet your car is immaculate. Not a speck of dust, or a greasy finger mark.'

'I believe in being tidy, yes. Just like I believe in being punctual. Standards are important.'

He noticed her body stiffen. 'If you have something you want to say, just say it. Like I said, we need to be honest with each other.'

How could he voice his fear, that she might not be professional enough, or experienced enough, to deal with the danger he was most terrified of, when he couldn't articulate that specific threat? 'I don't understand the fascination with confectionery,' he said instead.

Her sidelong glance told him she wasn't convinced of his reply. 'Why, were your parents dentists?'

'No.' He turned his head, looking out of the passenger window, and held his breath while he waited for her follow-up question.

'Of course, they weren't. Sorry, for a moment I forgot you were posh.'

She'd read his biography, then. At least he'd be spared the family questions. 'How about your parents? I suspect they weren't dentists, either.'

'No.'

It was the same single-syllable answer he'd given, yet from someone so loquacious up to now, it was a clear signal she didn't want to talk about them. 'Whatever they did, I feel sorry for them. I bet you were a handful when you were younger.' His eyes zeroed in on another stray wrapper and he missed the way her expression shuttered.

'Why would you say that?'

'You have to ask, after what happened in the car park?' He screwed the wrapper up and placed it in the empty cup with the rest of his catch. 'There's a hint of mischief, of a trouble-maker, about you.'

'You're wrong.' Her clipped words took him by surprise. 'What you saw in the car park was the result of a vow never to allow myself to be pushed around, bullied, or walked over ever again.'

Zac cursed inwardly, annoyed with himself. It seemed he'd done what he hated others doing to him. Made a judgement without the facts. 'Sorry. I actually meant my remarks as a compliment. It's refreshing to meet someone so . . . unconventional.'

Her hands slowly relaxed the vice-like hold they'd had on the steering wheel. 'Unconventional? Is that your fancy way of saying I'm odd?'

'No. It's my fancy way of apologising.' Interested, he angled his head towards her. 'Collier said you'd been in the army. Did that have something to do with this vow?'

'In a way, yes, because it gave me a means of escape. Mainly I joined for the thrill of doing something different, something physical. Challenging myself. I mean, I was never going to sit at a desk, that's for certain.'

'No.'

She slid him a look. 'You don't think I could hack it in an office?'

'I think that would stifle your . . . spirit.'

'It would certainly drive me crazy.'

Suddenly the mood in the car changed and he watched, part in fascination, part in fear, as she checked the mirror and quickly switched lanes. For the next few minutes she alternated her focus between the road ahead and the rear-view mirror, turning right when the sat nav said left, an intensity to her bearing that hadn't been there before. Yet when she finally spoke again, it was as if nothing had happened. 'What about you? Why did you get into acting?'

'I enjoy it.' He swallowed, relieved to find he still had some saliva left after the heart-bumping few minutes. 'Are you going to tell me why we're going the wrong way?'

She appeared briefly confused. 'Oh, you mean the right turn? A white Golf has been behind us for the last five minutes. I wanted to check if it was following us.'

'And was it?'

'If it was, it decided not to make it obvious.' He felt his palms begin to sweat and when he didn't reply, she spoke again. 'Not the answer you were looking for?'

'A simple no would have worked.'

'It would also give you a false sense of security.' Her voice was strong and steady. Clearly he was the only one in the car rattled by what had happened. 'Look, whoever's leaving you those love notes managed to find out where you live,' she continued in that same, matter-of-fact tone. 'As I assume you don't make the information public knowledge, either they've hacked into some database to find it, or they've asked the right people. Or they've followed you home.'

He felt everything inside him clench and tighten. Considering the perks of his life, being paid a stupid sum of money for doing what he loved, he could concede that he deserved the reporters and the cameras with their prying lenses. At least there were rules governing how far they could encroach. The stalker was different, though. The person who'd walked right up to his front door and left the note clearly didn't follow rules.

Once again, he felt the slippery coils of fear wrap around his gut. Who was doing this to him? Were they doing it to scare him, or did they have a more sinister motive? And if the latter, would Kat Parker, with her disorganised ways and her whole three years of experience, really have a chance in hell of stopping them?

'You've gone quiet on me.' She laughed softly. 'Maybe I should say "even quieter", because you don't seem the type who likes to talk.'

Zac massaged the back of his neck in a bid to rub out the tension. He was getting overly paranoid. This was a fan who got a kick out of leaving him notes. In a matter of days, the police would discover who it was and order her to keep away. 'I'm trying to get my head around it all.'

'Will it help if I tell you we see this a lot? The stalker is usually found quickly, given a restraining order and never heard from again.'

'It would help if you'd left out the *usually*.'

'Ah, but then I'd be lying, and that's something I promise not to do.'

He wondered if she was aware her hands had gripped the steering wheel again. 'I can tell you I've never lost a . . . client.'

Her hesitation, almost imperceptible, did nothing to allay his fears. She hadn't lost a client, but she had lost someone? 'But were any of those clients in danger? Were they being stalked?'

'Danger doesn't always come waving a big red flag.' Halting at a traffic light, she turned those sharp brown eyes on him. 'I might be untidy, and today I might have turned up late, but I can also tell you – stuff that – I can *promise* you, none of it is a reflection on how I operate in my job. I'm bloody good at what I do.'

'Ah.' He shifted on the seat, feeling about three foot tall. 'What gave me away?'

'You thought I *wouldn't* pick up on that dig about standards?'

'I'm sorry. I . . .' His brain came up blank. He had nothing that could explain his snotty comment. Nothing that wouldn't leave him open to further questions about why he was so paranoid she wasn't up to the job. 'I'm sure you're eminently capable,' he finished lamely.

As Kat pulled up outside the swanky modern apartment block in Highgate, she mentally high fived herself. Yep, just as she'd imagined. She'd like to bet inside it was all wooden floors, stainless steel fittings and . . . minimalism. Was that a word? She was pretty sure it was. Also, pretty sure nobody would ever accuse her of it.

Parking in the private underground car park, she noted the lack of security. No CCTV, no electronic gate. There was a key fob entry system, but all the stalker had to do was wait for someone else to enter or leave and walk in after them. There was no reception area, no door man.

Mr Edwards was going to have to move out. And she could just imagine how happy he was going to be about that. The guy was already quietly freaking out after the not-sure-if-it-was-a-tail incident. Well, she assumed he was freaking out but it was hard to tell because at times his thoughts were locked away so securely – not just in a vault, but within a castle with the steel portcullis down and the drawbridge up – it was impossible for her to get a read on him.

She did know he wasn't impressed with her so-called standards, though, or her relative inexperience, and it rankled. He was finding her guilty without any evidence. *There's plenty to be had if he knew where to look.* Yeah, that thought could go and take a running jump. She hadn't been at fault.

She hadn't.

At least that's what everyone had told her.

When they reached the door to his apartment, he gave her a wry smile. 'I'm heading for 24/7 room service and a chocolate on my pillow, aren't I?'

Taking the key from him, she opened the door and motioned for him to wait. When she was satisfied it was clear, she waved him inside. 'Was my expression that obvious?'

His gaze captured hers and once again she felt the power of his attraction. It wasn't just that his eyes were a pretty shade of green. It was the pull of them. 'The curl of your lip did rather give it away.'

Oops. Not the time to tell him the sneer hadn't been about the security, but about the soulless looking apartment block. 'I can't understand why the security on these modern places is so lax. Surely that's the advantage of buying one.'

'You make it sound like the only advantage.'

Oh crap. 'No. I mean I can see why you like it.' She walked back into the open plan living area, with its gleaming – she'd guessed it – wooden floors, huge glass windows, weird modern art, fancy leather sofa with two strategically placed cushions. And complete absence of any clutter whatsoever. 'It's very you.'

Whatever he thought of her remark, he kept it to himself. 'I'll throw a few things in a suitcase.' He nodded over to the clinical looking open plan kitchen. 'Feel free to make yourself a drink.'

'You've got to be kidding.' She stepped towards the spotless worktop. 'Where's your mug tree? The tea and coffee canisters? This morning's breakfast things you've not had time to clear away?'

With a resigned sigh, he pressed a hand against one of the shiny white doors. When it glided open, she saw two rows of neatly stacked black mugs. 'These *modern* places have plenty of cupboard spaces, so no need for a mug tree.' He pushed open an adjacent door. 'Or tea canisters.' Finally, he gave a unit near the sink a gentle pull, revealing a dishwasher. 'And if you give yourself enough time in the morning, you can clear up before you leave.' He smirked. 'And avoid being so late you have to pinch someone's car park space.'

'Sarcastic sod,' she muttered under her breath as he walked away. Her heart bumped as he halted.

'I heard that.'

'Heard what?' She gave him a wide, innocent grin. 'I'm too scared to make a mess in there, so I'll just . . .' She pointed to the sofa. 'Try to sit as neatly as I can on your sofa while I wait.'

He shook his head, and she could have sworn she heard the words, *sarcastic sod* thrown back at her, though it was hard to be sure. Apparently, he was a master at hiding his thoughts even when he said them out loud.

Gingerly she went to perch on the sofa. After two minutes of looking at her phone – one message from Mandy, apologising and saying she'd pulled herself together and one from her niece saying she'd be late home because she was seeing a friend after school – Kat pushed it into her pocket and skimmed her eyes across the living space. They rested on a glass-fronted cabinet at the far end. Intrigued to see if there was anything inside that would give her a hint of the man she'd been assigned to protect, she strolled up to it.

Her jaw almost hit the floor when she saw the contents.

Teapots?

And not clever, modern, arty teapots either. Fussy, old fashioned . . . let's be honest, totally naff teapots. The type your granny would have used, back in the days when she'd also have shoved a hand-knitted tea cosy over it.

Utterly spellbound, Kat opened the door and, not daring to touch, feasted her eyes on them. One, two, three . . . crikey moses, there had to be a dozen of them.

'I'm done.'

Guiltily Kat stepped away and turned to see Zac standing in the middle of the living room, staring at her. At his feet was a very expensive looking leather holdall. He'd changed out of his suit and into a pair of grey tailored trousers and a meticulously ironed pale-pink collared shirt. Over his arm was a suit carrier with, she guessed, several more designer suits, pressed trousers and collared shirts.

'Right then.' *Ask about the teapots.* She had to, right, because it would look odd if she didn't mention it. Never mind the fact she was bursting to know the story behind them. 'I was just admiring your teapots.'

'So I see.'

She might have guessed Mr Closed Book wasn't going to make this easy. 'Have you been collecting them long?' She bit into her cheek to suppress the giggle bursting to explode. Was she really having a conversation with heart-throb actor Zac Edwards about his teapot collection?

'I've had them a while, yes.' His eyes held hers, and she had to admire his acting skills. Whether he was amused, angry, or just mildly irritated, she hadn't a clue.

'You know what I'm dying to ask, don't you?'

'Yes.' He picked up the holdall and turned towards the front door. 'What I don't know, is why you're holding back.'

'Because I don't want to piss you off. Protection duty only works if the bodyguard and the client get on.' He put his hand up to open the door, but she shook her head. 'From now on, that's my job. I go in and out first, check it's clear, and then you follow.'

He uttered a mild expletive but dropped his hand and took a step back.

Once they were back in the Jeep, he cleared his throat. 'Ask the question. I made you uncomfortable earlier; it's only fair you get a shot back.'

She glanced at his handsome profile. 'Why do you collect teapots?'

'I don't. They're my mother's.' Immediately he slid a phone out of his trouser pocket. 'Excuse me while I make a call. I need to let my manager know what's happening.'

It was clear she'd had her question, and the subject was now closed. A real bummer, because his answer had sparked a swarm of further questions. Not least why on earth the classy Lady Edwards had collected so many tacky teapots. And then palmed them off to her son.

Chapter 5

The afternoon's filming had been tough. Or maybe Zac hadn't been as focused as he should have been. Twice he'd forgotten his lines. Twice. He never forgot lines. He always turned up to filming impeccably prepared.

Overprepared. An image of Kat and her none-too-subtle smirk came to mind. Okay, so he had a thing about going through his lines ten times before the shoot. It wasn't odd, it was being professional.

Except that today, his preparation had been disrupted, and his professionalism called into question. Not in so many words, but Zac hated being the one filming had to stop for. The one at fault.

Maybe this was what his stalker really wanted. To disrupt his life so much he'd no longer have a career.

The thought didn't help his mood as Zac trudged wearily off set. 'Zac, darling.' Sophia Layton, who played his love interest in the film, caught his eye. With blonde hair, blue eyes and high cheekbones, she was classically beautiful. And she knew it. 'The crew and I were talking about going out for drinks on Friday. We're hoping . . .' she smiled, showing a set of perfect white teeth. 'I'm hoping, you'll join us.'

Usually he'd say yes, not because he liked socialising particularly, and definitely not because he wanted to pick up on the promise in Sophia's eyes. It was more that he saw filming as teamwork, and he was a part of the team. But as of this morning, things had changed. Now he wasn't sure he had the autonomy to agree to a night out, or whether he needed to check with his bodyguard first.

The thought of having his life dictated by a security company stuck in his throat. 'Sure,' he told her, acutely aware of the irony. He'd spend the evening trying to avoid Sophia's advances, while being watched by a woman who'd avoided his.

'And if you ever want to go through your lines with someone.' Sophia fluttered her eyelashes. 'Remember I'm always available.'

'Thank you, but I'm good.' He had enough problems of the female variety at the moment with his stalker and his bodyguard. 'Today was an anomaly.'

He'd make damn sure of it.

Kat was waiting for him outside his dressing room. Ignoring the way his pulse raced that little bit faster when she smiled, he went to open the door, but she shook her head.

'Bodyguard's first.' After doing a quick sweep of the room – he guessed out of habit, because security within the studio was so tight she'd agreed she wasn't needed while he was here – she nodded for him to come in. 'Is it a wrap?'

'For today, yes.' He stepped inside and ran a hand over his

face, his fingers sliding over make-up. Nice. God, he needed a shower. Usually he'd take one before he left. Then again, usually he didn't have a woman waiting in his dressing room. A woman who wasn't beautiful like the one he'd had to kiss this afternoon, on set, yet who he found far more interesting. 'I could do with a shower. If that's possible.'

As he met her eyes he saw a flicker of . . . was it amusement? Or something else? He wanted to believe she was imagining him in the shower – that's certainly where his mind would have wandered had the boot been on the other foot. Yet he'd had no hint that she found him attractive. He knew her sister did, because her sister had *dragged* Kat to watch his film. So from current evidence, far from imagining him showering, it was more likely she was silently laughing at this weird shyness he'd developed.

'No problem, I'll wait outside.' She was halfway towards the door when she stopped. 'By the way, I've booked you into a hotel that we've used before. You're on a private floor, with its own gym, that can't be accessed without a special lift key.'

He grimaced. 'My own personal, five-star prison cell.'

The look she gave him was heavy with sympathy. 'It's not forever. And you're not under lock and key. If you want to go out, just let me know and I'll make sure either I or Mark accompany you.'

'Mark?'

'Yes. He's coming by the hotel so you can meet him. I'll be your main point of contact, but Mark Evans will provide cover when I can't.' She shot him a grin. 'He's also the boss man, so feel free to big me up whenever you get the chance.'

She slipped out and Zac headed to the adjoining shower feeling . . . flat. An evening in a soulless hotel. If he wanted to go out, he couldn't just open his front door. He had to phone and wait for a babysitter. Some people – Kat no doubt one of them – would call his apartment soulless, but at least it was his. His sofa, his bed.

His things.

He groaned as he stepped under the hot spray, his mind going back to this morning. A thousand questions had been in Kat's eyes when he'd caught her looking at his mother's teapots. He could only hope she kept the other nine hundred and ninety-nine to herself.

Zac's eyes strayed towards the Aston Martin as he walked into the car park. Newer than his, but the sleek lines were similar enough to cause a pang in his chest.

'Is my car still in the Vision Films car park?'

Kat ushered him into the Jeep before jumping into the driver's side. 'Yes, why? Worried she'll get wet if it rains?'

He sighed, letting her have her fun. He was too fed up to argue.

'I can arrange for her to be taken back to your place, if you like,' Kat said quietly a moment later as she drove out of the studio gates.

'Which place would that be? My home, or the place I'm going to be living?' And yes, he knew he sounded testy.

'Your home. Putting her in the hotel car park would be the equivalent of sticking a big sign outside the hotel saying *Zac Edwards is staying here*. As we've gone to all the trouble of booking you into a private floor, and ramming the whole *Make sure none of your staff tell anyone he's staying here* speech down the manager's throat, that seems a little counterproductive.'

'The first two words were sufficient.'

Her lips curved. 'I make it a rule never to use two words when twenty is so much more satisfying.'

'Satisfying for whom?'

Her laughter filled the car. 'Me, obviously.'

'What happened to keeping the client happy?'

'Technically the client is Vision Films.'

He guessed he deserved that. And heavens above, he was being a grumpy sod. What had he got to complain about, really? The inconvenience of having to live in a five-star hotel for a short while? Yeah, it was no wonder his cheery bodyguard was already fed up with him. He didn't like himself right now, either. 'Tell me how this works with you and Mark.'

She slid him a brief look. 'What do you want to know?'

'Do you have some sort of rota?'

'Nothing so formal. I'll take most of the shifts, but if you're going out every night he'll be there to pick up some evenings. We also try to alternate weekends.'

'I won't be out every night.' With a sigh, he remembered the chat with Sophia. 'But I am going for drinks with the crew on Friday.'

'Okay, no problem.'

What about spontaneity, though? What about meeting a woman he fancied and asking her out for a drink? *Like he'd been seconds away from doing with Kat.* He wasn't a womaniser, but he wasn't a monk, either.

She indicated and turned into a side street before speaking again. 'I can almost see your mind working.'

God, he hoped not. 'Yes?'

'We're discreet. If you want to . . . date, we won't cramp your style.'

He shook his head, amused despite himself. 'You assume I have style.'

'Are you kidding? A man can't look like you and not have style.'

The moment the words were out of her mouth, Kat kicked herself. She really needed to employ that filter. The poor guy already had an overly keen fan on his hands. The last thing he needed was his bodyguard, the one hired to protect him from the fan, fangirling all over him.

At times it was hard not to be a fan, though. Like when he'd returned to the dressing room wearing the tightest of T-shirts, amply showcasing the famous Edwards physique. So yes, her mind had done a little wandering when he'd mentioned having a shower.

'When I saw you again this morning,' his quietly spoken words broke through her smutty thoughts, 'it's fair to say I'd harboured hopes that you'd let me show you my . . . style.'

'Oh?' she squawked, totally blindsided, which made him laugh.

'Not so quick with the chat now, I see.'

'I, umm, the hotel is just ahead.' Out of the corner of her eye she saw the laughter on his face at her glaring change of subject, but she ignored it. Just like she'd have to ignore his comment.

He's a job, Parker. Get that into your damn head. 'I took your bags up earlier when I checked you in.' That was better. Nice and professional. 'You should have everything you need.'

'Thanks.'

She didn't dare look or speak to him again, so it was in silence that she parked the Jeep and escorted him up to his private floor.

After doing another cursory check of his room – she'd done a proper check earlier when she'd dropped his things – she waved him in. 'Mark will be here in a few minutes to introduce himself. He just needs to ask you a few questions and we'll be out of your hair. But if you want to go out—'

'Call you. I know the drill.' He slipped off his jacket and laid it neatly over the back of the sofa before undoing the cuffs of his shirt and rolling them up. It was almost surreal watching him. As if she had a front-row spot at a 3D film. She'd never met an actor so captivating in the flesh.

'What sort of questions?' His voice brought her out of her daydream. She must have looked blank because he added, 'You said Mark needed to ask a few questions?'

'Yes, just to see if you have any ideas about who could be behind the stalking.' As she spoke, Zac moved to stand behind the sofa, his hands resting on the back. His eyes fixed on a spot over her left shoulder.

'If I did, don't you think I'd have mentioned it to Jerry Collier earlier?'

Kat couldn't explain why she thought it, but her gut said he was hiding something from her. 'Any smart, sensible guy would have done so, yes.'

Now she had his full attention. And to give him his due, the gaze that locked with hers didn't waver. Then again, he was an actor. 'As I'm both sensible and smart, we can assume I'm as much in the dark about who's doing this to me as you are. So, what questions does Mark want answers to?'

'Whether you can remember anyone who might have given you cause to think they could turn psycho on you. In particular any women you've met and maybe had a drink with. Dated.' She paused. 'Have slept with or are sleeping with.'

He let out a muted oath before turning towards the window, leaving her with a view of his ramrod straight back.

Bugger. She should have waited for Mark. Clearly she had the tact of a charging rhino. 'Look, I know this is difficult, but any information you can provide us will help the police track this person down.'

'How far back do I need to go?'

She could understand his annoyance. This time yesterday he'd been an actor whose movements were followed by the press. Now he was an actor followed by the press, a stalker and a bodyguard. He must feel his privacy had been violated enough already today.

Yet her sympathy was tempered by the belief he wasn't being totally open with her. 'The notes started a few months ago, so I would say six months is enough. For now.' She could feel the tension pinging across the room. 'If it helps, you can talk to Mark alone. I don't need to know.'

Finally, he turned, slipping his hands into his pockets. 'You think discussing my love life with a complete stranger will *help*?' His eloquent eyes looked so wounded, and guilt pricked.

'I don't know.'

With a sigh, he went to sit on the sofa. 'Can we just get it over with now?'

'Sure. Whatever you want.'

'I want for this to be over.' He drew in a breath and let it out slowly. 'Sorry. I just . . .' He dragged a hand through his hair. 'It's been a long day.'

'Tomorrow will be easier. And the day after that, if they've not caught Lipstick yet, you probably won't even notice I'm around.'

His eyes met and held hers. 'I very much doubt that.'

The dip in his voice, coupled with the way his gaze didn't leave hers, sent her pulse skittering. Crap, was he flirting with her again? Or did he mean he couldn't fail to notice her because she was such a pain in the arse intrusion on his life?

It had to be the latter. She *needed* it to be. 'So, those names.'

'Yes.' With another deep expulsion of breath, he took out his phone and began to scroll, presumably through his contacts. 'I dated Chloe Patterson for a while. It ended six months ago. Amicably, I thought.' He glanced briefly at her. 'I'll ping the contact through to you.'

'Thanks.' God, this was stickier than a vat of treacle. 'Any others?'

'There have been a couple of ladies I've . . . had a drink with since.' She felt her phone beep twice. 'I've sent you the contacts.' He paused, eyes on his phone and not on her. 'There was one other, Hannah, but I don't have her number. I met her at a party. She was waitressing. My manager will have the details of it if you feel the need to track her down.'

Oh boy, the tacky one-night stand. She didn't know who was more embarrassed, him for having to admit to it, or her for having to ask about it. 'Anyone you're seeing currently?'

He gave her a hard stare. 'No.'

His annoyance was palpable. Then again, she had just asked him if he was sleeping with someone, despite knowing he'd been flirting with her. 'Have you any reason to think someone you know might be the stalker?'

'For Christ's sake.' He leapt to his feet. 'I don't treat women like shit.'

It was the first time she'd heard him sound anything other than polite. 'I'm not suggesting you do.'

'No?'

'No,' she asserted. 'I'm trying to do my job. The police will want to know, and we figured you'd find it easier discussing it now, than at the police station.'

Once again, he ran a hand through his hair, walking a few strides away before turning. 'Sorry. It's just this is very . . . awkward.'

'Tell me about it,' she said on a sigh. 'It's why I'd planned to leave it to Mark to handle.'

'Oh?' Some of the tension on his face eased. 'I didn't have you down as a coward.'

'I'm not, but I am a mouthy ex-soldier. Delicacy and diplomacy don't come naturally.'

'And they do to Mark?'

The thought made her laugh. 'You've got me there. He's also ex-army and worse than I am.' Zac had been forced to admit things he hadn't wanted to. Perhaps it was time she did the same. 'Look, the truth is, for you and me to work, we need to develop a rapport. I didn't want to risk ruining any hope of that by asking these questions.'

The sharp buzz of the doorbell interrupted any answer he may have planned. 'That'll be Mark.' She walked to the door and as she checked through the peep hole, Zac spoke again.

'For the record. There's already a rapport. And this hasn't dented it.'

Relief and something else, something unwanted, fluttered through her as she opened the door to let her boss in.

The guy who strode purposefully into the room was tall and wide and . . . well, the phrase 'built like a brick shithouse' could have been coined for him. Her former CO when they were in the army, Mark had helped her through one of the toughest times in her life, so she knew, first hand, he was far less scary than he appeared. Of course, it also meant he'd seen her at her worst, which was proving to be a tough obstacle to overcome.

In four strides, he crossed the room towards Zac. 'Mark Evans.' He stuck out his hand. 'Good to meet you.'

'Zac Edwards. And nothing personal, but I'd rather not be meeting you.'

Mark gave Zac a brief smile. 'Not the first time I've heard that.' He motioned towards the sofa and armchair. 'Shall we sit?'

Kat cleared her throat. 'I'll leave you both to it. Mark, I've got the information we needed.' His eyes flared with surprise, but she ignored his unspoken question and turned to Zac. 'I'll see you tomorrow. Message me with the time you want picking up, or if you need to go out for any reason.'

'Sure. And Kat,' those eyes met hers. 'Thanks.'

What on earth was he thanking her for – poking round his house, hounding him for details of his sex life? Still, she smiled, relieved there was no hard feeling. 'No problem.' He made a movement to stand – no doubt to walk her to the door, because he seemed to have impeccable manners – so she signalled for him stay where he was. 'Don't worry, I'll see myself out.'

Though his body settled back into the sofa, she felt his eyes remain on her as she opened the door.

She also felt a tingle resonate throughout her body as it reacted to his gaze.

Chapter 6

It was Friday morning. Four days since Zac had met Kat in the lift, decided he wanted to ask her out, then found out she was going to be his bodyguard. Four days of not driving his own car. Of living in a hotel. Of being quizzed about his friends, his acquaintances. His sex life.

Four evenings spent stuck in his hotel room feeling frustrated because he couldn't go for a run, or down to the bar for a drink. Not without disturbing Kat.

And he still didn't know who was stalking him, so he still didn't know how much danger he was really in.

'I'm out tonight,' he reminded Kat as they walked into the underground car park together.

'Umm.' Her eyes scanned the concrete underbelly of the hotel, and Zac belatedly realised it was the wrong time to ask her anything. He was slowly learning she could switch off and on at will, and anywhere in the open, like a car park, she was as focused as a laser beam. It was reassuring, though he'd be far more reassured when they told him who the stalker actually was.

Or would he? A cold shiver ran down his spine as his

thoughts hurtled towards that worse-case scenario, before he yanked them back.

Once they were in the Jeep and heading down the road, Kat finally responded to his earlier comment. 'It'll be Mark on duty tonight.'

A surprising lump of disappointment settled in his gut. 'Hot date?'

Her laughter vibrated around the Jeep; it was that facet of her that he was starting to appreciate. Her vibrancy, her zest for life. 'Not unless you count going to the cinema with my fourteen-year-old niece as a date.'

'Is this the same niece who lives with you?'

She flicked him a glance. 'So you do listen to some of the stuff I say.'

He listened to everything, every word, because the banter with Kat, the repartee during their car journeys, was fast becoming the highlight of his day. 'You must be going to the cinema with Debs then, she of the one-syllable answers.'

She pursed her lips and shrugged, clearly doing an impression of a typical teenager. 'Sure.'

'I can see why you chose the cinema.'

'Exactly. The thing is, when she's not being monosyllabic, she's actually funny, sassy and off the scale smart. I know I'm biased, but she's the most amazing young person, she really is.' Pride and affection wound through her voice. 'She just needs more confidence. Mandy, my sister, her mum, she's tried hard but between work and battling her addictions, it's been tough.'

'And the dad?'

Kat snorted. 'That waste of space didn't hang around when he found out Mandy was pregnant. Oh no. He disappeared faster than a . . . damn it, I can't think of anything witty.'

'England's chances of regaining the Ashes?'

She gave him a wide-eyed look. 'Oh God, please don't tell me you're a cricket fan.' Before he could reply, she was answering her own question. 'Of course you are. The posh background.' She waved down at his tailored trousers. 'The natty dressing. The way you do everything slowly, patiently, never in a rush. You're bound to love cricket.'

'Fast isn't always better.'

She rolled her eyes at his double entendre. 'Only a cricket lover would say that. Fast is exciting, thrilling. Adrenalin pumping. Lewis Hamilton, sweeping through Maggots, into Becketts and then haring onto the Hangar Straight. That's sport. Not five days of men standing around in a field wearing white trousers.'

'You've made your point,' he said dryly, trying not to feel too entertained. His journeys to the studio were going to be infinitely duller when he no longer needed a bodyguard. 'Have you always lived with your sister?'

'I've always shared a house with her, yes. When I was in the army I was away a lot so she and Debs would get used to me not being there, and then have to readjust.' Her eyes flicked between the rear-view mirror and the road ahead. 'It's not always been plain sailing, but we're a unit. Having shitty parents brought us closer together probably, so we have something to thank them for, at least. What about you? Have you any siblings?'

He forced himself not to react. Giving himself a moment, he picked up three Starburst wrappers and screwed them into a ball. 'A brother and a sister, yes. We're not close.' Because he didn't want to give her any chance to question him further, he changed the subject onto something he did want to talk about. 'You laughed when I asked if you had a hot date. Are you dating anyone?'

For the first time since he'd known her, Kat didn't reply straight away. She'd openly spoken about her family, her job, her life as a soldier. Not, it seems, about her love life. 'Aren't you supposed to be learning your lines?'

He looked down at his forgotten script. Funny how his rule of reading through ten times had slipped since she'd started driving him to the studio. 'It's a fair question,' he reminded her. 'You grilled me on my romantic history.' Even now, he cringed at the memory of *that* conversation. He wasn't a guy who usually went for the quick and easy. He preferred to do the choosing and the chasing, because that way he knew if he was successful, he was wanted for himself, and not the fame that came with him. He'd succumbed to the overtures of the bold, busty Hannah, though. And the embarrassment, the shame of that sleazy encounter had burned through him when he'd spoken to Kat about it. He'd not even dared to look at her, fearing what he'd see on her face. *Womanising actor who deserved to be stalked.*

'No,' Kat said heavily. 'I'm not dating anyone.'

'Why not?'

Suddenly the car swerved as Kat pulled out to overtake the slow van in front of them.

'Whoa.' He grabbed onto the handle above the door to steady himself.

She glanced sideways. 'You're looking a little pale over there.'

'I'm trying to persuade my breakfast to remain in my stomach.' When he was certain there were no more overtaking manoeuvres ahead, he began to breathe again. 'Rather an extreme way to avoid the question.'

'I'm not avoiding anything. Just making sure nobody is following us.'

'And now we've ascertained there is no evil plot to kidnap me . . . Why aren't you dating anyone?'

'Because nobody has asked.'

He angled his head to look at her and found she was staring ahead, an amused expression on her face. 'And if someone were to ask?'

'It would depend on the someone.'

It was on the tip of his tongue to ask, *If that someone was me*, but it was too obvious. He'd already made his attraction clear, and she'd not taken the bait. Pushing any further would embarrass them both. Worse, if she knocked him back, it would make their current situation intolerable.

'Well I hope, when you find the someone to say yes to, he shares your love of . . .' he indicated towards the inevitable carnage in the centre console of the Jeep. 'Mess.'

She laughed, as he'd hoped she would. 'Being messy is right up there on my list of attributes for the perfect man.'

He decided not to ask what the other attributes were. No doubt they included loving motorsport, not being an uptight, cagey bastard, and not being in the public eye.

Kat glanced at her watch, and then at Debs who was sat on her bed, fingers flying over her phone.

'You realise the film started five minutes ago.'

Her niece's eyes didn't stray from the screen. 'You said that already.'

'No, five minutes ago I said the film was about to start. You said to give you two minutes.'

'Oh my God, just chill.'

Kat leant against the wall. 'I don't mind being late. It's my default position. But I'm not going to pay full price to see half a film, so if you'd rather stay here messaging your friends, that's cool with me. I'll go and get myself a beer.'

Debs huffed but stood up, squeezing her phone into the pocket of a pair of jeans so tight, Kat wondered how she could breathe. 'Whatever. Let's go.'

Her niece was silent on the way there, which wasn't especially unusual, though the edge of tension Kat could see around her mouth, was. 'Are you okay, Munchkin?' she asked once they'd parked and were walking towards the huge cinema complex.

'Sure.' Debs heaved in a shuddery breath. 'And stop with the stupid name. I'm not six anymore.'

More's the pity. Six-year-old Debs had been cute as a button. Teenage Debs was a stroppy, hormonal disaster. 'Who were you messaging?'

'Mind your own business.'

If Kat didn't know her niece so well, hadn't lived with her for all of her fourteen years, she might have left it there. 'Was it your mum?'

Debs glared at her. 'So what if it was? I'm allowed to message my own mum, aren't I?'

Kat's heart melted at the vulnerability behind Debs's stubborn stance. 'You are. And you're also allowed to be angry with her. And to tell me about that anger, because much as I love your mum, I feel it too.' Debs didn't reply, just stared ahead with a sullen expression on her face. 'But once you've got the anger out of your system, you also need to understand that your mum doesn't want to be away from you. She loves you. The fact that she's prepared to put herself through this shows you how much, because she wants to change. She wants to be the mum you deserve.'

'You said this already.'

'I know I did. I also said when she does come home, she'll be fitter and stronger than she's been for a long time so it will have been worth it. I figured it was a good time to remind you.'

'Fine.'

A lump shot into the back of Kat's throat as she saw a single tear creep down her niece's cheek. 'Hey, come here.' Dragging Debs into her arms, she soothed a hand up and down her back. 'It's going to be okay.'

'You said that last time,' Debs mumbled into her neck. 'And the time before that.'

Damn, so she had. 'Okay, you've got me. Those times I was hoping she'd be okay. This time I know she will be.'

Debs sniffed, finally pulling away. 'How?'

Kat gazed directly into her niece's dark-brown eyes. Eyes like hers, and like Mandy's. 'Before, she went because we asked her to. This time *she* asked to go. She wants to get better.'

The sad look Debs gave her tore at her heart. 'I can't stand it, the way she gets when she drinks.'

Kat squeezed her hand. 'I know. She doesn't mean to upset you. When she's sober, she's mortified that she has. But she was unlucky enough to get our father's genes and it's hard for her. Really hard, Debs. You have to remember that. She's going to need all our support to get through it.'

'Yeah, I know.' Debs sucked in a breath, wiped her eyes on the sleeve of her jumper, and looked around her.

'It's okay, nobody's looking.'

'You don't know that.'

Kat smiled. ''Course I do. It's my job to assess the surroundings.' She linked arms with Debs as they picked up the pace towards the cinema. 'Come on. At this rate, we really are going to only see half a film.'

'It's alright. It's Thomas Sangster. He's not like my favourite actor.'

'Who is then?'

'Dylan O'Brien. Zac Edwards is fit, but a bit old.'

Kat ground to a halt just before the cinema entrance. 'Zac Edwards?'

'Duh, yes. He's fit.'

'You mean he works out a lot.'

Debs rolled her eyes. 'Fit as in hot. Good looking.'

Well, what do you know. Smiling to herself, Kat ushered Debs into the lobby and handed over her debit card. 'Be a sweetie and collect the tickets from the machine. I just need to message someone about work.'

As Debs flounced off, Kat sent off a quick text to Zac.

Guess what? My niece thinks you're fit.

She knew he was out having drinks with the crew, so she was shocked when she received an instant reply.

Guess what? I am fit.

Laughing, she fired another back at him.

Does your fit self, fancy doing me a favour?

Once again the reply was immediate.

Name it.

She'd only known him five days, yet he was offering to help before he even knew what she wanted. Was he for real? Because she didn't want to think about how much that meant to her, she deflected.

Lend me the Aston to go rally cross racing?

His reply had her shaking her head in amusement.

Do I have to be in it too?

He was *kind*, she realised. Beneath the glossy layers of celebrity was a funny, kind man.

That was a joke. The favour I really want is for you to phone my niece and say hello.

She pinged him the phone number just as Debs walked back to her with the tickets.

'Here.' As she thrust the tickets at Kat, miraculously, her niece's mobile started to buzz.

'You'd better get that.'

Debs frowned, digging out her phone. 'It's an unknown number.'

'It's okay, I'm here. Put it onto me if you think it's dodgy.'

Debs pressed answer. 'Hello.'

Kat couldn't hear the voice on the other end. She could only watch the changing expressions on her niece's face – confusion, disbelief, wonder – and hear her responses. 'No way?' Pause. 'Is this a joke?' Debs, eyes wide, stared over at Kat. 'She never said.' Pause. 'I'll tell her. My mates will go mental. And my drama teacher. She's always banging on about taking us there but never has.' Pause. 'For real? Gucci.' Laughter. 'Yeah. Bye.'

Kat smiled to herself as saw her niece's hands tremble as she pushed her phone back in her pocket. 'Everything okay?'

'OMG, Kat. Why didn't you tell me? Zac fucking Edwards.'

'Language.'

Debs giggled, jumping up and down like a big kid. 'I mean, I've just been talking to *Zac Edwards*.'

'What did you have to tell me?'

'What? Oh, he said you have to bring me down to the studio one day. He'll show me around. And I can bring my school mates, if I want.' She put a hand to her head, clearly still in shock. 'I mean, I can't believe this, he said *he's* looking forward to meeting *me*.'

Kat could just imagine it. The smooth language. Those impeccable manners. 'Did he know what Gucci meant?'

Debs snorted, her whole face looking so much more alive than it had five minutes ago. 'He said something like "Can I presume that's a positive?"' She giggled. 'He's dead posh, isn't he?'

'He certainly is.' Kat glanced at her watch in horror. 'And we're dead late for this blasted film now.'

Debs shrugged. 'It's Gucci.'

And then she laughed, and while Kat knew this wasn't over, that Debs would have some difficult times ahead, at least now, tonight, she was reassured to see her niece with a smile on her face.

Chapter 7

Zac was, unusually for him, running late. Something his bodyguard had been happy to point out when she'd knocked on his hotel room five minutes ago to find him not yet ready. His main bodyguard, he should add, not the tall, silent guy he'd had to put up with Friday night, once at the weekend, and just now on his way back from the studio.

'Mark said you had another note today, delivered to the studio.' Kat's voice echoed through to his bedroom where he was currently dragging a shirt off a hanger.

'Yes.' Fear crashed down his spine as he recalled the note. *I came to your place to see you. They told me you'd left. Are you avoiding me?* It wasn't so much the words, as the implication. Someone was watching him.

Who? And more importantly, why?

'Have you had any more thoughts about who it might be?'

His hands stilled, and as his heart began to thump, Zac was grateful for the wall that separated him from Kat. 'Why do you ask?' Damn, that wasn't the right answer. 'I'd hardly keep it to myself if I had, would I?'

'Only if you're a total idiot.'

She'd said something similar before, yet Zac refused to believe he was an idiot. He was an actor trying to protect an image he wasn't ready to see destroyed on a wild, highly improbable, obsessively anxious hunch.

'How's it going with Mark?' Kat's voice cut through his paranoid thoughts. 'I bet you two were chatting away on the journey here.'

Shrugging on the shirt, he walked out to the sitting area where she was waiting, feet up on the footstool, thumbing through the newspaper the hotel conveniently placed outside his room every morning. 'You know we weren't.'

She smirked, though the expression slid from her face as her eyes settled on him. Or more precisely, on the part of his chest revealed by the shirt he hadn't buttoned up yet. He was vain enough to know he looked good without his shirt on – hell, he spent enough hours in the gym working at it. Even more hours recently, since it was one of the few things he could do, without having to call for an escort.

'Eyes on my face,' he said mildly.

Of course, Kat being Kat, wasn't embarrassed to be caught out. 'Don't fret, Mr I-can't-act-a-scene-without-taking-my-shirt-off. I've seen it all before.'

'But not in the flesh.' He slowly – and yes, deliberately – began to do up the buttons.

'Not yours, maybe, but I've seen plenty of others.' When his brows shot up to his hairline, she groaned. 'I was in the army, remember? I've seen enough male chests to last me a lifetime.' As if to prove she was totally unfazed, she glanced back down at the newspaper. 'So, back to my original question. How are you and Mark getting on?'

Disappointment curled inside him. Ridiculous. Did it matter that she wasn't interested in him? Wasn't it better this way? He had enough going on in his life right now without further complicating things. 'Mark is fine. We're getting on . . . fine.' All of it true. The big guy was exactly how he'd imagined a bodyguard would be. Strong and silent.

Kat burst out laughing. 'Come on, admit it, you miss my chat when I'm not around.'

He was acutely aware he didn't just miss her chat. He missed *her*. 'Mark is like me. He understands the need for quiet reflection.' Before she could call him on his bullshit, Zac headed back into the bedroom to retrieve his jacket and tie. When he came back out, she was on her feet.

'Ready?'

He threaded his tie as he walked towards her. 'As ready as I'll ever be.'

She looked at him askance. 'You're not looking forward to the launch of your very own brand of fragrance?'

He huffed out a breath. 'It's not mine. I'm merely the face behind the name.' On the back of the success of *The Good Guy?* the perfume company had done a deal with the film company, and tonight was the big promotional shindig for the launch of a male fragrance of the same name.

'Ah, but what a face.'

Her smile was teasing but it was hard to smile back. Being idolised for how he looked was an uncomfortable fit. Much like a cheap suit.

'You need to lighten up by the time we get there,' she told him once they were in the car. 'Or they'll have to change the name to The Morose Guy.'

'Sorry.' He settled back into the passenger seat – a hired Range Rover – and wondered at how quickly he'd become used to being driven around. Or was it Kat he'd become accustomed to? 'Where were you this afternoon?'

'So you did miss me.' He saw the moment she became aware that her statement was too personal, and clamped her mouth shut.

'I missed your driving,' he corrected, though if he'd thought the comment would have been well received, he might have agreed with her statement. 'Had you driven me back, I doubt I would be running late.'

'Ah, good spot. Debs had a parent–teacher meeting at the school, so I agreed to do tonight if Mark covered me for that.'

'Gucci.'

Kat burst out laughing. 'You have no clue what that means, do you?'

He smiled. 'None whatsoever.'

'She's still talking about the day she spoke to you. You're like some sort of superhero in her eyes now.'

'Perish the thought.' He turned his head to stare out of the side window, not wanting Kat to read his thoughts. To see how insecure he was, beneath the polish. Being acclaimed for his acting was one thing; he craved it. The rest, the attention that came from people's impression of who he was from the parts he played, or from his appearance. That he had a hard time dealing with.

They didn't know him. Very few people did, and while that was deliberate, it was also, at times, very lonely.

It was manic. Sitting in the Range Rover, Kat eyed up the crowds with mounting apprehension. The people she'd previously provided protection to had attracted nowhere near this interest. People lined either side of a narrow, cordoned-off area leading to the entrance of The Old Billiard Room – the venue for the fragrance launch. Ninety-nine percent of the waiting throng were female, many bearing placards, some of which were quite clever – *Good Guy, be My Guy*; some straightforward – *I love you Zac*; and a few downright dirty – *Zac, shag me*, being the politest.

She brought the Range Rover to a halt directly outside and glanced at her passenger. He'd been very quiet since she'd mentioned Debs and she wondered if it was because he wanted to back out on his offer to show her round the studios – an offer Kat had no intention of holding him to – or if there was something else going on inside that handsome head of his.

'Ready?'

Almost on cue, as if a director had said, 'Action', Zac sat up straight and gave her a flash of that sexy smirk. 'Are you?'

She eyed the clamouring crowd and did a bit of spine straightening of her own. 'Of course.'

'Then let's go and meet the fans.'

She jumped down from the car and, giving the area another sweeping look, went to open his door.

Immediately flashlights lit up the dusky evening, and Kat froze, her heart pounding. Shit, no, this wasn't going to happen.

She was not about to have a panic attack. The flashbulbs were from paparazzi cameras. There was no gunfire, no lurking terrorists.

As she forced herself to be calm, she reflected on how stupid it was that she hadn't prepared herself for this . . . and that she even needed to. It had been over three years since she'd left the army. That part of her life was done, she'd moved on.

'Kat?' Zac gave her a quizzical glance.

She nodded, focusing on breathing, in and out, slow and steady.

'Are you okay?'

'Sure.' There, she'd found her voice. And now her heart rate was starting to come under control. 'Just hadn't realised you were so popular.' As if to prove her point, the fans started to shout his name. 'Go on then, don't keep them waiting.'

Pulling herself together, Kat scanned the crowd. She couldn't afford to get distracted. Zac's life might depend on her.

She swallowed down another bubble of panic. She'd told Mark she was ready for this. Damn it, she *was* ready.

While Zac worked the fans, a handshake here, a selfie there, Kat kept her eyes trained on the faces.

'Hey, Edwards, what's this new aftershave like?' A middle-aged guy pushed his way to the front. 'Will it make the missus go wild for me?'

Zac gave the man his small, polished smile. 'Why not try it and find out?'

'Not at those rip-off prices. You must get some freebies. How about throwing a bottle my way? Keep her happy?'

Okay, she didn't like how close he was getting. 'Back away, sir.'

At just under six foot, the mouthy guy looked down at her. 'And who are you? No, wait, don't tell me. You're the bleeding bodyguard.' He started to laugh. 'Bloody hell, that's priceless.' He spun round to address the crowd behind him. 'Look here, ladies. The big action hero you're all drooling over is such a wimp he needs a woman to protect him.'

Beside her, Zac went rigid, but she admired his restraint when he merely turned away to shake the hand of a fan on the other side.

That's when the jerk doing the taunting decided he didn't like being ignored. 'Oi, I'm talking to you.' Ducking under the rope, he made towards Zac.

Kat acted on pure instinct. In two seconds, she had the guy face down on the pavement, pulling on his right hand as she edged it higher up his back. 'Let me go, you bitch.'

'Ask me nicely and I might.' Adrenalin surging through her, she tugged harder on his arm.

'Fucking hell, that hurts.'

'Oh, I'm sorry. I didn't realise a mere woman could hurt a big strong guy like you.'

A moment later the event security staff came running over and Kat gladly handed him over. 'He's all yours.'

Suddenly a hand gripped her arm and she turned to find Zac staring at her, his eyes full of concern. 'Are you okay?'

'Of course.' Her lip curled in disgust as she watched the man being escorted away.

'Christ, Kat.'

He looked shocked, rattled. Exactly how she'd felt when she'd first faced the crowd. 'Let's get you inside, before any other tossers decide they want to end up face down on the pavement.'

Being the star he was, Zac immediately plastered a smile on his face and waved at the crowds on either side as she escorted him inside the building. Once there, he was swamped by the organisers and Kat hung back, watching from a distance as he was introduced to people, photographed, and generally treated like visiting royalty. Every now and again his eyes would land on hers and she wondered what he was thinking.

In taking down the troublemaker, had she reassured Zac she was capable of keeping him safe?

Or instead was he remembering her wobble at the beginning, and the snide comments from the mouthy guy. Were they reinforcing his concerns about having her as his bodyguard at all?

Two hours later, Kat escorted Zac back to the Range Rover. He looked tired, so she left him to his thoughts as she drove him back to the hotel and then walked with him into the lift.

When he still didn't say anything after she'd done a sweep of his room and signalled it was okay for him to come in, she decided it was time to hit the issue head on.

'The guy hurling all that abuse on the pavement was a moron.'

Zac shrugged off his jacket and loosened his tie. 'Agreed.'

'So you can ignore everything he said. Like having a female bodyguard makes you look like a wimp.'

'What?' A mixture of shock and confusion spread across his face. 'You think that bothered me?'

Crap, if it wasn't that . . . Kat felt a ball of unease settle in her stomach. 'Something did, because you've not said a word all the way here.' He shook his head, exhaling heavily as he threw his jacket onto the sofa. 'And you always hang your jacket up.'

'Jesus.' He tugged a hand through his hair before heading towards the minibar. 'Do you want a drink? Someone told me it was one of the perks of living in a hotel.'

She could have murdered one, but she had to shake her head. 'No thanks. I'm on duty.'

'I'm here, safe and sound in my hotel room. You're off the clock.'

'I'm also driving. But I'll take a Coke, if there is one.'

He reached inside and drew out a miniature of whisky and a small Coke, pouring hers into a glass and handing it to her before pouring his own. 'Cheers.' He perched on the arm of the sofa and gave her a small, tight smile. 'Here's to my bodyguard, keeping me safe.'

He was being ironic. Damn it, he was going to pull her up on her mini panic attack. Feeling her hands start to tremble, Kat quickly put down her drink. 'Just say what you want to say.'

'I just did.' He raised his glass towards her. 'A toast to my bodyguard.'

'How many drinks have you already had?'

He raised a brow, looking offended. 'You think I'm drunk?'

'I don't know what to think,' she muttered, taking a big

swig of the Coke. 'But if you're going to talk in riddles, it's time for me to leave.'

He sipped at his whisky, his eyes on her, the look brooding and unnervingly intense. 'He could have had a knife. Or a gun.'

The bottom fell out of her stomach. Any minute now, he was going to tell he wanted her replaced. Slowly she turned. 'I realise that. And I can imagine how terrifying it must be, knowing someone might want to hurt you.'

'You think *that's* what spooked me out there?' Suddenly he jumped to his feet and stalked over, putting his hands on her shoulders. When he looked down at her there was an urgency, a roughness to his expression she'd not seen before. 'Fuck, Kat, he could have hurt *you*.'

Her heart lurched at the emotion swirling in his eyes. 'He couldn't. He *didn't*. I'm good at what I do.' *When I'm not distracted.* Kat shoved the unhelpful, yet grimly accurate, thought away.

Zac huffed, glancing away for a moment, before settling those stunning eyes back on her. 'I didn't think about it before, but now it's all I can think about.' His hands shifted to curl around her upper arms and his gaze landed on her mouth. 'I don't want you putting yourself in danger to protect me.'

Inside her chest, her heart beat like a crazy thing. Was this all part of his ploy to get rid of her? Or was he worried about the thing he was hiding from them – she wasn't daft, she knew there was something he wasn't telling them. Was he worried that might put her at risk, too?

Or, God, the hooded eyes, the parted lips. Was he going to *kiss* her? Involuntarily, her own lips began to tingle in anticipation. It was wrong, so very wrong, yet part of her wanted it to happen. Wanted to feel that sensual mouth against hers.

This man with his fussy ways and careful words. Dry humour and kind actions. She was getting frighteningly attached to him.

Taking a step back, she forced her mind to focus back on what he'd said. 'You want to swap bodyguards? Have Mark find you someone else?' The thought stung.

'The thought has crossed my mind.'

'I see.'

'No, you don't!' With a hiss of frustration, he swirled round and smacked his hand against the opposite wall.

Always so measured, so in control, it was a shock to see this other side of him. 'Zac?'

His back facing her, she watched the rise and fall of his shoulders as he drew in a deep breath and slowly let it out. When he turned towards her again, he looked calmer.

'Sorry. Seeing you in action today, it rattled me.'

'What did?' *The way I froze, like a startled rabbit? Please don't say it, please don't—*

'The way you put yourself between me and that mouthy git.'

He hadn't noticed her scared bunny impression. Relief flooded through her. 'If it had been Mark grappling the jerk instead, would you still have been rattled?'

'No.'

She huffed. 'So it's a gender issue.'

He laughed, but not in an amused way. More . . . baffled.

'No, Kat, it's not a gender issue. It's a *you* issue. I like *you*. I don't want *you* to come to any harm.'

Deep inside her chest she felt a squeeze. 'Thank you, but I know what I'm doing.'

'We don't know who we're up against though, do we? We don't know what *they're* capable of.'

He was worrying her again. 'What are you saying?'

With a shake of his head he walked towards the door. 'I'm saying I don't want to be responsible for you being hurt.' Hand on the handle, he glanced over at her. 'I'm saying for both our sakes, I hope you're right when you say you know what you're doing. Goodnight, Kat.'

Her mind was a whirl of emotions as she rode back down in the lift. He'd hinted at it before, but now she knew. He liked her.

It shouldn't matter, yet it did.

Did he like her enough to trust her with the information he was clearly hiding though, because she really, really needed him to do that. Only then would she know the true scale of the challenge she was facing and whether she was as ready as she'd promised Mark. Or as capable as she'd claimed to Zac.

Chapter 8

The following day Zac was in his dressing room when he received a call from the police, who wanted to let him know they were working with UK Security and doing all they could to track down his stalker.

Three of the names he'd provided had checked out, they'd reassured him, though they were still trying to trace Hannah. Could he give them a description of her?

And even though their *encounter* had been between two consenting adults. Even though they'd both got what they'd wanted out of it; her to have sex with a celebrity, him a welcome distraction from a party filled with pretentious luvvies he'd hated every minute of and only gone to because his manager had told him to. Even then, knowing they'd parted amicably, her with a smile on her face, he'd felt seedy talking to the cop. Especially when he couldn't, for certain, say whether her eyes had been green or brown.

Surprising, because it was often the eyes that attracted him first.

Kat, who'd he'd nearly kissed last night, had eyes that were a deep, luscious brown. Warm eyes, to match her warm soul. Eyes he'd nearly lost himself in.

Frustrated with the way his thoughts were turning, he jumped to his feet, only for his phone to ring again.

It was twenty minutes later before he was able to get back on set. A lot longer before he was able to get the phone conversation out of his head for long enough to focus on the scene they were filming.

'You were distracted this afternoon.' Tom, the assistant director, caught up with Zac moments after he'd called a wrap on the day.

'Sorry.' Annoyed at his piss poor performance, Zac gave Tom a tight smile. 'It won't happen again.'

'Hey, I'm not concerned, not for the film. You're one of the most professional actors I've worked with. I'm concerned for you. Is this stalker getting to you?'

Zac shook his head. 'I just had a phone call that threw me for a loop, that's all.' Deciding maybe he could use the excuse Tom had handed him, Zac added, 'The police phoned to update me on progress so far, or should I say lack of progress.'

Tom gave him a sympathetic look. 'They'll catch them soon enough, and in the meantime UK Security will take care of you.'

Which was half the damn trouble, Zac thought as he made his way back to the dressing room. He had a stalker who might, or might not, be related to the past he'd wiped clean, and who might, or might not, want to seriously harm him.

Then he had a bodyguard he liked – *really* liked – but who he could be putting in terrible danger.

On top of all that, his bodyguard was also a woman who, through professionalism or lack of interest, was determinedly keeping her distance. Hell, he'd nearly kissed her last night, before she'd coolly taken a step back.

Added to that heady mix was the phone call he'd taken earlier, reminding him where he needed to be this weekend.

It was the last place he wanted someone watching him closely.

When he'd finished his shower, he found Kat waiting for him outside.

What was it about her?, he mused as his eyes fell on her trim form, dressed as usual in black. Uniform or personal taste, he didn't know. Only that the colour suited her, emphasising her luscious dark eyes.

'Straight home?' She winced. 'Sorry, straight to the hotel?'

'Unless you have a better idea.'

She pursed her lips. 'Well, it's a lovely evening. Shame to spend it cooped up inside when you could be strolling along the river. Perhaps ending up in a pub with a . . .' She considered him. 'Gin and tonic?'

It sounded like heaven. But. 'Are you with me in this scenario?'

'Well, I'm on duty, so the G&T would need to be a Coke, but otherwise, you bet.'

This was part of her appeal, he realised. She didn't wait for life to happen, she grabbed at it. 'And if I'm recognised?'

'You've got some shades?' When he nodded, she added, 'I can lend you a baseball cap.'

'Sold.' Feeling his mood lift, Zac followed her down the corridor towards the car park.

Twenty minutes later, he was walking alongside the River Thames with Kat, watching the sun glisten off the water. The evening was warm and still, the only sound the gentle chug of a river barge as it eased its way downstream.

He sucked in a deep, life affirming breath, only to catch her smiling at him. 'What?'

'You were really wound up when I first saw you. Now you've relaxed.'

He eyed her speculatively. 'Is that why you suggested a walk?'

She gave him a smug smile. 'Of course.' They walked in silence for a few minutes. 'Is there anything on your mind? Anything I can help with?'

Find the stalker so I don't have live in this awful, twisted fear not just for my own life, but yours. Words that would shatter the peace. Unfair words, too, because it wasn't her job to work out who was following him. 'I've got to attend a family function on Saturday.' He kept his eyes forward, his body language deliberately casual. 'My mother holds this annual charity ball. It's a private party, in my parents' house, which is in the middle of nowhere.'

'Is that your way of saying you don't want me or Mark there?'

He gave her the cocky smile he was famous for. 'I knew you'd see it my way.'

'Oh no. No, no, no. And in case you misheard it, I'll repeat. No.' Those brown eyes flashed darts at him. 'Vision Films are paying us to guard you 24/7. The only reason we're not camped outside your hotel room is because Collier is happy with the security arrangements of a hotel with a private floor.'

'Fine. You or Mark can drive me there, drop me off and pick me up later.'

She blinked. 'That's not how this works. I decide how to handle your security, not you.'

'Of course.' He forced himself to smile. 'It just seems overkill to take a bodyguard to a charity event held at my parents' estate. The stalker is hardly going to be invited.'

He wasn't sure what was at the bottom of the assessing look she gave him. Only that he found her scrutiny uncomfortable. 'In the last note you received, the stalker asked if you were avoiding them, so would it be fair to conclude they're watching you?'

'Possibly.'

Kat gave a huff of annoyance. 'You're deluding yourself if you think there's any other explanation, but let's explore this further. Your biography states you were brought up in a manor house in West Buckinghamshire, so even you have to admit anyone determined enough can find out where your parents live. As for the stalker not having an invitation, the Queen didn't invite Michael Fagan into her bedroom at Buckingham Palace, but she still found him there.'

Frustration bubbled. 'Come on, Kat. The worst thing that happened to the Queen was the country got to know what type of nightie she wore.'

'Only because the security staff got lucky. It could have been so different. Fagan could have had a knife or a gun.' She levelled him a look. 'I suspect someone lost their job over it.'

He laughed in disbelief. 'You're really going to use *that* argument?'

She shrugged. 'I'll use whatever it takes.'

He knew when he was beaten. Knew too, that if he protested any further, she'd start to wonder what he was hiding. Still, if he had to have an escort, he'd at least make it on his terms. 'I'll accept a protection detail, as long as it's you.'

She eyed him suspiciously. 'Why?'

'Because if I'm bringing someone, they're coming as my date.'

'Oh no.'

'Oh yes,' he insisted. 'I take a bodyguard to a private charity function, people will think I'm a paranoid tosser or an arrogant prick.' He let his eyes skim over Kat's bewitching face. The angles that shouldn't work, but did. The eyes that held him hostage. They were by the river, in the setting sun, with nobody watching them. He was damned if he was going to waste the opportunity. Deliberately he softened his voice. 'I take you, and people will think I'm a lucky bastard.'

Kat almost swallowed her tongue. Good God, what did she say to that?

'You're flirting again. We can't.'

'I've not seen any rule to that effect.' His eyes danced as he trailed his forefinger gently down her cheek, causing a flurry of sparks to race across her skin. 'Or any rule stating I'm not allowed to kiss you,' he murmured, those magnetic green eyes skimming over her mouth before lifting to meet hers. The hunger she saw, the intensity, made her breath catch.

'Please,' she croaked, her pulse racing at what had to be a million beats a minute.

'Please, you want me to kiss you?'

His voice had lowered an octave and she felt herself slowly drowning under the power of his sexuality. 'No,' she managed, before she went under.

A frown appeared between his eyes. 'Are you sure, because your body is telling me something else.'

'My body can't be trusted.' With herculean strength, she tore her gaze from his. 'Please don't make this hard.'

His lips quirked and he glanced down. 'Well, it's not hard yet, but it's getting there.'

With a growl of frustration, she pushed at him. 'I'm being serious.'

Sighing, he rubbed at the back of his neck. 'So am I.'

'What do you mean?'

Placing his hands in his pockets, he took a step away from her. 'I'm very attracted to you, Kat.'

She swallowed, her heart beating erratically. 'Thank you. I'm flattered, I really am.'

'Are you attracted to me?'

Oh shit. 'How could I not be. I mean, look at you. All those shiny good looks—'

His jaw muscle twitched. 'Cut the crap.'

Beneath his annoyance, she saw a vulnerability she'd not expected. Yet she couldn't be seduced by it, or by him. She just couldn't. 'Look, whatever seduction routine you've got going on inside your head—'

'*Seduction routine.*' He jerked backwards, shaking his head. 'You think I'm that cunning? That I *planned* this? You're the one who suggested the walk.'

'I know, I'm sorry.' Agitated, she glanced towards the river, watching a group of ducks as they glided serenely by. 'What I'm trying to tell you is, if you want to seduce me, it will work.'

He stilled. 'It will?'

'Yes.' As his mouth started to curve into that sexy small smile, she added, 'But I'm asking you, please, not to.'

His answering sharp exhale sounded like a clap of thunder against the tranquillity of the setting. As she held her breath, waiting for him to reply, the air between them hummed, like power lines from an electricity pylon. The more he stared at her the more she knew, without doubt, that if he decided to kiss her anyway, she'd melt against him.

Damn, that pissed her off. She didn't want a man to have that sort of hold over her again. The sort of hold that would lead her to forget right from wrong, sensible from stupid, and just give in to what her body wanted.

Maybe, further down the line, to what her heart wanted.

'Am I allowed to ask why I can't seduce you?' he said eventually.

'Sleeping with the client is tacky and unprofessional. I don't want to be that person.' She swallowed, focusing on keeping her voice steady, her emotions on lockdown. 'More importantly, it's a distraction. And distractions can get you killed.'

He gave a little shake of his head, as if he didn't believe her. But then a guard came down across his face and he stared towards the riverbank. When he spoke again, it was as if the whole conversation hadn't happened. 'I believe you promised me a gin and tonic.'

She told herself she was relieved he hadn't pressed it.

Relieved he hadn't kissed her, even though her lips felt deprived of his touch. 'I promised you a pub. You're responsible for your own drink.'

A twitch of those delicious lips. 'Who said having a bodyguard is no fun?'

They started to walk again, an underlying . . . *tension* was too strong a word for it . . . a sizzle, an awareness between them that, while it had always existed, she'd been able to push to the back of her mind. Now she'd have to find a way to cut through it, so she could get them back on the polite yet friendly footing her equilibrium desperately needed.

'You do realise I'm not here for your entertainment,' she remarked after a while.

'More's the pity.'

Ignore him. 'I'm here to keep you safe.'

He slid her a sidelong look. 'Explain how you driving like a lunatic, keeps me safe.'

Better, she thought. 'I drive like a competent professional who's undergone extensive advanced driving tests.'

'Is that so?'

'It is. So, about that offer you made to lend me the Aston to go rally cross racing.'

As his laughter filled the air between them, Kat relaxed. Perhaps by tomorrow their almost-kiss would be a distant memory.

Chapter 9

Kat rechecked her image in the mirror. There was no escaping the fact. Dresses just weren't for her. The same body that looked okay in jeans and leggings was too muscular, too athletic for a dress. She was a soldier, pretending to be a lady and failing miserably.

'I thought you said you had to leave at six?'

Kat caught sight of her niece in the mirror reflection. 'I did.'

'Then stop looking at yourself and get in the car. You look fine.'

'Is that the best you can do? Fine?'

'What do you want me to say?'

'That I look elegant?' She turned away from the mirror, and the clear evidence to the contrary.

Debs shoved her hands on her hips. 'You want me to lie?'

What was the point? It hardly mattered what she looked like tonight, did it? This was just a job.

Except he'd called it a date. And she was meeting Zac's parents.

She gave herself a mental slap. Since that awkward conversation on the riverbank, things were back to normal between them. Fine, normal was pushing it. Normal meant she wasn't aware of his eyes on her, her body didn't react to his nearness. She didn't think, far too often, about what it would have felt like to be kissed by him. So, no, things weren't as they had been, weren't *normal*, but he hadn't flirted, hadn't acted in a manner outside the boundary of client and bodyguard. He was doing as she'd asked, and she needed to find a way to do the same. His life might depend on it.

Worms of worry wriggled around in her belly and Kat pressed a hand to it, pushing them away. Inhaling a deep breath, she walked purposefully into her bedroom and grabbed at her handbag and the black wrap she'd pinched from her sister's wardrobe.

'What time are your friends getting here?' she asked Debs as she came back out.

'They'll be here in a bit. And yes, we'll be careful. We won't invite anyone else, we won't open the door to anyone.'

'And?'

'We won't drink, won't smoke, won't do drugs.' She rolled her big brown eyes. 'Won't have any fun.'

'Good. Mark's coming round to say hello later, so when he phones, you can open the door to him.'

'OMG, you did not get your boss to come and check on us.'

'No.' She searched around on the hall table for the hire car key. 'I got my friend to drop by on his way back from a function.' Damn, where the hell had she put it?

Debs picked a key off the coffee table, waving it in the air. 'Looking for this?'

'Thanks.' Dashing to take it from her, Kat almost turned her ankle. 'Ruddy hell. How does anyone walk in high shoes?'

'You think they're high?' Debs looked down at Kat's three-inch black strappy sandals in disgust. 'People wear higher shoes than that to school.'

There was nothing like a sarky teenager to crush your fragile confidence. 'Thanks, your comments on my attire have been noted and ignored. Now, I'm off. Be good.'

'You too.' Debs began to giggle. 'You know, considering you told me you don't fancy Zac Edwards, you're weirdly worried about how you look.'

'I don't want to *embarrass* him. We're pretending I'm his date.' And God, how had she let him persuade her into that? She was hardly the type he usually had draped over his arm. 'I realise how ridiculous that seems.'

It was too late to change now, so she'd just have to go as his overdressed bodyguard. With heels that were too high to do anything useful in, like walk or run. But apparently not high enough when it came to looking elegant.

As she hurried towards the door, Debs's voice carried over to her. 'You don't look elegant, but you do look okay. You know, for you.'

Kat burst out laughing. 'Thanks, Munchkin.'

As Kat waited outside Zac's hotel room she knew she was fidgeting but she couldn't help it. The dress felt too tight, the sandals too uncomfortable. She wanted her boots. Then the door swung open, and all thoughts of how she looked, how she felt, flew out of her mind.

'Oh my flaming God.' She gaped at the vision in front of her, dressed in an immaculate fitting black tux, crisp white shirt unbuttoned at the collar, black silk bow tie loosely hanging round his neck.

He gave her a quizzical, highly sexy smile before his eyes made their own bold appraisal.

'You don't have to say anything nice,' she told him quickly. 'You've seen this dress before and besides, Debs has already told me I look okay, for me, which I'm taking as a compliment.'

'I think I can do better than that.'

His dryly amused charm woke the dormant butterflies in her stomach. 'No, that's the whole point. You don't need to. I know I look okay.' She hoped she didn't sound as flustered as she felt. 'Now, are you ready? I mean, you look ready, well apart from the sexy undone tie thing you've got going on.'

'Sexy, huh?'

'Please, you know perfectly well how sexy you look. So let's just . . . go.' *Breathe, Kat, breathe.* He'd turned her into a rambling, hormonal mess and she wasn't happy about it.

'By all means.' Still looking amused, he ducked back inside to pick up his wallet, tucking the hotel key card inside. 'I assume you'll want to lead the way?'

Nodding curtly, she opened the door, taking her time to check the corridor. The routine action helped calm her, a timely reminder this was far from a date. It was work.

She'd taken a step towards the lift when she felt the warmth of his body press lightly against her back, and the classy smell of his expensive aftershave drift up her nostrils. 'You look stunning, Kat Parker.' Her knees buckled and as she stumbled, he smirked back at her. 'Everything okay?'

Inhaling sharply, she gathered herself. 'Fine, thank you. I'm not good in heels, as you already know to your cost. They should come with a health and safety warning.' *As should he*, she thought crossly. It was one thing telling herself he was a client, a job. Now she needed to make sure her body understood it, too.

Zac took another long sidelong glance at the lady driving him. And she really looked like a lady tonight. Not a slick, highly polished lady with hair artfully styled and make-up professionally applied. No, Kat, with her *stuff convention, this is me* attitude, was her own woman. It gave her a vibe, an edge, that was so sexy, it was impossible not to keep staring at her. He itched to tear down the barriers she'd put up. Ached to explore both the body and the mind of this fascinating, unique woman who could floor a man in the blink of an eye, yet who couldn't take a compliment on her looks.

Who acted so tough, yet who came over soft and sentimental when it came to her niece.

Kat didn't feel the same pull towards him, though. The excuse she'd given by the river, of him being her client, simply didn't ring true. A woman who had no compunction pinching a car park space, who'd blithely turned up late to a client meeting, wasn't someone cowed by rules.

So though she was attracted to him – he could read those signs – she didn't like him enough to want to cross the line she'd drawn. He needed to respect that and stop fantasising about her.

Fuck, it was hard though. Especially when she spoke to him the way she was now.

'So, tonight. I don't really have to go as your date.'

The question, which should have been there, was buried deep beneath the combative tone. It made him want to kiss the attitude right out of her. 'We've agreed this already. You, Kat Parker, are my date this evening.'

Her huff was one of pure annoyance. 'Fine. But what about your parents? We're not going to lie to them, surely.'

He was grateful she was driving, so wasn't watching him too closely. 'They know you're my bodyguard, but nobody else does.'

'They're Helena and William Edwards, yes?'

'Yes.' It was so close to the truth it actually felt like it was, which was why he had no qualms repeating the story whenever he was asked about his background. So why did the lie now stick in his throat?

'What about any other family? I think you said you had a brother and a sister?'

'I'm not sure if they're going.'

Dread seeped through him. Why the hell had he agreed to come? *Because William and Helena asked you, and you can never say no to them.*

Damn it, this was why he hadn't wanted a bodyguard with him. Hadn't wanted anyone from his new life, mixing with his old.

'You've gone all quiet on me.' Kat's amused voice broke through his panicking thoughts. 'And you're looking all . . . twitchy.'

With a determined effort, he relaxed his shoulders. 'I'm not.' He flicked her a glance. 'I'm remembering how unspeakably dull these occasions are, so if you want to drop me off and go somewhere more exciting for a few hours, feel free.'

This time she was the one who appeared to tense. 'You know I can't do that, so repeating the wheedle isn't going to work. But I can go as your bodyguard if, you know, you're having second thoughts about the date thing. Which I totally understand and actually think would be a far better idea—'

'Why would I be having second thoughts?'

She indicated to turn down a narrow country lane, and his heart beat a little faster. They were nearly there. 'Well, something's worrying you. I thought maybe you were thinking it was a bad idea to pretend I'm your date.'

'Whatever is going on in that head of yours,' he rebuked mildly, 'stop it. I'm proud to have you on my arm, as my date.'

He could have sworn there was a hint of a blush on her cheeks, but it was too dark to tell for sure. 'I hope you're still saying that when I've tripped over the shag pile rug because of these ruddy shoes.'

Laughter burst out of him. 'I can promise you there will be no shag pile rugs. Only very expensive wool rugs from Persia.'

That elicited a groan. 'Did I mention how clumsy I can be?'

'I'm well aware,' he answered dryly.

'Ah, yes, I'd conveniently forgotten that little encounter. And I have to warn you, if the choice is spilling drink all over your parents' Persian rug, or all over you, you're in for another dousing. I will take it easy on you, though, and stick to water, so at least you won't stink like a wine cellar while you're schmoozing with your parents' honoured guests.'

He started to laugh again, but then the Edwards Estate came into view and the laughter died. One glance at the shock on Kat's face, though, was enough to shove him out of his worry pit. To think she'd actually believed the reason he was acting so twitchy, as she'd called it, was because he didn't want to introduce her as his girlfriend. Did she really think he was that shallow? Or was this vital, sexy woman not as confident as she let on? One thing he was certain about: no way was he going to let his own unease about the situation lead her to think she was anything less than the rather amazing woman he was fast discovering.

Kat swung the hired BMW 5 series – she'd taken to insisting on using different cars – into the gravel drive and parked it by the entrance where a valet waited to park it. After she'd handed over the keys she stood awkwardly, staring at the house.

'You know I checked this out on Google maps, but seeing it in real life is something else. It's a flaming stately home.'

Zac put his arm around her, resting it against the small of her back. 'It's a house. One a little larger than most.'

'I'd be fine if I was in my leggings and boots.' She gave him an accusing stare. 'You made me put on this stupid dress and pretend I'm something I'm not.'

'I don't want you pretending anything. Be yourself.'

She made a noise of irritation. 'What if they ask me what I do?'

Gently he pressed his hand against her back, leading her – or more accurately pushing her – towards the entrance. 'You can be a bodyguard. Just not my bodyguard.'

'Then how did we meet, hot shot?'

He smirked back at her. 'I believe you threw your drink over me.'

Her answering bad-tempered hiss made him smile.

'This is a bad idea,' she muttered as she stepped gingerly over the gravel towards the short path.

He bent his head towards her, feeling a dart of satisfaction when her body shivered as his lips touched her earlobe. 'Relax, Kat.' Because he enjoyed the feeling of being so close, of touching her, he added, 'You should know it's doing my ego good to be the one calming you for a change.'

Her brown eyes darted to his. 'When have I ever had to calm you? You're always so cool, so smooth, it's like somebody irons you before you go out.'

He laughed, flattered. 'All that is on the outside. You're steady where it counts, on the inside.' He'd witnessed it himself, at the launch of the fragrance, when she'd taken the guy down in the blink of an eye and then carried on as if it was no big deal.

While he'd spent the rest of the evening haunted by what might have been.

'Zac, my dear, there you are.' Helena Edwards appeared in the entrance, a wide smile on her beautiful, refined face. 'It's so good to see you. I know this didn't come at a good time, but I'm thrilled you could be here.'

'Helena.' He reached out to kiss her cheek. 'You know I wouldn't miss it. I'd like to introduce you to Kat Parker.'

'Kat, how do you do?' Helena gave Kat a quick peck on the cheek. 'Come on in. I'll just go and find William. Why don't you wait for us in the drawing room?'

He could feel Kat's eyes on him, and the sense of foreboding from earlier returned. Keeping his hand on her back, just above the gentle curve of her buttocks, Zac led her into the room on the right of the hallway and carefully closed the door.

Immediately her gaze locked in on her surroundings, taking in all the details he now took for granted: huge stone fireplace, oil paintings, period detailing on the cornices over the door, the windows and on the ceiling.

'Kat.' He touched the tip of her nose, bringing her eyes back to his. 'There might be things you see tonight, things you hear, that don't add up.' Her mouth opened, no doubt to ask him if that included the way he'd just greeted his mother as Helena, so he placed a finger on her soft, soft lips. 'Please keep any questions to yourself.'

Hurt flashed in her eyes and guilt washed through him. Here he was, pulling the loathsome *respect my privacy, I'm a celebrity* card when she'd shared so much of her life, been so open with him.

But he had to protect himself, didn't he?

'Are there any other rules I need to know before I meet your parents?' There was a bite to her voice he'd not heard before.

'Of course not,' he protested, but already she'd taken a virtual and a literal step away from him.

And before he could do anything to mend some of the damage, the door opened and William and Helena Edwards walked in.

Chapter 10

Whatever Kat had been expecting from Zac's parents, this wasn't it.

They were well spoken, yes, refined. Elegant.

They were also . . . well, her English teacher had hated the word, far too bland, but Kat had been crap at the subject so she stuck with what she knew. His parents were really *nice*.

Maybe she should have expected it, because when Zac wasn't being a total arse, like he'd been five minutes earlier, he was nice, too. All those careful manners, the way he'd guided her in with his hand on her back. The kind things he'd said.

Until he'd cut her to the quick by not just shutting her out but slamming the door on her. Of course he was perfectly within his rights to ask her to keep her nose out of his business. Doing that hot on the heels of telling her he wanted to seduce her, though? It felt like a slap in the face, and while she was angry at herself for allowing her feelings to get caught up, she was also angry at him for sending conflicting messages.

Involuntarily she glanced over Helena's shoulder, to where Zac was talking with William. When he caught her gaze, his expression turned pained, his eyes full of apology.

Yeah, well tough luck. He could stew for a while.

'Zac told us he didn't want anyone else here tonight knowing you're his bodyguard, so I'll say this now.' Helena's voice brought Kat's attention back to her hostess. 'Thank you for keeping Zac safe.'

'It's what I'm employed to do.' She smiled, hoping it came across as confident and professional and not the smile of a woman who'd had to convince her boss she was ready for the task.

'This person leaving him notes, it's all very worrying. We wish we knew who and why they were doing it.'

'The police are working hard on it. I'm sure it won't be long before there's a breakthrough.' It was funny, with Zac's reluctance to talk about his parents, and then hearing him refer to them by their first names, she'd expect Helena and William to be more distant, yet nothing could be further from the truth. Maybe the first-name thing was just what posh people did, because the affection they had for him, and he for them, was very clear. 'I was wondering, do you have a person in charge of security tonight? I'd like to have a quick word.'

Helena paled a little. 'Are you expecting trouble?'

'Not at all,' Kat reassured her. 'Just making sure all bases are covered.'

'I'll ask Samuel to make himself known to you. I'm afraid we need to head back to our guests now but do come and join us in the ballroom when you're ready.' Kat's face must have done a little paling of its own, because Helena smiled kindly at her. 'I promise nobody will bite. They're all looking forward to seeing the young lady Zac has brought with him.'

'Oh, crap.'

Helena laughed. 'I take it pretending to be his date wasn't your idea?'

Kat ran her eyes over her black dress and down to her apparently not very high sandals. 'If you knew the real me, you'd know this is not my idea of fun.'

'You have no need to be nervous, my dear.' Helena touched her lightly on the arm. 'You're far lovelier than the last woman he introduced us to.'

Not knowing quite what to say to that – the high five she wanted to give Helena was clearly inappropriate – Kat smiled awkwardly.

When his parents had shut the door behind them, Zac came to stand in front of her. 'She's right, you know.'

'You're only saying that because you know you pissed me off.'

He laughed, that low, soft chuckle that did things to her insides she really wished it didn't. 'I'm saying it because it's true. Chloe was . . . high maintenance.'

'For that read, she was glamorous.'

'For that read, she was more interested in where I could take her, and who I could introduce her to, than me.'

Kat felt an immediate blast of anger that anyone could treat him like that. 'Then she was a shallow, small-minded trollop.'

Zac's smile beamed right into her eyes. 'Well put.' Before she knew it, his hands had moved to cup her face, the sensation warm, intimate and so very right, despite the alarm bells ringing in her head. 'You, on the other hand, Kat Parker, are a delight. You make me want things I know I shouldn't.'

Her breath hitched as he bent so that his face was only an inch from hers. Oh God, those eyes, they weren't just green, they had specks of gold, of burnished orange. 'I . . .' her words were swallowed by her gasp as he edged even closer. So close she felt the warmth of his breath flutter across her face.

'You?' He smiled, eyes crinkling in the corners. 'If I'd known how easy it was to render you speechless, I'd have done this a week ago.'

And while her heart hammered against her ribs, he planted a feather-light kiss on her lips.

Before she had a chance to complain, or, damn him, to drag him closer, because despite the fact he'd barely touched her, that was the most erotic kiss she'd ever experienced . . . before she had a chance to do either, he'd taken a step back.

'We . . .' She cleared the unwanted constriction from her throat. 'We agreed you weren't going to do that.'

He took her hand, tucking it under his arm. 'We agreed I wouldn't seduce you.'

'Then what the blazes do you call that?'

Another smile, with an edge of smirk. 'That was me relaxing you. Now, let's go and show our faces.'

She didn't know whether to laugh, to elbow him in the ribs, or to scream. Was it just a game to him? Was she simply a puppet he could manipulate at will?

But then she remembered his words. *You make me want things I know I shouldn't.*

She was the one who'd pulled away at the river. Who'd told him no.

Maybe he was feeling this . . . thing between them as

much as she was. And that was the scariest prospect of all, because after what she'd just experienced, she knew everything she'd said by the river was true. If he set out to seduce her, he would.

Zac kept his arm protectively around Kat as he listened to Penelope and Harold Foster, long-time friends of Helena and William, talk about their latest holiday. Protectively was, perhaps, stretching it. The only danger she faced was boredom, but he would take any excuse to keep some of part of his body in contact with hers.

Apparently, spring was the perfect time to cruise around the Aegean islands. Zac didn't doubt it, but he didn't need the information backed up with quite so much detail.

Though her expression didn't show it, Kat had to be equally as bored. Over dinner she'd been animated, wowing the septuagenarians on their table, but she'd not said a word for the last ten minutes. Not since they'd been ensnared by the Fosters en route to escaping outside.

He allowed his hand to drift upwards, towards the bare skin at the V of her back. It was unfair of him to touch her there, when he knew she couldn't protest, couldn't move away.

But he couldn't help himself.

Especially when her body did another of those tell-tale little shivers. It gave him hope that he could eventually wear her down, though it was a selfish thought. She didn't want that from him.

'Good Lord, fancy seeing you here.' Zac froze at the sound of the distinctive upper-class voice. 'Penny, Harold, excuse my poor manners in interrupting, but I'm so shocked to see this fellow. I thought we'd be too mundane for him, now he's joined the celebrity classes.'

'Antony.' Zac nodded stiffly at William and Helena's son. Manners dictated that he should formally introduce Kat, but for once he didn't give a damn about what was right and proper. He just wanted away.

'Brother.' Antony's lip curled. 'That is what we're calling each other these days, is it? I forget mother's latest instructions.'

'You can call me what you like.' *You and Isabelle always did.* 'Sorry we can't linger, but I've promised to show my date around the garden.'

Ignoring the knowing glint in Antony's eye, Zac pulled, perhaps a little too strongly, on Kat's arm.

'Whoa, hang on a minute.' In the heels she hated, but he appreciated, Kat struggled to keep up with him. 'Since when have I become Alan Titchmarsh?'

He forced himself to slow down. 'Alan . . . who?'

'You know, the gardener. Alan Titchmarsh. You said I wanted to see the garden.' She huffed. 'Don't make me explain the joke. Just tell me why I'm hurtling towards the rhododendrons.'

'I decided I didn't want to make polite conversation any longer.'

He eased her through the orangery, where everyone was milling, and out onto the patio. It was a warm summer evening and this part of the garden looked particularly impressive, with a trail of lights leading up the path towards the summer house. Either side of it, flower beds teemed with colour.

He felt a tug on his hand and glanced down to see Kat looking at him in concern. 'Is everything okay?'

The words *Everything is fine* circled in his mind, but such an obvious lie would only push her further away. While he couldn't be honest, he could at least not lie so terribly. 'Sorry. Antony and I don't get on, as you'll have gathered.'

'He did seem a bit of an arse.'

The blunt words made him smile. 'You mean you weren't taken in by his dashing blond looks and baby-blue eyes?'

'Are you kidding? Since I've had to follow you around all day, I've become immune to good looks.'

He caught her eyes, holding them. 'Is that a dare?'

'Absolutely not.' He continued to stare at her, letting her see his attraction, how hard it was to hold back from dragging her away from here and doing to her what his dreams had started to taunt him with. Swallowing hard, she averted her gaze. 'So, Antony is the brother. Where's the sister?'

The question hit him like a bucket of cold water, and he took a step back. 'I suspect Isabelle is around somewhere. They usually hunt in pairs.' Kat's sharp look made him realise what he'd revealed. 'They're twins,' he added, as if it would explain everything.

Kat's gaze shifted past his shoulder. 'Does she look like her brother?'

'Blonde and blue-eyed, yes.'

'Then I think she's heading towards us.'

Zac turned and his insides plummeted as he spotted Isabelle walking through the open orangery doors and onto the patio.

'Antony told me you were here.' Her eyes narrowed as she glanced at Kat. 'He also told me you'd brought a date.'

'Not a dried, wrinkled one, I hope.' Kat, clearly deciding to ignore the tension so obviously snapping between him and Isabelle, reached out her hand. 'Hi, I'm Kat.'

'How do you do? I'm Isabelle.' She shook the proffered hand and glanced between the pair of them. 'Well, this is truly fascinating. I don't believe I've ever met one of Zac's dates before.'

'Not even the infamous Chloe?'

Zac knew Kat was trying to help, but he didn't need it. What he needed was to get away from Isabelle and her taunting look, Antony and his sneering comments, and all reminders of the half-truths, the lies he was peddling, even to Kat.

'Nope, I wasn't allowed to meet Chloe. Mum and Dad had dinner with her I believe, but Antony and I weren't invited.' Isabelle's lip curled up at one side. 'I think Zac was afraid we'd scare her off.'

'I don't scare so easily,' Kat asserted.

'I'm sure Zac will be pleased to hear that.' Isabelle swung her laser-bright focus back to him. 'Won't you, dear brother.'

The poached salmon he'd eaten felt too heavy in his stomach, the champagne too fizzy. 'I believe the music is about to start. We should head back in.'

'Oh, I think Mum will forgive us for not being the first on the dance floor. We're having such a lovely time catching up, after all.' Isabelle took a sip out of the champagne flute she was carrying. 'How long has it been since we last saw each other? Five years?'

He wanted to say *Not long enough*, but that wasn't how Isabelle or Antony played these little games. They liked to pretend to be nice, to be civil, while slowly plunging in the knife. 'Six.'

'Doesn't time fly.' The expression on her face as she studied him was coolly condescending. 'I hear you've been busy making films, which must be the perfect career choice for you. You always did enjoy being someone you weren't.'

He flinched, and her lip curled even further. Damn it, he was thirty now, not thirteen. Her catty remarks shouldn't have the power to hurt him anymore. 'And you always enjoyed being a bitch. Goodbye, Isabelle. It's been fun catching up.' He was so wound up now, his muscles were making knots on top of knots. Clasping tight to Kat's hand, he marched them back inside, through the orangery and into the adjoining ballroom where a small band had started to play.

'If we bump into her again,' Kat muttered, 'I'm warning you now, she's going to end up flat on her back with my knee on her neck.'

'If we bump into her again, we're going home.'

'That works for me, too. At least then I can get out of this dress and maybe, you know, start to breathe again. Once you relax that death grip you've got going on.'

Slowly Zac ground to a halt. 'Sorry.' Reluctantly he let go of her hand. 'I'm so angry right now, I want to scream.' His eyes travelled across her face, noting the fire still in her eyes. 'Yet one look at you and suddenly I have this mad urge to smile. Why is that?'

'Duh, that's obvious. Because I'm funny.'

'Funny, I concur.' He slid a hand across her cheek and gazed into those deep-brown pools. 'Yet also utterly enchanting.'

He watched as her eyes fluttered closed. When they opened again, they pleaded with him not to say anything more. Reining in his frustration, he held out his hand. 'Come and dance with me.'

'Me? Dance?' She gave him an incredulous look before glancing down at her feet. 'In these toe crushers?'

Ignoring her protest, he led her towards the floor where a dozen or so couples moved to a variety of techniques, from the awkward sway to the full-blown waltz. 'You don't need to dance. Just . . .' He placed her hand on his chest, over his heart, which still hadn't fully calmed since the spat with Isabelle. 'Just let me hold you for a while. Please.'

Her eyes searched his, and he guessed she must have read the same desperation for human contact, for comfort, that he felt in his gut because she nodded her head.

Moments later, they were face to face, chest to chest, hip to hip. As he eased his arms around her waist, drawing her closer, he felt some of the tension slide away. When her hands moved from clasping his biceps, to wrapping around his neck, he inhaled a deep breath and began to relax for the first time that evening.

His pleasure was cut short when the music ended and Samuel appeared.

'Sorry to disturb you. I thought you should know, we had an uninvited guest.'

Kat stiffened, moving away from him and following Samuel off the dance floor. 'Did you get a name? A description?'

Samuel shook his head. 'No name. We approached the car, as we were suspicious, because it was so late arriving. The lady – that's about all I can tell you for sure, it was a female with long hair – immediately turned the car round and disappeared down the drive. It was so dark we didn't even get a number plate. Sorry.'

Kat cursed under her breath. 'Not your fault. Thanks for letting me know.'

'Probably just someone who got lost,' Zac murmured as Samuel drifted off. 'I'd make a joke about women and navigation, but I fear I might find a knee in my groin.'

'Usually you'd be right, unless you're making the joke to hide the fact you're worried.'

'I'm not worried,' he said softly. 'I've got you.'

'No.' Kat jerked her head away from his gaze. 'You should be worried. It makes you more vigilant. We both need to be on our toes.' She cursed again. 'I should have been out there, keeping watch.'

'But nothing happened.' Why wouldn't she look at him? 'Kat?'

Finally, her eyes met his. 'Don't you see? I was distracted tonight. I was dining with you, dancing with you, but I'm not your flaming date, Zac. I'm your bodyguard.'

Guilt from the lies he'd been telling, anger from the meeting with Isabelle and Antony, frustration at the situation with Kat. It all mixed into a heady, emotional cocktail. 'Then swap with Mark,' he demanded, taking hold of her shoulders. 'Get someone else to be my bodyguard so you *can* be my date.'

It was the wrong thing to say. She shook his arms off and glared up at him. 'You assume I want that.'

Ouch. Now he could add hurt to his simmering emotions. 'I apologise,' he bit out. 'I didn't realise the idea was so abhorrent.'

'It isn't.' She released a long, exasperated breath. 'But this is my job, Zac, and it's important to me. This assignment is important to me.'

'I see.' He jammed his hands into his pockets. 'I'm more important to you as a client, than as me.' *And why not?* he thought bitterly. It's not like it was the first time he was wanted because of what he was, not who he was.

'God, Zac, that's not what I'm saying here. Why are you being so bloody infuriating?'

'I didn't think I was.' Aware they were starting to get looks now, Zac forced his shoulders to relax, his mouth to smile. 'I thought I was being truthful.'

'Truthful?' He received his same, forced smile, thrown back at him. 'Is this the same truth that means I can't ask about what I've seen tonight?'

He hung his head. '*Touché*. I know you have questions and I want to answer them, but . . .' He trailed off, his throat closing up as fear, dread and guilt all tightened around him. Was he ready to open that can of worms?

'You don't trust me.'

'That's not it,' he shot back. 'I trust you with my life, Kat.'

She averted her eyes, staring at the band rather than at him. 'How can I protect that life, if you don't give me the full facts?'

He could understand her argument, but signatures in pink lipstick, a woman driving the car tonight. It all pointed to the stalker being a female fan. And if that was the case . . . 'I don't know who's stalking me, Kat.'

She didn't reply and the silence grew heavy between them, at odds with the surrounding music and laughter. Instead they were stuck in a bubble of distrust and anger, when all he longed to do was tug her back to the dance floor and wrap his arms around her.

'I'll make my excuses to Helena and William,' he said finally, aware the evening was lost.

The bigger question was whether his bodyguard was lost to him, too.

A week or so ago, he'd have jumped at the chance to get someone more experienced. Now he realised he'd been overly paranoid. The person stalking him clearly wasn't that of his worst nightmare, and his fears had lessened enough to make him selfish. If he had to have a bodyguard, he wanted it to be Kat watching his back, Kat driving him around. Kat sticking to him like glue.

He wanted her in his life, and if this was the only way it was going to happen, then it sucked, really bloody sucked. But he'd accept it over the alternative.

Chapter 11

Kat kept her eyes fixed on the road as she drove Zac back to the hotel. It was Friday; almost a week since the charity function at his parents' house.

Well, estate.

And were they even his parents? Ever since the visit there, her mind had replayed snippets of conversations, leaving a confused mess of contradictions in their wake.

Brother? That is what we're calling each other these days, is it? I forget mother's latest instructions.

And the equally unsettling *Acting must be the perfect career choice for you. You always enjoyed being someone you weren't.*

Clearly Zac was carrying around a big, dirty secret. It hurt, both professionally and personally, that he wasn't prepared to let her in on it. Professionally, because his secret felt like an unexploded bomb hanging over them. One of those frigging IEDs in Afghan. She knew it was there, but she didn't know if it would explode in their faces and if it did, how much damage it would do.

The thought brought back horrifying flashbacks; deafening bangs, panic, blood, debris . . . a shudder ran through her.

Definitely not the time to be taking a trip down that memory lane. 'The police think they have a lead on your stalker,' she said when she thought she had her voice under control.

'I'm aware.'

Zac sounded clipped and distant. Exactly as he had been all week. It was like the dance, when she'd melted against him – yes, for a moment there, Kat Parker had flipping *melted*. Anyway, it was like that hadn't happened.

Get someone else to be my bodyguard so you can be my date. It was like that hadn't happened, either. And yes, she'd panicked at the idea, both of dating him and of giving up this chance to prove herself. She was starting to think the result though, this awful tension between them, was worse than doing as he'd suggested.

'You know all about Hannah's waitress friend, then?' she prompted, pulling up at a red light and sliding him a look.

He gave her a small, unamused smile. 'If by that you mean have I been informed that another waitress at the event was annoyed I'd picked Hannah to leave with and not her, then yes.' When she didn't say anything, he gave a sharp bark of laughter. 'Ouch, Ms Parker. I can see the judgement in your eyes from here.'

'Then you need to get your eyes checked. I'm not judging.' She focused back on the traffic lights, moving off when they turned green. 'But okay, I am wondering why a guy like you, a guy who values his privacy, decides to have sex with a waitress he picked up at a party.'

For a long while he didn't speak. Then he sighed. 'After Chloe—'

'The trollop.'

'Yes.' Unlike when she'd said that at the party, there was no answering smile. 'After her, I suppose I was looking for a more honest interaction. Two people clear on what they wanted. Even if it was just sex.'

A glance at his handsome profile and she ached, just a little, for him. While it was clear Chloe hadn't hurt his heart, she had dented his ego. Perhaps made him re-evaluate his self-worth to an extent that he was reduced to a tacky one-night stand.

She'd not helped either, she thought with a pang of guilt, remembering how he'd taken her comment about how important the assignment was to her. Yep, he wasn't the only one with secrets that had the potential to blow up in their faces.

'By the way, I'm out tonight.'

His statement, seemingly coming out of the blue, rocked her back. 'Okay. Let me know what time to pick you up and where we're going.'

She was aware of his eyes on her. 'What happened to Mark?'

'Mark provides cover when I can't. Tonight, Debs is at a party so I'm home alone. I might as well work it. Save the favour for another day.'

'Well, I'm sorry for making you *work* on a Friday night,' he said tightly.

'I didn't mean it like that.'

'Like what? That escorting me is a chore? But why wouldn't it be? I am just a job to you, after all.' Before she had a chance to reply he added, 'I'd like to leave at 7.30 p.m. The destination is a club in Berkeley Square.'

Swallowing down her annoyance – a rare feat – she gave him a cool smile. 'How exciting. Little old me gets to go to a private members' club.'

'I suspect you're used to it, in your line of work.'

There he went again. She waited until they were parked and in the lift on the way to his suite before speaking again. 'Can we stop all the snide remarks. They're doing my head in.'

He shrugged his shoulders in an elegant gesture of indifference. 'I'm doing as you requested. Keeping things professional. Client and bodyguard. Of course, that assumes you still want to be my bodyguard, but as you're still here I guess this assignment really is important to you.'

There he went again, twisting what she'd said. 'It is. You're important to me,' she added quietly, hoping he would understand the two weren't mutually exclusive. 'Clients and bodyguards can be friends, you know. They can like each other. They don't need to go around with a stick up their arse.'

He raised an eyebrow. 'Is that what you want? For us to be friends?'

'I thought we were moving towards that, yes.'

Though he nodded, he didn't reply, which infuriated her more. They'd been so close on Saturday. Heck, she shouldn't remember it with such clarity, her heart shouldn't flutter when she thought of it, but he'd called her, bolshie Kat Parker, *enchanting*. And now this? Was Zac Edwards, seriously hot film star, really upset that she'd wanted to remain his bodyguard rather than his date? It didn't make sense. Unless his frosty show was about something else.

'You do know I won't say anything about what I heard on Saturday,' she told him as the lift doors opened and she walked with him towards his suite.

'Of course.' They came to a halt outside his door and he leant against the wall. Debonair, smooth as hell. 'There must be rules about that sort of thing. And despite evidence to the contrary, apparently you like to stick to rules.'

Debonair, smooth, yet also pretty obnoxious right now. Choosing to ignore him, she put the key card in the lock and marched inside, doing her usual check. When she'd finished, she waved at him to enter. 'I'll see you here at 7.30.'

Bristling with annoyance, and hurt more than she wanted to admit, she strode towards the door. 'Wait.' A beat later he added, 'Please.'

'Fine.' She folded her arms as she turned to face him.

The action brought a glimmer of amusement to eyes that had been cool and flat for the last few days. 'I'm not sure I like your body language. It's a little off-putting.'

'Tough. What did you want? Because I've got a lot to do between now and 7.30.'

'Yes. Sorry. I . . .' His shoulders rose and fell, and his eyes slowly met hers. 'I've spent the last week trying to convince myself I don't want you. It's not easy.'

Oh God. She'd not expected that. 'I know.'

His eyes flared at her admission. Instead of taking the opening, though, he gave her a sad smile. 'I'll try to be less of a git about it from now on. See you later.'

'Yes.' As she walked back to the car park, she told herself this was exactly what she wanted.

Funny, it didn't feel that way.

It felt even less like what she wanted a few hours later as she watched the actress he was filming with – Sophia somebody – and another woman flirt their pert little arses off in front of him. It made her wonder if he'd come here deliberately just to prove there were plenty of other women all too happy to date him. To jump into bed with him, from the look of it.

She knew she had to ignore the darts of jealousy. To stop wondering what she and Zac would have been doing now if she'd asked Mark to replace her. Whatever the outcome, though, it would have been temporary. This job, proving to Mark and to herself she could handle it. That was her future.

Zac stifled a yawn. Coming here had been a seriously bad idea. One hatched in desperation on the journey home when he'd found himself irked at Kat's obvious disapproval of his one-night stand. Then even more irked, that he was irked. Her opinion of him shouldn't matter so much. Determined to move past this rather terrifying obsession with Kat, he'd decided to accept Sophia's invitation to join her and her friend at the club.

So far all the evening had done, though, was remind him why he was so obsessed with Kat in the first place. Sophia and her friend were easy on the eye, pleasant enough to talk to, but they didn't make his skin tingle, or his pulse race. They didn't make him laugh or want to hang on every word they said.

They didn't *interest* him.

The one who did was sitting at the other end of the bar,

her attention bouncing between him and her phone. Occasionally she'd shake her head when a guy came up to her, no doubt to offer her a drink.

'You should come for a visit to LA when filming is over.' Sophia fluttered her eyelids at him. She had huge blue eyes, but he hankered for velvet brown. 'I've got this amazing pad right on Malibu beach.'

'Sounds good.' Because he had no intention of taking her up on her offer, he swiftly changed the subject. 'Would either of you like another drink?'

He'd just given the order to the bartender when Kat appeared by his side. 'Sorry to disturb you, but can I have a minute?'

Any clever retort he might have come up with died the moment he looked into her eyes. 'Of course.' Nodding to the two ladies, he slipped off the bar stool. 'What's wrong?'

'I've just had a call from Debs.' She bit down on her lip, clearly agitated. 'She's scared the party she's at is getting out of hand, so I need to go. I've called Mark and he'll be here soon. Please don't get yourself into any trouble between now and then.'

He told himself it was the thought of escaping the women at the bar, and not the worry in her eyes, that prompted his next words. 'Cancel him. I'll come with you.'

'Don't be daft.' Her eyes strayed to the bar, and Sophia who was watching them with undisguised interest. 'Stay and enjoy yourself.'

'Who said I'm enjoying myself?' Not, perhaps, the brightest move to let that slip, but there was too much pretence in his life already. 'Give me a second to settle the bill and say goodbye.'

Five minutes later they were bombing west down the motorway towards Windsor.

'You really didn't have to come with me.' Kat's profile looked strained as she focused on the traffic. 'I can handle a bunch of stupid teenagers.'

'You think I don't know that?'

There was a pause before she asked, 'Were you really not enjoying yourself, because that isn't the impression I had.'

He leant back against the passenger seat. 'I'm an actor, Kat. What you see isn't always the truth.'

She didn't reply and his words were left hanging ominously between them. He wanted to take them back, to say something glib instead, like *That's why I'm a hotshot actor.* Because then she might have smiled and given him a mouthy reply.

And then things might have gone back to how they were before he'd started to fall for her.

But no. He'd gone for something too close to home to be comfortable, for either of them.

It was only when Kat pulled up outside a tall Victorian terrace forty-five minutes later, that she spoke again. 'Stay in the car. I'll just be a minute.'

He gave her a searing look. 'I realise you're a bodyguard and I'm merely your client but Christ, Kat, don't cut off my balls completely.'

Not waiting for her reply, he dug in the glove compartment

for the baseball cap and shades she insisted he keep there and jumped down from the Jeep.

'I'm not cutting off your balls, you dumb arse,' she hissed as he walked round the bonnet towards her. 'I'm protecting you.'

'Protecting me from whom, exactly? Because I don't see the stalker following us out here, do you?'

She gave him a look of disbelief. 'You really want to have your name splashed all over the papers, associated with an out-of-control teenage party?'

Her eyes flashed, her expression tightened, but she wasn't the only angry party here. 'Do you really think you need to tell me how to manage my own image?' He jammed the baseball cap on his head, and the glasses on his nose.

'Fine,' she ground out. 'But if there's any manhandling needed, it's to be done by me.'

'*Manhandling?*' He looked towards the house, where the heavy beat of rap music filtered through an open window. 'Please tell me you're not going in there in full combat mode.'

'Of course not.' She raised her chin. 'Not straight away, anyway.'

'Not at all.' Kat's obvious need to protect her niece, and to tackle anyone who got in her way, positively vibrated through her. Realising he had to go carefully, Zac placed his hands on her shoulders in a placatory gesture. 'Debs is in there, yes? Frightened, no doubt, yet she won't want to lose face in front of her friends. And that would definitely happen if her aunt bulldozed her way in and hauled her out.'

'Bulldozed is way too strong.' Kat narrowed her eyes, her

expression hardening. 'I just want to put the fear of God into the jerk who thought it was a good idea to bring alcohol to a party for fourteen-year-olds.'

'Like that never happened at the parties you went to.'

'Of course it did, but I grew up in a shit neighbourhood.' Kat drew in a shaky breath. 'This is Windsor, for crying out loud.'

'And teenagers are teenagers, wherever they're brought up.'

Her lip curled in disgust. 'Even in mansion houses?'

'Yes.' If only an alcohol-fuelled party had been the scariest thing he'd witnessed. 'We're doing this my way.'

'Now wait a minute—'

He'd done with trying to reason with her. 'You have your skill set,' he cut in. 'And I have mine. I'm going to knock on the door and pretend to be an off-duty policeman. While I'm *calmly* pointing out how much trouble they could get in if they don't quieten things down, you're going to sneak in, find Debs and take her out of the back door. Then we'll call the real police.' When she stared at him blankly, he gave her shoulders a squeeze. 'Agreed?'

Her shoulders relaxed a fraction. 'I guess that could work.'

Hallelujah. Before she could change her mind, Zac marched off down the path and rang the bell.

Chapter 12

For once, Zac was the one driving. Kat had started towards the driver's seat, her arm around a very subdued Debs, only to hear Zac curse, his expression hovering between incredulity and disgust.

'You sit at the back with Debs,' he'd ordered. 'I only had one drink at the club, so I believe I can just about be trusted to get us back in one piece.'

He was probably still in a funk from being asked to stay in the car. Or maybe it was the same funk he'd been in all week. *I'm trying to convince myself I don't want you.*

She felt a flutter deep in her belly. If that was the reason behind his mood, it was fair to say he wasn't the only one trying to convince themselves.

From the front seat, Zac cleared his throat. 'Which house is yours?'

'Number twenty. Red door. Wreck of a front garden that Debs is going to sort out this weekend.'

Debs sat bolt upright. 'No way.'

'Yes, way. Your punishment for tonight's shenanigans.'

'That's so not fair. I didn't know they were going to be stupid.'

'You knew older boys were going to be there.'

She stuck out her bottom lip. 'So?'

'So, I hope you've learnt your lesson.' As Zac pulled up outside, Kat touched a hand to her niece's cheek. 'You're fourteen, Debs. Too young to be mixing with seventeen-year-olds.'

'Yeah, well, boys my age are lame.' Debs climbed down from the Jeep, tears streaming down her cheeks. 'And stop telling me what to do. You're not my fucking mum.' With that she ran up the path.

Sighing deeply, Kat followed her, aware of Zac a few steps behind them. He should be where she could see him. Hell, he should still be in the club, chatting to the delightful Sophia, with Mark watching over him. Nothing about tonight seemed to be working out as planned.

The moment Debs opened the front door, she scarpered inside and ran up the stairs to her bedroom.

The sound of her door slamming reverberated through the house.

'She's not wrong,' Zac said quietly, his tall frame blocking the front doorway. 'I was pretty lame at fourteen.'

'Yeah? And what about when you were seventeen? What was foremost in your mind then, when you'd had a skinful?' The fear she'd felt ever since Debs had sent her that text was finally escaping the box she'd slammed it into. 'No, it's okay, no need to answer. I know exactly what boys think at that age. And I don't want that for my niece.' Damn, now her voice was shaking. 'I want Debs to have a proper childhood. Not one sullied by growing up too fast, having sex too early with older guys not interested in anything else but their next lay.'

Aware she'd said too much, Kat dropped her handbag onto the coffee table and then thrust off her jacket and threw it onto the sofa. She almost jumped out of her skin when a pair of arms circled her from behind. 'Hey.' He planted a gentle kiss on the top of her head. 'I'm sorry.'

Tears welled and Kat blinked desperately. She was not going to cry. 'Why are you sorry? I bet you weren't getting girls drunk when you were seventeen.' A strangled laugh left her throat. 'God, you wouldn't have to get them drunk. I bet even then they were flinging themselves at you.'

His chin rested on the top of her head and when he spoke again, she could hear the smile in his voice. 'I didn't have any trouble getting a girlfriend, no.'

'I bet you didn't.' Feeling too vulnerable for such an intimate embrace, she stepped away from him. 'I used to hate guys like you. Posh rich guys with gleaming looks and a cocky attitude.'

His answering smile was strained. 'Then it's a good job you didn't know me back then.'

She snorted. 'Like we would ever have bumped into each other. My shitty estate was a world away from your manor house.'

Another tight smile, and she wondered if he was embarrassed by his upbringing, angry at the way she'd pushed him away, or just annoyed at her jibes. Jibes that weren't fair, because he'd never acted entitled with her, never treated her as anything other than an equal. 'Sorry, that sounded really bitchy. I didn't mean it as a dig. Just an observation.'

He nodded, slipping his hands into his pockets and giving her a quiet study. 'If we had bumped into each other, I'd have wanted to get to know you, Kat Parker.'

Oh no. She couldn't handle him flirting. Nor could she handle the kindness in his eyes. Ignoring her quivering, squirming insides, she forced out a laugh. 'If your official age is correct, it makes you two years younger than me, so I'd have been sixteen to your fourteen. I'd have eaten you alive.'

He smiled, eyes still pressing hers. 'And I'd have enjoyed every minute of it.'

Holy shit, he was too good at this. Feeling herself flush, she turned and walked into the small open-plan kitchen, reaching for the kettle as if it was a lifeline. Distraction. That's what she needed. 'Do you want a drink?'

He shook his head. 'I'm fine, thanks.'

She settled the kettle back on the worktop. 'Well, make yourself at home. I need to go and check on Debs and then I'll take you back to the hotel.'

'Remind her I owe her a visit to the studio. We talked about her bringing her drama class, too. If she's still keen, we could organise something next week.' Her look of surprise must have shown on her face because he sighed. 'You thought I'd forgotten.'

'Well, not forgotten exactly. I thought you'd offered just to, you know, be kind.'

'It's not very kind to offer and then not deliver on it.'

Perhaps not, but many celebrity clients had done exactly that – tickets to their shows, autographs – and not followed through. She was starting to realise Zac wasn't someone she could neatly put a label on. 'Okay, as soon as I've checked Debs is okay, we'll head off.'

His jaw clenched and he dug a phone out of his pocket. 'No need. I'll order a taxi.'

'No, you won't.'

He gave her a look of disgust. 'You can't seriously expect me to drag you away from your niece to play chauffeur?'

'And you can't seriously expect me to let you make your way back to the hotel unprotected.'

Cursing, he thrust a hand through his hair. 'I don't want to be a burden, Kat. Debs needs you. Go to her.'

Immediately her irritation slipped away. He wasn't trying to be difficult. He was trying to help. More, in offering to take Debs round the studio, and in coming with her tonight, he was being *kind*. 'I'll go, as long as you promise not to leave.'

He exhaled, shoulders sagging in defeat. 'Fine.' He glanced towards the sofa currently piled high with newspapers, magazines and clothes. 'I'll try and find a few square inches to sit on.'

And there it was again, finally. The dry humour she hadn't realised she enjoyed, until she'd had a week without it. 'Feel free to move things.'

'Good Lord, no. I don't want to ruin your system.' With that delicious quirk of his lips he smiled back at her, and for a brief, tantalising moment, the worries over her niece, over Zac and how to protect him, even the worries about her growing feelings towards him, drained away.

As Kat climbed the stairs, she felt as if a small weight had been lifted from her.

Zac shifted on the sofa, his arm brushing against the precariously piled magazines on his left. He tried to read the title upside down. *F1 Racing*. He should have guessed.

A thought hurtled through his mind and he hit the search

engine on his phone. When he'd found what he wanted, he tapped out a message to his assistant. Then slumped back against the sofa and sighed.

He felt like a nuisance, a responsibility. An obligation Kat needed to fulfil, even though she clearly already had enough on her plate.

Hell, when he'd held her, she'd almost cried. Even now, the memory of the way her body had shuddered, far too briefly, against his, cut him to the quick. It was that very vulnerability, the warmth, and yes, the *softness* that lay beneath her tough exterior, that tugged at something deep inside him; a reminder of the journey she'd taken to become this brave, bold, big-hearted woman he was enthralled by. Let down by her parents during her childhood, and from what she'd just hinted, let down by early boyfriends, too. Yet she'd come through both with her sense of humour, and her love of life, still intact. It was no wonder she wasn't interested in the fickle celebrity with a posh upbringing a world away from hers – she didn't need the angst. She might find him attractive, but Zac knew he was a long way from the type of guy she wanted. That lucky sod would be strong and steady. A guy as fearless as she was, happy in his skin. A man like her, who knew exactly who he was.

Not an insecure actor still playing a part.

On that miserable thought, Zac leant his head back and closed his eyes.

About twenty minutes after she'd left him, he heard footsteps and opened his eyes to see Kat walking down the stairs. She started when she saw him, a clear sign she'd forgotten he was still here. Another job to tick off before she could finally get to bed.

'Is Debs okay?'

'She will be.' Kat perched on the arm of the armchair. Possibly because the chair itself contained a few days' worth of post, an iPhone charger and a water bottle. 'She's a lot like her mum, when she was that age. Mandy was always flying off to some party, mixing with older guys. Drinking. It's why she ended up pregnant at nineteen.'

'And you? Where were you when Mandy was out?'

Kat grimaced. 'With her, of course, which is why I know it's such a bad idea for Debs.'

He wanted to carry on talking to her, two friends chatting, not bodyguard and client, so he chose his next words carefully. 'I guess the alternative, staying at home, wasn't an option?'

'Not if I wanted to avoid being yelled at, treated like a skivvy or seeing Mum being a doormat to my drunk bully of a father, no.'

Though he'd half-expected the answer, it still made him wince. 'I suspect now you could take your dad down with a flick of your wrist. Have you ever been back?'

'I've thought about it, many, many times. But no.' Her eyes avoided his as she stood. 'Are you sure you don't want a drink?'

She was open and direct, so it wasn't hard for him to know when there was something troubling her. Rising from the sofa, he moved to stand next to her, tucking his hand under her chin so her eyes were forced to meet his. 'What is it?' She shook her head and tried to move away but he held her by the top of the arms. 'Tell me.'

'Why? It's not like you're going to reciprocate, is it? You're not exactly Mr Chatty when it comes to talking about your life.'

He flinched, knowing he deserved the jibe. Never had he hated the lie he was living, more. What harm would it do if he told her? So what if she let it slip, if she told others? Did it matter anymore?

Yet if he was only ever going to be a job to her, was it worth the risk? Especially as she'd see him in a different light, probably a less favourable one, cutting his already low chance with her down to zero.

'I feel guilty, alright?'

Kat's voice shook him out of his internal ramblings. 'Guilty about what?' he asked softly, dismayed at the tortured expression on her face.

'Guilty about leaving Mum. We left her with him.'

She made to move away again but he kept his hands on her arms, knowing full well if she wanted to escape, she could. 'Your mum wanted to stay. If she hadn't, she'd have left, too.'

'No, you don't understand. Dad . . . he was a bully, sure, but he had this sort of power over us. It was like we were programmed to do what he wanted.' She inhaled an agitated breath. 'Mandy and I, we hated it, but we still did what he told us. When we asked Mum why she put up with it, why she stayed with him, she just smiled and said where else would she go.'

Zac understood all about powerful, bullying fathers, though of course he couldn't tell her that. William Edwards was about as gentle a man as it was possible to meet. 'You're stronger than your mum, Kat.' Relaxing his grip on her biceps, he slowly ran his hands up and down her arms. 'You can't blame your eighteen-year-old self for getting away as soon as you got the chance.'

'No.' She blinked those dark eyes. 'But I can blame adult

me for not going back to check on her.'

Her expression was wracked with guilt and he ached for her. 'Sometimes, in order to cope with our present, and look ahead to our future, we have to put the past behind us.' Nobody knew that better than he did. Nobody.

Of course, Kat was far too smart to miss the words he hadn't said. 'Is that what you've done?' Before he could answer, she shook her head and stepped back. 'Nope, forget it. That's probably one of those super-nosy questions I'm not allowed to ask. You being a celebrity and all that.'

'Kat.' Frustrated, he reached for her hand. 'Yes. That's exactly what I've done.' He hesitated, and answered more honestly, 'Am trying to do.'

Nobody was more surprised than he when a slow smile slid across her face. 'There, that wasn't so hard, was it? Admitting that teeny-weeny bit of information about yourself?'

'I'd tell you more,' he answered quietly, bringing his face closer to hers. His eyes dipping down to her soft lips. 'But I'm only a job to you.'

Her breath hitched. 'You know you're more than that.'

'Do I? Am I?' He bent his head, his lips daring to touch hers. When she didn't pull back, he tried again, this time bringing his hands up to clasp her face. To draw her closer. When her lips parted, he groaned, his tongue diving into the sweet depths of her mouth. Christ, she tasted even better than his imagination. Before he knew it, her arms were winding around his neck, and he wasn't the only one moaning in pleasure. Wasn't the only one trying to press closer and closer. To take more and more.

On a gasp, Kat pushed him away, her eyes fevered, her breathing heavy.

'I don't want to hear how that shouldn't have happened.' His voice was almost a growl.

'I know.' She lifted a hand to her chest, clearly trying to calm herself. 'I guess at least now you have your answer.' When he looked at her questioningly, she gave him a wry smile. 'I've never kissed a client before. Ever.'

Satisfaction burned through him. Enough to ease some of the ache. 'Good to know.'

'Good for you, maybe,' she muttered, picking up the handbag she'd abandoned on the coffee table. 'Now I really do need to take you back.'

'I could always stay.'

She hiccupped out a laugh. 'Oh sure, because that's a really sensible option after what just happened.'

'It doesn't have to be in your bed.' Though his blood flashed hot just thinking about it. 'I could sleep on the sofa.'

'Oh no you can't. I'm not having those pheromones of yours sneaking through my bedroom door. You need to take them away from me.'

'They are pretty strong,' he agreed, perhaps a little too smugly. 'Are you sure the hotel is far enough?'

She shook her head in an *I can't believe he just said that* gesture and marched towards the door. As they settled back into the Jeep, Zac felt the first sprouts of hope nudging through the despair of the last week.

Yes, she'd stopped the kiss, but she had let him kiss her. More than that, she'd been as into it as he had.

Chapter 13

It was Monday evening and Kat was doing her usual sweep of Zac's hotel room as he waited outside. Thankfully Mark had done the weekend protection duty, giving Kat two precious days to get over spilling her guts to him about her mum. And *that* kiss. Unconsciously she paused, placing a hand to her chest, willing her heart to slow. Crap. Two days was nowhere near long enough recovery time.

Considering everything that had happened on Friday, she'd expected today to be awkward, yet it hadn't been. Zac had been . . . well, back to his usual self. Smooth, quiet except for the odd dry comment. Occasionally he'd flashed his sexy smile but not once had he mentioned the kiss..

Maybe he'd forgotten about it. Maybe he wasn't obsessing about every moment like she was. And wow, that hurt, but there was no place for her feelings in this current arrangement with Zac. As achingly, gloriously perfect as it had been, there wouldn't, *couldn't* be a repeat.

Opening the door to his bedroom, Kat noted the total lack of any clothes lying around with a wry smile. In fact there was a lack of any personal items other than the toiletries and shaver she could see in the en suite.

Her eyes skimmed over the tidy surfaces and onto the carefully made bed – she'd like to bet he'd done that himself – before zeroing in on a white card lying on top of a pillow. She took one look at the bold pink lips and cursed. Violently.

Did you think you could escape me? Now I know where you sleep.

How the hell had the stalker followed Zac here? Hot on the heels of that question, was another, even more sickening one. Had she cocked up? Was it her fault?

'Err, hello.' Zac's voice echoed through from the sitting room. 'Can I come in or are you still removing the bogeymen from under my bed?' A second later he walked in, his eyes dropping to the card in her hand. 'It's another note, isn't it?'

'Yes.'

He cursed and turned full circle. When she went to follow him, she found him sitting on the sofa, head in his hands.

'Sorry.'

He lifted his eyes to hers. 'Why?'

'They should never have found you here. Maybe I didn't notice we'd been followed.' The sick feeling magnified and dread pooled in her stomach; she'd let him down. Put him in danger. 'Damn it, I should have swapped cars more often. Been more careful.'

Shit, how was she going to tell Mark?

'Maybe they haven't followed me at all,' Zac countered. 'Maybe they trawled all the five-star hotels until they came across one where someone was willing to talk for a fee.'

Rubbing a hand across his face, he let out a sharp, frustrated exhale. 'Christ, Kat. This isn't your fault.'

Kat wasn't sure Mark would see it that way. Heck, she wasn't convinced of it, either. But Zac was looking shaken, so she pushed aside her doubts and sat next to him, bumping her arm against his. 'I like your version better.' He attempted a smile, but his glorious eyes were flat, and his handsome face etched with strain. 'I won't let them get any closer. I promise.' She meant it. The crappy doubts could go and take a running jump.

'I know you won't.' His unflinching gaze, the certainty in his voice . . . her chest tightened in response. 'But it's just a nutty fan. The closest I'm likely to come to danger is being kissed to death.'

She sensed he was trying to convince himself, though it was hard to tell, him being such a good actor. She'd not actually appreciated how good he was until he'd knocked on the door at the party the other night. To the teenager who'd opened the door, Zac had been that off-duty cop. No question.

Still, she didn't want him to act in front of her, and especially not over this. Complacency could get him killed. 'I know you want to think it's just a harmless fan, but what if it's not? What if instead of planning to kiss you to death, they're planning to knife you to death?'

He visibly paled beneath his tan but she hardened her heart. His safety was her priority. Not his feelings. Not making him comfortable.

'Obviously you can't stay here tonight.' Kat rose to her feet. 'Gather your things while I make a few calls.'

He inclined his head in acceptance, the weary nod of a man who'd been blindsided. It took all of her effort not to fling her arms around him and hug him tight.

While Zac packed, Kat phoned Mark. He answered on the second ring and swore like a trooper when she told him about the note. 'I could have cocked up. I could have been followed,' she admitted.

'Do *you* think you made a mistake?' Instantly her mind flashed back to another time, when she'd asked herself that question over and over again. 'Kat?'

She swallowed, shaking off the memory. 'No, I don't.'

'Then you didn't. This person must have paid someone off in the hotel. Hopefully we'll get a good look at them on the CCTV.'

The certainty in his voice helped to settle her stomach. 'Thanks for the show of confidence, boss.' She glanced again at Zac, who'd finished packing his case and was now watching her from the bedroom doorway. 'Do the police still think it's the waitress from the party?'

'They do, but she gave a false name and address. They've had to get a photofit drawn up from the staff who worked with her. Her long hair fits the description of the driver who turned up at the Edwards function. They're sending me a copy tomorrow so you can keep an eye out and show Zac. See if it sparks any memory. Meanwhile we'll get the hotel CCTV reviewed.'

'Okay.' It was progress, she guessed. 'Any suggestions for where I should take Zac tonight?'

Mark sighed down the phone. 'The flats are both occupied. Guess it will have to be another hotel.'

Kat's eyes flicked over to Zac. His shoulders, usually so straight, sloped a little, and the film-star face staring back at her was etched with tension. The last thing he needed was being bundled off to another faceless hotel. 'I've got a better idea. I'll take him back to mine tonight.'

Zac's eyes widened in shock, the look almost comical. Ignoring him, she focused on what Mark was saying.

'Are you sure that's wise?'

'It's only one night. We'll sort something else out tomorrow.'

'What's wrong with a hotel?'

She read the subtext from Mark's question, and it annoyed her. With Zac listening, though, she could hardly blast back with the answer he was looking for. Just because she'd offered to put Zac up in her home, didn't mean she was becoming attached. Didn't mean she was doing anything as stupid as falling for him. 'He's been staying in a hotel,' she answered evenly, 'and look how well that turned out.'

Mark let out a heavy sound of annoyance. 'Fine. As long as you know what you're doing.'

'Of course I do.' As she ended the call, she realised it was the first time she'd ever lied to him.

Zac stepped warily through the front door of Kat's house. The second time he'd been here in the space of a few days. The first had just been a stop off, but this? He really wasn't sure why he was here.

'Mark isn't happy with this arrangement, is he?'

Kat, busy clicking switches to turn off the alarm and whatever other security feature she had set up on a state-of-the-art-looking panel, gave him a cool look. 'Your safety is my responsibility. It's my decision.'

'He's the boss though, isn't he?' Zac paused, perfectly aware it was none of his business. Damn it though, he needed to know. 'Unless he's something more?'

She stopped fiddling with the switches and stared up at him. 'Did you really just ask if I'm shagging my boss?'

'No.' Feeling acutely uncomfortable, he shifted on his feet. 'At least not in so many words.'

'Unbelievable.' Muttering under her breath, she marched into the living area, throwing her handbag onto the coffee table again, just as she had the other night. Given the table's appearance, it clearly had a function beyond that of a resting place for hot drinks. 'So you think I got this job because I agreed to sleep with him?'

'Good God, no.' Annoyed with himself, Zac dropped his holdall on the floor. 'You appear to get on well. That's all I meant.'

'We do.' She busied herself flicking through the mail she'd picked up when she'd come in, then checking her phone.

Zac stood like a lemon watching her, wondering how to ease the tension he'd just created. 'Sorry, it was a crass comment.' He paused, raking a hand through his hair. 'I made it because I was jealous.'

'Jealous?' Incredulity spread across her face. 'We're not . . . I mean, you and I aren't . . . Holy Moses, Mark and I aren't, either.' He'd never seen her so lost for words. 'You have to be with someone to be jealous,' she said finally.

'Clearly not.' His eyes tracked hers as she walked into the kitchen and went to open the fridge.

She paused, staring into it, clearly trying to gather herself – maybe to rein in her temper – before turning back to him. 'Don't do this.'

'Do what? Check out my competition?' He was out of order, he knew it, but he was tired, scared, and angry that his life had come to him having to spend the night in another place that wasn't his home. Worse. In a place where he wasn't wanted, but was staying because he was the owner's *responsibility*.

She huffed, pulling various things out of the fridge and thumping them down on the worktop. 'There is no flaming competition, because you and I aren't doing this.'

He dragged in a breath, forcing himself to calm. None of this was Kat's fault. Not the fact the stalker had found him again, nor the searing jealousy he'd felt when he'd seen her speak to Mark on the phone. The fond way she'd called him *boss*.

'Okay, message received.' Zac's gaze skimmed over the ingredients she was wrestling with: pasta, bacon, cheese and green beans. 'Look, you don't need to cook for me. Let's get a takeaway. My shout. The least I can do for inconveniencing you like this.'

Slowly she closed the fridge door. 'You're not an inconvenience.'

'Sure, I'm not. Babysitting your client in your own home is exactly how you want to spend your evening.'

Finally, her face lost its anger and she gave him a wry smile. 'I guess I deserved that.' With a sigh, she began to chuck the ingredients haphazardly back into the fridge. He itched to point out the cheese should go on the top shelf, and vegetables on the bottom, but he needed to mend fences, not build them, so he shut up.

'Okay.' Pushing the door closed, she folded her arms and leant up against it. 'First, thank you, we'll go for the takeaway option. Debs will be delighted, but I'm paying.' When he baulked, she put up her hand. 'I'll claim it back on expenses.'

He nodded, happy to concede that one. 'Second?'

'Second, Mark and I have never been, nor ever will be, in a relationship.' She looked him square in the face. 'He was my CO in the army and helped me through some tough personal stuff while I was in Afghanistan. When I left to join life as a civilian, I couldn't settle.' She shrugged. 'Funny fact, I'm not cut out to spend my days monitoring bloody CCTV. Mark heard how unhappy I was, and when he offered me this gig I snapped his hand off. So, if we sound close, it's because we are. Fighting alongside someone does that.'

Once again, he felt the sharp bite of jealousy. Not close in the way he'd thought then, but they clearly shared experiences, shared a *bond*, he had no hope of emulating. She'd needed Mark, and he'd been there for her. Zac couldn't imagine Kat ever needing him.

It was time to change the subject. 'When will Debs get home?'

'She's doing her homework at a friend's house. At least that's what she told me.' Kat glanced at her watch. 'I expected her back half an hour ago.' Waving towards the sofa, she told him, 'Sit yourself down. I know, I know, you'll have to remove a ton of crap first, but just dump it on the floor. I'll go and get Mandy's room ready for you.'

He hadn't thought it possible to feel even more of a burden, but apparently, he'd been wrong. Kat was stuck with sorting him out when what she'd really wanted to do was check on her niece. 'I'm not sure what getting the room ready entails, but I don't care about any clutter.'

'Says the man who didn't even mess up his hotel suite.' Suddenly she smiled, and the warmth from it seeped into his heart, causing it to lift. As if, for that suspended moment in time, there was nothing dragging it down. 'Don't stress, Mr Neat and Tidy, I'm not about to do a major overhaul. I'll just remove any obvious signs of underwear.'

'Ah, okay.' It was the most eloquent response he could come up with, considering she was smiling at him, and talking about underwear.

She'd only been gone a few minutes when the front door opened and Debs walked in, doing a double-take when she saw him. 'Oh, hi.'

'Hello. Again.'

She smiled tentatively. 'Is my aunt here or—'

'Yes, I'm here.' Kat marched back into the living room, hands on her hips. 'What time do you call this, Debs?'

As Zac silently squirmed on the sofa, Debs squared up to her aunt. 'A bit later than you said.'

'Thirty-five minutes later.'

'So? I was doing homework.' Debs dumped her rucksack onto the floor. 'I thought you'd be pleased.'

'Were you really doing homework?'

'Sure.'

She might be keen on drama, but Debs would have to improve her acting skills, Zac thought as he watched the interaction. She was obviously lying.

'Pick up your rucksack and let's go to your room,' Kat told her. 'You and I are going to have a talk.'

Zac immediately jumped to his feet. 'Don't.' When they both turned to look at him, he gave them a weak smile. Heavens above, how had it come to this? The uninvited, unwanted, inconvenient guest. It was excruciating. 'You talk down here. I'll go out for a bit.' When Kat glared at him, he exhaled roughly. 'Okay, I'll go to my room. Mandy's room.' Embarrassment vied with frustration and he snatched up his case. 'Please, use your sitting room, in your house. I'll get out of your way.'

Utterly and completely fed up with the situation, he trudged upstairs and opened the door to the pretty pastel-pink room that was his for the night. Taking off his shoes, he lay down on the double bed and stared up at the ceiling, wondering how many more beds he was going to have to sleep in until he could finally lie in his own.

Wondering too, if he had any chance of sleeping in the one down the corridor. The one that belonged to Kat.

Chapter 14

Kat ignored the tug on her heart as Zac, head bowed, walked out of the room. He would have to wait. First, she had a rebellious teenager to deal with.

She went to sit next to Debs on the sofa and looked into her niece's annoyed brown eyes, choosing her words carefully. 'I don't want to fight with you. Just remember, I was fourteen once. I know what the temptations are.'

'Yeah?'

'Yes. I went around with boys older than me, too. They were your mum's friends and I thought I was cool, hanging out with them. Some of them were older than Mandy, too.'

'So?'

'So, I missed out on a good part of my childhood. Instead of fun things like shopping and going to the cinema, I spent my time in dodgy houses, drinking vodka disguised in Coke because I couldn't stand the taste. I was forced to grow up too soon and looking back on it now, I regret it.'

'Fine.' Debs avoided her eyes. 'Consider me warned.' She jumped up and went to pick up her rucksack. Kat guessed she could at least claim that victory. 'So, anyway, Zac Edwards.' Debs slung the bag over her shoulder. 'What's he doing here?'

'He's staying with us tonight.'

Her niece's eyes rounded in shock. 'OMG. Are you two like, you know—'

'Absolutely not,' Kat cut in, feeling a flash of heat she hoped to God wasn't showing on her face. 'He's my client, Debs. But someone broke into his hotel room, so he can't stay there tonight. I figured you wouldn't mind if he crashed in your mum's room.'

Debs snorted with laughter. 'Wicked. Wait till she finds out she had Zac Edwards in her bed. She'll go nuts.'

'You have to promise not to say a word of this to anyone, Debs, not even your mum. Not until the person following him has been caught.' She mimed zipping her mouth shut. 'Okay, now to the good stuff – we're ordering take-out. What do you prefer? Chinese, Indian? Pizza?'

'Pizza.' A slow smile spread across her niece's face. 'I'm going to be sharing pizza with Zac f . . .' she caught Kat's stern look. 'Zac frigging Edwards. Holy shit.'

Maybe she hadn't got through to her about the older boys, but at least they were still talking. And as she'd provided Zac frigging Edwards, Kat was confident she'd earned some major cool points.

As for Zac frigging Edwards himself . . . Kat's stomach knotted as she walked towards Mandy's bedroom. She'd been a crap host, no question. He might have hacked her off with his comment about her relationship with Mark, but she'd more than paid him back, making him feel like a . . . how had he worded it? An inconvenience. Considering the shock he'd just had, that had been pretty damn rude. Especially since he'd admitted his snide remark had come from jealousy.

Her heart twisted. The police needed to find this damn stalker soon because it was becoming harder and harder to keep a lid on the bubbling attraction between them. Every time he said one of his long words, every smile, every glimpse of vulnerability beneath the shiny surface . . . each one nudged her deeper into feelings she was terrified of. She didn't want to get hurt, but equally she didn't want him getting hurt either, emotionally or physically. And right now it was the physical hurt she needed to focus on.

Taking a deep breath, she knocked on the door.

'Come in.'

The sight of him lying on a white duvet with pink flowers, his head resting on the fancy iron bedstead, all set against pastel-pink walls, made her smile. 'Well, isn't that a pretty sight.'

'An unusual compliment, but I'll take it.' He shifted so he was sitting upright, knees bent. 'Have you and Debs finished . . . speaking?'

'Yep. She's looking forward to having pizza with Zac frigging Edwards.'

He gave her a small, wary smile. 'That's good. I think.'

Kat took a further step in and leant against the wall. 'I'm sorry about earlier. I didn't mean to make you uncomfortable. Apparently, I'm a crap host.'

He shook his head, forearms resting loosely on his knees, which belied the twitching muscle in his jaw. 'I'm in the way. I should just check myself into another hotel.'

'Sure, because the stalker can't get to you in a hotel.'

He glanced away, eyes on the wall. 'I was unlucky.'

'You were lucky,' she corrected. 'Lucky you weren't in the room when they left the note.' The thought of what could have happened sent a cold shiver through her. 'Look, you're absolutely not in the way. Debs and I have had our spat, and now we're looking forward to pizza. If I have to tell her Zac frigging Edwards won't be sharing it with us after all, we'll be heading for another row.'

'I suppose we can't have that.' With a grace of movement she'd come to expect from him, he swung his legs off the bed and stood, looking somehow even taller, even more male, surrounded by the feminine décor. 'I presume it's safe to head back to your living room?'

She waved him forward. 'Not only is it safe, I've created a space for you on the sofa.'

'I'm touched.'

They shared a smile and because she wanted to keep looking at him, and smiling at him, a little too much, she forced herself to turn away and walk towards the door.

'Kat.' When she halted, he was right next to her, those vivid green eyes gazing into hers. 'Thank you.'

'For?'

'Putting me up.' He exhaled heavily. 'The realisation that this person has gone to the effort of breaking into my room . . . it's knocked me back a little. I'm glad I'm not stewing by myself in another hotel room tonight.'

'So am I.' She meant it. A note on his pillow was a major escalation. Proof that the stalker was no longer content to keep their distance. It wasn't surprising it had shaken Zac in a way none of the other notes had. It had scared the crap out of her, too. Yet even as he'd absorbed this gross invasion of his privacy, had no doubt finally begun to realise the danger he was in, his first reaction hadn't been anger. It had been to reassure her it wasn't her fault. A generosity of spirit, an unselfishness, that once again tugged at those feelings she was trying to fight.

'Kat.'

Her breath caught as he touched his fingers to her cheek. 'Please.' God, she didn't even know what she was asking for . . . him to stop, or him to carry on. For him to *kiss* her, because that's what her body was aching for.

'I know.' He sighed and bent to touch her forehead with his, those warm hands cupping her face. 'I know,' he said again, whether to remind himself, or reassure her, she didn't know.

The air around them fizzed, a palpable sign of the chemistry between them. When he straightened, his eyes found hers, the green mixed with flashes of gold and orange, like leaves caught up in the autumn wind. The longer he stared, the more the colours darkened. And the more her heart thumped.

Just when she thought he was going to kiss her, he cleared his throat and took a step back. 'No mushrooms.'

The rapid change of pace, of topic, left her reeling. 'Sorry?'

'On my pizza.'

'Oh, right.' She struggled to pull herself together. Later she'd be grateful he'd not pushed on what he had to know had been an open door, but now all she could feel was a crushing disappointment. 'What have mushrooms done to offend you?'

He mock shuddered. 'They're slippery buggers.'

This was what was needed, she told herself. Dial down the emotion, dial up the friendly banter. 'Well you'll have to pick them off, because Debs and I like our pizzas fully loaded.'

His lips twitched. 'Of course you do.'

'Why of course?'

'Because you're the antithesis of me.'

She shook her head. 'I swear to God you make up half these words just to confuse me.'

He smiled, but there was something else going on behind his eyes. They looked . . . sad? 'I'm merely pointing out the obvious,' he told her as they made their way back into the open-plan living room. 'That you're my opposite in almost every way.'

Her mind stuck on his hesitation over the word *almost*, but now wasn't the time to ask. Not with Debs in the adjoining kitchen, rummaging in the cupboards for some glasses. She swirled round when she heard them, a glass in each hand. 'What would you like to drink Zac . . . er, Mr Edwards.'

'Please, call me Zac.' The film-star smile was back in place, all signs of his earlier wobble, vanished. 'And I'll have whatever Kat is drinking. Though I may regret saying that.'

Debs stared back at him, the glazed look on her face causing Kat to bite into her cheek to stop herself laughing. How bloody lovely to see her niece as a star-struck teenager instead of the usual older-than-her-years act she put on.

But then he turned his smile on her, and the desire to laugh died, because apparently he had the ability to turn her into a star-struck teenager too. 'Zac's safe,' she finally managed. 'I've run out of Sambuca. There's some lager in the fridge.'

Last night had turned out to be unexpectedly enjoyable, once Debs had overcome her surprising shyness, and Kat had reassured Zac he wasn't entirely unwelcome. Oh, and once he'd pummelled his libido into submission for long enough to convince himself he didn't want to storm down the corridor, march into her bedroom and make love to her. Yes, considering all that, it had been a surprisingly good evening.

This morning, though, that was another matter entirely. Awkward wasn't a strong enough word for how he felt now, sitting on the bed in Kat's sister's room, pretending to practise his lines when really, he was listening to Mark and Kat argue in the downstairs living room about where he should stay tonight.

Of course, he could have shut his door, but he justified keeping it slightly ajar on the grounds that he was the subject matter under discussion.

'Another hotel is far too obvious,' he heard Kat argue. 'The stalker will just find him again.'

'They won't have long enough.' Mark's gruff voice this time. 'The hotel CCTV was no damn use, other than to confirm it was a woman with long hair who knew exactly how to avoid the cameras seeing her face. At least we have a photofit now, though. We know who we're looking for.'

'Not true. We have a photofit of a suspect, with no concrete proof she's actually the stalker.' Kat again. If Zac closed his eyes, he could picture her face lit up with the vibrant energy that was so much a part of her, whether she was angry, or happy, or anything in between. 'And so far, the stalker has been pretty flaming elusive.'

'You really think the answer is having him sleep here, in your house?'

Zac jerked upright. Was Kat seriously suggesting he stay here? With her?

'I do. It's easy for me to protect him as I'm with him 24/7, plus this place is like Fort Knox. You know that, you put all the security in place for me. Cameras, alarms, motion sensors. Unlike a hotel, nobody's coming in unless we invite them. He'll be safe here until a flat becomes free, or we find another safe house.'

Dear God, she was serious. Zac ran a hand over his face, shocked to find it trembling. Should he feel delighted, or terrified? He was in so deep already, this might push him into an obsession he couldn't back away from.

And if she was offering to give up her own privacy, to have him stay when he knew very well it was the last thing she wanted . . . he felt the beginnings of a cold sweat. She must really think he was in danger.

'Are you sure it's his safety that's at the front of your mind, Kat?' The heavy tone in Mark's voice signalled his displeasure. They might never have been an item, but it was blindingly obvious Mark had feelings for her.

'You know me better than that,' Kat retorted.

'Yeah, I know you, Kat Parker. That's why I'm asking the question.' A pause, which might have been a hesitation. 'I was there, remember. I don't want you going through it again. *Any* of it.'

Going through what? Zac was torn between wanting to hear more and guilt that he was eavesdropping on such an intimate moment. In the end, guilt won and he leapt to his feet and started to walk down the stairs. He was nearly at the bottom when he heard Kat reply quietly, 'Neither do I.'

Had he inhaled too loudly? Did the stair creak? Whatever it was, suddenly two pairs of eyes, one steely grey, one dark brown, swung in his direction.

'I fancy a cup of tea,' he said lightly, acting for all he was worth. 'Can I get either of you anything?'

They shook their heads, and he was hyper-aware of their eyes tracking him as he walked over to the kitchen. Mark was clearly annoyed at being interrupted, or annoyed at Kat, or both. Kat looked . . . damn, she looked upset. Whatever *tough personal stuff* Mark had helped her with, had clearly been traumatic.

It seems he wasn't the only one keeping secrets.

'Have you decided where I'm sleeping tonight?' he asked innocently as he waited in the now strained silence for the kettle to boil.

'Yes.' Kat gave Mark a look before turning her attention to him. 'We think it's best if you stay here for a few days. Easier and safer.'

He'd known the answer, and the twin emotions of joy and dread sat uncomfortably in his stomach.

'Is that okay with you?' Mark this time, his gaze sharp. 'It's not ideal, so if you want to say no—'

'I'm fine if Kat is.' No way was he going to be intimidated into staying somewhere else.

'Okay then. Seems it's decided.'

Zac pretended to focus on making his drink – teabag into mug, add hot water, clearly very taxing – while Kat showed Mark out.

'You could do with a teapot,' he remarked mildly when she walked back into the room.

'Maybe you can lend me one of yours. I seem to remember you having quite a stash.'

Bollocks. He'd forgotten what she'd seen on that first day. 'I'd be happy to.' He gave her a wide smile to prove the point.

'Oh, for God's sake. I'm not stupid. You can cut the crap.'

'Sorry?'

'You were listening to me and Mark, weren't you?'

Ah. 'Maybe?'

She huffed. 'You sneaky bastard. I forgot how easily the sound travels upstairs from the living room, though I did kind of assume you'd have the decency to shut the bedroom door.'

'You were talking about me,' he protested.

'Well, whatever you overheard, forget it. The only reason I'm offering for you to stay here is because I believe it's best for your safety. Okay?'

'Understood.' He hesitated, then figured, to hell with it. 'It seems we might have more in common than I thought.'

She glanced at him warily. 'You've decided you like mushrooms after all?'

'No.' He swigged at his tea. 'We both have areas of our lives we're keeping hidden from each other.'

A strangled laugh left her throat. 'Oh no, you don't get away with that. There's lots I don't know about you, and you don't know about me. The difference is, you're choosing not to tell me something that could impact your safety.' Her eyes zeroed in on his. 'You're stopping me from doing my job properly.'

His heart sank. It always came back to that. No matter how close he felt they were becoming, he was still a job to her. 'The police sent me the photofit of the suspect, Kat. I don't recognise the woman.'

'*If* she's the stalker,' Kat muttered, clattering plates and mugs into the dishwasher. 'Right, let's get you to the studio.'

He took a final gulp of tea before relinquishing the mug to her. 'I see my tidy habits are catching,' he remarked, keen to divert the conversation. 'Is now a good time to ask if I get the same service here as the hotel? I've become rather accustomed to a daily laundry service and a chocolate on my pillow every night.'

She looked like she didn't want to smile, but he saw when she lost the battle, and amusement entered her eyes. 'There's a perfectly good washer dryer, and I'll point you to the tin of Quality Street left over from Christmas.'

'I don't suppose there are any purple ones left?'

'You've got to be kidding. I can offer fudge, coconut and one or two orange creams.'

He winced. 'Thanks, but I'll pass.'

'Thought you might. I expect you're more of a Thorntons man.'

'Charbonnel et Walker, please. If it's good enough for her Majesty . . .'

Finally, he pulled a full smile from her. 'God, Edwards, you're such a snob. How are you going to cope slumming it with us?'

If only slumming it was all he had to worry about, he thought, his eyes skimming over the sexy curve of her buttocks as he followed her to the door.

Chapter 15

A few days ago, he'd been a man who lived in a hotel. Temporarily, sure, but it had become his substitute home; a place where, despite its lack of personality, he'd felt comfortable. He'd even developed a routine; exercise in the morning, shower in the walk-in shower cubicle with the half a dozen jets. Order room service breakfast: fruit and cereal, followed by toast. At the end of the day he'd shower again – it was a very good shower – go through his lines and order more room service. Maybe watch a film before he went to bed in the super-king bed with its 400 thread count bedding.

But then the crazy stalker person responsible for all this upheaval in his life had conned their way into his suite – apparently by pretending to be a new housekeeper – and he was no longer a hotel dweller. In the space of a few weeks he'd gone from a man living in his own place, to a man dossing down at his bodyguard's house. The same house she shared with her teenage niece.

Luxury had flown out of the window, and while he didn't need it – he'd lived a good part of his life without it – he did miss the order. Walking into a space and knowing exactly where everything was.

He also missed his privacy. He was very happy for the company, but there were times he needed more space than the four walls of Mandy's bedroom provided.

Take tonight, his third night in his new accommodation. Debs had come back late again, and Kat and she were currently having a shouting match downstairs. This time he had shut his door, but he could still hear it. It wasn't so much that he minded the noise. More that, beneath the anger, he could hear the distress in Kat's voice.

'Yeah well, guess what, you're still not my fucking mum, so you still can't tell me what to do.'

Zac winced as he heard footsteps thump up the stairs, followed by a door slamming.

Gingerly he opened the door to his room and walked out onto the landing.

'I suppose you heard all that.'

Kat's voice sailed up to him. Deciding it was an invitation, he went down to join her. 'It was hard not to. Even with my door shut.'

She sighed deeply, her dark eyes full of misery. 'Sorry.'

'Don't be. I've heard plenty of rows in my lifetime, though teenage ones are new to me.'

'They're the worst, because they're so flaming stubborn.'

Kat's body trembled as she inhaled, and Zac ached for her. It was obvious to anyone who saw Kat and Debs together how strong their bond was. How much Kat loved her niece. 'Am I allowed to hold you?' Not giving her time to answer, he wound his arms carefully around her very still body. 'Just like this. Nothing more.'

He held his breath, aware there was a high chance she'd push him away, but after a few seconds she surprised him by exhaling softly and resting her head against his chest.

He had no idea how long they stood like that. Only that everything seemed to melt away and the only thing that existed was Kat, and how good she felt in his arms. How right, even though everything about it should feel wrong. They had nothing in common. Were only here, together, because he was her assignment.

Yet despite being effectively homeless, and with a stalker who seemed to be turning more and more sinister, he was, in that moment, the happiest he'd ever been.

Kat took a moment to just *be*. To breathe, relax her shoulders and appreciate how good it felt to be held by a strong pair of arms. Okay, by *Zac's* arms. His heart thumped steadily, comfortingly as she pressed her head against the muscled wall of his chest. His smell wrapped around her; essence of Zac, mixed with a dose of expensive cologne. A combination both heady and reassuringly familiar.

How long had it been since anyone had done what he was doing now? Taking some of the strain away, just by holding her.

His hand began to move in slow circles along her spine, and Kat melted into him that little bit more. God, that felt good.

This – the enforced intimacy – is exactly what Mark warned you against.

Guiltily Kat jerked away. Mark was right, if she went down

this path it was all likely to blow up in her face again. Worse, she realised sickeningly, it could be Zac's face it blew up in.

Aware of Zac's confused eyes on her, she moved over to the sofa, almost falling on it as her legs buckled. 'Thank you,' she managed, desperately fighting off the rising panic. When he raised an eyebrow, she added, 'For the hug.'

'It was hardly a hardship,' he answered dryly, coming to sit next to her. Close, but not touching. 'Do you feel any better for it?'

'Sadly, Debs is still mad at me for not being her mum, and I'm still mad at her for being so stupid.' *But God help me, I enjoyed every moment of your arms around me.*

He eased his long legs out in front of him, and Kat tried not to notice that he'd taken off his socks. How was it fair that even his feet were attractive?

'Is she still hanging around with guys she shouldn't be?'

Kat dragged her eyes from his slender feet, to his face. 'Of course. Why would she take any notice of me? I'm just the pain-in-the-neck aunt who keeps on at her to do her homework, tidy her room.' Seeing Zac smirk, she added, 'I know, I know. Seems like double standards, but at least I don't leave my clothes lying around.' Another twitch of his lips. 'And you can take your mind out of the gutter, Mr Edwards.'

'Noted.' They shared an amused smile and for a few grateful beats Kat thought they'd waded out of the emotional minefield. But then he sighed and leant back against the cushion. 'Have you told Debs what happened to you?'

Feeling defensive, Kat drew her knees up to her chest. 'I've told her I hung about with boys too old for me, yes.'

'And the rest?' There was so much compassion in his eyes, she found it hard to look at him. 'Maybe if you tell her about your own experience, she'll take more notice.'

'I should never have told you that.' Kat stared down at her hands. 'It was way too personal a conversation to have with a client.' Yet she'd blurred the line so many times now.

'I'm more than a client, and you know it.' There was no anger in his voice, just a statement of fact.

'You shouldn't be, and that's entirely my fault.' She jumped to her feet, frustrated at how badly she was handling the situation. Hadn't history given her enough warnings of how dangerous it was to get involved with a man she had a responsibility to keep safe? 'Anyway, thanks for the advice. I'm sorry you had to hear the shouting match.'

'No problem.'

The shrewd look he gave her made her feel off kilter. 'I bet you miss your hotel room now, huh? All that peace and quiet, no clutter.'

'You think it bothers me to sleep in a house with noisy inhabitants and clutter?'

Calm green eyes zeroed in on hers and though she wanted to move away, she found it impossible to untangle herself. 'I think it must do, yes.'

'You're wrong.' He unfurled his long, lean body from the sofa and her heart gave a powerful thump as he walked towards her – no, stalked towards her. 'This is what bothers me.'

Before she knew what was happening, his mouth was on hers.

It was like a repeat of their last kiss, only better. Hotter.

Longer. His hands held her head steady, his lips teasing and nibbling before his tongue plundered. The heat of him, the soft feel of his mouth, the sounds he made, the press of his taut, hard body against hers. She couldn't move, couldn't breathe. Could only absorb everything he gave her like a parched flower, deprived of water for too long. She needed to stop him, this wasn't helping either of them, but she didn't have the willpower. Fighting him, fighting this, was too hard when all she wanted to do was give in.

His hands dropped to her hips and he angled his body, thrusting unsubtly against her. Holy hell, the feel of him. It was like a fire had been lit inside her. Yet as her fingers curled into the softness of his hair, and her body pushed back against his, it was he who eased away. His fiery gaze that trapped hers, his ragged breaths echoing around the room. 'The knowledge that you don't want me to do that,' he said, his voice rough with unfulfilled need, 'is what bothers me.'

Panting heavily, Kat took a step away, and then another, until she could lean her weak, trembling body against the kitchen breakfast bar. Would she have stopped, if he hadn't? To her shame, she didn't know. 'Just because I don't want you to do it, doesn't mean I don't want it.' *Want you*. 'And you kissing me like that, and looking at me like you are now, doesn't help.'

His mouth curved and there was mischief in his eyes now, alongside the heat. 'It doesn't? Good.'

She ignored the flutter in her chest. 'But neither does it change anything. You and me . . . it can't happen. I need to keep an emotional and professional distance to do my job.' A fact she'd conveniently forgotten a few minutes ago.

'Come on, I know you, Kat.' There was an edge of annoyance to his voice now. 'Something else is stopping you.'

His insightfulness was scary, yet she couldn't let this softly spoken, smooth talking, drop dead gorgeous actor make her forget the harsh, harrowing lesson Afghanistan had taught her. 'Why would I risk my career and your safety for a quick fling?'

He frowned, eyes seeming to caress her face. 'How do you know that's all it will be?'

'You said it yourself. I'm – what was that fancy word? Your antithesis? We're a million miles away from being compatible.'

'Being opposites doesn't mean we aren't compatible.' His gaze zeroed in on her mouth. 'I've found at least one thing we're extremely compatible at.'

He started towards her and for a heart stopping moment she thought he was about to kiss her again, but then he changed direction and walked past her into the kitchen. 'Why don't you go and check on Debs while I cook us something for dinner.'

Yet again he'd successfully turned the tables on her, leaving her disappointed she wasn't being kissed rather than grateful. 'Well, well, Zac Edwards can actually cook?'

'Why is that such a shock?'

'Because you're a film star born with a silver spoon in your mouth. Why would you ever need to cook?'

His answering smile didn't reach his eyes. 'Because even actors have to eat.'

'Fine. I'm not going to argue if you want to take over the kitchen.' Probably she sounded ungrateful, but she didn't like the way he kept unbalancing her. 'I've already taken some chicken and vegetables out of the fridge.'

'So I see.' He pulled a sharp knife out of the block and, with a quick flick of his wrist, expertly peeled and sliced an onion.

'Well, you seem to have that under control,' she murmured, unable to take her eyes off him. Zac frigging Edwards was in her kitchen, barefoot, shirt sleeves rolled to reveal tanned forearms. He glanced up, and a sexy little smirk played across his face as he saw her watching him. 'Did Mark tell you the hotel staff confirmed the woman who conned her way into your hotel suite matched the police photofit?' There, that's why she hadn't left yet. Not because she was busy ogling him.

'He did, yes.' With a clearly practised move, he deftly scraped the onion into a frying pan. 'But I gather there's still no name or address.'

'True. The net is closing in, though. It won't be long before she's spotted.'

He arched an eyebrow. 'Are you saying that to reassure me, or reassure yourself you won't have to put up with me much longer?'

As her feelings were too confused to know for sure, she turned and headed up the stairs. When she'd argued with Mark for Zac to stay with her, it had been with the purest of intentions. She genuinely thought he was safer here than in a hotel.

Now she was starting to think Mark was right to be concerned, because now there was no break from Zac, no space. No time to get her hormones under control until she saw him again.

Pushing her muddled thoughts to one side, she went to knock on her niece's room.

'Can I come in?'

'Sure.'

Kat drew in a breath and stepped inside. Debs was lying on her bed, computer on her lap. 'What?'

Swallowing her frustration, Kat perched on the end of the bed. 'There's more to the story I told you before, about me hanging around with older guys.'

It clearly hadn't been what Debs was expecting. 'What do you mean?'

'I mean I lost my virginity to a drunk seventeen-year-old when I was fifteen.'

Debs blinked. 'So?'

'So, I wish I hadn't. He didn't deserve that gift. He bragged about it at school the next day and I got myself a reputation I hadn't bargained on.' Seventeen years later and the taunts, the jeers, were still vivid. 'He didn't care about me, only about getting his end away.'

'Yeah, well, you're just salty 'cos he turned out to be a dick.'

'Salty?'

Debs raised her eyes to the ceiling. 'Duh. Angry. Bitter.'

'Yes, I'm angry he was a dick, but when I was your age I didn't realise that. I thought he cared about me because that's what he told me.' She placed a hand on her niece's arm. 'Now I know if he had truly cared about me, he wouldn't have pushed.' Debs blinked again, and this time Kat was sure she saw tears in her niece's eyes before she quickly averted them. 'Debs, is someone pushing?'

'Maybe.' She choked on the word and then let out a sob, tears spilling from her eyes and pouring down her cheeks.

Her heart bursting, Kat shuffled up the bed and held her in her arms. 'Hey, shh. It'll be okay.'

'I wish Mum was here,' Debs mumbled against her shoulder, her voice breaking.

'I know you do. But she'd be so proud of you for not giving in to this boy. For waiting until it really feels right for you, not for him.'

Debs clung to her until the sobs quietened. Then, wiping her eyes with the back of her hand, she gave Kat a watery smile. 'Sorry for being a bitch.'

'And I'm sorry for shouting at you.'

She sniffed, her eyes not meeting Kat's. 'Do you reckon Zac heard any of that stuff?'

Kat smiled and kissed the top of her head. 'Of course not. He's downstairs cooking dinner.'

Chapter 16

Kat wanted him, but only for a quick fling. And she didn't want that enough to risk losing her job.

The thought rankled as Zac sat next to her in today's hire car, an Audi, pretending to go through his lines on the way to the studio. It seemed he didn't actually need to go through them ten times to know them. Four was quite enough.

'Will we be allowed to watch any filming?' Debs's voice piped up from the back seat.

'The director says yes, but we'll have to confiscate your phones before we go in. Security is pretty tight on set.'

'OMG, that's so cool. The class are like so excited. I thought Miss was going to faint when I told her about it.'

Miss, who Zac understood was Mary Worthing, would be meeting them at the studio with fifteen of Debs's classmates. It's fair to say Jerry Collier had been less than impressed at Zac's offer to show a school drama class round. Since everyone on set, including the director, had been happy to allow it, Collier had finally relented, though not without an unsubtle dig. *Better make sure none of them turn up to stalk you later.* As if it was Zac's fault this woman was stalking him.

There were times he wondered if it was. In trying to be

who he was expected to be, had he inadvertently led her to think he liked her? When he'd been shown the photofit, he couldn't even recall seeing her at the party. Yet she'd obviously felt so . . . upset? Hurt? So angry he'd chosen Hannah over her that she'd decided to stalk him?

The thought settled uneasily on him.

As they turned into the studio, Kat slowed, her eyes darting between the rear-view mirror and ahead.

'What is it?'

She shook her head. 'Nothing.'

'But?'

'But, there's been a car following us for the last few miles, and I'm sure it had a female driver, though it's hard to say. Damn thing kept so far away I couldn't even make the number plate.' When he snapped his head round to take a look, she added, 'It turned off.'

'Okay.' He exhaled the breath he hadn't realised he'd been holding and received a questioning look.

'Are you alright?'

'Of course.' The lie slipped from his tongue like one of the lines he'd been learning. Knowing his stalker wasn't an over-eager fan but a woman who believed she'd been snubbed, a woman who might want to do him harm, scared the shit out of him. Not, of course, that he was going to admit it to Kat.

Kat slotted the Audi into a space by the entrance to the main admin building and the three of them walked inside where they were met by a group of overly excited fourteen-year olds. And a young teacher with big baby-blue eyes who couldn't stop thanking him.

'Really, this is so, so kind of you. The class has talked of nothing else since they found out they were coming.'

'It's my pleasure,' Zac told Mary Worthing for the third time, giving her his trademark smile. 'Sally,' he nodded towards the studio guide, 'will take you round because she knows far more about what goes on here than I do. When she's finished, she'll bring you to the set we're currently using, and the class can watch for a short while. If they've not had enough by then.' He flashed another smile.

'Oh, of course they'll want to see that. Watching you in action is the highlight.' She must have realised how that sounded, because she blushed.

'I hope I won't disappoint then, Mary.'

'I'm sure you could never disappoint.'

There went that blush again. To save them both any further embarrassment, Zac waved over to Sally. 'I think everyone is ready for their tour.'

As the giggling group headed off – following many surreptitious, and a few glaringly obvious glances in his direction – Zac exhaled in relief.

'You're such a flirt.' Kat rolled her eyes. 'I bet Miss Worthing hasn't blushed that many times since she was at school, though from the look of her it wasn't that long ago.'

The thought of his stalker flashed through his mind. 'I wasn't flirting.'

'Sure you weren't. *I hope I won't disappoint.*'

Kat fluttered her eyelids at him, clearly expecting him to laugh, but for once he didn't find her funny. 'I was trying to be nice.'

The amusement in her eyes faded. 'Hey, what's wrong?'

'Nothing's wrong.' He straightened his shoulders. 'I need to get on set.'

'Then we'll go. As soon as you tell me what's bugging you.'

'You're not in charge here. If I want to walk to the set, I will.'

'You'll have to get through me, first.' She planted herself in front of him. Five foot six to his six foot three, yet the determined set of her jaw, the fire in her eyes, were reminders that if she wanted to, she was quite capable of taking him down. 'Are you regretting offering to show Debs round?'

'Of course not.'

She gave him a shrewd look. 'Then it's about the woman stalking you, isn't it?' Dark eyes searched his and Zac found it hard to look away. 'What are you thinking? What's got your boxers in a twist?'

'Christ.' He managed to drag his gaze away from hers. 'Please leave my underwear out of this. I can promise you, nothing's in a twist.'

He could almost see the cogs in her brain sliding over each other. 'We now know for certain Miss Lipstick was a waitress at the party,' she mused. 'And we also know she wasn't happy that you chose Hannah to go back with, so we can assume she's no longer a fan, but a woman with a grudge. Just now you got all panicked when I suggested you'd flirted with the teacher.' Kat let out a long, drawn-out breath. 'Bloody hell. You think it might be your fault you've got a stalker, don't you?'

* * *

Kat's heart went out to the man standing in front of her. On the outside, a glossy film star, cool, unruffled, smooth. But inside, a surprising tangle of insecurities.

His eyes avoided hers. 'It's time I was on set.'

'Not until you look at me.' A pair of wary green eyes settled slowly on hers. 'It is not, I repeat not, your fault that Lipstick Lady is stalking you. She's clearly deranged.'

'Clearly.'

Kat sighed and began to walk towards the exit. 'FYI, the way you were with Mary, that was charming. Don't stop being charming.'

'Charming, huh?'

She tried not to smile. 'Some people call it that, yes.'

'And you? What would you call it?'

Instantly her pulse kicked up a gear. A moment ago she'd been – yes, okay, she was big enough to admit it – she'd been annoyed to see him flirt with someone who wasn't her. Now he was back to flirting *with* her, and she didn't know how to handle it. 'It doesn't matter what I think.'

He made a noise of frustration. 'You know that's not true. What you think is starting to matter to me more than almost anything else.'

'It shouldn't.' Panic bubbled inside her. 'It can't.'

He gave her a humourless smile. 'If only it was that easy. Flick the switch, turn off the feelings.' They reached the door and he inclined his head. 'After you, I believe.'

He said nothing more on the way to the set, and for once Kat was out of conversation. It was becoming alarmingly clear that no matter how much she tried to pretend it wasn't happening, this attraction wasn't disappearing. Instead it was growing, on both sides.

And her refusal to acknowledge it was starting to really piss him off.

Two hours later, Kat stood with the class at the back of the huge stage, unable to take her eyes off Zac. The assistant director had explained they were filming an early scene, where Zac's character meets his love interest – played by Sophia Layton – for the first time, in a bar. Zac had changed into a pair of faded jeans, tough cowboy boots and a tight-fitting white T-shirt. Something the girls around her definitely appreciated, from the gasps and giggles when he walked on set.

As for her, it turned out she wasn't able to turn off her feelings, despite her desperate need to do exactly that. She found it impossible not to look at him, and not to want. The same magnetism that had drawn her to him at their first encounter, when she'd spilt champagne over him, was now vividly alive on set. It meant it was hard, really bloody hard, to watch him flirt with Sophia . . . to see him *kiss* her. It seemed too real. She knew exactly how it felt to have those lips on hers, so to see him place them on another woman's mouth, was excruciating. Especially as she knew that woman was after him for real. The urge to run onto the set and shout stop. To push them apart, put the actress in a headlock . . .

Yep, she was losing her mind over the man.

Finally, *finally*, the director announced cut.

Mary, who'd been standing beside her, let out a wistful

sounding breath. 'He's quite something to watch, isn't he?'

Kat felt like a tigress, slowly drawing in her claws. 'He certainly is.'

Mary's eyes drifted back to Zac. 'But it's not just about acting, is it?'

'Sorry?'

'To make it onto the big screen you have to have that something extra, don't you? A star quality, I guess people call it. A gloss, an aura.' She laughed. 'Oh God. I sound giddier than my pupils.' She slid Kat a smile. 'I understand from Debs that you're his bodyguard. Maybe when you're around him all the time, you become used to it.'

At that moment Zac glanced over, his eyes coming to rest on Kat. He didn't smile, didn't do anything other than hold her gaze for a few humming seconds before turning back to talk to the director.

Kat felt Mary staring at her, and when she turned, the teacher gave her a knowing smile. 'Or perhaps the aura becomes more potent.'

Zac's filming went on into the early evening. Debs and the class had long since gone. When he messaged to say it would be a late finish, Kat went home and threw together a corned beef hash – go her, she knew how to cook for a film star – before deciding to pick Debs up for a change.

'I would've come straight home,' Debs protested when she climbed into the Jeep.

'I'm not picking you up for that reason. Zac's working late, so I have some free time.'

She screwed up her face. 'Is that because of us? Did we put him behind schedule?'

Kat hadn't even thought about that possibility. 'I'm sure it's not. Even if it was though, it was his choice to invite you.'

Debs gave her a look, a devil-like gleam in her eyes. 'You know he only did it to impress you, right?' Kat felt her cheeks heat, which was enough to send her niece into fits of laughter. 'OMG, Kat. He fancies you and you fancy him. I know it.'

Kat spent the rest of the journey assuring Debs there was no fancying being done on either side, though from the twinkle that persisted in her niece's eyes, she wasn't sure she'd convinced her.

Hardly surprising, considering she hadn't convinced herself.

Now it was eight o'clock, and she was back at the studio to pick Zac up. He was freshly showered and giving off too many pheromones for her weakened state.

He was also, she noted as he stared straight ahead when she climbed into the driver's seat, still upset with her. *What you think is starting to matter to me more than almost anything else.* His shocking words had circulated through her head on a loop all afternoon. Couldn't he see she needed to keep him at arm's length to do her job? The thought of her failing again, of taking her eye off the ball for that split second . . . her hand trembled as she put the car into gear. Damn, she couldn't afford to be thinking like this.

Nor could she afford for him to wriggle any further under her skin. Her heart was damaged, *she* was damaged. There were far easier women for him to throw his undeniable charms at.

'I made a corned beef hash for dinner,' she said finally into the silence. Then cringed. She sounded like his wife.

'Next you'll be telling me you ran me a bath.'

'Only showers in our place. Sorry.'

'As if that was the only thing stopping you.'

Her hands gripped tighter to the steering wheel. 'Please, can we just get back to the way things were.'

'And what way was that?' She felt the intensity of his stare. 'You pretending not to want me? You kissed me back, remember.'

God, she did remember. All too clearly.

As she dug around for a suitable reply, the sound of his phone echoed round the car.

'Saved by the bell,' he murmured, staring down at the caller ID. 'Excuse me, I need to take this.'

He greeted whoever was calling with a smooth hello, but after that, there was silence. And when she pulled up at a red light and glanced sideways at him, his face had drained of colour.

'What is it? What's wrong?'

After uttering a faint, 'I can't talk right now, I'll call you back,' to whoever had called, Zac slowly slid the phone back into his pocket. 'Nothing that concerns you.' He turned to her, his expression tight. 'As your *client*,' his emphasis of the word sliced right through her, 'I believe I'm entitled to a modicum of privacy, at least.'

Chapter 17

The moment he bit out the words, Zac regretted them. Still smarting from Kat's continued need to push him away, snapping at her had been an instinctive reaction, but also a mean one. She might not want him as he wanted her, but he thought she did at least like him, and wasn't finding this any easier than he was.

The call from Helena had blindsided him though, and he simply couldn't cope with Kat's concern right now. It would take all of his focus, all of his strength just to keep it together until he could make it into the four walls of Mandy's room, shut the door, and phone Helena back to get the full, gut wrenching picture. After that . . .

He drew in a sharp breath and let his head fall back against the headrest. *One step at a time.*

At least his being a sod to Kat had, for once, shut her up. Knowing he'd upset her gnawed at his insides, but he was incapable of even the most banal conversation right now.

'Would you like me to heat up the corned beef hash?' she asked with cool politeness as they walked into the house.

'No . . . thanks.' The thought of eating made his stomach churn. 'I need to make a call.'

Very aware of her eyes on him, he dashed up the stairs and into the room he'd temporarily commandeered.

'Helena.'

He sounded breathless and didn't know whether it was from the flight of stairs, or the fear currently clawing at his insides.

'Zac, dear, I'm so sorry to be the bearer of such awful news. The liaison officer was trying to reach you, but I told them I would pass the information on.'

'It's okay, what did they say?'

'He's going to be released early. They couldn't give a date yet, all they could say was his release had been approved.'

Fuck.

He sunk into the bed, weighed down by a wave of hopelessness. His carefully crafted life was about to get smashed wide open.

'We don't know what his frame of mind will be,' Helena said softly. 'He's been in prison for nearly twenty years. It's bound to have changed him. He probably won't even want to look for you.'

'Perhaps.' But the thought that he might, had plagued Zac for years. Hell, when he'd started receiving the notes, signed in *pink lipstick*, for God's sake, his paranoia had been so acute, his first thought had been that the bastard was somehow behind them.

'Even if he does want to search you out,' Helena continued in that same calm tone, 'twenty years has definitely changed you. You even have a different name, Zac. He won't recognise you. With luck, he'll live the rest of his life without troubling you.'

With luck. He wasn't sure how much he had left in supply. His whole career was based on luck; the right place at the right time, with the right director. God knows, twenty years was a long time though. Long enough for his life to have changed beyond all recognition.

'Darling, you need to push it to the back of your mind for now. For all we know, there'll be a change of mind or circumstance and he won't get released after all.' Zac wasn't sure she believed her own words, but he appreciated her trying. 'Now, tell me how the filming's going?'

'It's going fine,' he answered, grateful for the change in topic. 'We're on track, which is a major plus.'

'And your stalker? Are they any closer to catching her?'

He pushed himself up on the bed, shaking off the doom that had cloaked him since answering Helena's call in the car. 'The police have a photofit, which is a step forward.'

'I'm sure they'll catch her soon, though I suppose that will mean you have to say goodbye to that lovely bodyguard.'

Zac managed a small smile. 'That wasn't very subtle.'

'Oh, I don't know. I thought it was a very clever way of asking you if you have plans to see Kat when this is over.'

He raised his eyes to the ceiling, wishing it was that easy. The client–bodyguard issue would be over, but whatever else was holding Kat back – indifference, wariness, a mistaken belief that they weren't compatible – that would still remain. 'It's not all in my hands.'

He heard the smile in Helena's next words. 'So I was right, you do like her.'

'Yes, I like her.' It had gone beyond like, but as the deeper feelings appeared to be all on his side, there was no point piquing Helena's interest. 'Tell me what you and William have been up to recently. Didn't you go to Venice?'

By the time Zac made it back downstairs, only Debs was in the sitting room. Walking into the kitchen, he noticed the corned beef hash on the side, with a note giving instructions on how to heat it up.

Debs glanced up from the TV, which was currently showing a group of men and women in their twenties wearing very little and sitting around a pool, showing off the most appalling fake tans. 'Kat's in the study. You know, in case you wanted her for anything.'

'Thanks.'

He needed to make peace, so after scooping a portion onto a plate and zapping it in the microwave, he grabbed a fork and carried it down the hallway towards the study. Swallowing down a quick mouthful, he knocked on the open door.

Kat, laptop in front of her, looked up from behind the desk. 'Hi.' She focused back on the screen. 'Thought it was time I caught up with my emails. Well, those that aren't trying to sell me bitcoins, or encourage me to join a sex romp with some dubious Russians. How's the corned beef hash? Sorry it's nothing fancy but I thought it would at least make a change from pasta.'

Shaking his head, he leant against the doorway. 'No apology necessary. Your job description says you have to protect me, not feed me.' He forked up another mouthful. 'Besides, this is surprisingly tasty.'

'Surprisingly? Well gee, thank you. Complimented and insulted in the same breath.'

The fact that she was even talking to him, never mind feeding him, told him he was a lucky bastard, and she had a very forgiving nature. 'I wanted to apologise for my behaviour earlier, in the car.'

'Before or after the phone call?'

Ouch. Shame rolled through him as he remembered he'd been a prick before the call, too. 'Both.' He swallowed another mouthful while he considered his next words. 'The truth is, I'm not dealing with this situation well at all. The stalker, why they're doing it, and what they want from me. Living out of a suitcase.' He met her eyes. 'Wanting something I can't have.' Inhaling a deep breath, he pushed off the doorframe. 'But I shouldn't have taken it out on you. Especially since you've just given me my first taste of corned beef hash.'

'Apology accepted.' Her features softened. 'And if you need me to be a punch bag now and again, no problem. I can take it.'

'Thank you.' He didn't want to hit her though, he thought despondently. He wanted to do far more pleasurable things.

'About the phone call.' It was typical of Kat that she brought it up rather than leaving the issue to fester. 'Clearly there is something wrong, and while I don't need to know what, I'd like to know if there's anything I can do to help.'

For a split second, he thought of telling her. Thought how good it would feel to unburden himself to someone who might understand, even if it would change her view of him. But trusting her with that was a further step on the road to intimacy, and it was a road she'd made clear she didn't want to travel with him. 'Thank you, but I'm fine.'

He thought he saw a flicker of disappointment, but it could also have been annoyance. Or relief that she could get back to her Russian sex fests.

Sharing bathrooms was a tricky business. It was one of the reasons Kat and Mandy had decided to build Debs her own en suite when she'd turned eleven. That way they each had their own bathroom. Kat's bedroom already had an en suite, and from that moment on, Mandy had been able to commandeer the main bathroom.

The bathroom that was now Zac's.

It had been working out fine, until this morning, when Kat noticed a large pool of water on the floor of her en suite when she went to take a shower. It looked like the loo was leaking.

Deciding to use the one in Debs's room instead, she knocked on the door, only to hear Debs turn on the shower.

Great. Waiting was a possibility, but time was ticking on, Debs was a notorious hot water hogger, and Zac, Mr Punctual, would have a fit if they didn't leave at 7.30 a.m.

As he was always so punctual though – way beyond punctual, bordering on ludicrously early – he would surely have finished in the bathroom?

Tentatively she walked down the corridor. His room – *Mandy's* room – was at the end, with the bathroom next to it on the right. All was quiet, and the bathroom door open. Thankfully she stepped inside it.

And screeched to a halt.

Zac stood at the sink, cleaning his teeth, a white towel around his hips, showcasing a neat, sexy backside. Above it, tanned, naked skin stretched across broad shoulder blades forming a triangle of masculinity that made every part of her sit up and take notice.

Their eyes caught in the mirror.

'Crap, sorry. I didn't realise you were in here.'

Slowly he turned, and greedily her eyes fixed on his chest. More precisely, on the drops of water that slid over the curve of his pecs, down the hard ridges of his six pack, and into the trail of brown hair arrowing beneath the towel.

A rush of heat pooled between her legs.

'In the context of fairness, I think it's only right that you take your shirt off, too.'

Guiltily her eyes jumped to his as a hot flush crept across her skin. 'Sorry?'

'I'm happy for you to stare at me,' he pointed out mildly, 'as long as I can do the same.'

'Oh no, no way.' She backed up a step, and then another. 'I couldn't possibly compete with all *that*.'

His right eyebrow shot up, and his mouth curved, just a little. When she checked out his eyes, they sparkled with silent laughter. 'I beg to disagree.' He placed his toothbrush back in the holder and leant against the sink, arms folded across his chest. Biceps bulging. 'Though really there's only one way to find out.'

'I've got a leak. In my en suite.' She seemed to have difficulty talking.

'Oh dear.' His eyes tracked around the bathroom. 'You're welcome to share.'

She swallowed, but the saliva had disappeared from her mouth. 'Share, no. Use, when you've finished, yes.'

'Oh, you don't have to worry on my account.' He turned again to face the mirror, his eyes finding hers in the reflection. 'I'd rather share than be late.'

'Of course you would,' she muttered, throwing her towel onto the side of the bath. 'Shout when you've finished.'

'Oh, I'm done.' But he remained where he was. A bulk of pure, rippling manhood.

'You don't seriously expect me to have a shower while you're still in here, do you?'

He gave her another small smile in the mirror before bending to splash water on his face. 'Expect, no.' Dragging a hand towel from the rail, he dried himself. 'Hope?' This time he grinned right into her eyes. 'A man can always hope. I'll see you at 7.30 by the front door. Don't be late.'

'I wouldn't dream of it.'

When he'd left, she sagged against the door. There was no doubt what her top priority was today. Finding a blasted plumber.

Chapter 18

Buoyed by their encounter in the bathroom yesterday morning – Kat might say she wasn't interested, but her eyes had said something else when she'd come across him – Zac decided he was going to make the most of the weekend. Sunday was already taken care of, unbeknown to Kat, and today. Well, he was going to head to the beach.

And because he knew Mark was busy, it meant Kat would have to come with him.

'Seriously.' Kat, dressed today in jeans rather than black trousers, though still with the obligatory black T-shirt, gave him one of her searching looks as she walked into the kitchen. 'You want to head to Brighton for the day?'

'The sun is out. It's summer. The beach seems a good place to head.'

'Sure, if you've got kids.'

He gave her a dazzling smile. 'Excellent. We can take Debs. And she can take a friend, if she wants.'

'Now wait a minute.' He'd never seen so much suspicion in a pair of eyes before. 'First you want to head to the beach.

Now you're playing happy families. Only we're not a *family*. I'm your bodyguard.'

'A fact you've made very clear.' Choosing to ignore her, he took a bite of his toast. 'I've arranged a picnic.'

'For crying out loud.' She made a strangled sounding noise. 'This is getting worse. Next you'll be telling me to pack my bikini.'

'Well, I wouldn't be averse to seeing you in one.' He wasn't a hundred percent sure what she said next, but it sounded suspiciously like a strong swear word. 'Though wearing one is entirely optional,' he added, before she burst a blood vessel.

'Well, gee, that's mighty kind of you.' She ran a hand down her face in what he suspected was an attempt to gather herself, before muttering, 'I need to see what Debs has planned.'

The girl herself chose that moment to wander into the kitchen and glare accusingly at Kat. 'I couldn't get back to sleep after you woke me when you used my shower.'

'Sorry Munchkin. The plumber is coming on Monday.'

'Your aunt is welcome to use my bathroom.' Zac gave Kat an innocent look. 'I believe yesterday proved there's plenty of room in there for both of us.'

Kat did something very rare. She started to blush.

'Err, is there something I need to know?' Debs looked at them both questioningly.

'Only that Zac is a major wind-up merchant.' Kat gave him a dirty look before turning back to her niece. 'I went to use the bathroom yesterday, not realising Zac was already in there.'

'Oh.' She started to giggle. 'Was he, like, you know, in the shower or taking a p—'

'No!'

Zac couldn't help smirking at Kat's horrified expression. It was rare to see her so unbalanced.

'He was cleaning his teeth, that's all. Now,' she continued hurriedly, clearly anxious to end the line of conversation. 'Zac wants to go to the beach today, so I need to go with him. He's suggested you and a friend come along too, if you want to.'

'Really?' Her clear excitement was a pleasure to see. 'That sounds well good. I'll message Anna.'

As she darted back up the stairs, Zac glanced at Kat. 'At least someone is looking forward to the trip.'

'So it appears.'

Kat's less than enthusiastic response to the whole idea started to prick at his happy bubble. 'Come on, out with it. You're not usually so hesitant about voicing your opinion.'

'I'm just wondering what, exactly, you're trying to do?' She started to pace back and forwards. 'First the sudden desire to head to the beach, then winding Debs up about what happened in the bathroom.' Her eyes drilled into his. 'It's not a flaming joke, Zac. This is my job.'

'You think I don't know that? You've reminded me often enough.' Irked, he jammed his hands into the pockets of his shorts. Ralph Lauren would be livid.

'Then what are you playing at?'

'I'm an unwanted guest in your house. What am I supposed to do this weekend, Kat? Sit around and get in your way? I thought at least this way we could both have a reasonable day.'

She stopped the pacing. 'And that's all this is? It isn't you trying to . . .' She bit into her lip, glancing down at the floor before meeting his eyes. 'Trying to take me on a date?'

It was exactly that, and it frustrated him no end that she clearly found the idea so abhorrent. 'If it was, you'd run a mile, so no. It's just a day at the beach.'

Her shoulders relaxed and she gave him a hesitant smile. 'Okay then.'

Relief vied with simmering disappointment. He'd get his day with her, just not the way he wanted it. 'Excellent. We can go as soon as the hamper is delivered.'

'Hamper?' She stared at him wide-eyed. 'You've seriously ordered a *hamper*?'

'Why not?'

'One of those wicker jobs with the plates, cutlery, glasses and carefully folded check napkins?'

'Yes.' He was starting to feel defensive now.

'We're going to sit on Brighton beach eating a posh person's picnic? Smoked salmon and roast beef with a side order of caviar. All topped off with, let me guess . . . champagne?'

Irritation pricked, along with a sense of acute disappointment. She was taking the piss out of him now. 'Unless you have something against the idea.'

'Of course not.' She looked at him questioningly. 'Where is this hamper of untold goodies coming from?'

And now he felt every inch the entitled prick she clearly thought he was. 'Fortnum and Mason.'

'Of course, it is.' She half laughed, shaking her head. 'Jesus, Zac. How much has that cost?'

'It hardly matters, does it. I'm paying.'

'But you didn't need to do that. We've got a fridge full of stuff. We could have made sandwiches.'

He'd wanted the day to be special, though. Damn it, he'd wanted to treat her. 'My mistake,' he said stiffly. 'Should there ever be another occasion, I'll make sure to check with you first.'

'No, it's not that. It's your day, you should do as you want.' As if aware she'd upset him, she smiled. 'I'm sure Debs and her friend will get a real kick out of it.'

But not you. Feeling foolish, he turned away from her and, for want of something to do, began to fill the kettle.

A moment later, her phone rang. Digging it out of her jeans pocket, she glanced down at the caller ID. 'Sorry, I've got to get this.'

He thought he heard her say 'Hello Mark,' before she went into the study and closed the door behind her.

Maybe he'd be sharing the blasted hamper with Mark now, Zac thought grimly as he waited for the kettle to boil.

They'd walked along the prom, skimmed stones in the sea and eaten the picnic. Now Debs and Anna had decided to go on the pier, leaving Kat and Zac to chill out on the beach.

Breathing in a lungful of sea air, Kat lay back on the blanket. There was no sand between her toes, no swishing of palm trees. Instead seagulls squawked, fighting over a bag of discarded chips, and pebbles dug into her back, yet they hardly registered.

This, right now, felt like a little taste of heaven.

The sky was a stunning shade of blue, the sun was warm

on her skin, and – forgetting who he was for just a moment – the man lying next to her, took her breath away. In chino shorts and a turquoise T-shirt that fitted snugly across his pecs, he was on a level of attractiveness far beyond anything this beach had ever seen. Even with a baseball cap jammed on his head, and shades covering his face.

'Is that a sigh of boredom?'

As he angled his face towards her, Kat huffed out a laugh. 'Hardly. It was an *I'm relaxed*, sigh.'

'So this non date isn't so terrible, after all?'

Her mouth itched to smile. 'Not so terrible, no.'

'And the picnic? Was that bearable?'

There it was again. The edge to his voice. She thought she'd heard it when she'd been taking the mick out of him earlier. 'It was delicious.' When he didn't reply, she glanced over to find him staring up at the sky. 'I'm sorry if I sounded ungrateful before.'

'No matter.'

But it did matter, she realised belatedly. Unwittingly, she'd hurt him. The private Zac Edwards was clearly more sensitive, perhaps more insecure, than his public persona suggested. 'It was a sweet thought. Debs really—'

'Enjoyed it,' he interrupted. 'You said. So did she. Several times, I believe.'

'I enjoyed it, too,' Kat added quietly, which finally got him to look her way. 'It's just I'm not used to being . . . well, I suppose cossetted. Fussed over. Wined and dined.'

'You should be.' His eyes pressed hers. 'If I dated you, Kat Parker, I would wine and dine you every night.'

That's not me. She was about to tell him, when she realised it would only encourage a conversation she didn't want to have. Instead it was time to broach one they needed to have. 'Do you remember the call I had earlier?' She levered herself up onto her elbows. 'It was from Mark. Apparently, a note from our lipstick friend was delivered to the Vision Films offices this morning, addressed to you.'

His body tensed. 'And?'

'It said *You can run from the hotel, but you can't hide.*'

'I see.' He drew his hands up behind his head, his face turned once again towards the sky. 'Was there anything else the pair of you discussed that concerned me?'

'Whoa, hang on a minute.' She sat upright and stared down at him, frustrated to find the sunglasses made reading his expression almost impossible. 'Where did that come from?'

'It came from you locking yourself in your study to discuss a matter that concerned me.'

'I didn't know it concerned you, until I spoke to him,' she countered, wondering at his reaction. She'd expected him to be upset, worried, but not this. Not the anger, directed at her.

'So you always speak to Mark behind a locked door, do you?'

'Yes.' Annoyed now, she glared into eyes still shielded by shades. 'Often the things we talk about, the safety of celebrities, of people in the spotlight, are highly sensitive. I've got into a habit of always making sure I'm away from prying ears when I answer his calls.'

Silence. Just the rise and fall of his chest as he inhaled a few deep breaths before slipping off his sunglasses. 'Shit.'

Slowly, avoiding her eyes, he, too, sat up, drawing up his legs and resting his forearms on them. 'Sorry.'

Unsure what was going on in his head, she nodded. 'Accepted.'

He gave her a small smile before turning his attention towards the gently rolling waves of the English Channel. 'I'd like to blame my fit of pique on the shock of the note, but it would be a lie. Truth is, I find myself annoyingly, frustratingly, jealous of Mark.'

Thump went her heart. 'I told you before, we're not—'

'I know.' He turned to her, and the sombre look in his eyes squeezed her heart. 'Sadly, it doesn't appear to help.'

'I'm . . . crap, I don't know what to say.'

For a long while they both stared out to sea, the only sounds those of the waves, and the hovering seagulls. Was it fair of her to let him keep going out on a limb, voicing his feelings, when she kept hers all screwed up in a tight ball? Because while she couldn't act on them, she could at least share some of them.

'That time Debs and her class came to the studio.' Kat was aware that his head turned sharply to face her, but she couldn't look at him. 'I didn't like seeing you flirt with the teacher.' She paused. 'And I didn't like watching you kiss another woman on set.'

'No?'

When she got up the nerve to look at him, there was no smug smile, as she'd expected, and as she could have coped with. Instead his eyes held a hopefulness that made all her worries leap back into life. 'That doesn't mean—'

'I know.' Once again, he interrupted her. 'But it's comforting to know I'm not the only one suffering.'

They remained in silence for a few more minutes, their attention on the sea. Kat was so lost in her thoughts, she gave a start when she felt a warm hand curl around hers.

'Relax, I'm only helping you up.' He jumped nimbly to his feet and gave her hand a gentle tug. 'I thought we could pack up the car and then take a stroll. Maybe find Debs and Anna on the pier.'

'Okay.' She scrambled up with considerably less grace. 'But only if you buy me a hot donut.'

'Seriously?' He screwed up his face in disgust. 'All that fat, all that sugar?'

'Are you saying I need to watch my weight?'

'What? No, God no.' His eyes ran down her legs – he'd somehow managed to convince her she couldn't go to the beach in jeans and boots – and then back up to her face. 'You look perfect to me. I just meant, all that *mess*.'

With that, and the accompanying expression on his face, Kat couldn't help it. She burst out laughing. 'Oh my God, Zac Edwards, it's high time I got you crumpled and dirty. And before you look too excited about the prospect,' she added as she saw the corner of his mouth lift in a smirk, 'I mean we're going to paddle in the sea, where I might accidentally splash you, so be warned. Then we're going to stuff our faces with donuts on the pier and let the sugar stick to our lips, and the grease stain our clothes.'

'Clearly an experience not to missed.' His vivid green eyes rested on her mouth. 'Do I get to lick the sugar off?'

Hot damn. A slow sizzle began in the pit of her stomach. The man was incorrigible. Funnily enough though, she could have fended off that, fended off the handsome flirt.

It was the other side of Zac. The man who'd ordered the picnic because, she suspected, he'd thought she might like it. Who'd listened to her worries about Debs, held her and then encouraged her to talk to her niece about her own experiences. The man who'd been brave enough to open up to her about his feelings despite getting very little in return.

It was that man she was finding she had no defence against.

Chapter 19

Yesterday, the hiccup over the hamper aside, had been a good day. A particular highlight had been Kat's admission that she'd been jealous watching him kiss Sophia on set. Even that had been eclipsed though, by her reaction to his statement about where he was planning to spend Sunday.

'You're going to *Silverstone*?' she'd repeated when they'd arrived home last night.

'Yes. I'm not sure whether you or Mark will be accompanying me. If it's you, I have a spare ticket for Debs.'

'Oh, it will most definitely be me,' she'd answered, just as he'd anticipated.

He was well aware the reason for her eagerness was the lure of the race, and not his company, but he'd long since left his ego behind when it came to Kat. If he had to bribe her to drop her guard with him, so be it. He was optimistic that he could worm his way under her skin. He had to be, because he was well and truly hooked. There was no stepping away from this now, not for him.

He didn't even mind that Debs was with them, because he'd started to enjoy her company. At times stroppy, many times unintelligible – teenage speak was a very different language – he'd found making her giggle to be surprisingly rewarding.

'Holy cow, this is really happening,' Kat exclaimed as she expertly slotted their hired Range Rover Evoke between an Aston Martin and an Audi Q8 in the VIP parking. 'We're at flaming *Silverstone*.' She angled her head towards the back seat to look at Debs. 'Can you believe it?'

Whatever Debs said, Zac didn't hear. He was too lost in the excitement shining in Kat's eyes when she turned back to meet his. And in the warmth of the smile she directed at him, which made everything in his chest lift and swell.

'Will we get to go to the pit lane?' Debs asked once they were seated on the shuttle bus, her voice almost breathless with excitement.

'I believe so.' He didn't really have a clue. Only that he'd asked for three of the best tickets he could get, money no object.

'And we watch the race from the Drivers' Lounge?'

'So I was told.'

'Where's that on the track?'

Ah. As he didn't want to admit he didn't know, he smiled. 'I believe your aunt is the expert in Formula One.'

Kat cast a brief, questioning glance in his direction before answering her niece. 'It looks over Stowe Corner through to Club Corner.'

Debs squealed. 'Frigging awesome.'

Kat grinned back at her. 'It's a tough job, being Zac's body-guard, but hey, I guess someone has to do it.'

The reminder that she was only here because she had to

be, rankled, but Zac pushed the niggle away. 'Tough is rather a strong word,' he protested evenly. 'I'm sure you've faced more difficult assignments.'

For a split second she hesitated, but then her eyes found his. 'I suppose that depends how you define difficult.'

He felt a pulse of satisfaction on realising the *difficult* moments she was referring to.

In no time at all they were stepping onto a wide terrace, overlooking the track. Debs immediately dashed over to the viewing area, and began taking photos to post on her Instagram page.

'Any moment now I'm going to wake up and find this is all just a dream,' Kat murmured, her sweeping gaze taking it all in.

'*This* is what you dream about?'

The grin she gave him was wide and uninhibited. 'Oh no, I'm not going to answer that.'

He led her over to a seating area and accepted two glasses of champagne from a passing waiter. When he set them down carefully on the table in front of them, he couldn't help but smile. This was where it had all started.

Kat caught the direction of his gaze. 'Me, you, and champagne. You're not feeling so relaxed now, I bet.' She nodded to the Tom Ford blazer he'd chosen to wear. 'How badly do you think it will stain?'

'As unlikely as this may seem, I really don't care. I've developed a fondness for the drink, no matter where it ends up.'

Her answering smile, full of amusement, and yes, of affection, caused his heart to lodge in his throat.

As if aware she was dropping her guard too much, she averted her gaze and scanned the terrace. 'Well your jacket is safe today because I'm on duty. I'll have to pass on the champagne.'

Irritation rippled through him and he had to actively force his muscles to unclench. She might be on duty, but the smile she'd given him a moment ago had gone beyond client and bodyguard.

'It was kind of you to include Debs today,' Kat said into the now rather strained silence. 'She enjoyed yesterday, but today. It's like *the best day ever*.' She mimed her niece's voice with uncanny accuracy.

'Good.' As his sole motivation for the day had been to spend some time with Kat, the thanks made him uncomfortable.

'When did you get the tickets?'

'I decided I wanted to come a while ago.'

'What if Mark had been covering the weekend instead?'

He leant forward to take a sip of champagne, not sure where she was going with this. 'Then I'd have had a spare ticket. Perhaps have invited one of the crew to join me.'

'Do you come here a lot then?'

He took another swallow of champagne. 'Not a lot, no.' Desperate to change topic, he glanced back at her. 'Did I tell you how good you look today?'

Though she suited the black she usually wore, it was a treat to see her in the bright cherry-red summer dress she'd put on. It was simple, but it suited her athletic frame. And the colour made her skin glow.

'Only twice now.' Humour made her eyes sparkle.

'Three times a charm?'

Laughter rolled out of her. 'Oh, you're that alright.' She glanced down at her watch. 'I think we need to go and find Debs. The pit lane tour starts in five minutes.'

'This from the lady who turned up late for our first meeting.' He nodded towards his half-full glass. 'I haven't finished my drink.'

'I don't know how to say this politely but sod the flaming champagne. We're going to be walking down the *pit lane*.'

With that, she grabbed hold of his hand and yanked him to his feet. With one last longing look at the gently fizzing contents of the champagne flutes, Zac followed her.

Kat was inclined to agree with Debs; this was the best day, ever. And the race hadn't even begun. The thrill of walking down the pit lane, spotting famous faces, stepping on the same tarmac that Hamilton and co. had stepped on. Of looking down on the track from what had to be the best place to view the race.

Of sharing all this experience with her giddily excited niece, who seemed younger, and happier, than she had in a long time.

Then of course there was the smoothly handsome man next to her. A man who turned the heads of nearly every female in the VIP enclosure, yet who, for some inexplicable reason, seemed only to notice her.

'It looks like they've started,' Zac remarked, eyes on the cars streaming past them.

Kat eyed him quizzically. 'It's the warm-up lap.'

He returned her look with a bland smile. 'Sure, I know that.'

Possibly, she thought, though she was beginning to suspect his knowledge of Formula One was very much on the basic side.

Soon she was too absorbed in the race to wonder about anything other than would Hamilton achieve what the vast majority of the crowd were hoping for – a British win. It was gripping, nose to tail racing. Watching it on the television hadn't prepared her for the electrifying thrill of seeing the cars thunder past. To *feel* that speed. The noise levels had been cut a few years ago but to Kat, who'd never been to a race before, the scream of the engines still sent shivers down her spine. When she glanced sideways at Debs, who was to her left, her niece had a look of sheer, unadulterated awe on her face. 'OMG, this is so cool.'

Kat grinned back before turning to look at the person to her right. Only to find his eyes fixed firmly on her.

His mouth curved in a slow smile. 'Is it how you imagined?'

She laughed, the sound breathy with excitement. 'Better.'

'Good.'

She turned back to watch the rest of the race, and though she couldn't be certain, she had a feeling his eyes remained on her more than they did on the track.

'Hamilton was awesome. He must really love winning here,' Debs remarked as they finally drifted back towards the car park. Her niece was clearly still on a high, because not only was she engaging in conversation, she'd not looked at her phone once, other than to take photos.

Kat watched as Zac gave Debs a small smile. 'He must.'

'What do you think of McLaren this season?' Kat directed her question at Zac. 'Reckon their car is any better?'

His eyes blinked, and for a second she was sure she saw panic, but then all his acting skills came into play and he gave her a smooth smile. 'Just a smidgen, maybe.'

'To think, they used to have Button and Alonso driving for them. I mean. I can't even remember the names of the drivers they have now. Can you?'

Zac furrowed his brow, giving every impression of a man thinking hard. 'No, I'm afraid I can't.'

'What about the names of the Ferrari drivers?'

Debs opened her mouth to answer, but Kat shot her a look. 'Let's let Zac answer this one, shall we? If he can.'

He narrowed his eyes at her. 'What is this, a test?'

'In a way, yes. And I've got a strong feeling you're going to fail. So, Edwards, the names of the two Ferrari drivers you watched today. I'll even give you a clue. One of them came third.'

His lip curled in a gesture of disdain. 'I'm not interested in third place.'

And with that, she started to laugh. He really hadn't watched the race at all. 'Wow, you're acting your socks off, aren't you? You might not be interested in who came third, but if you were at all interested in Formula One you'd have probably been to Silverstone before, you'd definitely have known where the seats you'd bought were on the race track, and you'd not only have known the names of the Ferrari drivers, no matter where they came in the race, you'd be able to list all the drivers on the track today.'

Zac didn't reply. Instead he walked swiftly towards the car.

'Don't think I'm letting you off the hook,' she murmured as she turned on the engine. 'I want to talk to you when we get back.'

'I'll look forward to it,' he drawled, eyes straight ahead.

By the time they made it back to the house, it was late. Debs was quiet as they walked inside and Kat started to worry something was up until she saw her niece taking several glances at Zac, before inhaling a deep breath.

'Zac . . . I mean Mr Edwards.' Zac gently shook his head in admonishment at her. 'Zac,' she began again, rolling her eyes, this time looking a little less nervous. 'Thank you for taking me today. It was, like, so fun.'

'I'm glad.' Then he smiled, and if there was one thing guaranteed to add the final sparkle to her niece's already brilliant day, it had to be receiving a wide, genuine smile from Zac Edwards. 'Thank you for coming with us. Taking you,' his gaze drifted over to Kat, 'taking both of you, was entirely my pleasure.'

Her niece's cheeks flushed. 'I'm going to catch up with Anna, now. 'Night.'

Kat watched Debs climb the stairs, and the moment the door to her room shut, the air seemed to spark into life, crackling with an energy that sent goosebumps racing across her skin. 'Would you like a drink?' she asked Zac. 'Something to eat?'

Zac shrugged off his jacket, folding it neatly and placing it over his arm. 'I'm fine, thank you. I think I'll just head to my room.'

'Oh no. You're not getting away that lightly. We need to talk.' As dangerous as the atmosphere felt between them, she needed to know why he'd gone to Silverstone today. 'So, I repeat, do you want anything to eat or drink?'

He gave her a long, guarded look. 'Why do I feel like the condemned man being asked for his final requests?'

'I'm not about to condemn you. Just to interrogate you.'

'Now I feel much better.' With great precision, he rolled up the cuffs of his shirt. 'I'll have whatever you're having.'

'A Jägerbomb and a packet of pork scratchings?'

He baulked. 'Is there an option B?'

'A glass of red with some cheese and crackers?'

'Much better.'

She waited until the food was on the coffee table and they had a glass of wine in their hands before asking the question she hadn't dared ask in front of Debs. 'So, tell me, Mr *I've just paid an obscene amount of money for 3 VIP tickets to Silverstone*. Do you actually like motorsport?'

'I don't dislike it.' He took a careful swig of his wine. 'Cricket is more my sport. More finesse. Less . . . speed.'

'So if you're not a fan of F1, why did you go to Silverstone today?'

His lips formed another wry smile. 'I could argue that it's the place to be seen, but we both know it would be a lie.'

Her pulse started to hammer. 'You went because I like it?'

Slowly his eyes, his beautiful, beautiful eyes, met hers. 'Yes.'

And even though she'd half expected the answer, hearing him say it so clearly, caused her heart to jump. 'When did you book the tickets?'

'Does it matter?' He looked down at the glass of wine in his hand. 'It was the day we picked Debs up from the party. While I was waiting for you to finish talking to her in her room, I noticed an F1 Racing magazine on the sofa. One of the many items on the sofa, if I recall.'

The last sentence was his way of lightening the atmosphere, of changing the subject. Even as she allowed herself to laugh though, and allowed him to smoothly move the conversation on, Kat kept coming back to what he'd just admitted. Even before that first kiss, he'd liked her enough to book the tickets because he thought *she* would enjoy it. It was a thoughtfulness, just like with the hamper, that she'd not expected, and though it warmed her to her core, it also scared the living daylights out of her. Were these really the actions of a man who only wanted sex? A quick fling with his bodyguard while he was under her protection?

She didn't know him well enough to be certain. Maybe he treated all the women he fancied like this . . . and the fact she was including herself in that category, hardly seemed possible.

When the wine had been drunk and the crackers eaten and cleared away, Kat hovered at the foot of the stairs. She didn't want to tease, to suggest something she couldn't deliver on. Yet it felt wrong to end the day without him knowing exactly what it had meant to her.

'Before we go up, there's something I want to say.'

A slow smile spread across his face. 'If it's your bed or mine, I'm easy either way.'

She had to work hard to push the images of him naked, in her bed, out of the way. 'Yesterday, and then, wow, today. It's been a very special weekend. I wanted you to know that.'

He nodded, his gaze meeting hers. 'Special for me, too.'

She should leave it at that, though somehow it didn't seem enough. 'I can't remember the last time I felt so . . . so . . . oh God, I don't know the words.' Frustrated with herself, she looked him straight in the eye. 'Nobody's ever done that for me before.'

'Treated you?' When she nodded, he gave a slow shake of his head. 'Then it's beyond time someone did.'

It was so easy to get swept up in his looks, but it did him a disservice. It was fast becoming clear that inside, he was pretty special, too. 'I want to kiss you.' When his eyes rounded she smiled, 'But you have to promise not to kiss me back.'

'I'm sorry?'

'If you do, it will get out of hand, and I can't risk it. So, will you promise?'

Slowly his Adam's apple moved up and down. 'I'll try.'

Softly, gently, she pressed her lips against his, feeling the tingle from it all the way to her toes. For a few breathless seconds, she held her mouth there, her head spinning, her heart melting. When his hands slid to her hips, pressing her against him, she let out a moan pleasure. Then heaved her body away.

'Thank you,' she whispered.

Then she darted up the stairs before his hot, beguiling eyes drew her into something she absolutely couldn't afford to succumb to.

Chapter 20

Zac was into his fourth week of being the victim of a stalker. His fourth week of needing a bodyguard.

His fourth week of knowing Kat.

Was it possible to fall in love in that space of time? And despite not going further than two incredible, yet far too short, kisses?

He didn't think so, but that's not how his heart had felt yesterday, when he'd watched her watch the Grand Prix. A woman who grabbed life by the scruff of the neck, she'd been in her element watching the adrenalin-fuelled sport, her response to everything so animated, his heart had pumped that little bit faster every time he'd looked at her.

Even now, on a grey, overcast Monday morning, she made everything brighter. And that despite the text he'd just read from Helena, the words sending shivers down his spine.

We've been told if he's going to be released, it could happen any day now.

Feeling sick, Zac pushed the phone back in his pocket as Kat drove through the studio gates. He refused to worry about something that still might not happen. The man was part of his past, and there was no reason to think he wouldn't stay there.

Instead of dwelling on the bad, the nasty, he turned to watch Kat scan the studio car park, as she did every morning, before turning off the engine and climbing out of the car to open his door.

'One day I'd like to open a door for you.'

'Hmm.' Whether she heard him and chose to ignore him, or just didn't hear, he wasn't sure, because her focus wasn't on him, but on the car park.

'I hate always waiting for you to open the door for me,' he complained. 'It's horribly unchivalrous.'

He caught her lips twitching. 'God, Zac, you and your weird way of talking.'

'Weird? I take exception to that. I speak the Queen's English.'

'That's what it is, huh?' She wasn't listening, not really. Her attention was on the rows of cars.

'Kat? Is everything okay?'

'Probably.'

'Not exactly the answer I was hoping for. In fact, you're starting to freak me out a tad,' he told her, worry settling like cold porridge in his stomach.

'As long as it's only a tad.'

Suddenly Kat swore violently and as she shoved him hard onto the floor he heard the crack of gunfire echo around the car park.

His heart began to pound, the sound a loud, insistent throb in his eardrums.

'Are you okay?' Kat's voice echoed above him.

'Yes, fine.'

While he continued to cower on the floor – he wasn't proud of it, but his instinct was to hide from gunfire, not leap up and face the shooter – Kat talked on her phone, her words precise, her tone calm. He'd barely been able to squeeze his two words out.

'The police have been called. Security are out there now, doing a sweep of the car park.' She reached down for his arm. 'Can you get into the car and lie down across the back seat?'

'Of course.' He manoeuvred himself inelegantly into the back of the car, then froze when he saw Kat climb into the front and wriggle across into the driver's seat. 'What the hell are you doing?' he demanded. 'And keep your bloody head down.'

'It's not me they want.' She turned on the ignition and thrust the car into reverse. 'I'm driving to the entrance so we can get you safely inside.'

He had no time to argue. A squeal of tyres on tarmac and he was hurtled against the back of the seat.

A minute later she bundled him inside. He was mortified to find his legs trembling.

'Let's get to the dressing room.' Kat was like the strong, fearless lion to his wimpy newborn lamb. 'You look like you could do with a sit down and a drink of something strong enough to blow your knee-caps off.'

'Actually, I'd like to retain them, if it's all the same. They're the only thing keeping my legs from giving way.'

Her eyes met his, soft and sympathetic. 'Okay, we'll make it a strong coffee. Attack the whisky when we get home.'

Home. The word had come out naturally, and why wouldn't it, because it was home to her. Still, his chest warmed at the idea of going *home* with her.

Kat pushed him onto the sofa and then fussed around making him a coffee from the machine in the tiny kitchenette. The more he sat there, thinking about what had just happened, the more his stomach churned and the sicker he felt. Unable to hold it any longer, he rushed to the bathroom.

Not only the guy with the wobbly legs then, the one who'd frozen at the sound of a gun going off. He was now the guy who'd humiliatingly, ignominiously, thrown up.

After rinsing out his mouth and splashing water on his face, he sucked in a deep breath and walked back out.

The sympathy on Kat's face when she saw him, only made him feel worse. It was sexist, male chauvinist bullshit but damn it, he wanted to be the strong one. The one who looked out for and protected her.

'It scares the crap out of you, doesn't it, hearing gunfire?'

'Apparently.' Though equally apparently, it had only scared the crap out of him. He fell back onto the sofa, hunching forward, forearms resting on his thighs, trying to find his equilibrium.

'Do you want this coffee I've painstakingly prepared or will it, you know, make you—'

'Have another humiliating heaving episode? Quite possibly.' He gave her what he knew was a weak smile. 'But I'm willing to risk it if you are.'

She pushed the mug into his hands, then surprised him by perching on the coffee table in front of him and looking directly into his eyes. 'There's nothing humiliating about being scared when someone's firing a gun at you.'

He couldn't hold her gaze. He felt too vulnerable, too disgusted with himself. 'You weren't.'

'That's where you're wrong.' She held out her hand, and he was shocked to see it tremble. 'See, I'm having a wobble too, and the shot wasn't even directed at me.'

'Fuck, Kat.' He rubbed a hand across his face, struggling to compose himself. 'Someone tried to kill me.'

'Yeah, but they didn't. And now the police are out there, hunting them down.'

'They didn't because of you.' How shameful that it had taken him this long to realise it. 'You saved my life.'

She shook her head. 'Hey, no need to get all dramatic on me. All I did was shove you onto the floor.' Her gaze fell to the dust on his black jeans, and then up to his now creased shirt. 'FYI, the crumpled look is surprisingly good on you.'

He knew she was trying to lighten the mood, but his mind kept going back to what had happened. 'You risked your life to drive me to the entrance.' While he'd been cowering on the back seat. Once again, his stomach churned. 'Christ.' His chest heaved on a shuddering breath and he flung his head back against the sofa, squeezing his eyes shut.

Kat was desperately trying to hold it together. She knew if she allowed her brain the chance to relive that moment in the car park, she'd turn into a jabbering wreck. Instead she forced it to focus on what needed to be done, rather than what had already happened. And as she watched the shame rolling through Zac, she knew exactly what that was.

'Stop it.' She must have said it a little more sharply than she'd intended because his eyes flew open. 'First off, I didn't risk my life when I drove the car. Whoever was shooting wasn't aiming at me.'

'And of course you knew they had perfect aim?'

If they had, you'd probably be dead. Her stomach lurched and she put a hand over it to try and settle it. 'I took a calculated risk. One of many I've taken over the years.'

His face paled and he pinched the bridge of his nose. 'That doesn't help.'

'Doesn't help what?'

He sat bolt upright, agonised green eyes slamming into hers. 'It doesn't help my twisting guts to know you put yourself in danger for other people, not just me.'

Oh no, she wasn't having this. She'd had this discussion once before in her life, when a guy had tried to wrap her in cotton wool. Tried to pull her out of the line of fire. 'Were you listening to me? I said I took a *calculated* risk. I know what I'm doing.' *You said that last time, too,* she realised belatedly, sickeningly. *And look how it turned out.*

A low, unamused laugh rumbled out of Zac. 'I'm not saying you don't. I just . . . Jesus.' His eyes bounced around the room before finding hers again. A stormy green whirl of feelings, they reached right into her. 'I can't stand the thought of you being hurt.'

Emotion balled in her chest, squeezing the air from her lungs and suddenly Kat felt as if the walls were closing in on her. She stared back at him, not knowing what to say. Only knowing that hearing the gunfire, and seeing Zac lying on the floor, had terrified her so much that for a moment, she'd not been able to breathe.

It was a feeling that went far beyond what a bodyguard should feel for a client.

A feeling she'd felt only once before in her life, and vowed to never, ever, put herself through again.

But the heart couldn't be controlled.

'I overstepped again, didn't I?' Clearly taking her silence as irritation, she watched as he mentally and physically withdrew from her, sliding a big steel guard around his emotions. 'Sorry.'

'Don't be.' She reached out to clasp a hand around his clenched fist before dropping a gentle kiss on his knuckles.

His gaze arrowed in on hers. 'What was that for?'

'For caring about me. And to let you know I care back. When I thought you'd been shot, I totally freaked out.'

He gave her a wry smile. 'A silent freak out? It doesn't sound like the Kat Parker I know.'

'Yeah, well, thankfully for both of us, the training kicked in.' But it could have been too late. Despite her efforts to keep it locked up, the horror of the moment began to replay back to her. She'd allowed Zac to carry on talking when she should have shut him up.

She'd allowed him to *distract* her.

That bullet could have got him.

Bile rose in her throat and it took all her effort to swallow it down. When her phone rang, Kat snatched at it, desperate for the diversion. A chance to regroup and put her professional head back on.

She relayed what had happened to Mark almost robotically, her need to keep her emotions battened down drowning out everything else.

'That was Mark,' she told Zac once she'd ended the call. 'Security and the police are prowling the area, but so far they've not found anything. The police are anxious for us to give a statement when you're ready.'

Zac had slumped forward, forearms resting on his thighs. 'Fine, though all I did was hide out of the way.' His self-disgust was clear.

'You followed my orders,' she corrected. 'And that helped both of us get out alive.' *Though I nearly ballsed up. Nearly got you killed.* She fought the voices in her head. Later she'd give in to them, let them have their say, but for now, the man beating himself up, needed her. Walking back over to him, she placed a hand gently on his face. 'The first time I heard a gun go off, I almost shit myself. The first time I heard the enemy firing a gun at me, I think I did.'

'Yet you remained in the army for twelve years.' He clasped a hand over hers, the feel of it warm and strong. 'You're incredible, Kat Parker.'

The sincerity in his eyes made her heart bounce, but he didn't know the full story. 'I'm a long, long way from incredible,' she told him, fighting to keep the tremor out of her voice. 'Some people would argue that making magic on the big screen, bringing so much depth and warmth to a character that people flock to part with their money to watch you, is incredible.'

He dismissed her words with a slow shake of the head. 'I don't care about some people. I care about you, and what you think.'

'I—'

He'd never know what she would have said, because there was a sharp knock on the door, followed by an authoritative female voice. 'It's DS Spencer. Can I come in?'

Giving Kat an ironic smile, Zac went to open the door.

I think you're spell binding. That's what she'd have told him.

And I'm desperately trying not to fall for you. That's what she'd have kept to herself.

As Kat did her usual recce of the studio grounds and car park the following day before she was due to pick Zac up, she had a fleeting glimpse of a female figure sitting in a car. It was unusual because with six acres of gorgeous grounds, workers at Pinewood usually went outside to think, or for some peace and quiet. They didn't sit in their car on a sunny day in the middle of July.

Security at the gate confirmed they'd let her in because her ID card had shown she was staff, yet when she asked them to check the plate, they were puzzled to see the car wasn't registered.

As suspicious as Kat now, they agreed to call the police.

Ten minutes later, the woman in the car was arrested.

Not only did she fit the image of the photofit, in her handbag was a note, signed with a lipstick kiss. It read, *Now I want to meet you in person.*

The conviction that they'd found the shooter was strengthened when the police discovered a gun hidden in a drawer in her house. The fired bullet had yet to be discovered, but all the evidence pointed in one direction.

The danger was over. Zac's stalker had finally been found.

Chapter 21

He didn't have a stalker anymore. It was official.

Yesterday evening, when Kat had told him they'd arrested a woman that fitted his stalker's description in the car park, Zac's relief had been tempered; *arrested* didn't mean they had their woman.

This morning, when he bumped into Kat in the kitchen, she had better news.

The woman had confessed to stalking him.

'Why?' It was the question that had hovered in his mind for the last four weeks.

'The official line from her is that she wanted to get close to you. She took the job as a waitress so she could meet you, then got royally hacked off when you flirted with Hannah. After that she set out to make sure you took notice of her.'

He supposed it made sense. 'And unofficially?'

'She's got a screw loose.'

He huffed out a laugh. 'Are you saying a woman needs to be mentally unstable to want to get close to me?'

The wary glance she gave him made his insides sigh. After

the way she'd held a palm to his cheek and kissed his knuckles yesterday, his hopes had foolishly started to rise.

'You know I'm not saying that,' she replied, taking the milk and butter out of the fridge. 'Stop trying to trip me up. I said the woman's got a screw loose because this isn't the first time she's stalked an actor.'

'I'm not special then?'

Kat heaved out a sigh. 'Oh for pity's sake, cut the crap. You should be happy. This is good news. Jerry wants to see us to review the situation, now the danger is likely over.'

Slowly her words began to fully sink in. He was no longer in danger. He could go back to his apartment, back to living his life the way it had been, without fear, without restrictions.

So why was he not excited? Why did it suddenly feel as if all the joy had been sucked from him?

He forced himself to smile. 'I guess that means you lose your annoying house guest.'

'Maybe.'

'Only maybe?' And damn it, there it was, that slippery hope. 'Are you planning on kidnapping me?'

'In your dreams, sunshine.' Sighing, she went to fill up the kettle and load up the toaster. 'We need to talk to Jerry and Mark, but I'm not comfortable assuming the shooter and the stalker are the same person.'

'You think someone out there still wants to kill me?'

His mounting panic must have shown on his face because her expression softened. 'I'm not saying that, not exactly. Just that we should consider all the angles before dispensing with your protection.'

Okay, that he could cope with. In fact, he allowed himself a small smile. 'Have you considered one angle might be, you don't want to let me go?'

She focused on pouring boiling water into two mugs, and not on him. 'Why would I want to keep protecting such a pain in my backside?'

'Because you like me?'

She let out a spluttering noise, halfway between strangled laughter and a sob. 'Of course I like you, Zac Edwards.' Before he could push further, she changed the subject. 'I'm seeing Mark and Jerry after I've dropped you off at the studio.'

'Should I start to pack?' The thought didn't fill him with any joy.

'Let's wait until after the meeting.' She glanced at the clock, her expression giving nothing away. 'Besides, Mr Punctual, we need to be out of the door in ten minutes.'

He took the mug of tea and plate of toast she placed in front of him, wondering at how easily they'd slipped into the domestic routine. 'That's impressive time keeping, Miss Parker. Next you'll be putting magazines into racks and hanging coats on pegs.'

She gave an exaggerated shudder. 'Please. It's clearly time you and I parted company. Your nasty habits are starting to stick.'

Probably it was a joke, yet as Zac took his mug and plate back upstairs to finish getting ready, her words pricked. He was happy, beyond happy, not to have a bodyguard any longer, but he was nowhere near ready to part company with Kat.

* * *

Kat tried not to wilt under the glares of the two men sitting opposite. She and Mark had met up with Jerry in his office ten minutes ago. That's all the time it had taken for her to realise she was fighting a losing battle.

'The woman was found in the car park the next day, Kat. The very same car park the shot was fired from. She's admitted stalking him.'

'Stalking him, but not shooting him.'

'Because shooting him would be attempted murder.' Jerry pinned her with his hard stare. 'Of course, she's only going to admit to stalking, it's a much lighter sentence.'

'But it doesn't make sense,' she argued. 'She's been sending notes, that's all. The last one we found on her said she wanted to see him. Why would she come back to the car park where she'd attempted to kill him, only to slip a note under his dressing room door asking to see him?'

Mark grunted. 'Because she's deranged?'

'She's not that unbalanced.' Kat tried to keep the annoyance out of her voice. 'We need to find the bullet. Only then can we be certain if it was her or not.'

'The police have done a search and not been able find it yet.' Jerry jumped up to his feet, and Kat fleetingly wondered if it was so he could look down on her, and thus bend her to his will. 'What are you saying, Kat? That we need to keep a bodyguard on him indefinitely, just on the vanishingly remote chance there's been a second person stalking him?'

When he put it like that, maybe she did sound paranoid. But this was Zac's safety they were discussing with such cold matter-of-factness. 'I thought you wanted to protect your asset?'

'Look, I'm not trying to be callous,' Jerry countered. 'I know we're talking about a human life here, but we're also talking about a cost, and putting him under a continued restriction he won't thank us for. If I felt there was still a real threat, I wouldn't hesitate, you know that. But we have a woman who's confessed to stalking Zac, turning up in the same car park where a gun was fired the day before. We've even found a gun in her house. If the police are satisfied she's both the stalker and the shooter, then so am I. It all adds up.'

Kat ignored Mark's warning look. 'Not all of it. There's still the matter of why she'd want to kill him. She's stalked before and not tried to shoot anyone. Why kill Zac when she wanted to meet him?'

'Why does anyone try to kill another human?' Jerry pulled his phone out of his pocket and glanced down at it. 'Look, I'll have another chat to the police, but for the time being, I'm suspending the contract.'

Kat had always got on with Jerry. She believed they'd built up a level of trust between them, so it frustrated her that he couldn't see what she could. 'I think you're making a mistake.'

Annoyance flashed across his face. 'Noted.'

Mark gave her a *For God's sake, shut up* glare, and as Jerry's stance had turned from relaxed to rigid, Kat had to concede this was a battle she wasn't going to win. Reluctantly she followed Mark out.

When they reached the reception area, her boss turned on her. 'Are you trying to piss off our most valuable customer?'

'Are you trying to get Zac Edwards killed?'

Mark stilled, his expression hard. 'What's got into you? You don't usually overreact like this.' A pair of piercing blue eyes stared into hers. 'What's going on between you and him?'

'Nice. If I was a man, would you still be asking me that? Telling me I'm overreacting?'

He swore under his breath. 'Don't play the sex card with me. You know I don't give a toss what gender you are.' His voice softened. 'I care about you, Kat. And this isn't like you.'

'Looking after the safety of my client isn't like me?'

'Come on, you know what I mean.'

'You know what, I don't. You're going to have to spell it out for me.'

'Okay.' He thrust his hands in his jeans pocket. 'I'm worried you've become too close to Zac and now you're trying to cobble together an excuse to keep being his bodyguard.'

She'd known the words were coming, but they still felt like a slap around the face. 'Well, gee, thanks for your faith in my judgement.'

'Don't.' Mark's jaw clenched. 'You know I trust your judgement. It's why I gave you the assignment in the first place.'

'And I was right, wasn't I? I told you I was ready for the step up. I told you to trust me.' *Though maybe he shouldn't have.* The emotion of the last twenty-four hours started to catch up with her and Kat heard the shake in her voice.

'I did trust you,' Mark said quietly. 'I do trust you. So much so that I know you're wrong in thinking you made a mistake yesterday. Most people wouldn't have been alert enough to react to the shot at all, never mind have time to push the client out of the way.'

Because she needed to believe him, Kat looked Mark

straight in the eye. 'You mean that? You're not just saying it to make me feel better?'

'I mean it,' he answered firmly. 'But I also mean it when I say your judgement on Zac's continued need for a bodyguard is wrong. It's become clouded by your feelings.'

Tears burnt the back of Kat's eyes. 'You really believe I'd let myself fall for another guy, after what you saw me go through?'

Mark's shoulders slumped, the fight seeming to drain out of him. 'You can't control feelings like a tap, Kat. I believe you don't want to fall for Zac, but that doesn't mean you won't. Or that you haven't already.'

Because she was scared he was right, Kat went on the attack. 'I'm perfectly capable of maintaining a line between professional and personal, and I've not crossed it.' Or had she? Wasn't kissing her client crossing the line? Ruthlessly she shoved the thought aside. 'Now if you'll excuse me, I have to go and tell Zac that I believe someone out there is still trying to kill him, but we'll no longer be providing protection.'

Mark muttered her name, but she ignored it and marched out towards the car park. Maybe Mark was right and she was overreacting, but she couldn't get the image of the gun firing, and Zac lying on the floor, out of her head. What if it happened again? What if next time, he didn't get out of the way?

Fear ripped through her and she stumbled, clutching at her chest as she tried to draw breath. She felt terrified for Zac, yet also for herself, because she had no other option left but to defy Mark. She'd take annual leave if she needed to, but she wasn't leaving Zac's side until she was convinced he was no longer in danger.

Zac waited in the doorway as Kat pushed all the buttons on the security panel. He was relieved to finally be back home – he caught himself – back at Kat's home. Returning to the studio this morning had been harder than he'd imagined. The moment they'd entered the car park, he'd had a nasty flashback and, like a lunatic, had frantically cast his gaze around the rows of cars, only calming when he'd caught the look of sympathy in Kat's eyes. Thankfully she hadn't called him out on it.

'Are you going to tell me the outcome of your chat with the merry men this afternoon?' he asked as he watched her tug off her boots and dump them haphazardly in the hallway.

'In a minute. Just let me sort out what we're having for tea and check in on Debs.'

'I thought you said she was having a sleepover at Anna's. Something about it being her friend's birthday?'

'That's what she told me, yes.'

'You don't believe her?'

'I want to, but I also know how fourteen-year-old girls think.'

Perhaps this was why Kat had been so unusually quiet in the car on the way back. 'Is there anything I can do to help?'

She gave him a wan smile. 'I'm going to phone her, but if I hear a loud party going on in the background, or the sound of male voices, I might take you up on that offer.'

'Well, as I didn't get a chance to shower at the studio, I'll take one now. I spent so much of the day being thrown in the lake, I fear I've got trench foot. Let me know if you need my muscle.'

He expected a comment along the lines of her being able to handle a bunch of teenagers, but instead he received a distracted nod of her head.

Fifteen minutes later he bumped into her on the landing as he was doing up his shirt.

Had he deliberately decided to walk out of his room before getting fully dressed? Quite possibly. His days with her were numbered – might actually be over already – and he was prepared to use all the ammunition he had to convince her what they had was worth exploring.

'How's Debs?'

'All good. I heard Anna's mum in the background.'

When her eyes didn't stray above his neck, he felt a dart of satisfaction. 'Should I do my shirt up?' he inquired mildly. 'You seem a little distracted.'

'Oh no, it's fine.' She took a step back, her gaze bouncing guiltily away. 'I told you before, I'm immune to all that now.'

'You are?' Her expression told him something else. 'What if I do this?' He reached for her hand and placed it on his naked chest, experiencing a scorching wave of heat where her fingers touched his skin.

'Still immune.' But her breath came out in short, choppy breaths, and her cheeks were flushed.

Slowly he moved her hand to cover his heart. 'Feel my heartbeat?' It was racing, thumping madly against his ribcage. 'That's how immune I am to you.'

He heard her sharp intake of breath and watched as she swallowed convulsively before finally raising her eyes to his. And snatching her hand away. 'We need to talk.'

Frustrated, he began to do up his shirt in stiff, jerky movements. 'Fine.'

'Please, don't be like that.' When she met his gaze, he was shocked to see the plea in her dark eyes. 'You know what you do to me, but that isn't important right now.' She drew her shoulders back. 'I need to tell you about the meeting with Mark and Jerry.'

Well, that successfully put a pin in his seduction hopes, and in his ardour. He wasn't sure which he dreaded more; being told the two men thought he was still at risk, meaning he'd keep Kat as a bodyguard.

Or being told he was no longer in danger and could go home.

Chapter 22

Kat was glad when Zac buttoned up his shirt. It was hard enough to tell him Vision Films no longer wanted to protect him, but she did. To do that when it was so blatantly obvious she couldn't take her eyes off him? That would raise more questions than she was ready to answer.

She waited until he'd sat down on the armchair, one leg neatly crossed over the other, hands resting loosely in his lap.

'Jerry believes you are no longer in danger, so he's terminated the contract with UK Security. Well, technically he's suspended it, pending any further information that might come to light, but it amounts to the same thing, I guess.'

His jaw tightened a fraction, but other than that, his expression remained frustratingly enigmatic. 'I'm free to go home then?'

'Yes.' Holy cow, where had these nerves come from? Her belly was alive with them, wriggling around her insides. 'But I don't think you should.'

His eyes snapped to hers. 'Why?'

'Because I don't believe the woman who's been stalking you is the same person who tried to shoot you.' She paused, taking care over her next words. 'I've asked you before, and now I'm asking again. Can you think of anyone who might want you dead?'

Her heart sank as he fidgeted on the sofa, his eyes avoiding hers. 'You think I'm that obnoxious?'

'I guess even at your most irritating, I wouldn't call you that. Annoying though? That I could go with.'

He arched a brow. 'Am I supposed to be grateful for that assessment?'

'Grateful, no, but you are supposed to think very carefully about my question. You see, there are things I know you keep private, things you refuse to tell me, that might be relevant.'

'As has already been pointed out, there are things I don't know about you, too.' Her gave her his trademark crooked smile. 'Ms Parker, is this your way of saying you're worried about me?'

Don't fall into his trap. 'I wouldn't be much of a bodyguard if I wasn't. Having spent the last month trying to protect you, I don't want all that hard work going to waste in one unplanned, careless moment.'

He shifted, sitting a little straighter. 'I'm torn between fear that you really think I'm in danger, and delight that you like me enough to worry about me.' He met her gaze. 'But if it takes me being a target to keep you close, then I'll happily accept it.'

'Jesus, Zac.' She leapt to her feet, the image tearing her up. 'Don't say things like that.'

'Don't say that I want to keep you close?'

His soft words caused a further squirming sensation in her stomach. 'I meant the target bit.'

He nodded, glancing down at his hands before looking back up at her. 'So it's okay to admit that, aside from the danger part, I'm very, very happy to hear you say you don't want me to leave?'

It had all been leading up to this moment, she realised. A month of attraction, of sexual tension, of near kisses, and two actual, humdingers of a kiss. She couldn't continue to put her head in the sand, to hide away from it. 'Yes, it's okay to admit that,' she whispered, half afraid, half thrilled by where this might take them.

Slowly he unfurled his long body from the sofa and stepped towards her, his eyes never leaving hers. 'Is it also okay to admit that I want you, Kat Parker?' His hand came up to clasp her face. 'And that once won't be nearly enough. In fact, I'm very afraid I'll find you utterly addictive.'

The warmth from his hand, combined with the intense heat from his gaze, made it hard to think. 'It's sounds like you're saying I'm a bad habit.'

His answering laugh was low and seductive. 'Nothing about you could be bad.' With a quiet intensity that made her skin prick, his eyes roamed her face before landing on her mouth. Then he bent and kissed her, very gently, on the lips. 'You realise you're not technically my bodyguard anymore, don't you?'

The husk in his voice made her knees buckle. 'Yes.'

'So the only thing stopping us now, is you.'

Her pulse rocketed, and as her legs began to shake she wondered if she was really ready for this. Really ready to make herself vulnerable again. Because no matter how much she might kid herself this would just be sex, sleeping with this man could never be 'just' anything.

'Kat?' His lips teased hers again, their touch like a drug,

melting her from the inside, blurring her thoughts. 'Are you going to stop this?'

She should, it had disaster written all over it. Kat Parker and the hot film star from the privileged background. It didn't make any sort of sense. Yet how could she possibly care about that, when her hormones were dancing and all these delicious feelings were coursing through her. 'No.' It was barely a whisper, so she cleared her throat and repeated it more firmly. 'No, I'm not going to stop it.'

His face broke into a smile as desire flared in his eyes. Then he pressed his lips to hers again.

This time there was no teasing. This time, when his mouth claimed hers, she felt his hunger, his need, which only served to heighten her own.

'Let's go upstairs,' he breathed, running his hands down her arms before capturing her hands in his. 'I want you on a bed, so I can take my time and enjoy you.'

As he led her up the stairs her heart began racing like the clappers, excitement mixing with nerves. Yet when he opened the door to her bedroom and turned to give her the small, sexy smile he was famous for, the nerves suddenly started to take over. Oh God, she was about to go to bed with Zac Edwards, heart-throb film star. What was he expecting when she took off her clothes? She didn't have the sort of loose-limbed, elegant body he must be used to. She was strong, not soft. Athletic, not graceful. And even if that went okay, if he *liked* athletic, it had been . . . holy shit, a scary long time since she'd had sex.

* * *

Zac took one look at the way Kat was chewing at her bottom lip, and his heart sunk like a lead weight. She was going to tell him to stop.

'Talk to me, Kat. What's going on in that head of yours?'

Her eyes flicked away from his and onto her bed. Her cluttered, unmade bed. 'Crap, look at the mess.' Immediately she began to pick up the clothes and straighten out the duvet. 'You should have warned me you were going to seduce me tonight. I'd have made sure to tidy up first.'

'Kat,' he said heavily, tugging at her hand until she dumped what she was carrying onto a small chair. 'I rather hoped we were going to be taking clothes off. Not tidying them up.'

'Of course.' Her eyes were too bright, her smile too wide. 'Taking clothes off, that's a good plan. Why don't you start?'

He couldn't fathom what was happening. If she were another woman, he might have said she was nervous, but Kat, confident enough to face down a would-be assailant, wasn't the nervous type.

'Hang on a second.' She jumped onto the bed, wriggling up until she was sitting with her back against the headboard. 'Okay, now you can start.'

'You want me to give you a private striptease show?'

She nodded, eyes not meeting his. 'Do you need music? I can go and get my phone.'

She started to move but he stepped up to the bed, blocking her way, afraid if she left, she'd never come back. 'I don't need music.'

'Okay, good.' She drummed her fingers against her thigh. 'I could hum, if you like? Or whistle. I'm pretty good at whistling.'

She *was* nervous, he realised with a shock. 'I think I can manage without the musical accompaniment.'

'Right.' She folded her arms and rested them on her raised knees. 'Whenever you're ready.'

Smiling, he slowly shook his head and went to sit on the bed in front of her. 'What happened to the woman I kissed downstairs?' He searched her eyes. 'Has she changed her mind? Because it's okay if she has.'

'No.' Her voice was reassuringly firm. 'Definitely not. I mean, Debs is away, I'm not your bodyguard anymore. You're . . . you know, you. No way am I changing my mind.' She waved a hand towards him. 'You should take your shirt off.'

He worked hard to keep his shape, and one of the benefits of that was he was comfortable in his skin, so he quickly undid the buttons and shrugged off the shirt. His reward was in the way her tongue crept out to lick her lips; a gesture he thought was totally unconscious.

'Can I touch?' Her eyes bounced up to his.

In reply he clasped her hand and placed it on his chest, as he'd done earlier. He knew she could feel the way his heart began to thump harder, reacting to her touch.

'My turn.' He nodded to her T-shirt. 'That needs to come off.'

She bit down on her lip again. 'Now?'

He laughed softly. 'Yes, now. I want to see you, Kat. I want to touch you.'

'Okay.' But she didn't move, just kept her hand on his chest, her fingers moving across his skin, leaving a tingle of excitement wherever they touched.

'Kat?'

'What if you're disappointed?' The words came out in a rush. 'I know I shouldn't think like that. I mean I work out, so I'm in good shape, it's just . . . it's just it's a different sort of shape to what you're probably used to.'

'Look at me, Kat. Look into my eyes. What are they saying?'

Her gaze flicked up to his but then settled back again to where her fingers touched his chest. 'I don't know, I'm too chicken to look into them right now.

'Then feel my heartbeat.' He pressed her hand further against his skin. 'What's that telling you?'

'It's jumping, like it would if you were scared. Or maybe nervous.'

'Or?' he prompted, moving her other hand further down so it was touching his abs. Instantly his heart rate kicked up a gear.

'Or you like me touching you,' she whispered, finally raising her eyes to his.

He smiled straight into those twin dark pools. 'I more than like you touching me, Kat. I *need* you to touch me. And I need to touch you, too. Please?'

Finally, she seemed to relax a little. 'Please, I like that.'

'I'll beg if it helps.'

She rolled her eyes. 'No begging needed.'

In a flash she removed her top, leaving him starting at a pair of perfectly sized breasts in a plain black bra. He slipped a finger beneath one of the cups and tugged gently. 'Can I?'

'Knock yourself out. I mean, not literally, but you know, go for it.'

He'd had romantic preludes to sex, frantic ones, but never anything like this. Never anything that had felt so real. A twist of his wrist and the bra fell onto the duvet. 'Christ, Kat.' His gaze swept appreciatively across her naked breasts and up to her eyes, which looked achingly vulnerable. 'You're stunning. I hope you know that?' His fingers brushed across the curve of her breasts, and then to her rose-pink nipples, and he drew in a sharp breath as a pulse of desire shot through him.

She touched him again. 'I can feel your muscles quivering.'

'They're enjoying your touch. I'm enjoying your touch.'

She smiled, a hint of mischief to it now. 'Time to see if the rest of you passes muster. Trousers off.'

'And she's back.' When she frowned at him, he smirked. 'The bossy Kat Parker I know left for a while, but now, thank God, she's back.'

'You like me bossy?'

Hurriedly he yanked off his trousers before pulling her down so she was lying on her back. Then he bent to kiss her. 'Bossy, argumentative, untidy . . . it doesn't seem to matter. I more than like you.' He kissed her again, deeper, for longer. 'I'm falling for you.'

He felt her stiffen, but he ignored it and kept kissing her until her body grew pliant again.

Chapter 23

Kat was lost in the happy bubble that was Zac and his incredible mouth. She couldn't ever recall kissing being so erotic, so mind blowing. Add to that the touch of his hands on her breasts, the feel of his hard, muscular length all the way along her body. The luxurious smell of his cologne.

'These need to come off.'

She felt his hand dip into the waistband of her leggings and bugger it, that small distraction, that loss of his mouth on hers, was all it took for the nerves to jangle again.

'It's been years,' she blurted, holding onto his wrist, stopping him from peeling her leggings any further. 'Lots of years. Too many years. I might have seized up down there.' She made the mistake of looking into his eyes, and oh my God there was so much going on in those brilliant green orbs. Desire, concern, affection. Hints of something deeper. *I'm falling for you.* His husky whisper from earlier floated through her mind and she slammed her eyes closed. It was all too much. 'I've probably forgotten what to do.' She was going to start babbling, she could feel it. 'Is there an instruction manual I should look at, you know, just to remind me again? I don't want this to be a rubbish experience. I mean obviously you won't be rubbish, it's just—'

'Kat.' Her eyes fluttered open, and immediately she felt herself drowning in swirls of green and burnt orange. His lips found hers again and it was as if that was all the connection she needed to turn her brain off.

This time he kept his mouth on hers as he drew the rest of her clothes off. By the time he finally slipped on a condom and eased his way inside her, she was too far gone to worry.

He let out a deep, guttural groan as he began to slowly pump his hips. 'You feel incredible.' The smile he gave her was both wicked and sensual. 'And I can confirm nothing has seized up. Everything,' he thrust again, making her shudder, 'everything is in perfect working order.' Another thrust, followed by a groan of pure male satisfaction. 'Absolutely perfect.'

Gradually his hips began to increase their pace, and desire, hot and frantic, began to claw at her, building until she wasn't sure who was groaning now, him or her. 'I . . .' His scorching mouth captured her words, her breath. 'Oh God, I . . .' Another wave hit her, and she dug her fingers into his hips, feeling herself coming undone.

And then she fell over the cliff, dimly aware of him following her.

'Hey there.' Kat blinked, and when she turned onto her side, she found herself staring into a pair of amused green eyes. 'Looks like I've finally found a way to shut you up.'

It was hard to focus on talking when her limbs felt like

overcooked tagliatelle, and the man she was staring at, with his mussed hair and crooked smile, was so flaming sexy. 'You think?'

'Of course, I can't be absolutely certain, until I give it another go.'

She experienced a bump of delight at the thought of doing it again. 'The instruction manual wasn't needed then.'

His fingers reached across to caress her face and she almost purred. 'Why has it been so long?' he asked softly.

'Ah.' Time to regret the earlier meltdown. Now she'd left herself wide open to a series of questions she really didn't want to answer. 'If I tell you that, will you tell me whatever it is you're keeping from me, because I know there's something.'

Slowly his hand dropped to his side. 'What do you mean?'

'I was there at your parents' house, Zac. I met your brother and sister. I know you have secrets, and that's fine, of course you do. It's not like we're in a relationship, I don't need to know your personal stuff.' She looked him straight in the eye. 'But that goes both ways.'

He let out a deep sigh and flopped onto his back. 'I'm not asking about your family life, Kat. I'm asking about your romantic history. You know mine.'

'The job makes it hard to have any sort of private life.'

Still on his back, he angled his head towards her, his expression clearly telling her the answer was a cop out. Well, tough. The more she shared, the more vulnerable she became, and she wasn't risking that for a man still clutching hard to his own secrets.

'According to Hollywood, bodyguards are always jumping into bed with their clients.'

'According to Hollywood, the world is protected by men either dressed as a spider, wearing an iron suit or wielding a big hammer.' She could see he was annoyed, and she didn't want him to be. This man had just magically, and patiently, made love to her. 'I've already told you, I've never kissed a client. Until you.'

He shifted so he was facing her once more. 'What about an ex-client?'

'Jeez, Zac, same answer. Only you.'

She marvelled that he was so bothered by the thought of her with other men. Was he really starting to fall for her, like he'd said? If so, this was more dangerous than she'd thought. She didn't want to lead him on, to give him any reason to think there was more between them than simmering sexual chemistry and mutual like and respect. There couldn't be anything more, because she couldn't go through all that again.

You hated seeing him kiss on set.

You kissed him even when he was your client.

A shudder ran through her. God, was she falling for him, too?

Zac watched Kat's lithe, toned body tremble. 'Hey, what's wrong?' Concerned, he wrapped his arms around her, changing their positions so she lay against his side, her head on his chest, her soft hair brushing against his chin.

'I just felt a chill.'

She was evading, just as he'd done when she'd asked, yet again, if he knew of anyone who wanted to kill him. He didn't though, not really. He had a fear, yes, but no evidence to back it up. Nothing to suggest it wasn't simply wild paranoia.

She was right about him hiding things from her though, and by not opening up, he wasn't helping convince her that what they had was more than sex. More than the fling he knew was all she planned. For the first time in his life, Zac wanted that *more*. He needed time with her before he could dump his life history on her though. Time for her to see him for who he was, without the gloss of fame. Or the tarnish of the past.

Drawing in a breath, he kissed the top of her head, catching a faint smell of her coconut shampoo. 'I can recommend something to warm you up.'

He felt her smile against his skin. 'I thought you might, but am I going to like it? Because right now I'm thinking food, preferably something with a bit of heat, like a curry.' Her stomach gave a little rumble, making her laugh. 'Oh God, that is so not sexy. I'm lying in bed with a naked Zac Edwards and my stomach is making "feed me" noises.'

'I was thinking more along the lines of you taking a hot shower. With me. But we can go with the curry if you prefer.' If she chose the latter, he wasn't sure his ego would ever recover.

She propped herself up on her elbow. 'So let me get this straight. You're asking me to choose between taking a shower with you, or a chicken jalfrezi.'

'It doesn't have to be a jalfrezi. We could opt for something milder. Like a korma.'

She screwed up her face. 'A korma isn't a curry. It's got no spice, no flavour. It's bland, boring, tasteless goo.'

'You'll find I'm less bothered about the attack on my favourite curry, than I am about the fact we're discussing curry at all.'

'Ah.'

'Yes, ah.' He tried to remove all trace of neediness from his voice. 'Have you *dismissed* the shower idea?'

'I wouldn't say I've dismissed it.' She sat up, dragging the duvet with her so he was deprived of the sight of her naked breasts.

'So taking a shower with me isn't unacceptable. It's just not as desirable as a chicken vindaloo.' Perhaps that would be his new tagline, he thought gloomily. *The film star not quite as desirable as a chicken vindaloo.*

'Chicken jalfrezi,' she corrected. 'The vindaloo takes my head off.' He was about to remark he wasn't sure whether that made the comment better or worse, when she burst out laughing. Proper, belly laughing. 'Oh my God, look at your face. You don't seriously think I'd rather eat a curry than have a shower with Zac Edwards and all his rippling muscles, do you?'

He'd rather hoped she wanted the shower with him, not the celebrity version of him, but considering a moment ago he'd believed he'd been beaten by a curry, perhaps he should count his blessings. Besides, this awful insecurity he'd just developed was of his own making. He'd been the one to spill his feelings, to tell her he was falling for her. Now, guess what, he'd left himself vulnerable to second guessing her every action, her every word, for a hint that she felt more for him than simply a passing attraction.

In cricketing parlance, he was an opening bat on a dodgy wicket who should have ducked the bouncer, but instead he'd decided to hit it for six. Now he was crossing his fingers he wouldn't find his stumps flattened, and the umpire raising his finger.

'After we shower, I'm taking you out,' he decided as he took her hand and led her to the en suite. If she wanted that celebrity version, he'd pull out all the damn stops and give it to her. 'And no,' he added when he saw her hesitate. 'You can't stop this. I'm officially no longer in danger, and you're officially no longer my bodyguard. Tonight, I'm in charge. I get to decide where we go, and I get to drive.'

She'd baulked when he'd suggested she might want to wear a dress, chuntering on about how uncomfortable they were, though she'd slipped her black number on anyway. And taken his breath away.

She'd complained when he'd snatched the Jeep keys off her, though she'd let him open the passenger door for her and only winced once on the drive into London.

When he'd pulled up outside The Ivy and given the keys to the valet though, she'd not said a word. Nor had she spoken when he'd taken her hand as they were escorted to the dining room, with its signature harlequin stained-glass windows, and to a discrete private booth.

And as they sat reading the menus, her head remained down, her eyes not meeting his.

'You're very quiet.'

She glanced up and gave him a weak smile. 'I'm trying to work out what on earth a Casterbridge steak is and how it differs from one from Tesco.'

'Casterbridge steak is from the West Country. The cattle

are grain fed. It's very tasty.' Slowly he put down his menu, all the joy from the day ebbing away. 'But that's not what's really on your mind, is it?'

'No.' Her neck, elegant, though she'd not thank him to point it out, moved as she swallowed.

The waiter came over and Zac did as he hated to do and ordered for Kat. 'Before you throw something at me,' he told her when the man had gone, 'I did that not because I don't think you're capable of making a decision on what to eat, but to get rid of him. So we could talk.'

'I'm sorry.' She sucked in a breath, her hand playing with the stem of her wine glass. 'Places like this make me uncomfortable.'

'By places like this, do you mean restaurants?'

'I mean pretentious places.'

'I see.' Stung, he reached for the glass of water. 'You don't like my choice of venue.'

She huffed, her eyes skimming around the room. 'I don't mean it like that. It's lovely. It's just . . .' Her eyes settled on his. 'It's not me. Putting on a dress, sitting here with more wine glasses than I can count, and more sets of cutlery than I own. I feel like a fraud. I don't belong here.'

'Yet you look like you do.' This time he glanced around the room. 'You're more gorgeous, more real, than anyone else here. You're the only woman I see.' It frustrated him to think she couldn't see what he did. And it hurt that she thought he was putting on a show. 'I came here because I wanted to take you somewhere as special as you are.'

'Oh God, Zac.' Her hand flew to her chest and he wasn't sure of the emotion that clouded her face. Was she horrified? Touched?

He shrugged, trying not to show how wrecked he felt. 'It's true.'

Her hand reached across the table to cover his. 'Then I thank you, truly, for the beautiful gesture.' She smiled into his eyes. 'For future reference though, I don't need any of this. I'm happy sat at home with an Indian takeaway. And you.'

The warmth from her smile lit him up inside and just like that, all was well with the world again.

But then his phone, the one he'd unthinkingly placed on the table, began to vibrate as a text came through. And when he gave the screen a cursory glance, that same world shattered into a million jagged pieces.

Chapter 24

Kat saw the blood drain from Zac's face, and automatically her eyes sought out the message which seemed to shine like a beacon on the table in front of them. Well, that was her excuse for reading it.

Sorry darling. He's out. Please call me when you get a moment. Xx

'Can I take it from your reaction that Helena isn't talking about your childhood tortoise escaping?'

He gave her a dazed look. 'I didn't have a tortoise.'

'I kind of guessed that.' Bollocks to it. Swanky surroundings be damned. She wasn't going to sit here and politely wheedle this out of him. 'Look, if you don't want to tell me what's going on, fine. Just because you slept with me, doesn't mean you owe me any insight into your deep dark secrets. But if this has anything to do with your safety, if it could explain why someone tried to shoot you.' Fear that he might really be in danger began to gnaw at her insides. 'If that's the case then you flaming well owe me an explanation. I can't protect you if you shove a blindfold on me.'

He hunched forward, burying his face in his hands for a moment, his shoulders moving as he dragged in a few breaths. Then he rose to his feet, his eyes turbulent and troubled. 'I'm sorry. I can't do this right now.' Jamming the phone into his jacket pocket, he reached out a hand to help her to her feet. 'Looks like you'll get your wish for a takeaway, after all. I need to get back so I can phone Helena.' He threaded a distracted hand through his hair. 'Then I'll answer any questions you have.'

After settling the bill, he walked stiffly beside her towards the valet, all the grace, the elegance gone from his bearing. Instead he looked not just shocked, but defeated, which sent another pulse of alarm shooting through her.

As they waited for the Jeep to arrive, he turned towards her. 'For the record, I didn't just sleep with you, Kat. I fell for you.'

Kat pressed a hand to the pain in her chest. Her heart was really taking a hammering tonight. And if his words weren't enough to leave her feeling battered, drowning in emotion, there was also the message in the text. Who the hell was *He* and where had he just come out from?

The return journey was silent, except for the sound of Classic FM coming out of the radio. Zac's choice. Music was obviously another thing they didn't have in common.

As soon as she opened the front door, Zac shot up the stairs. Too pumped up to sit and do nothing, Kat marched into the study and called the one person she could always rely on to understand her. The big sister who, despite her own struggles, was always there for her, even if *there* was currently a rehab clinic.

'You went and *slept* with him?'

Kat raised her eyes to the ceiling. Typical of Mandy that that was the piece of information she'd taken away from the ten-minute update she'd just given her. 'Yes. And if you're going to tell me I'm stupid, don't bother, I know. But you try spending 24/7 with a guy who looks like sex on legs and resist him.'

'So it's just sex.'

She wanted to answer yes, because this moment, this brief flash of brilliance, was never going to last. Yet if she couldn't be honest with Zac, she should at least be honest with herself, and her sister. 'Truthfully, I think I've totally bollocksed this up and developed feelings for him. Maybe he has some for me, too, though equally maybe I've become a habit. He has been stuck with me pretty much all the time.'

Down the phone line, Mandy let out a snort of laughter. 'You're really trying to tell me the guy who's just taken you to The Ivy, of all places, even though you didn't appreciate it . . . the same man who doesn't even like Formula One, but took you to Silverstone . . . who got you a picnic hamper from Fortnum and flaming Mason . . . you're saying he's doing all that because he's got used to having you around? You know how totally dumb that sounds, don't you?'

Kat sighed, leaning back against the chair and closing her eyes. 'He's a film star, Mandy. He does this sort of stuff all the time. It doesn't necessarily mean anything.' Yet even as she said it, the words sounded hollow. *I wanted to take you somewhere as special as you are.*

Was she putting her head in the sand about his feelings for her because she was too afraid to acknowledge they were real? She didn't want another relationship. She didn't want to fall in love again, only to have it leaving her emotionally eviscerated.

Yet did she really have a choice? The ache in her heart said otherwise.

'I know you're scared, Kitty Kat.' Mandy's voice was in her ear again. 'You have every right to be. But, aside from being a mega-gorgeous rich film star, Zac sounds like a pretty okay guy. Debs raves about him.'

He's more than okay. He's kind and funny and, beneath his sexy surface, achingly, touchingly, vulnerable. Words that didn't help her tortured emotions one little jot. 'This is the same Debs who wants to spend time with a guy who's three years older than she is and treats her like shit,' she said instead. 'I hardly think she's a good judge.'

'She promised me she isn't hanging round with him anymore.' Mandy paused. 'In fact, she told me you'd had a word with her and it had made her think, so we have you to thank for that.' Kat felt a lump rise to her throat. Had her niece really listened? 'She also said there was a cute actor on set when her class went to watch Zac filming, and if you can bag a film star, maybe she can, too.'

Kat lurched upright. 'For God's sake, I haven't bagged anyone. Besides, Debs doesn't know what's going on with Zac and me. Nothing happened while she was here.'

Mandy's laughter exploded down the phone. 'Sex might not have happened, but Debs kept telling me she was sure Zac fancied you. Why do you think she's having a sleepover? She said, and I quote, "I'm gonna stay over at Anna's so Kat can do the whole Netflix and chill thing with Zac." In case you don't do teen speak, that means—'

'I know what it means,' Kat cut in, feeling hot and cold all over. 'Look, I've got to go. You take care. Remember, you're nearly halfway through and the worst is behind you.'

Kat said her goodbyes, a sting hitting the back of her eyes. She missed her sister, though it was a relief to hear Mandy sounding stronger every week. Hard to believe she'd been away a month.

It meant she'd known Zac for that long, too.

Long enough for her defences to crumble. Long enough for her heart to ignore her brain and become entangled with a dangerously attractive man who kept secrets.

Zac walked slowly back down the stairs, a mixture of dread and fear settling like boulders on his shoulders.

The fear was not only for his life, but that he'd drag Kat into his mess, too.

The dread was because he'd lost his opportunity with her now. Not only would she see him differently, she'd turn back into his bodyguard. Not his lover.

Was he adding two and two and making five? After the phone call with Helena, he could no longer stick to his assertion from earlier that he didn't know anyone who'd want him dead. He did know someone, had known him all his life.

And apparently over the weekend, that person had been released from the safety of his prison cell.

Lost in his awful thoughts, he almost collided with Kat as he reached the bottom stair. He wasn't so deeply buried in his own quagmire that he didn't notice the sadness in her expression. 'Is everything okay?'

'I think I'm supposed to ask you that, but yes, thanks, it's all good. I've been on the phone to Mandy. She's fine,' Kat added, correctly interpreting his silent question. 'It just makes me realise how much I miss her. We're not just sisters, we're best buddies.'

'Does she know I'm inhabiting her bedroom?'

'Of course. She's wondering if you'll still be there when she comes back.' Immediately she put a hand to her face. 'And crap, that second part was supposed to be a joke. Obviously, you won't be here in another month, and equally obviously it's not good taste for me to be talking about you sleeping with my sister when you and I have just, you know, had sex.'

His heart fell. 'That's all it was, sex?'

She breathed in deeply, as if struggling with how to answer him. When she finally whispered '*No*,' hope wormed through him, though it was halted by her next question. 'Are you ready to tell me what's going on?'

'Ready, no.' It was his turn to take in the deep breath. 'Willing, yes.'

'Okay, go and sit down. I'll be there in a minute.'

Confused – she was the one who'd wanted to talk, wasn't she? – he went to sit back on the sofa where a few hours ago he'd been optimistically planning a relationship with her. One where he took her to restaurants, held doors open for her. Looked after her.

None of which she seemed to want from him.

He did manage to drag out a smile when he saw what she was carrying.

'It's single malt.' She settled the whisky bottle on the table, along with two glasses. 'Courtesy of an ex-client. He told me it was the best whisky money could buy.'

'Macallan,' he said appreciatively, eyeing the label. 'He could be right. You've not drunk much of it.'

'I save it for occasions when it's warranted.' She poured them both a healthy measure before sitting down next to him. 'And this feels like one of them.'

They clinked glasses and he took a large sip, welcoming the burn as it travelled down his throat. As he wasn't one for long-drawn-out explanations, Zac put down the glass, drew in a breath, and started to speak. 'The *he* in the text refers to my father, my real father. He's just been released from prison.'

He tried to read the expressions flitting across her face, but there were so many he couldn't keep a handle on them.

'Okay, I was bracing myself for something bad, and that certainly slots right in.' She drank a mouthful of whisky, and then started to cough. 'Shit, that stuff is lethal. I'm sure it's stripping the skin off my throat. Right then.' She coughed again. 'You'd better start from the beginning. Unless you only want to tell me the bits that are relevant to why your dad might want you dead? Because I'm guessing that's the reason you've decided to talk to me.'

Had she not heard what he'd been saying to her, or was she deliberately ignoring it because she didn't want to hear? 'I'm not telling you this as your damn client. I'm telling you it because I don't want any more secrets between us. You're important to me, Kat. I want today to be the start of you and me, not the end.' He drew a hand across his face, trying to quell the churning in his gut. 'My dad is Jimmy McCarthy. He was put away for murder when I was ten.' Knowing he couldn't get through this if he looked at her, he kept his focus on the glass in his hand. 'Mum admitted later he'd been dealing drugs for many years, and by the time he was locked away he headed up a pretty large crime ring.' He gave her a weak smile. 'So you see, I'm not posh. Far from it. I'm the son of scum.' He took a swig of the whisky, hoping it would settle his stomach. Discussing his murdering father was excruciating enough. He didn't want to add throwing up over her sofa.

'You're not your father, Zac.' Kat's expression wasn't just full of sympathy, it was full of understanding. 'If you were, it would mean I'm a bullying alcoholic, and I flatly refuse to be anything like mine.'

Her eyes met his and he felt the weight of her unasked questions. 'You're not usually so reticent. Go on, ask away.'

'What happened to your mum? How did you end up with William and Helena? Why do you think this man, who's not fit to be called your father, might want to kill you? Because I'm guessing you do, considering the timing of his release.' She gave him an unapologetic smile. 'You did say to ask.'

He had, and weirdly, now he'd got the worst part over, he wanted to talk. To get everything out there so she could see who he really was.

If she liked him anyway, maybe they did have a future.

And if she only wanted to protect him? Well, at least he'd have a future.

'My mum . . . who was incredible, by the way. She thought her husband went out to work at a garage. She didn't have any idea it was only a front. Anyway, she worked as a housekeeper for William and Helena. Had done since before I was born. When my father was put away, they urged her to come and live in a cottage on the estate.' A lump settled in his throat. 'We had a good two years together. Mum was happier than I'd ever seen her and the eggshells we'd always been treading on had been locked away along with my father. But then Mum got sick.'

'Oh shit, Zac.' Kat's hand reached out to touch his arm, the gesture both instinctive and comforting. 'I don't think I'm going to like the next part.'

'No.' He took a swallow of the Macallan, mentally thanking her foresight. 'She died of oesophageal cancer six months later.'

Her arms wrapped around him and she squeezed tightly. 'Bloody hell, Edwards, if you make me cry, I swear, I'll never talk to you again.'

Her eyes glistened and he felt both honoured and unbearably moved by her compassion. 'Then please don't, not on my behalf. I've led a pretty charmed life ever since. Helena and William were kind enough to take me in and became my legal guardians. They even arranged to have my name changed so it looked like I was part of the family.'

'Looked like.' Kat glanced up at his inadvertent slip and gave him a shrewd look. 'I'm guessing it didn't always *feel* that way?'

'No.' He'd tried to make himself belong. From the age of thirteen he'd started to change the way he spoke, how he dressed. He'd learnt to hold his tongue, to open doors for ladies, to keep his room meticulously tidy.

Her expression softened. 'You know what, I think I understand some of your weird quirks now.'

'Excuse me?'

Her elbow found his side in a gentle dig. 'Come on, you know what I mean. All that obsessive neatness, the smart clothes. The careful way you speak. It was all to help you fit in, wasn't it?'

'Perhaps.' It had been more to ensure they'd have no reason to chuck him out, but he preferred her version. 'I take exception to *obsessive*, though. And *weird*.'

She grinned back at him. 'Noted. I bet Antony and Isabelle didn't help. I thought they were obnoxious as adults. I can't imagine how shitty they were as kids.'

He smiled, appreciating both her phrase and the fierce look in her eyes. 'Pretty shitty.'

'God, I wish I'd been around then. I'd have sorted them out.'

Placing the glass back on the table, he pinched the bridge of his nose. 'I don't need you to fight my battles, Kat.'

'I know.'

'Do you?' It was one thing being his bodyguard – at least that was her job, what she was trained for – but now he felt his masculinity draining away.

She blew out a breath. 'I fight for the people I care about, you idiot. It's the way I'm made. It doesn't mean I think they aren't strong or capable. Just that I want to *help*.'

'People you care about,' he repeated, trying to quell the hope sneaking back into his heart. 'Does that, by any chance, include me?'

She gave him a playful shove. 'Do you think I'd have invited you into my bed if it didn't?'

He shifted to face her, planting a soft kiss on her lips. 'Does the invitation still stand?'

'I suppose it could, if I was properly persuaded.'

He smiled, angling his head so he could kiss her properly. When he drew back, he was pleased to note he wasn't the only one breathing heavily. 'Invite me to your bed,' he whispered, trailing kisses across her face. 'Let me sleep with you. Wake up with you.'

'Ummmm.' He eased up on the kisses, drawing back, and her eyes blinked open. Warm, brown and delightfully fuzzy. 'Why did you stop?'

'I wasn't sure what ummmm meant.'

She put a hand behind his head and pulled him towards her. 'It means, get your very fine arse upstairs.'

Chapter 25

When Kat opened her eyes the following morning, for a few seconds she thought she was dreaming.

A lean male body, his skin a rich golden tan against the white of her duvet, lay in bed next to her, the duvet pooled by his stomach. Unable to resist, she ran her fingers gently over the curves and ridges of his chest. She was no longer his bodyguard. As long as she was careful with her heart, she could touch as much as she liked.

When her fingers trailed lower, finding him beneath the sheet, his eyes blinked open.

'Good morning.'

'It is so far.' His voice was raspy and she didn't think it was because he'd just woken up. Leaning up a little, he sought out her eyes. 'Are we still okay? No regrets about last night?'

Her hand squeezed him beneath the sheets. 'You really need to ask?'

He laughed softly, pushing his hips further into her grip. 'You might just be using me for sex.'

'And if I am?'

His eyes burned into hers. 'You can use me as much and as often as you like.'

Laughing, she wriggled over him, her breasts crushed against the wall of muscle that was his chest, her core aligned with the heat of him. 'Then I think I should start now.'

His answer was a deep groan, before he clasped her head and stopped any further talk by giving her a searing, scorching kiss.

It was only later, when they were having breakfast in the kitchen, that Kat remembered the question from the previous evening that he hadn't answered. The one sex had, unbelievably, managed to push to the back of her mind.

'Why do you think your father wants you dead?'

He stilled, mug of coffee halfway to his mouth. 'I see the honeymoon period is over already.'

'Come on. Someone out there wants to kill you. Nothing's going to stop me from worrying about that, not even sex.' Her eyes met his and she smiled. 'Though you did a pretty good job of trying.'

'I did, didn't I?' He returned her smile before letting out a sigh and lowering the mug. 'Honestly, I don't know if my father wants to kill me. I only know he came out of prison at the weekend, and on Monday someone took a shot at me. The police believe the shooter was Lipstick Lady, so we may be worrying about nothing.'

She searched his face. 'You don't believe that any more than I do.'

His shoulders sagged a little. 'I no longer know what to believe. When the notes first started to appear, I dismissed them, but as they became more sinister I started to wonder, what if?' He looked over at her. 'That's when I was pleased, in a way, to get a bodyguard.'

'Even if it was a messy, inexperienced one.'

He smirked. 'Even then.' As fast as his smile had come, it vanished. 'But my father was safely locked away in prison, and all the evidence pointed to the stalker being a female fan, so I kept quiet, figuring I was being paranoid. Now he's out, and the timing for the shooting . . . well, it could work.' He dragged a hand down his face. 'To really answer your question, I saw . . . things as a child that I shouldn't have done. My statement helped put my father away.'

She experienced an alarming wrench on the heart she'd promised to be careful with. 'I want to ask the question, but I'm not sure I can bear to hear the reply.' When he didn't volunteer anything, she placed a hand over his. 'What did you see?'

'What do you think I saw? I told you the type of guy he was. Of course, back then I thought he was a garage mechanic, so when school finished early and Mum wasn't around to pick me up, I walked to the garage.'

A shadow crossed his face and she clutched at his hand, her heart breaking for the boy who'd had his innocence, his childhood, snatched away from him. 'You don't have to tell me. Not if it's too painful.'

'I don't want secrets between us.' He stared down at their hands, then back up at her, his voice now flat and emotionless. 'The door wasn't fully closed so I peeked around it, expecting to find Dad with grease on his overalls and a spanner in his hand. Instead,' he paused to swallow. 'Instead I saw him with a knife in his hand, and blood on his shirt. A body at his feet, the throat cut.'

Kat couldn't stop the gasp that escaped. He'd seen things, horrific things, no ten-year-old should be subject to. And the mother he'd adored had been snatched away from him soon afterwards. So much for the privileged life she'd all but accused him of having.

Suddenly Kat had a fierce desire to visit Helena and William and wrap her arms around them, because it was they who'd rescued him and turned Zac's life around.

'What happened then?' She continued to hold tight to his hand, unwilling, unable to let him go.

'I scarpered. Thankfully nobody had seen me, so I started to walk home.' He gave her hand a gentle squeeze and stood up. 'I must have looked a state because one of the other mums stopped and offered me a lift home.' Picking up his dirty plate, he took it over to the dishwasher. She suspected it was so he wouldn't have to look at her. 'Of course, nobody was in, so she asked me where my mum worked and took me to the Edwards Estate. Helena answered the door, took one look at me, and immediately called for someone to get Mum.' He smiled, though it didn't quite reach his eyes. 'Helena told me later that I'd scared the bejesus out of her. She'd never seen a face look as pale as mine. Apparently while she was waiting for Mum to come she kept looking for signs of a cut because she was sure I'd been bleeding to death.'

'Dear God, Zac, the stuff you've lived through.' Kat couldn't put it into words how gutted she was for him, yet also how proud. 'I can't believe you've turned out so, well, normal.'

He began to laugh. 'You didn't think that when you stuck your nose around my apartment.'

'Oh my God, the teapot collection.' Another fist seemed to wrap around her heart. 'They weren't Helena's, of course they weren't. They were your real mum's.'

'Yes.' His eyes skimmed past hers and to the clock on the wall. 'And now I need to get moving or I'll be late on set.'

He'd had enough of talking about his past. Though Zac had meant what he'd said, and he didn't want any more secrets, he also didn't want to be an object of pity for the woman he was more than halfway in love with.

Kat jumped to her feet. 'No way are you driving yourself to the studio when it's likely someone out there wants you dead.'

Tension caused every muscle in his body to tighten. 'This isn't your call anymore.'

'Like hell it isn't.' She marched over to the hall and began to tug on her boots. 'I'm driving you, no argument.'

Now, he felt a fizz of anger, along with the tension. 'I thank you for the offer but I'm perfectly capable of dialling a taxi and getting myself to work. I'm no longer your responsibility, Kat. Mark's probably got your next client lined up already.' He felt a stab of envy for the lucky sod she'd be assigned to. They'd get to spend far more time with her than he would.

'I'll phone him later and tell him I'm taking annual leave.' Her chin jutted stubbornly towards him. 'You might as well give in gracefully because this is going to happen.'

He recalled her words from yesterday, about her fighting for the people she cared about. Was this desire to protect him a reflection of that, and not of how she saw him? It would be easier to believe if he hadn't spent a good chunk of last night and this morning telling her about the worst part of him. The DNA he carried. The scared little boy who'd wet his pants when he'd seen his dad and the blood. So much blood.

'Fine, I'll come with you this morning.' He'd yet to pick his car up from his place, and he was already running later than he liked.

After bounding up the stairs to grab his wallet, he found her standing by the door, arms crossed, looking distinctly unhappy. 'I'm not having this argument every morning. Please, let me do my job until this is really over.'

Her eyes pleaded with him, yet none of this sat well. 'I'm grateful you want to protect me still, I really am. But I don't want you to see me as a job. Or as this . . . weak person who needs looking after.' He touched her lips with his in a light kiss. 'I want you to see me as a man, Kat.'

Her gaze flew up to the ceiling and she let out a huffing noise. 'You seriously think I see anything else when I look at you? Can I take you back to an hour ago, when we were in bed, and my hand was wrapped around your—'

He silenced her with another kiss, one that got his blood thickening and his heart pumping. 'I'm seconds away from saying forget the ruddy studio and hauling you back upstairs.'

'Surely you wouldn't do that, Mr Edwards.' Her voice sounded breathless even as her eyes danced. 'I know how much you hate being late.'

'Don't tempt me,' he muttered, kissing her again. It was only years of discipline, years of making himself into the model son, that enabled him to finally break away.

Later, in the car, he mulled over her words, beginning to realise the implications – the full implications – of what she'd said. 'The part about you still doing your job.'

She glanced over at him. 'Yes?'

'That means you drive me to work and back every day.'

'Correct.'

'And I still can't open doors, go out by myself. Or sleep in my own bed.'

'Still correct.'

It was testament to how deeply he was falling for her that none of that bothered him now, whereas four weeks ago, it had made him livid.

His next question didn't just bother him though. It filled every nook and cranny of his mind so that nothing else mattered but her answer. 'Does it also mean I can't sleep in your bed?'

He held his breath, every muscle fibre pulled tight. But then the glorious sound of her laughter echoed around the car. 'I think that ship has sailed, don't you?' After indicating to turn into the studio, she gave him a brief sidelong glance. 'If you think I'll be able to resist you now I've slept with you, you must think I'm a lot more stubborn, or a hell of a lot stronger, than I really am.'

It wasn't quite the *Of course we'll be sleeping together every night, try stopping me,* he'd hoped for. But he'd take it over the alternative.

Chapter 26

It had all the hallmarks of a chilled Friday night. The three of them – Debs was back from her sleepover – were sat in the lounge, pizza (one without 'slippery buggers') in front of them, *Avengers: Endgame* showing on the TV.

'Is this really the best that Walt Disney Studios has to offer?'

Debs dragged her eyes away from the screen long enough to pull a face at Zac. 'This is the best film, ever.'

'It is?' He reached for another slice of pizza, and Kat sniggered as she watched him carefully cut off the stringy cheese rather than leave it hanging so it would run down his chin, like a normal person. 'Should I make sure to wear blue tights and a cape in my next film?'

Debs gave him a big eye roll. 'Superman isn't Marvel, he's DC Comics.'

'Of course, he is. My mistake.' He bit neatly into the pizza and then wiped his hands on one of the paper napkins the pizza company always provided, yet surely nobody ever used. His meticulous actions brought another smile to her face, but then she remembered their conversation yesterday. His tidy, careful actions might well be amusing, she'd even say charming, but the reason behind them, the desire of a twelve-year-old boy to fit into his new family, was heartbreaking. How many of his quirks stemmed from that desire not to be an outsider? Punctuality, manners. His overpreparation in going through his lines? And what about his insecurity, so surprising in such a talented, good-looking guy? He hid it well, but now she looked back at the way he'd treated her: Silverstone, The Ivy, the over-the-top picnic hamper. She'd thought it was a demonstration of their differences, but actually, they weren't that different. They both came from troubled families. Flashing his money at her was perhaps simply his way of masking his need to feel accepted. To feel loved.

Unconsciously she rubbed at the ache in her chest.

'Indigestion?' Zac gave her a smug smile. 'That's what you get for eating so fast.'

'I like my food hot.'

Debs started to giggle. 'She likes her men hot, too.'

Zac's gaze shifted to Kat's, his expression one of pained confusion. *Does she mean me?* she could see him asking. *Does she know?*

Kat shrugged her shoulders before looking at her niece questioningly.

'I'm not dumb. I knew there was stuff going on with you two, and then I spoke to Mum.' Debs grinned. 'She told me you're now, you know—'

Bonking, fucking, shagging. Kat realised with horror she had no idea what Debs was going to say.

'Dating,' Zac cut in. 'Your aunt and I are dating.' He glanced down at the pizza, and then at the television screen. 'Though I'll be happier taking her on a date that doesn't involve comic characters or food eaten from a cardboard box.'

Debs frowned. 'But I thought they caught the stalker?'

'They have,' Kat reassured her. God, this was awkward. 'We thought it would be safer for Zac to stay here for a few more days, just in case there's more than one person who might want to . . . harm him.'

Zac cleared his throat and stood up. 'Excuse me a minute.' He glanced towards the TV. 'No need to pause the film. I think I can just about keep up with the plot.'

She watched as he walked towards the stairs in that elegant, fluid gait that was so ridiculously sexy.

'Is he okay?'

'You know what, I'm not sure. You carry on watching the film. I'll go and check.'

Debs smirked. 'Is that like another way of saying you're going to go and—'

'No.' Kat shook her head. 'Watch the film. Eat pizza.'

She found Zac sitting on his bed – crap, she was starting to think of it as his, and not Mandy's – his shoulders hunched forward, eyes staring at the floor.

'Hey.'

He jerked upright and gave her a small smile. 'I thought you were watching the best film, ever.'

Concerned, she went to sit next to him. 'I thought you were, too.'

'Technically, I was watching a Marvel film. The best film ever—'

'Isn't what I'm interested in at the moment.' She reached for his hand and clasped it in hers. 'What's wrong?'

He huffed out a laugh. 'What's wrong? I'm sitting eating pizza on my lap on a Friday night with a woman I'm falling in love with, yet I can't take her out. Worse, she's forced to look after me out of some vague notion that I'm in danger, and though I want to dismiss that, I also know my father's out of prison, and two days after his release, someone tried to shoot me. On top of all that, Debs is only fourteen, and she doesn't know what's happening. On one level that feels right, because I don't want to scare her, but on another level that feels so very wrong, because if I am in danger, isn't me staying here putting her in danger, too? Putting you both in danger?'

'Wow, that's a lot of words for a guy who's usually so measly with them.'

He let out a long, deep sigh, closing his eyes for a moment before looking straight into hers. 'I don't feel in control of anything right now. Not my life, not my feelings.'

A woman I'm falling in love with. She tried to think back to his other points, but her mind wouldn't budge from those words. It wasn't the first time he'd said them, but she'd brushed over them before. No woman believes what a guy says during sex. This time there was no convenient excuse. This time she had to listen, and she had to act, because he couldn't do this, couldn't fall in love with her. God, the thought of hurting this man who'd suffered so much, tore her in two. Yet if she didn't find a way to get him to slow down, she was going to.

With care, and a gentleness she hadn't realised she possessed,

Kat cradled his face in her hands. 'Stop overthinking this. We're eating pizza and watching a movie. It's what most people do on a Friday night.'

His smile was achingly sad. 'It's not that simple.'

'It can be, if you let it.' And she needed it to be that simple, because if she thought too deeply about what he'd said, both the falling in love and the putting them in danger, she'd feel panicked, too.

'Okay.' He drew in a breath, then gave her a weak smile. 'Maybe it will help if you kiss me.'

'You think?' She gave him a platonic peck on the lips. 'How's that?'

'Not quite what I was aiming for.' This time he took over. With one hand behind her head, the other resting gently on her face, he proceeded to kiss her until her heart was pounding, her insides melting, and she was ready to climb into bed with him and beg him to finish the job. 'Now that,' he breathed when he finally let her go. 'That is how you stop me thinking.'

The film had finished, the pizza had been eaten, and Debs had gone off to her room. Zac stretched out his legs and tried to ignore the discarded pizza boxes. He'd already gone to pick them up twice, and both times Kat, who was now lying across him, had told him to leave them.

'You're looking at them again, aren't you?' She prodded his too-full stomach. 'This is like therapy for you. You're not allowed to pick them up until tomorrow morning.'

'Tomorrow?'

His face must have signalled his horror, because she let

out a big, booming laugh. 'Oh my God, Zac, it's not that terrible.' She waggled her eyebrows at him. 'And I bet I can think of a few ways to make you forget they're there.'

As arousal pulsed through him, he felt a buzzing against his thigh. 'Is that you vibrating with excitement, or me?'

'Who would call at ten o'clock on a Friday night?' With an annoyed huff she sat upright and pulled her phone out of her pocket, her face turning from scowl to frown when she read the screen. 'Hi Mark.'

Immediately Zac shifted. He wasn't going to sit here and listen to her talk to the guy, no matter how platonic the relationship was. But when he moved to stand up, she pushed him down again. 'Yes, he's here with me.' A pause and he tried to read the expression on her face. All he could make out was confusion and worry. 'Sure, we'll see you soon.' Ending the call, she looked his way. 'I don't know what's going on. Only that the police called Vision Films to get hold of you, and Jerry called Mark, and he's coming over. With a detective.'

A chill went through him, but he tried to smile through the fear. 'As you said, just your average Friday night.'

Sympathy edged into her eyes. 'Okay, maybe it's taken a turn, but we had a few hours, at least.'

'Indeed.' He could feel the knots in his stomach tightening. 'At least I can tidy up the pizza boxes now.' Though even that had lost its appeal. Who gave a fuck about pizza boxes when the police had such a serious message to deliver, they were coming round on a Friday night?

'Oh no you can't, it will ruin all that therapy. I'll do it.' Kat jumped up and started to pick them up. 'You sit there and . . .'

'Panic quietly?'

He received another sympathetic glance. 'I was going to say sit there and look pretty, but you can do both, if you like.'

The words didn't do much for his ego, implying he had about as much use as a blasted ornament. 'They've come to see me,' he said to her retreating back as she carried the boxes into the kitchen. 'You don't have to stick around.'

'Oh, right. Thanks for the let-off.' She walked back towards him, eyes flashing with annoyance. 'I'll just go upstairs and what, wash my hair?'

'I didn't mean it like that.' Clearly fear and frustration were poor companions. 'Just that I'm not your damn responsibility.'

'No, you're not, though apparently, according to what you told Debs, you are my damn boyfriend.' She seemed to catch herself. 'Well, sort of, in a loose sense. Anyway, I want to be here, okay?'

'Boyfriend, huh?' Why, considering everything that was going on, did he suddenly feel the urge to smile?

She raised her eyes to the ceiling. 'Look, you don't have to stress about the term. You told Debs we were dating, and dating's what girlfriends and boyfriends do, so I guess it just came out.'

'I *like* how it came out.' He rose from the sofa and went to stand next to her, clasping her hands in his. 'I like thinking of you as my girlfriend.' After giving her a soft kiss, he drew his gaze up to her eyes. 'Do you like thinking of me as your boyfriend?'

Her eyes refused to meet his, and his heart began a slow shrivel in his chest. He was racing ahead, telling her he wanted a relationship, admitting he was falling in love with her. She hadn't come out of the starting blocks yet.

The clang of the doorbell crashed through the silence. As she went to answer it, he realised none of it really mattered, because he had a terrible feeling he knew what the police needed to see him so urgently about. And if he was right, there was no way he could stick around Kat any longer. No way on God's earth.

Chapter 27

Kat led Mark and the detective into the living room, but decided to stand. It gave her a feeling of equality, compared to sitting down like the little woman.

You sit there and look pretty. Her words to Zac a few moments ago reared back at her, and shame rolled through her. He had to have known it was a joke, surely? But then she'd gone and refused to answer his comment about being her boyfriend. Hell, she'd not even had the decency to look him in the eye. She was failing this incredible man left, right and centre, and just at a time when he really needed her.

The realisation was agonising. So, she was terrified of a relationship. Big bloody deal. What she was doing to him wasn't only unfair, it was cruel. It was time to be honest with him and admit why she was the world's biggest coward when it came to giving away her heart.

But that talk would have to wait. From the way Mark was giving her a hard, searching look, and the way the police detective was clearing his throat, there were more important things to focus on.

'Please, go ahead.' She smiled at the detective. 'My niece is upstairs but she's in the middle of an online game with her friends so I'm sure she won't disturb us.'

The guy glanced from her, to Zac and back to her, and she realised he was wondering why she was there.

'Whatever you need to say, you can say it in front of Kat.' A wry smile crossed Zac's face. 'She'll only drag it out of me the moment you're gone, so she might as well hear it first-hand.'

Seemingly satisfied, the detective turned to Zac. 'We received some information from our colleagues in Birmingham earlier today which we believe has direct relevance to you. A man by the name of Frank Sterling was found murdered in his house this morning.'

Zac hung his head before placing his hands over his face.

'I'm guessing by your reaction that you know why we're here.'

With what looked to be considerable effort, Zac slowly straightened. 'How . . .' He cleared his throat and tried again. 'How was he murdered?'

'A bullet to his head.'

Zac swallowed. 'Not a slit throat.'

'No. More like a professional hitman.'

The blood drained from Zac's face. 'You think . . . fuck.' He reared back, slumping against the back of the sofa. 'You think my father put a hit on him?'

'We do.'

Dread, cold and sick, pooled in Kat's stomach. 'Who was this guy? Why do you think your dad would want him killed?'

Zac looked to the police detective, presumably giving him permission to talk.

'Frank Sterling was a drug dealer who used to work for Jimmy McCarthy. He gave evidence at the trial. According to Sterling's statement, he'd gone into the back of the garage to pick up a fresh load of supplies when he heard shouting. He saw McCarthy slit the guy's throat and freaked out. Fearing he might be next on the list, he went straight to the police and gave a statement.'

'And now he's dead.' Fear rose again, clawing at her with painfully sharp nails. It didn't take a genius to work out what that might mean for Zac.

'It might be he was killed for another reason. He was dealing again, so maybe a rival gang wanted him out of the way.'

'But it's likely he was shot on demand. My father's retaliation.' Zac's voice was hard and emotionless.

'Yes.'

Mark, who'd been quiet up until now, spoke into the grim silence. 'Vision Films have renewed the contract with us. From now on we'll be working with the police and providing round the clock security.'

'Fine.' Zac kept his focus on Mark. 'I'll need a secure place to stay, starting from tonight.'

'We have a flat free now.'

'Good. I also want to be assigned another bodyguard.'

Mark raised his eyebrows. 'As well as Kat?'

'Instead of Kat.'

She froze. 'Why?'

Though she willed him to look at her, Zac ignored her question, instead directing his own at Mark. 'Will that be possible?'

When Mark nodded, yes, Kat felt like she'd been sucker

punched. All the breath left her lungs and she struggled to fill them again. How could Zac claim to be falling for her when he didn't trust her enough, *respect* her enough, to help him now that they knew the danger was horribly real?

Yet as the pain threatened to overwhelm her, she reminded herself how badly she'd let down the last person she'd cared for. The last man she'd fallen head over heels in love with. It hurt, boy did it hurt, but maybe it was better this way.

'I'll pack up my things.'

Dimly she was aware of Zac standing and climbing the stairs. Of the detective having a last few words with Mark before giving her a nod of acknowledgement and leaving the house.

'You look like you've seen a ghost.' Mark came to stand next to her, his eyes scrutinising her face.

The idea made her want to laugh – a hollow, bitter laugh. 'Maybe I have.'

He frowned, squeezing her arm, the gesture both gentle and compassionate. 'Talk to me.'

'I don't need to.' She couldn't handle his kindness right now. Not when she still had Zac upstairs, getting ready to leave her. She'd get through that, then she'd shed a tear. In private. 'You know what I'm thinking. You've told me how stupid it would be for me to get involved with another guy, especially if that guy was about to get himself shot.' Oh crap, she hadn't meant to say that.

Mark sighed. 'You crossed the line with him after all, didn't you?'

'No. Sort of.' She huffed. 'Oh, for God's sake, I slept with him, that's all. And only after the contract was terminated.'

Mark's hand wrapped more firmly around the top of her arm, his expression more sad than angry. 'I'm not calling into question your professionalism. I'm looking out for you, as a friend. I want to know if you've developed feelings for him, and he for you?'

'You don't have to worry on that score. Whatever has gone on is clearly in the past. He doesn't even trust me to protect him anymore.'

'It's not a question of trust.' Zac, jacket on, bag in hand, looked cool and disgustingly handsome as he stared at her from across the open-plan living area.

'No? The moment the danger is terrifyingly real, you decide my house isn't good enough for you. I'm not good enough for you?'

The muscle in his jaw seemed to be working overtime as he strode towards them, his eyes flicking down to where Mark continued to hold her arm. 'That's nonsense and you know it. I can't possibly stay here now. It would put you and Debs right in the bloody crosshairs.' He turned to Mark. 'I'm ready to go.'

Mark nodded. 'Okay. Wait here while I check outside.'

As Mark slipped out, the tension between her and Zac grew more and more taut.

Finally, Zac cleared his throat. 'Would you say goodbye to Debs for me. Please.'

'Is that goodbye, goodbye or just, you know, goodbye for now and maybe I'll see you again sometime if I have a spare few minutes and nothing to do?'

'Stop it.' His green eyes flashed angrily at her. 'You're well aware this isn't what I want. I'm trying to do the right thing.' Another emotion came and went in his eyes, something tormented and raw. 'I'm trying to keep you both safe.'

Mark bounded back up to the door. 'You're good to go.'

Zac nodded, and with one final searing glance at her, he followed Mark out.

Kat quietly shut the door. Then slipped onto the floor and let the tears fall.

Zac lay on the strange bed, in the soulless room, in the tiny apartment, and felt his heart shatter. The place was as far removed from Kat's cluttered, homely house as was possible to be. A police officer was positioned outside, which was meant to reassure him, but actually only put the fear of God into him. It was one thing the film company paying a security company because they wanted to protect their asset. Quite another knowing the police were worried enough for his safety, they were prepared to spare some very stretched resource on protecting him.

It was after midnight when Mark knocked on the door and let himself in. The same Mark who, only a few hours ago, had held Kat's arm in a proprietary manner that had triggered Zac's jealousy radar. He'd wanted to snatch the hand away and tell him never to touch her again, Kat was *his* girl. Yet she'd declined to call him her boyfriend so he was, in fact, only a guy she'd slept with. And yes, he'd overheard her telling Mark exactly that.

Except there had to be more, didn't there, because why else had she been so livid at him for leaving?

Because she thinks you don't trust her, professionally. He sighed, running a weary hand across his face. Yeah, there was that.

'I've brought some basics to keep you going,' Mark shouted from the living area cum kitchen cum only other room in the place.

Zac levered himself off the bed and went to meet him, staring into the bag Mark had placed on the kitchen worktop. There were food essentials – milk, bread, cheese, fruit – along with toothpaste, deodorant, shower gel and a few magazines.

'Thanks.' He mustered a weak smile, reminding himself none of this was Mark's fault.

'Have you any plans for the weekend?' Mark asked, his manner business-like. 'Anywhere you need to be?'

It was only then Zac realised tomorrow was Saturday. Marvellous. 'I've got a charity function Sunday night that I need to be at.' Other than that, he had the choice of being bored to death within these four walls, or going out and literally facing death. If he decided to take the second option, it wouldn't even be Kat trailing around with him, because he'd dismissed her – that's how she'd taken it, though it was far, far from how he'd intended it.

'Is that all?'

'A workout at the studio gym tomorrow would be good.' How had lifting weights become the highlight of his weekend? 'If I can be picked up around ten?'

'Fine. It'll be me or a guy called Simon. He'll have ID on him and I'll text you in the morning to confirm. Anything else you need?'

Kat. Her name hovered in his mind, in his heart. He needed her right now more than he'd ever needed anyone. Just a dose of her calm, her funniness. Even her anger would be better than this emptiness. 'No, I'm good. Thanks.'

'Okay then. See you tomorrow.'

Mark headed towards the door and Zac felt the silence, the oppressive loneliness, start to close in around him. 'Wait.' Mark halted, turning expectantly, and suddenly Zac didn't know what to say.

'Yes?'

'Sorry, I just . . .' *Feel horribly lonely, and you're the closest thing I have to Kat, so I need you to stay a while?* Words he could never admit. 'Will Kat be assigned another client?'

'It's what she does, so yes.'

Of course, it was. Dumb question, born of weariness, of fear, of an ache in his chest. 'You're aware that my asking for someone else isn't a reflection on her ability.'

'I'm aware she's damn good at her job, yes.'

The edge to Mark's voice told Zac all he needed to know. 'Is she aware you're in love with her?'

Mark reared back, his usually phlegmatic face showing signs of shock. 'Where the fuck did that come from?'

'You probably think it's none of my business, except that I'm also in love with her, so that makes it my business.'

Zac had a sense that Mark didn't know whether to punch him, or commiserate with him. 'I'm not discussing this.'

Zac laughed humourlessly. 'You think I *want* to?' He leant against the wall, feeling dragged down by tiredness. 'Look, if there's history between you, that's nothing to do with me. But if it's not consigned to the past, I want to know.'

Mark made a scoffing noise. 'If you think she's sleeping with us both, you don't know her at all.'

'I know she's sleeping with me.' He wasn't a man prone to one-upmanship, but he enjoyed saying it. 'I want to keep it that way.' *Though I'd like to know if I'm about to get my heart pulverised.*

'You'd better not get yourself killed, then.' Mark gave him a flinty stare. 'And if you hurt her, I might have to kill you myself.' He marched to the door and let himself out without a backward glance.

Though Zac wanted to dislike the guy, he found he could only respect a man who carried a torch for the same woman he loved. And yes, he was no longer falling in love. He'd already fallen.

Chapter 28

Debs slung her overnight bag onto her shoulder. 'Come on, Aunty Kat. It's lame to be late.'

Kat paused, in panicked search of her car keys, to give her niece a glare. 'Who told you that?'

'Zac. Well, he didn't say lame, more like one of those fancy words he uses, like "It's good manners." Oh no, wait, he used an even posher word. "It's correct etiquette," I think he said.'

'Did he now.' She tried to be annoyed, to tell herself he'd been taking a swipe at her. All she felt though, was a huge pang in her chest.

'It's weird without him.' Debs shuffled the bag's strap further up her shoulder. 'Like, I dunno, too quiet.'

She shrugged her shoulders, clearly as baffled as Kat as to why their Saturday morning hadn't felt the same. It wasn't as if Zac had been a noisy housemate. He'd spent a lot of time in his room – damn and blast, in *Mandy's* room – reading lines.

She'd known he was there, though. And when she'd offered him a drink, he'd given her that heart stopping smile. The one that made every part of her tingle.

Shoving the thought aside, she reached down the back of

the sofa. 'Bingo, found them.' Clutching at the keys, she walked with Debs to the door. 'You're sure you're okay with this?'

Debs rolled her eyes. 'Duh. Anna's mum is going to drop us off at the shops. You've given me money to spend, then a few others are coming over for a sleepover, and Anna's mum and dad said we can put the tent up in the garden if we want. Sunday we're going to the lido. It's going to be epic.'

Kat's niggle of guilt receded a little. She wanted to be there for her niece while Mandy was still in rehab, but she couldn't deny she also wanted to be there for Zac. She'd gone through his last words to her over and over, and now wondered if she'd got it spectacularly wrong yesterday. Maybe it wasn't that he didn't trust her, as he'd stiffly pointed out. More that he really did want to keep her out of harm's way.

Though the thought still made her bristle – she wasn't a woman who needed to be mollycoddled – it also made this burning need to see him, the one that had kept her up all night, even more acute.

After dropping Debs off at Anna's parents' house and showering them with thanks for letting her niece stay for the weekend and for taking her to school on Monday, Kat messaged Mark.

Is he back from the gym?

Immediately a message came back.

Just dropped him off. He's taking a shower so you might want to leave it a few minutes. Or not.

A smile snuck up on her as she remembered the shower she'd taken with Zac. It slipped when she read Mark's second message.

Are you sure it's a good idea?

With a sigh, she typed back:

No.

A good idea was to take yesterday as goodbye and forget all about him. That way she could protect both of them. It was also cowardly. She'd been too blindsided by what she'd seen as his rejection last night to think straight. This morning her head was clearer, and she couldn't just leave things the way they were.

Taking a deep breath, she added:

But I'm doing it anyway.

Fifteen minutes later she nodded to the officer guarding the corridor and rang on the bell to the company flat.

'Yes?'

She'd forgotten how low and sexy Zac's voice was. 'It's Kat.'

Silence. It started to unnerve her and by the time he finally opened the door, her heart was hammering so much she felt like she might be sick. That was until she saw his face; the surprise but also the unbridled joy. A joy he couldn't seem to mask, much as he was trying to.

'What brings you here?'

'Am I allowed in? Or is that honour only for those with the correct visitation rights?'

He pulled the door further open and it was only then that she took in the rest of him. Hair still wet, bare chested, he wore only a pair of less than immaculate jeans, their top button still undone. The scent of shower gel clung to his skin.

Her hormones started to jiggle. Suited and booted Zac Edwards was exquisitely gorgeous, but hastily put together Zac Edwards was sex personified.

He seemed to notice she was staring, because he reached to do up the button on his jeans. 'Sorry. I'd only just stepped out of the shower.'

There was a joke to be made, but Kat's tongue was still stuck on the roof of her mouth. It was only when she walked past him and into the small living area that she finally managed to unglue it. 'You didn't need to dress on my account. I'm used to seeing you in a towel.'

'And without a towel.'

His gaze burned into hers and she knew he was remembering their time together. Their *naked* time. But then he averted his eyes, and a guard came over his face. 'Please, take a seat. I'll grab a shirt.'

'Err, it's me.' She watched as he darted into the bedroom and came out wearing a T-shirt. 'What's with all the formality?'

He gave her a small, tight smile. 'Forgive me, but when you say it's you, is that the you who seems happy enough to invite me into your bed, or the you who wants to keep me at arm's length?'

The barbed comment ripped through her, hurting not because it was sarcastic, but because it was true. 'The first one,' she told him softly, taking the few steps needed to bring her face to face with him.

His eyes lasered in on hers. 'And once we've been to bed, what then, Kat?'

That, she thought despairingly, was the one question she was terrified to answer.

Zac watched the shadows cross Kat's face with mounting despair. She clearly didn't want what he wanted, so now the only question remaining was why she'd come here at all, instead of leaving things as they were.

'I don't know what comes next.'

Her quietly spoken words took a moment to permeate through to him. 'Do you want to know, or are you too afraid to find out?' Maybe that was a dumb question, because Kat wasn't afraid of anything. 'Let me rephrase. Do you want to give us a try, or is this goodbye?'

The thought of saying goodbye tore at his heart, yet he wasn't sure he could manage what he knew Kat would see as the alternative: a short-term fling based on nothing but scorching-hot sex.

'I didn't have you down as a poet.' Her smile, cautious and uncertain, didn't diminish his mounting frustration, a fact she must have sensed because she gave him an apologetic look before walking towards the sofa and sitting down in the middle of it. 'Sorry, that was me trying to deflect the question because I'm too much of a chicken to think about the answer.'

'You, a coward? Give me a break.'

She curled her feet under her, giving him a lovely flash of her bare legs – she was wearing jeans shorts with ragged ends and a white T-shirt instead of the usual black. 'Physically, I'm brave.' When her eyes met his, he ached at the sadness lurking there. 'Emotionally, I'm a train wreck.'

Aware she was finally going to open up to him, he moved to sit next to her. 'Does this have anything to do with the tough personal stuff you mentioned happening in Afghanistan?'

She stared back at him. 'You remember me saying that?'

'I remember everything you've said.' Because he wanted to ease some of the tension, he added, 'Though some parts are more of a blur than others.'

She let out a short huff of laughter, then sighed, leaning into him slightly. 'The short answer is yes, my tour of Afghan did scar me, and I don't just mean the one I have—'

'On your right knee.' He shifted her legs so they rested across his, and traced the outline of her scar. 'I remember kissing it.' His gaze travelled up to her face. 'I remember kissing all of you.'

Her breath hitched, and though he desperately wanted to kiss her again now, he wasn't sure where he stood, so he gave her legs a gentle squeeze. 'Will you tell me what happened?'

'I want to, but I might not be able to get through it without it turning really messy. It's been years since I voiced it out loud.'

Once again he gave her calves a squeeze. 'I've got you. I'm not afraid of your mess.'

That received a wry smile. 'Okay, don't complain I didn't warn you.' Her shoulders rose as she took in a breath, and then the words tumbled out, each one causing his heart to break for her that little bit more. 'I did what you're not supposed to do and I fell for this guy in my regiment. And by fell for, I mean the whole thing. The mind, the body, the heart. I'd had a few boyfriends before but this was the first time I'd felt this way, like the day was dimmer, duller, when I didn't see him. It wasn't against the rules, he wasn't my superior officer, but it's not ideal. You want to be one of the guys, to be treated equally, and part of that deal includes giving and receiving a lot of flack. Wes didn't like the guys giving me shit, so it created a bit of tension.'

Wes. Zac stored the name away. He now had a name for the man responsible for hurting her.

'Anyway, we were on tour in Afghan when our team was sent to meet a guy who'd agreed to give us some intel. Trouble is, when we got to his village, we were ambushed. As the sniper, I was supposed to provide cover for the guys as they went in, but I . . . but—' Suddenly she broke off, burying her head in her hands. When he reached for her, she shrugged him away. 'No. Bollocks to this.' Sitting bolt upright, she stared back at him, swatting at the few stray tears that trailed down her cheeks. 'I failed him, okay? I was the one there to protect them, but I didn't.'

The torment in her eyes sent anguish hurtling through him. 'I know you well enough to be certain you did everything you could possibly do.'

'Yeah, that's what everyone told me. "Parker, you got three of them. You weren't to know there was a fourth."' To his despair, she shifted her legs off him and drew them up and under her chin, clasping her arms around them in a protective, defensive gesture. 'Well guess what, it doesn't help. Not when you know that instead of checking for a fourth, you were checking if the man you loved was still on his feet. And especially not when you see that man drop dead in front of you from a bullet you were supposed to stop.'

He felt useless, utterly unable to think of anything he could say or do to help, though at least now he understood some of her motivation behind keeping him at arm's length.

'Would Wes be happy to see you blaming yourself like this?' he asked after a while.

She snorted. 'Of course not. He was so laid back it was a wonder he managed to stand upright. He's probably up there rolling his eyes and telling me to take a chill pill.'

'He sounds like a good guy.' Zac held off on the obvious observation, that *laid back* Wes also sounded like the sort of guy who wouldn't mind mess, creases in his trousers or being late. In other words, the total opposite of him.

'He was the best,' she agreed softly.

And there it was. Finally, he had the reason why he'd never be anything more than a brief fling to her. She was still in love with Wes.

Chapter 29

She hadn't intended to tell Zac all that. Gripping tightly to her legs, Kat waited as the heartache that always took hold when she thought of Wes, began to recede. All the while she was acutely aware of Zac sitting next to her, and of the compassion she knew was in his eyes, if only she dared to look into them.

'Sorry. I didn't come here to give you a history lesson in the life and loves of Kat Parker.'

He angled his body towards her. 'Then why did you come?'

Oh God, this was so flaming hard. Jumping up from the sofa she walked over to the pathetically small kitchen and filled a glass with water she had no desire to drink. 'I came to tell you I won't accept being shrugged off, like a coat that's no longer needed.' Gripping the glass, she turned to face him. 'Your safety is my responsibility, damn it. Not Mark's, mine.'

He gave her an incredulous look. 'I think you'll find I'm responsible for my safety. Not you, not Mark, not the police. Me.'

'I'm your bodyguard.'

'You were.'

Anger began to take hold and she welcomed it. Far better to vent than to spill her guts and cry. 'How can you claim you're falling for me, when you don't even respect me, or what I do?'

'Don't *respect* you?' He cursed under his breath. 'I'm in awe of you, Kat. Have you forgotten it was only a few days ago your observation skills, your quick thinking, saved my life?'

'Then why won't you let me be there for you now?' To her dismay, her voice started to crack. 'What if you're shot at and I'm not around to stop it? I've already failed one guy I was in a relationship with. Don't make me fail again.'

He sat very still, only his eyes moving as they searched her face. 'Saving me won't bring Wes back.'

'You think I don't know that? Nothing will bring him back, a fact that haunts me every single day.'

Zac visibly flinched. 'I'm sorry for what you went through, truly sorry.' When his eyes locked onto hers, they were full of sadness. 'But don't ask me to put your life in danger, just to protect mine.'

'I want to be there for you. I *need* to be there.' She didn't know what was happening between them, but she knew that.

He rose swiftly to his feet and marched over to her, cupping her face. 'And I need you to be safe.'

The emotion churning in his eyes snatched her breath away, but she couldn't let his needs drown out her own. 'Then we're at an impasse, but I should warn you that I'm not a quitter. And I'm certainly no good at being told what to do. Wes tried that, tried to get me to leave the army. I didn't quit for him and I'm not going to quit for you.'

His gaze roamed her face, skirting over her eyes, her nose, her cheeks before settling on her mouth. 'What if I asked you to kiss me? Would you at least do that?'

The plea in his voice tugged hard on her heart, and the husky tone tugged places much lower down. 'I might.'

'Only might?'

'It depends on what happens after the kiss.'

His eyes turned a shade darker. 'Whatever you want to happen.'

Because she knew it would drive him crazy, she licked her lips. 'Do I get to see you naked?'

'Only if you reciprocate.'

Maybe it was wrong to dive into sex when there was so much still hanging between them, but Kat had done enough talking for now. All she wanted to do was lose herself in him. 'I'm down for that.' She smirked. 'As long as you go first.'

He didn't immediately reach for his T-shirt, like she'd expected him to. Instead he continued to stand still, his eyes blazing into hers. 'Christ, Kat.' His voice turned gruff, his eyes hooded as he placed a hand on the small of her back and pulled her against him. 'I want you. I can't imagine a time when I won't want you.'

Desire burned through her, heating her blood and weakening her knees. 'Then take me.'

It was all the encouragement he needed. Immediately his mouth captured hers, devastating in its intensity. As his tongue swept across her lips, then plundered, the kiss turned from hot to scorching, from hungry to greedy.

'Bedroom,' she panted, grabbing at his hand, but he shook his head.

'Here. Now.'

He reached for the hem of his T-shirt and yanked it off in one fluid, X-rated gesture that left her staring, trance-like, at the defined muscles of his chest.

'Eyes on mine.'

She licked at her lips again. 'Nope, no way. I prefer this view.'

Suddenly she found her shirt being dragged off and her bra unclasped. As he bent to run his tongue across her nipple, he let out a deep, heartfelt groan.

After that, there were only moans, and sighs, and the exquisite feel of skin on skin.

Zac knew nothing was settled between them. Knew too, that despite the wholehearted way she'd just made love with him, Kat was still holding onto the part of her he wanted the most. Her heart. A part he now suspected he'd never touch.

But she was here now. Tomorrow he might find himself at the mercy of a paid killer, so really, now was all he had. And he was determined to make the most of it.

'How long can you stay?'

At some point after the first round of what he knew had been desperate-to-have-her sex, they'd moved from the living room to the bedroom. There he'd managed a more dignified, more elegant, repeat. Now she was tucked against his side, his arm around her waist, his hand trailing circles on the soft skin of her stomach.

'Debs is at Anna's for the weekend, if that's what you're asking.'

His fingers dipped further, and he felt her muscles twitch. 'Okay, I'll reword. How long will you stay?'

'This might sound like I'm not answering your question, but stick with me. Mark says you need to go to a charity ball tomorrow evening.'

'Yes. I'm supporting a local event in aid of Cancer Research. I'm apparently part of the auction.'

She leant back, amusement on her face. 'Holy moly, are they going to auction you off to the highest bidder?'

'Not exactly. They're auctioning off the first five dances.'

'Wow, very Jane Austen. What's the going rate for a dance with Zac Edwards?'

'For you?' Her lips were soft and slightly swollen from his kisses, her flawless skin flushed, those eyes dark and mysterious. 'For you, nothing.'

She huffed out a laugh. 'Oh boy, you're such a charmer. I'll have to save my dance for later though, because I'll be working.'

'You have a new assignment?' *Please let it be a woman. Or a man over fifty.* No, Clooney was in his fifties and still making women swoon. *A man over seventy.*

She gave him an impatient look. 'Weren't you listening to me earlier? I already have a client. He's obsessively tidy but easy on the eye.'

Slowly the penny began to drop. 'I told you, Kat—'

'No,' she interrupted. 'I told you. I'm not quitting.' She turned her head away from him and, to his shock, he felt her body tremble. 'I won't be responsible for the death of another guy I . . . I . . . oh crap, okay, I didn't want this to happen. I didn't want to fall for you, but it looks like it's happening anyway.' When she faced him again, her eyes glistened. 'If you go and die on me I'm going to be so pissed off with you – so no, you're not getting rid of me. I need to keep you safe, and I need to prove to myself that I can do this.'

She was falling for him. Joy hummed through him. 'Okay.'

'Okay?' She eyed him suspiciously. 'That's it? No more argument about keeping me tucked safely out of the way?'

'If I say I don't want you put at risk, will you take any notice of me?'

Her mouth lifted in a cute little smirk. 'A good point, well made. If I say you should cancel tomorrow and stay here, where it's safe, would you do it?'

'I've made a commitment to attend.'

'And I've made a commitment to protect you.'

He sighed, aware he was never going to win the argument. Deciding it was altogether more enjoyable to make peace instead, he wrapped his arms around her and drew her against his side. 'Fine.' He could trust her to keep them both safe, but if the worst happened, and a bullet headed their way, he'd make damn sure he took it. 'Did I ever get an answer to my question? How long will you stay?'

'Now we've cleared that matter up, I can say I'm with you all weekend.'

'Good.' He let the news settle over him; an oasis of bliss in a desert of unpleasantness. It gave him an idea. 'I won't be a second. Don't go anywhere.'

'What, not even to pee?'

God, this woman could make him laugh and frustrate him both at the same time. 'Just make sure you're still on my bed when I come back. Please.' He let all his desire for her, his hunger, show on his face. 'I've not nearly finished with you yet.'

Grabbing his phone from the bedside table, he darted into the living area and phoned the number Mark had given him to call if he needed anything.

'What is this?'

Kat had just walked out of the shower. She had a white towel around her, her short hair was glistening wet, and she looked like the sexiest thing he'd ever seen. Her eyes weren't on him though, they were on the table he'd set up in the corner. The one he'd covered with a white tablecloth and set with candles and a vase of red roses.

'It's dinner.'

'Dinner,' she repeated, as if she'd never heard of the concept.

'French onion chicken with Gruyère cheese is bubbling away in the oven. The chilli prawn bruschetta are ready whenever you are.' He walked over to her and traced his finger along the top of the towel, over the gentle curve of her cleavage. 'You don't need to change on my account.'

'You've made this for me?'

He'd had quite an afternoon. After making love with Kat a third time – he'd not been kidding about not being nearly finished with her yet – she'd left him to go home and pack a weekend bag, giving him just enough time to prepare the meal. When she'd come back, she'd taken a shower; that's when he'd laid the table. 'I have been known to use a kitchen from time to time.'

'No, I don't mean that. I mean . . .' she trailed off, shrugging. 'You *made* this for me. You didn't send out for a takeaway.' Her eyes wandered over to the table. 'You sent out for candles and ingredients. And roses.'

'Have I overstepped some line I'm not aware of?' He tried to read her expression, but all he could see was confusion. 'I wanted to do something nice for you. Our last date didn't go so well, so I thought I'd have another try at wooing you. This time without the overpriced restaurant you clearly didn't enjoy.'

'You want to woo me.'

He brushed his thumb along the frown line between her eyes. 'This isn't news to you, Kat. I told Debs we were dating.'

'I know, but I thought that was just your polite way of saying we're having sex.'

'And the part where I told you I was falling in love with you?' He tried to keep his voice even. 'Did you think that was just about sex, too?'

Her eyes fluttered closed and she bit into her bottom lip. When she opened them again, he saw more than confusion. He saw pain. 'I'm sorry.' She ducked her head, resting her forehead against his chest. 'Oh God, I don't know what I'm doing. After Wes . . .' She paused, clearly trying to rein in her emotions. 'After Wes I closed myself off. No way was I going to go through that again. But then you came along, with your natty clothes and your gleaming good looks. Your fussy ways and your bone-dry humour. And your rare thoughtfulness.' She tilted her head back to face him. 'Damn it, I could ignore the others, but not that.'

He held his breath, searching her eyes. 'What are you saying?'

She dipped her head to kiss his chest. 'I'm saying thank you for going to this trouble. Thank you for wanting to woo me.' Once again, she looked over at the table. 'I've never had candles set out for me before.'

'It's not too . . .' He hesitated, half afraid he'd got it wrong again. 'Too pretentious?'

'Oh no, no, no, no. It's perfect.' She wrapped her arms around his waist. 'I was a bit of a cow in The Ivy, wasn't I?'

He smiled and kissed the top of her head. 'I would never compare you to a member of the bovine species.'

Her soft laughter rippled through him. 'Well thank you, kind sir. Still, I know what I said then hurt you, and I didn't mean it to. I just wanted to make it clear that you don't need to flash your cash around to impress me.' She smiled up at him. 'In case you missed it, I'm already impressed.'

He had to swallow down the lump of emotion. 'You are?'

She gave his ribs a dig. 'Yes, Zac Edwards, I'm impressed by you, not your money, not your fame, but you.' Once again, her eyes drifted over the set table. 'You know, I've never been wooed. Wes wasn't the romantic sort, and after him, well, I didn't let anyone get close enough to try.'

He brushed a hand over her hair, and down the side of her face. 'Will you let me get closer? Will you let me in?'

The world around him seemed to go into freeze-frame as he waited for her reply.

'I don't need to let you in,' she whispered. 'You're already there.'

Chapter 30

Kat didn't want to admit it to Mark, to Zac, to anyone, but inside she was absolutely bricking it. Part of her was questioning her sanity. Why on earth had she insisted on being Zac's bodyguard still? She wasn't up against some vague stalker who liked to send notes signed with a kiss. They were dealing with a professional assassin, a paid killer. Was she really good enough to keep Zac safe, when a two-bit terrorist had beaten her?

'Are you listening to me?'

Mark gave her a hard look and Kat shook herself. They were sitting in the small living area of the flat Zac was holed up in, reviewing the plans for the charity ball tonight. Zac was in the bedroom, going through his speech. The one he'd apparently written a week ago, because he didn't wing it on the last minute. Of course he didn't.

'Sorry.' She focused back on Mark. 'I'll be providing close protection, the police and you will be on surveillance. I've got it.'

'Have you got it, really?'

Though the question was harsh, the voice he used was

more concerned than angry. 'I'm fine.' But then she remembered who she was talking to. 'I will be fine,' she corrected. 'Right now I'm having a teeny weeny crisis of confidence.'

He relaxed his stern features enough to smile. 'Teeny weeny, huh?'

'Yep, that's all.' Unwilling to make it into a bigger deal that it needed to be, she changed the subject. 'When are we doing a recce?'

He glanced down at his watch. 'Ten minutes work for you?'

She nodded, hating how nervous she felt. Before Wes's death, she'd never been afraid of anything. Since his death, the only thing that had held fear for her had been the thought of becoming emotionally attached to someone again.

Now she could taste that fear, and it wasn't fear of falling for Zac – it was too late for that. It was fear of failing him. Of losing him.

'Hey.' Mark took hold of the top of her arms, giving them a squeeze. 'You don't have to do this.'

'He's right.' Kat jumped as she turned to see Zac standing in the doorway to the bedroom. His eyes narrowed as he took in Mark's hands, but when he spoke again, it was in the same polite tone. 'If I thought for one minute you were having second thoughts because you were afraid of being shot, I'd be doing all I could to dissuade you. But it's not that, is it?' He stepped forward, slipping his hands into his trouser pockets. 'You're afraid I'll get shot, and you won't be able to stop it.'

'Now wait a minute.' Mark, who'd removed his hold of her arms, started to protest.

'It's okay, Mark. Zac knows about Wes.' She raised her eyes

to Zac's. 'So he also knows he's right. I am afraid I'll cock this up. Yesterday I had all this bravado, but today . . .' She huffed out a sigh. 'Today I don't know where the flip it's decided to hide, but I tell you, I'm going to find it again.'

Zac's lips curved in a small smile. 'I know, but none of that is an issue for me, because I have faith in you.'

For a split second her heart stuttered, and then seemed to swell as she absorbed his words.

Clearly clueless as to how deeply his comment had affected her, Zac stepped through to the kitchen and started to fill the kettle. 'Anyone want a drink?'

'No, thanks, we're off to do a check of the venue.' Mark caught Kat's eye and raised a brow, a world of questions in his stare, all of them involving her and Zac, and where their relationship – she could no longer deny she was in one – was heading.

'I don't have the answers,' she told Mark when they settled into his car.

It was a measure of how well they knew each other, that he didn't have to ask what she was talking about. 'But you stayed with him last night.'

'Yes.' She shot him a look. 'And I don't need to justify that to you.'

'I've not asked you to.'

'Maybe not, but you've got that disapproving expression on your face. The one that's tighter than a camel's bum in a sandstorm.'

'I don't want you hurt again.' His hands tightened on the steering wheel. 'I saw how Wes's death affected you, remember. I lived through it with you.'

'I know and I'll always be grateful.'

There was a heavy pause before Mark spoke again. 'But grateful is all you'll be.'

Instinctively Kat opened her mouth to say *yes*, but then paused, knowing the words that came out next would define their future relationship. Zac might think Mark had feelings for her, but she wasn't convinced. 'You know how important you are to me.'

He flicked her a look. 'Yeah, I guess I do.'

'And if you're honest with yourself, you also know that if there was anything more than a deep abiding friendship between us, something would have happened by now.'

There was silence while he negotiated the heavy traffic. It was only when he finally pulled up outside the hotel, the venue for the ball, that Mark spoke again. 'You're probably right, though it doesn't stop me wondering.'

She gave his side a gentle nudge. 'Come on. I'm like, I don't know, name me one of the toys you played with as a child. Not the best toy, the most exciting, but the go-to toy when there was nothing else better to do.'

'Lego? Action Man?

'Okay, that works, I'm like Action Man. You only decide I'm your favourite thing to play with in the whole wide world when someone else comes along and decides they want to play with Action Man.'

Laughter spluttered out of him. 'Jesus. I'm never going to look at Action Man the same way again.'

She grinned, but then reached to hold his hand. 'I'm right though, aren't I?'

He gave her a wry smile. 'I guess so. In the back of my mind I've always thought maybe we would, you know, one day.'

'But if we were meant to be, you wouldn't have waited. You *couldn't* have waited, because the brain doesn't get to choose who we fall in love with.'

'And is that how it is between you and Zac?' He didn't look hurt, which proved her earlier point. 'Do you love him?'

She thought of how she'd tried so hard to resist Zac, yet ultimately found it futile. She'd been the iron filing to Zac's powerful magnetic force. Unable to hold off, unable to resist. 'I'm not sure. Possibly, probably.' She sighed. 'Yes, okay. I love him.'

He was fine. It would be fine. Everything was . . . fine.

Zac knew if he repeated the words often enough, though they might not come true, they would at least take his mind off the alternative.

He glanced sideways at his driver. He'd never seen Kat so focused, her face so serious.

'I'm not going to be distracted by you,' she muttered, her eyes glancing quickly at the rear-view mirror. 'Your pretty face can stare at me all you like, but I'm not taking my eyes off the road.'

Smiling, he started to undo the buttons of his white Tom Ford shirt. 'Good God,' she spluttered. 'What on earth are you doing?'

'Proving I can distract you.'

It was only when she didn't laugh, he realised Kat was feeling the tension as much as he was. 'You know you can,' she whispered, eyes staring straight ahead. 'But please, I need to concentrate.'

He glanced down at his open shirt, feeling foolish. 'Sorry.'

'Don't be.' Another check in the mirror. 'Any other time I'd be more than happy to see you unbuttoning your shirt. Just not . . . now.'

'Not when you're trying to ascertain whether a trained killer is following us.'

There was a beat of silence before she answered quietly. 'Yes, that.'

Everything is fine. He repeated the words to himself, though now they sounded hollow, lacking any real conviction. He'd meant what he'd told Kat, he trusted her implicitly. It didn't mean he wasn't fully aware of the potential danger out there. No matter how good she was, how good Mark and the police were, it only took one lucky shot.

'We can always revert to plan B. Usher you in through the back entrance.'

They'd discussed it with him this morning, but Zac hated the idea of scuttling inside like a scared rabbit. 'No. If I do that this time, what about the next time, and the one after that? If someone out there is being paid to kill me, they won't just give up.'

'True, but equally you can't blindly carry on doing what you would normally do.' Her expression tightened. 'Unless you're deliberately trying to draw him out.'

He couldn't deny the thought had crossed his mind. He'd had enough of living the life of a nomad, a life so restricted he couldn't even pop to the shops without having to put in a request. And then finding his request turned down on the basis of it being not worth the risk.

'I want this to be over.' It was as close as he could come to admitting he wanted to put himself out there. He wanted the bastard to have a go, so they had a chance of catching him.

'I know.'

'What was the result of this morning's trip out with Mark?' There, he'd kept his voice nice and even.

She smirked, the tiniest lift of the corners of her mouth, yet enough for him to know his acting wasn't quite as good as he'd hoped. 'You make it sound like we went for a walk in the park.'

Another mirror glance, this time accompanied by a shift of lanes. 'Is anyone—'

'There's nobody following us. I'm just being super cautious.'

'Okay, good.' He allowed his heart to settle again. 'Back to the question.'

Another smile, this time with a hint of secrecy about it. 'It was . . . enlightening, I suppose you would call it. I'll tell you about it later, when—'

'We're not dodging bullets.'

'I was going to say when we've got more time.' She nodded to the sat nav. 'We're nearly at the hotel.'

'Right.' His heart began to batter against his ribcage.

'Are you okay?'

'Sure.' He discretely wiped the palms of his hands on his Tom Ford trousers.

'Not nervous about all those dances?'

This time it was her trying to distract him, and he latched

onto it gratefully. 'Are you questioning my ability to give value for money?'

Her smile was calm and steady. 'I can't imagine you providing anything less than full value.'

Kat indicated to pull up outside the hotel where there was a waiting crowd of fans several rows deep. Flashlights popped from the half a dozen photographers as the car came to a stop.

'I guess we should get out of the car.'

'I guess we should.' The Kat he knew and loved was back, her bravado found, her bearing confident and self-assured. 'We don't want to disappoint those rich ladies.'

'Quite.' Once again he ran his hands down his trousers. Then he took a deep breath, and another, before turning to her with the best smile he could muster. 'After you.'

Chapter 31

Kat had seen Zac Edwards act on the big screen, and she'd seen him act on set. Now he was acting his socks off right in front of her. The smile he'd given her in the car had been a little off, a little wobbly, but as soon as he'd stepped out and onto the pavement, the dazzle was in full force. To look at him now, smiling and laughing with the crowds, nobody would guess he'd just been wiping his sweaty hands all over his designer trousers.

He was, quite simply, magnificent.

She on the other hand, felt like a wreck. Everything she saw made her twitchy. An arm movement, a telephoto lens. A guy at the back of the crowd, who seemed to be just watching.

Watching.

The hairs on the back of her neck started to twitch and she spoke into her microphone. 'Not sure if I'm being paranoid, but there's a guy four rows deep in the crowd. Average height, short dark hair, grey lightweight jacket.'

Mark's voice came through her earpiece. 'On it.'

Glued to Zac's side as he posed for photos and scribbled autographs, she scanned the rest of the crowd. When she glanced back at where the guy had been standing, he was gone.

'Damn. I can't see him anymore,' she said into her mic. 'Have you got eyes on him?'

'Negative.'

Heart racing, she whispered to Zac. 'We need to move this along.'

He flashed her a quick look of alarm before nodding and giving the woman whose scarf he'd just autographed a practised smile.

They were now only a few yards from the hotel entrance. Kat knew Mark was in the crowd, checking everyone out. Knew too, that the police were watching surveillance footage from a van parked just up from them. None of it helped.

In the end, she felt she was almost pushing Zac towards the entrance and into the foyer which was decked with balloons and banners in the charity colours.

'Are we good?' His eyes looked very slightly wild as he gazed down at her.

'Of course.' She mustered her bright, bullshitter smile. 'You're with the best, Edwards. Never forget that.'

'I don't.' He cursed quietly on an exhale. 'What happened out there? Why the manhandling?'

Kat only had time to whisper, 'In your dreams,' to Zac because the organiser she and Mark had met earlier came rushing over to them all of a fluster.

'Oh, Mr Edwards, Zac, I hope you don't mind if I call you Zac? I'm Sally. It's such a thrill to have you here this evening. We've never had so many people queuing outside before. And as for the ticket sales. They've gone through the roof.'

Back to full-on charm mode, Zac reached for her hand,

then leant in for a quick kiss on her cheek. 'I'm honoured to be here and please, call me Zac.' He gave Kat a sidelong glance. 'Is there somewhere we can regroup before we head into the function room?'

'Oh, yes, of course, of course.' Sally, who had to be sixty plus but was acting like a sixteen-year-old on prom night, led them past the reception desk and into a small anteroom. 'Please, take your time. There's a bathroom just behind you. Someone will be outside to escort you to the main ballroom when you're ready.'

The moment she shut the door behind her, Zac collapsed onto the small sofa. 'Shit.' He squeezed the bridge of his nose. 'Maybe this was a bad idea.'

'You can't let Sally down now. I bet she's been saving for months to have that dance with you.'

He let out a strangled laugh. 'The way my legs are trembling right now, she'll be the one propping me up.' Once again he found her eyes, and once again he asked the question. 'What did you see out there?'

'It could be nothing.' It was honest, but she owed him more than a slick, professional answer. 'But there was a guy watching you. Don't get me wrong, I'm sure you appeal to both sexes, but he didn't fit in. He wasn't hoping for an autograph, wasn't holding a phone to take a photo. He was just staring.'

'Okay.' He ran a hand down his face. 'Do we know where he went?'

'No.' She wished she'd not taken her eyes off the bastard. That's if he was one, and not just a shy fan of *The Good Guy?* Dear God, this was hard. 'The police are looking through the surveillance footage so we'll know more later. For now, he wasn't dressed in a tux so we can assume he won't be in the ballroom.'

'Assume? That seems a little imprecise.' He rubbed the heel of his hand over his eyes and then rose swiftly to his feet and headed for the bathroom. A minute later he returned with his shoulders back and what she liked to call his game face on. 'Okay, I'm ready.'

She took a moment to walk up to him. To clasp his face and to kiss the lips she dreamt about when she closed her eyes. 'I'll be there, Zac. I won't let anyone harm you.'

His expression turned fierce. 'Look after yourself first.'

She rolled her eyes. 'That's not how this works.'

He gripped her left hand. 'It's how we work, Kat. Promise me you'll look after you, first.'

She could sense he wasn't going anywhere until she made the promise, so she did. With the fingers of her other hand crossed behind her back.

He'd done what he came to do. Zac couldn't promise the five ladies who'd paid a ridiculous sum of money to waltz with him had actually had their money's worth, but the dances were over, the champagne drunk and the attendees graciously thanked.

Now, as he sat at the table he'd occupied in between the dancing, he was finally starting to relax.

Kat, sitting to the left of him, was talking through some fancy wireless comms device. She caught his eye and nodded. 'Ready to leave? I'm going to take you out by the rear exit.'

He thought there was possibly a joke in there somewhere, but he was too exhausted to make it. Apparently dancing while wondering if there was a sniper targeting your back, was tiring work. 'You can take me wherever you want.' Perhaps he wasn't too tired, after all.

She held out her hand. 'Come on then Ginger Rogers. Let's get you out of here and into bed.' She gave him a wicked smile. 'See, you're not the only one who can do innuendo.'

'I'd rather you did me,' he countered, earning him a slightly disbelieving, but gratifyingly spontaneous, laugh.

Kat was all business again as they made their way through the still busy ballroom and stepped into the foyer.

And that's when it happened.

His world seemed to go into slow motion as Kat grabbed his arm and pushed him back into the ballroom. 'Stay behind me and walk quickly to the room on the left.'

He knew better than to ask questions when she was in full-on protector mode. Trying not to draw attention to them, he walked smartly towards the door used by the staff, acutely aware of Kat behind him, walking backwards as she monitored the main door and talked on the comms.

'He's been seen in the hotel,' she whispered as they hot-footed it through the staff area and into a small office used by the catering manager.

'Who has?' he asked, perhaps stupidly, as she did a quick search under the desk and behind the door, which she then kicked closed.

'The guy I spotted in the crowd when we first arrived. Police have been monitoring the hotel CCTV. They saw him walk into the foyer a few minutes ago.'

'Okay.' He tried to inhale properly rather than give in to

the short, panicked breaths his racing heart was trying to dictate. 'What do we do now?'

'We keep you safe while we search the building.'

His mind was taking longer to process information than usual. 'The *we* in that statement. That's you and me in a locked room, yes?'

'No. I'm the only one who's had eyes on the guy, so I need to get out there. Mark's coming to replace me.'

There were so many things he didn't like in that statement. Kat tracking down a potential killer was the most glaring, though feeling like a fraud while others, including the woman he loved, risked themselves to save his backside was also up there. 'I don't like it.'

'You don't like the idea of being locked up in a small room with Mark? He'll be gutted.'

He fought to keep his calm, when what he wanted to do was shake some sense into her. 'I don't want you out there while there's a killer on the loose.'

'Are you seriously forcing me to remind you once again that it's my job? Besides, if there is a killer out there hired by your father, he sure as hell isn't interested in me.'

Their staring match – who could glare the hardest – was interrupted by a knock on the door. Mark's voice came through the woodwork. 'It's me.'

Some of the anger left her face. 'You'll be safe here, and that's important to me.'

Important because she had deep feelings for him?, he wondered as she walked out. Or important because she needed to expel the ghost of Wes, the man she'd really loved?

Mark stepped inside and as he locked the door behind him, the room descended into silence. 'You and me, locked in a small room together. How delightful.'

'Don't get your hopes up, it won't be for long,' Mark responded in his usual gruff tone.

'Oh?'

'I told Kat the guy's vanished, but she won't have it. Wants to check for herself.' He gave Zac a cutting glance. 'Make doubly certain to protect your pretty arse.'

Zac gave him a tight smile. 'My arse thanks you for the compliment.'

After that, and Mark's answering grunt, they waited in silence, only interrupted by Mark's occasional mutterings into his comms.

It was twenty minutes before Kat returned, frustration etched across her face. 'I can't believe we didn't find him.'

Unbelievably relieved to see her back, Zac ached to kiss the annoyance right out of her, yet he wasn't sure how well that display of affection would go down while she was on duty. Even though he was the duty.

'My guess, for what it's worth, is he took a look into the ballroom, saw you were still with Zac, and decided it was too risky,' Mark stated matter of factly.

'What about the theory that he was a fan, looking for an autograph?' Zac pointed out. 'Or hey, maybe he worked here?'

Mark's lip actually curled. 'You don't believe the first, and if you really think we haven't shown his photo to the hotel staff, what are you doing continuing to trust your safety to the care of such numpties?'

While Zac wracked his frazzled brain for a suitably cutting response, Kat cut in. 'Gee, enough testosterone, the pair of you. At least now we have a photo of a suspect. It's one step closer than we were four hours ago.' She gave them both a sharp teacher-to-unruly-pupil look and nodded to the door. 'Now let's get out of here.'

As Mark marched out ahead, Zac took a moment to capture Kat's hand, and pull her towards him. 'I believe we were discussing you getting me into bed.' He touched his lips to hers for one too-short kiss. 'Are we still on?'

He'd hoped for a smile, but instead he got a weary sigh, her intense disappointment at not catching the guy still blindingly clear. 'If we can keep you alive long enough to get you into bed then yes, sure.'

He didn't care that Mark was no doubt pacing outside. He didn't care that Kat was itching to get her 'job' finished tonight. He took his time giving her another kiss, hoping she would feel his love for her in the tender press of his mouth on hers. 'Have faith,' he whispered as he drew back. 'My bodyguard is Kat Parker. No way am I getting shot.'

She raised her eyes to the ceiling, but when she looked back at him there was a slight flush to her cheeks, and when he smiled at her, she smiled back.

Chapter 32

Kat would never forget where she was when she received *that* phone call. The day was Monday, the clock on the bedside table read 12.24 p.m.

And she was rolling around in tangled, sweaty sheets with Zac Edwards, making the most of his rare morning off filming.

Self-disgust would come later, because it was the blood-curdling fear that blotted out every other feeling as she breathlessly answered the call from her niece.

'Hey, Debs, is everything okay?'

The lengthy silence kicked Kat's pulse into overdrive.

The reply, when it came in a cold male voice, sent her heart into freefall.

'I've got your niece.'

Terror hurtled through her as Kat instinctively gripped at the sheets, as if the man could see her naked body. 'Who is this?'

She was dimly aware of Zac, who'd been lying down beside her, jolting upright but she couldn't look at him. All she could do was focus on trying to remain calm when her stomach was pitching violently and her heart was pounding so hard she could hear it vibrating through her body.

'The name doesn't matter. Bring Zac Edwards to the location I'm sending through to you, and you'll get her back.'

Breathe. Breathe. 'I need to know she's okay.'

There was the sound of shuffling, then a muffled 'Kat.'

'Oh my God, Debs—'

'That's all your getting.' The male voice was back.

'She's done nothing,' Kat pleaded, knowing it was a waste of time but needing to try anyway because she'd never felt so desperate, so utterly frantic.

'True, but she's your niece and you're the one who's stopping me from doing what my client is prepared to pay a considerable sum for.'

Involuntarily her eyes found Zac's, and he must have guessed what was happening because he looked as unhinged as she felt.

'Midnight, at the park. No cops, or your pretty young niece takes the bullet instead.'

Abruptly the line went dead and as Kat clutched the phone to her chest, her only connection to Debs, a sob wrenched from her.

'He's got her, hasn't he?'

Zac's words didn't penetrate. She felt numb, paralysed with fear like she'd never known. Entering a terrorist stronghold in Afghan had nothing on this, nothing. At least then she'd felt in control.

Here, sitting on this bed, she felt utterly helpless.

'Kat.' Zac gripped her arms, forcing her to look at him. 'Has he got Debs?'

'Yes.' Who was this woman with the weak, trembling voice?

She pushed herself out of his grip and off the bed, wrapping the sheet tightly around her. 'While we were having sex, my niece was being kidnapped.'

He blanched, whether at her crude description, or the disgust in her voice, she didn't know, though she knew one thing. She'd never forgive herself for this, ever.

'How do we get her back? What does he want?'

'You.'

He nodded, as if she'd just asked him if he wanted a cup of tea. 'No problem, he can have me.'

'Just like that?'

His face contorted with anguish. 'Of course just like that. She should never have got involved in my shit.' His eyes, when they met hers, looked tortured. 'And that's on me, but I'll make this right, Kat. You have my promise. Whatever he wants, he gets.'

His agony was too much for her to watch, especially when she had her own guilt, her own self-loathing going on. 'I need to see Mark.'

'Of course.'

Clearly suddenly aware he was inappropriately naked, Zac reached for a pillow and held it over his crotch. The action made her laugh bitterly. 'Bit late for that, isn't it? I've spent all morning with it, when I should have been taking care of Debs.'

She knew she was being irrational – it wasn't his fault, it was hers – but the words wouldn't stop. At least when she was yelling at him, at herself, she wasn't thinking of Debs, and how terrified she must be.

Bile rose in her stomach and Kat rushed to the toilet, where she emptied the tea and toast Zac had made her earlier.

After that she turned the shower up to maximum heat and stood under it, hoping it would take some of the chill out this crippling cold dread. Yet when she stepped out of it, everything was the same. She was still the woman who'd irresponsibly brought Zac into her home. Who'd put his safety before that of her niece.

The woman whose stupidity, blindness, naivety, ignorance . . . she deserved every word that would be hurled at her. She was the one who'd put her niece's life in danger.

When she walked back into the room, Zac was dressed and sitting on the bed, staring at the floor, as if he hoped it would provide him some answers.

His head snapped up when he heard her. 'What can I do?' His eyes, heavy with pain, appeared sunken. 'Tell me how I can help.'

Hold me. For a brief moment she thought it, but how dare she ask for comfort when Debs was God knows where, at the mercy of an assassin?

'Stay put.' Her voice caught and she knew she was on the verge of tears. Something she couldn't give in to because they, like comfort, were a waste of her focus. She needed to expend every molecule of effort, of energy, on getting Debs safely back. 'Don't give me anything else to worry about.'

He gave her a tight smile. 'Seems to be my speciality, doesn't it? Hiding out of the way.'

His bitter tone said everything she needed to know. He

accepted she had to go, that she needed to discuss it with Mark, but he hated it too.

And he was blaming himself for what had happened every bit as much as she was.

He'd paced around the tiny flat for over an hour now. Zac felt not only helpless, but useless. Kat was at least out there doing something productive, finding a way to rescue Debs.

In a fit of pent-up frustration, he hurled the mug he was holding against the wall, watching as it shattered, leaving splashes of tea up the wall and broken fragments all over the floor.

Guilt. A deep, shameful, gut-wrenching guilt. That's what he couldn't, and maybe would never, escape from. He knew Kat was suffering her own version of it, aware that if she hadn't brought him into her home, Debs would never have become involved. Yet she'd done it with the best of intentions, to help protect him.

What had he done in return?

He'd brought his murdering, mobster father down on them. He couldn't get past the fact that when she'd invited him into her home, Kat hadn't known who he really was.

The sound of a knock on the door shook him out of himself and he strode towards it.

'It's me.'

He almost wrenched the door off its hinges as he flung it open to let Kat in.

'Any update?'

She shook her head, and he could see from the swollen eyelids that she'd spent at least some of the last hour crying.

The thought that Mark had been the one consoling her and not him caused a vicious twist in his gut.

'I'm so sorry. Here, let me hold you, just for a moment. Please.' He reached for her, needing to feel her in his arms, but she sidestepped away from him. If she'd slapped him round the face, it wouldn't have stung any more.

'We've been working on a plan.' She brushed by him and went into the kitchen, opening the door to take out a bottle of milk. 'Mark's coming here when he's made some phone calls.'

The twist in his gut tightened. 'Do I get to hear the plan? Or will I be required to sit quietly and stick my fingers in my ears when he gets here?'

Anger flashed across her face but then she closed her eyes and inhaled a deep breath. 'Okay, that's fair. This involves you and yet you're feeling left out of the loop.'

'Left out?' He wanted to take her by the shoulders and shake off this cool, don't-come-near-me guard she'd put up. 'I feel horrified, devastated, strung out. Guilty like you wouldn't believe.' He raked a hand through his hair, fighting to control his temper. Shouting would only drive them further apart, though at this point he wondered if that was actually possible. 'My hurt feelings aren't important,' he added more calmly. 'I only want to help undo the nightmare I've created.'

'You didn't cause this,' she told him flatly. 'I did.'

'It's you this man wants to kill then, is it? You whose father is pulling the strings?'

She slammed the milk down on the worktop. 'No, but it's me who brought you into my home. Me who connected you to Debs.'

He hadn't thought this could hurt any more, yet the knife she plunged kept slicing deeper. 'How can you possibly think you're to blame? You thought I was an actor from a respectable background, being stalked by a fan. You didn't know who I really was.'

He could feel his voice shaking and he hated the sign of weakness. Especially in front of this woman who was always so strong. Afraid he might embarrass himself further and actually cry, he turned sharply, intending to head to the bathroom.

A hand on his wrist stopped him.

'I know exactly who you are.' She swallowed, and her guard lowered enough for him to see how hard she was fighting not to buckle under the weight of the anguish she was feeling. 'You asked me what you can do. You can stay positive. Believe that we're going to get Debs back in one piece.'

He risked holding a hand to her face, and nearly collapsed with relief when she didn't smack him away. 'I do believe that. I believe in you.'

Tears welled and she blinked and looked away. 'I keep seeing her face, and she's terrified, Zac. What must she be thinking right now? Is he hurting her?'

Her anguish tore at him. He hated seeing her in this unbearable pain. Hated knowing he was responsible for it. Risking rejection, he slid his arms around her. 'Let me,' he whispered desperately as he drew her against him. 'Please.'

Her body stiffened and for a horrible moment he thought she was going to push him away. But then she shuddered and seemed to give in, her arms wrapping around his waist. He didn't know how long it lasted, only that for the first time since the phone call, he felt anchored.

All too soon she straightened and took a step back. 'I can't do this. Not now. I have to stay strong for Debs.'

He wanted to argue that it wasn't weakness to take comfort, but maybe he'd been the only one it had helped. Hell, maybe Kat couldn't find comfort from him, because he was the one who'd brought this on her.

'Zac?'

He blinked over at her. 'Yes, sorry.'

'I asked if you've eaten? Mark's just messaged to say he's on his way and suggested he pick up a pizza. He says we need the energy to think clearly.'

'Yes, sure.' Though the thought of eating anything, never mind the very thing he'd enjoyed sharing with Debs, churned his stomach.

Chapter 33

The plan would work.

Kat repeated that to herself over and over as she parked up at the specified location, ten minutes before midnight.

Next to her, his body taut, his expression masked, Zac stared straight ahead. She knew he still believed he was the one responsible for putting her and Debs through this. Later, she'd make sure he understood she didn't blame him. She hated herself for dragging Debs into this, hated herself for being in bed with Zac while her niece was being kidnapped, but she didn't hate Zac.

Now though, she had to be single-minded. It was the only way she could get Debs back.

It meant that if the worst came to the worst . . . her stomach lurched at the thought of making that split-second decision.

Put Zac in danger, versus get her niece back.

'Don't think about it.'

She glanced sharply at him. 'What?'

'You're thinking about what Mark said, about the fact you might have to put me in his line of sight before he'll release Debs.'

'That's not part of the plan.'

'This guy's a professional. He's not going to be swayed by you, no matter how persuasive I know you can be.' There was a pause before he turned to face her. 'If it comes down to protecting me or getting Debs back there is no choice, Kat. You know that. I know that.'

Emotion balled in her throat, but she couldn't deny his stark words.

'If it helps, I couldn't live with myself if she died.' His voice cracked on the last word, and Kat had to clench her fists to stop herself from throwing her arms around him and sobbing.

Mark's voice sounded in her earpiece. 'The drone's in position. You should be getting a feed now.' One of Mark's calls had been to organise a micro drone with a video camera that would fly over the park and send back footage to give them an idea of where Debs and the killer were. 'There's a van opposite the hut. I'll put money on him being in it. We'll check it out.'

Suddenly her phone began to ring. When she saw Debs's name come up on the screen, her pulse quickened.

'We're here,' she answered.

'I can see that.' In the army Kat had witnessed people getting shot, and had mixed with people who'd done the shooting, yet she'd never spoken to a cold-blooded killer before now. His voice was chilling. 'Tell Edwards to walk towards the hut.'

'No.' She willed her voice to remain strong and steady. 'Think again. The moment he gets out in the open, you'll kill him.'

'And I'll release your niece.'

She wasn't going to give Zac up without a fight. 'I've got no guarantee you won't kill her, too.'

'Why would I? I'm not getting paid for her death.'

'I don't even know she's alive now.'

The line went dead and a second later her phone pinged with a message. When she clicked on it, she couldn't stop the sob that left her throat.

'What is it?'

Zac's expression turned frantic and she instantly put a hand out to touch his arm. 'It's okay. She's alive. I just . . .' She gulped in a breath. Forced her mind to calm. 'He sent a photo of her. It's hard seeing her like that.' She turned the phone for him to see the photo of Debs, her hands tied behind her back, a gag around her mouth.

Zac's lungs heaved and a strangled, tormented sound escaped him.

The drone video footage showed movement. 'Mark, there's a man opening the back of the van.'

'Got it. We're in the bushes behind.'

Kat held her breath as she watched a girl being pulled out, knowing if she saw Debs being hurt, she was lost. Forget the plan, she'd charge over there, even though it would likely get them all killed.

Count to ten. Breathe.

'He's got an AK47.' Mark's voice in her ear confirmed what Kat could see on the video.

The gunman pushed Debs towards the hut and a minute later her phone rang again. She put it on speakerphone so Zac and Mark could hear.

'Drive one hundred metres towards the hut. I'll release the girl and you release Edwards.'

'No.' Kat's mind jumped through the possibilities. 'When Debs reaches halfway, I'll release Edwards.' It would at least give her a fighting chance.

'If you don't, I'll shoot your niece.'

The grim terms accepted, Kat ended the call, her hands trembling far too much for what she needed to do.

'He doesn't realise you have a gun,' Zac observed quietly as she drove the designated distance towards the hut.

'No.' She turned off the engine, which only served to magnify the sound of her wildly thumping heart. On her lap lay a military grade sniper rifle – another favour called in by Mark. 'But he has a telescopic sight so I'll have to be careful.'

Zac nodded, eyes fixed on the hut. 'She's coming.'

Kat's heart went into overdrive as she saw Debs walk towards them, hands still tied behind her back.

'Let her get halfway. When he shouts at her to stop—'

'I get out.'

'Yes.' She swallowed down her terror. From the drone video, she knew where the gunman was. It gave her an advantage. If she could get the rifle lined up without him seeing. If she could somehow manage to shoot him, before he shot Zac.

Inhaling a deep breath, she opened the car door, just enough so she could squeeze the end of the rifle through the crack.

Debs was about a third of the way now. Kat's stomach clenched, nausea threatening, but she couldn't think about it. Any second now she'd ask Zac to leave . . .

Zac swung the car door open and jumped out of the car.

'Over here,' he yelled, walking straight towards the hut and waving his damn arms about.

Kat had a split second to wonder what the hell he was doing. Another to line up her shot and shoot before the gunman lined up his.

It was a split second too long, because just as she heard her shot fire, she heard another shot.

And watched Zac fall to the grass.

The next five minutes happened in a blur. She couldn't remember getting out of the car, or Mark yelling into her earpiece that they'd got the gunman. She could remember, with absolute certainty, clutching an unhurt Debs in her arms.

And she could remember the feeling of absolute horror as she saw the blood on Zac's tailored blue shirt.

Zac winced as he stood up from the hospital bed. He wasn't going to recommend being shot, to anyone. Apparently, he'd been lucky. The bullet had gone right through him and missed anything vital, like his heart or his head, which was where the gunman had no doubt been aiming. Lucky for him, Kat's shot had reached its target before the gunman had fired, upsetting his aim.

She'd saved his life. For a second time.

'You're okay to go. Keep it clean and dry and apply the antibiotic ointment twice a day.' The nurse leaned towards him and lowered her voice. 'The person in charge of continuity might be cross with you, but your fans will love it.'

Zac glanced down at the bandage hiding the neat scar he'd gained. It probably wouldn't do his street cred any harm, though at the moment he was more focused on what he might have lost.

He hadn't seen Kat since he'd fallen to the ground last night.

Of course, she'd been busy with debriefs and taking care of Debs . . . even to his own ears the reassurances sounded horribly hollow.

After thanking the nurse, Zac made his weary way out of the hospital to the car park where a car waited to take him home. Finally, he was allowed back to his own place. In fact from now on, his life could return to normal, because while he'd been X-rayed and stitched up in hospital, the captured would-be assassin – he guessed he had Mark to thank for that – had apparently confessed to being paid by Jimmy McCarthy to shoot him. Following a failed attempt at the studio car park, and having been spotted at the charity auction, he'd decided the easiest way forward was to snatch Debs.

In a further update, the police had just phoned to say they'd picked up Jimmy McCarthy and would be sending him straight back to prison with no access to the outside world.

The upshot of it all was Zac no longer had a target on his back. He was free to come and go as he pleased. To drive his own damn car. To live in his own apartment rather than having to share with a woman and her teenage niece.

This time the pain in his chest had nothing to do with the bullet wound.

God, he needed to see Kat, yet logic suggested he should wait for her to come to him. After all, he'd laid his cards out, told her how he felt. If she could forgive what he'd done, how close he'd got to getting her niece killed, then she'd contact him.

If. It was the word he kept stumbling over. What if she never forgave him? The thought of sitting and hoping that every call, every knock on the door could be her, only to have those hopes dashed each time . . . He couldn't live like that.

Making a snap decision, he pulled Kat's contact details up on his phone and showed them to the driver. 'Can you take me to this address first?'

Half an hour later he was outside her house. After asking the driver to wait, Zac walked slowly up to the front door.

His heart pounded, his knees trembled and nausea cramped his insides. He felt like he was about to have a heart attack. Yet when she opened the door, all of it vanished in a rush of longing.

'Hey.' His eyes drank her in.

'How are you? Are you okay?' Her eyes ran up and down him, seeming to do their own inventory.

'A few stitches, that's all.' He willed her to look at him, to reach out and touch him, but she remained terrifyingly out of reach. 'Apparently, my fans will love the scar.'

'Another few inches to the right, and you'd be dead.' Her eyes slammed accusingly into his. 'What the hell did you think you were doing, taking off like that? The agreement was, you'd wait until Debs reached halfway.'

'It appears I can't judge distances very well.'

Her expression tightened. 'Don't take me for a fool. You deliberately went before I gave the go-ahead. Why?' He had the first hint of her emotional state when her voice shook over her next words. 'Didn't you trust me?'

'Of course I trusted you.' He forced a smile. 'Why else would I willingly walk into the line of sight of a professional killer?'

'Because you're stupid?'

Ouch, that hurt. He might be a mere actor, not a security expert, but he'd known exactly what he was doing when he'd jumped out of that car. His pulse sky-rocketed as he asked the question he'd been dreading. 'How is Debs?'

'She's dealing with something no fourteen-year-old should have to deal with.' Kat's voice caught. 'I don't know how she'll get through this.'

Pain lanced through him and Zac stumbled backwards. How stupid to think he could just turn up and expect everything between them to be okay. He'd done something monstrously unforgivable. He'd brought terror on the people who'd gone out of their way to help him. Kat and Debs had invited him into their home, and he'd repaid them by giving them mental scars that would last far longer than the flesh wound in his side.

'I'm sorry.' The words sounded so hopelessly inadequate. 'Please tell her that. Please tell her . . .' His chest felt so tight, he could barely breathe. 'Please tell her I never thought . . . I never wanted any of this to happen.'

The harshness left Kat's expression. 'I know you didn't, and this isn't on you. I regret letting you stay in our house.'

And the agony kept on coming. 'I understand, I do. I hate that Debs got involved.' Tears stung the back of his eyes. 'I also hate that your regret, was the happiest time of my life.' Emotion flickered across her face and he thought she might be about to step towards him, but he couldn't bear to receive the pity pat on the arm. 'Thank you for all you've done for me,' he managed, walking backwards. 'For opening your home to me.' He had to swallow hard to overcome the boulder that had lodged in his throat. 'For saving my life.'

With that he staggered towards the waiting car, almost hurling himself into it. He needed to get away from here, away from the place where he'd dared to dream, and back to the reality of his spotlessly clean, clutter free, unbearably lonely apartment.

As the car pulled away, he took a final lingering look at the house he'd lived in. The house where, for a very short time, he'd felt he'd belonged. The sight that greeted him shredded the last of his hopes. Kat stood on the doorstep, her arms around Debs. Both of them with tears streaming down their faces.

Chapter 34

'What did you say to him?' As they watched Zac's car drive away, Debs stared accusingly at Kat. 'I heard the last part, when he was saying he was sorry. What does he have to be sorry for?'

Kat hung her head, shame rolling through her. Why had she gone after him like that? Sure, she'd been angry with him – so, so angry at the way he'd nearly got himself killed – but that didn't excuse how she'd just made him feel.

As if he'd brought this on them.

'He asked how you were, and I gave him an honest answer, that you were dealing with stuff no kid should have to deal with.' Her breath caught as she tried to stifle a sob. 'But I think he thought I was accusing him.'

'It wasn't his fault.' Tears streamed down her niece's cheeks. 'It wasn't your fault, either. You both have to stop being so stupid.' Debs flounced back into the house and Kat thought she was about to storm off to her room but she didn't. Instead she turned and looked back at her with an expression far too old for her years. 'How am I supposed to get over this, to move on, if I can't talk about it without you being all stuffed full of guilt?'

Kat hadn't realised how much Debs had seen, but before she could apologise, her niece was talking again. 'Mum's as bad. She's blaming herself for not being here, as if that would have made any difference.'

Debs swiped a hand across her face, brushing at the tears, and Kat felt her heart squeeze. 'I'm so, so sorry. You can talk to me, of course you can. I *want* you to talk to me and I promise to keep my own guilt on a tight leash.' Raising her hand, Kat used her thumb to capture a remaining tear on her niece's cheek. 'I thought I was going to lose you.' She had to bite down on her lower lip to stop from crying. 'But here you are, braver and stronger than I'd ever given you credit for.'

A miracle happened and Debs started to smile. It was small, but it was the first one she'd given Kat since she'd wrapped her arms around her in the park last night, never wanting to let her go. 'I kicked him in the balls.'

Kat's eyes widened. 'Jesus Debs, he could have killed you.'

'Nah, he wasn't interested in me. He told me he wouldn't harm me. It was Zac he wanted.' Suddenly she pushed at Kat. 'See, that's why you and Zac are being so stupid. I was never in danger, not really. I mean, what if you'd not brought Zac here? What if he'd stayed in another hotel and the guy had killed him. How would you be feeling then, huh?'

Kat felt a small smile of her own forming, proof of her growing confidence that they would get through this. 'How come you're so smart?'

Debs shrugged. 'I dunno, I guess I was brought up by two smart women.'

They shared a hug, yet as she clung to her niece, Kat was sharply aware that Zac didn't have anyone at home he could cling to. Nobody who would tell him off for being stupid. Nobody to reassure him he hadn't done anything wrong.

Shouldn't he have you?

She felt another wave of shame. How hard must it have been for him to come to her today? Yet even feeling as horribly guilty as he had, he'd knocked on her door.

And she'd effectively accused him of putting Debs through hell, and then slammed it in his face. *Bitch* wasn't a strong enough word for her right now.

'Are you and Zac going to kiss and make up?' Debs asked as they wandered into the kitchen.

An image of Zac from a moment ago burned across her mind, his face stricken as he'd walked back to the car. 'I'm not sure it's that easy.'

'Why not?'

The simplicity of youth. Kat envied Debs in that moment. She'd have given anything not to be drowning in so many confusing emotions. 'I said some harsh words to him when he came here. I think we both need to cool off before any bridges can be mended.'

'Why were you so cross with him? What did he do? It wasn't about him involving me again, was it?'

'No.' Kat took Debs's hand and squeezed it. 'I never blamed him for that, only myself.' She walked over to the kettle and began to fill it. 'I was cross with him because we had this plan to get you back, and to protect him. He was supposed to wait until you got halfway, and then slowly, really slowly, on my count, step out of the car. That gave me time to line up the shot and fire before Zac was ever really in danger.'

'But he sort of jumped out and waved his hands in the air, didn't he?'

'Exactly. And when you were only a third of the way across.' Her stomach rolled as she relived that chilling moment. 'His stupidity could have got himself killed, and all because he didn't trust me.'

Debs looked at her as if she was an alien species. 'OMG, Kat, what is with you? Why are you being so precious? He did that for me. He wanted to make sure I was safe.'

On one level Kat knew that, but it didn't lessen her anger. 'The plan we put together was to keep you *both* safe. He should have trusted me to deliver it.'

Debs shook her head in a way that made Kat wonder briefly who the adult was. 'Maybe he didn't care about your dumb plan. Just about making sure I was okay.' Her voice wobbled. 'He was brave, not stupid.' She raised her watery eyes to Kat's. 'You're the stupid one for being angry with him.'

And this time she really did flounce off. Not that Kat could blame her. If she'd had a choice, she'd have flounced away from herself in disgust, too. The trouble was, her confrontation with Zac had been about more than annoyance that he hadn't done what she'd asked. In seeing him crumple to the ground, in fearing he'd been killed, her heart had literally stopped. It had been *déjà vu*. Wes, all over again.

It had taken that moment, that horrific feeling of thinking she'd lost Zac, to make her fully realise how deeply she'd fallen in love with him.

And that was why she needed space from him. Space to think. Space to wonder if she could really put herself through the agony of another relationship. One that, logically, had little chance of success. Her heart had already decided, but she was done being ruled by that, and her mind was far from certain she could do it.

Zac didn't know where else to go. The studio had told him to take a few days, but his four walls screamed back at him. Alone. You're all alone.

In the end he shoved a few clothes in a case – yes, he was willingly going to live out of a suitcase again for a few days – and jumped into the Aston.

It felt good to drive again. At least that's what he told himself as the car ate up the miles. Funny to think that when he'd first been assigned Kat as a bodyguard, he'd been so annoyed he wasn't allowed to drive his own car. Now he'd give anything to have Kat drive him.

No. For the sake of his sanity, he wasn't going to keep thinking about her. He had his life back on track now, didn't he? Soon he'd finish this film and start the next. That morning he'd called his manager and told her to accept a spot on one of those chat shows that kept asking him to appear. He wanted to come clean about his real background so anyone entering his life from now on knew exactly who he was, where he'd come from. And the inherent risks they could potentially be exposed to.

An hour later he swung the Aston into the Edwards Estate and brought it to a stop on the gravel drive by the entrance.

Even before he'd climbed out of the car, the front door of the house was flung open. *It's a bloody stately home.* Damn it, why could he still hear Kat's voice?

'Zac.' Helena dashed down the stairs and before he knew it, he was being pulled into a firm embrace. 'Oh my goodness, my dear boy, how are you?' Her eyes ran over him. 'You look tired, and a little on the thin side for my liking. I need to tell Maisy to change dinner tonight to something more fattening.'

'Whoa, calm down. I'm fine. Really.' Feeling a rush of affection, he gave her a quick squeeze. 'I'll have double helpings of whatever Maisy has already planned.'

'I suppose that will work, too.' He was surprised, when he looked into her eyes, to find them heavy with unshed tears. 'I was so worried when I got the call to say you'd been shot.'

'You needn't have been. It was a flesh wound, nothing more, though I have acquired a rather heroic scar.'

She smiled, threading her arm through his as they walked into the house. 'I would expect nothing less than heroic from you.'

He faltered as the word circulated around his head. 'There is nothing heroic about getting a fourteen-year-old girl involved in my mess.'

Immediately Helena stopped, her gaze searching his for a moment before she shook her head. And swore for the first time since he'd known her. 'I might have known you'd be taking the blame for what happened. Of course you would.' Gently she touched his cheek. 'I'm not sure if you remember, but for the first few years you lived here after your mother passed, you kept apologising for everything. If you needed new shoes because your feet grew too big. If you'd left a dirty sock on the floor in your otherwise far too tidy bedroom. When you knocked over a vase and broke it, even though Antony was the one at fault for chasing you indoors.' She reached up to kiss him. 'Like I told you when you were a child, not everything is your fault, Zac. And this certainly isn't. Your father hired a man to kill you, and that man chose to use Debs in order to get to you.'

'He wouldn't have even known about Debs if I hadn't agreed to live with them.' When she started to refute him, Zac squeezed her hand. 'I know that was Kat's choice, just as I know she's blaming herself for it. But I also know if I hadn't lied to her, if I'd told her who my real father was, she wouldn't have suggested I stay.'

'Fiddlesticks.' Helena gave him one of her steely stares. He'd not received many – most had been directed at Antony when they'd been growing up – but he felt the power of it now. 'Kat is a strong, independently-minded woman. She'd have trusted herself to keep you and her niece safe, whatever the circumstances. Besides, nobody could have foreseen that Jimmy would be crazy enough to seek revenge in this way. Neither the police, the prison wardens nor his parole officers saw this coming, and they knew him better than any of us. Now,' she guided him towards the living room. 'Enough of this nonsense. William will be pacing up and down, wanting to see you.' She gave Zac a soft smile. 'But I told him I wanted a bit of mother–son time, first.'

He came to an abrupt halt. 'I'm not your son.'

She placed her hands on his shoulders and gave him the

mother of all dirty looks, which should have looked ridiculous considering she was a foot shorter than him. 'Zac Edwards, I've thought of you as my son ever since you came to live in our home. We'd have adopted you, only your rotten father wouldn't let us. But we gave you our name, that should have told you how we felt. How much we both love you.'

'I . . . I didn't realise.' He felt choked, the emotion travelling hot and thick into this throat. All this time he'd spent believing he was a burden to them, yet he'd been *loved*. He tried to surreptitiously wipe his eyes, but she was too observant.

'Come here, you ninny.' She wiped away his embarrassing tears. 'Now go and put William out of his misery while I tell Maisie to bring us some tea and scones.'

Chapter 35

Kat stared at the woman on her doorstep. A stone lighter than when she'd left, her face less haggard, her eyes bright, her sister looked better than she had in a long, long time.

'You look . . .' Kat shook her head, the words getting all mixed up with the emotion of seeing her sister again. 'Flaming heck, Mandy, you look amazing.'

'I feel amazing.'

They shared a hug on the doorstep before Kat stepped back and yelled, 'Debs, you've got a visitor. She looks like someone I used to know, only younger. Not as young as me, obviously—'

'Mum!'

As mother and daughter shared an embrace, Kat had to look away for a moment. Along with the joy, the pleasure at seeing two of her favourite people so happy, was a dart of unwanted jealousy. Would she ever know that bond between mother and child?

The thought immediately turned her mind to Zac, and she had to work hard to shove it aside.

'What are you doing home?' Debs, bless her, looked totally overcome. 'I thought you had another three weeks.'

'I did, but I also needed to see my daughter.' Mandy cradled Debs's face in her hands. 'Kat told me you were okay but I had to check for myself.'

'So you're going back?'

'No, not as I have been.' Mandy clasped her daughter's hand. 'I'll go back during the day, but I'm coming home every evening from now on.'

The expression on Debs's face faltered. 'But won't that muck up your treatment?'

'No, sweetie. The clinic said I've been doing so well they were going to suggest this anyway.' Mandy held out her other hand to Kat. 'Come on you two, let's go and sit down. You guys have sooooo much to tell me.'

They talked, and talked. Debs became defensive when it came to questions about the party, and the older guy, but quietly admitted she'd told him she didn't want to see him anymore. She was going to focus on her exams because she'd decided she quite fancied being a lawyer. Or maybe a doctor. Or a pilot. She wasn't sure yet but she needed to max her GCSEs. Mandy and Kat shared a look of relief, mixed with pride.

As they relayed the trauma of the kidnapping, they all shed a tear. Debs confirmed she'd not at any point been hurt, and though she'd been terrified, she'd been more scared of what the man wanted to do to Zac.

'So, this Zac, who's been sleeping in my bed. From what you've both told me, he's a stand-up guy and as hot in real life as he is on the screen.' Mandy gave Kat a quizzical look. 'Where is he now?'

'Yeah, Kat, where is he?' Debs stared at her accusingly.

'I don't know.' It had been four days since he'd turned up on her doorstep and she'd hurt him with her thoughtless words. *Your regret is also the happiest time of my life.* His quietly spoken words were the last thing she remembered every night.

'Have you at least spoken to him since?'

'Yes.' Kat stood up abruptly. 'Look, I don't want to talk about this right now. There's too much crap going through my head. I said stuff I shouldn't and I really regret it, but I can't go ringing him up until I know what I want. I've hurt him enough.'

Mandy narrowed her eyes. 'Good God, Kat. You're scared, aren't you? You've fallen for this guy and you're terrified of, what? Him dying on you, like Wes did?' Kat whirled on her sister, ready to argue, but Mandy stuck up a hand. 'Okay, if it's not that, maybe you're terrified of ending up like Mum? Because I can really see that happening. You being a pushover and Zac turning into a drunken bully, dictating to you.'

Out of nowhere, Debs started to giggle. 'Yeah, he'd be like . . .' She tilted her chin and started to speak in a poor imitation of Zac. 'Kat, I believe I requested you get me . . . no, what's a fancy word for get?'

'Procure?' Mandy suggested.

'Yeah, yeah, that sounds right.' Debs started again. 'Kat, I believe I requested you procure me a glass of wine. Then Kat would be like, no, get it yourself. And Zac would get up and pour them both one.'

Mandy started to laugh along with her daughter. 'Is that really what he's like?'

'Sure it is. He talks all fancy and he's a total pussycat.' She gave Kat a sly look. 'At least with his girlfriend.'

'I'm not his girlfriend,' she started to bluster, then paused when she saw Debs and Mandy staring at her. 'Okay, I was, sort of. Maybe I still am, but I was pretty shitty to him when he came round, so maybe not.' She hadn't been there for him when he'd needed her the most. The shameful thought wouldn't leave her. Why hadn't she taken him in her arms and told him she loved him? That he wasn't to blame? Why had she chosen instead to make him feel as if he was?

'You are aware that if you want to remain his girlfriend, or even his friend, you need to give him a call.' Mandy gave her a searching look. 'Apologise for being shitty.'

Kat knew her sister was right, and maybe not just over her need to phone Zac. 'I might go out tomorrow. Give you and Debs some mother and daughter bonding time.'

'You know you don't need to do that.' Mandy looked questioningly at her. 'Where's this mysterious out, anyway? Are you planning to go and see Zac?'

'No, not yet.' She would phone him, though whether he picked up was another matter. 'I thought I'd go home.'

Mandy's eyebrows shot up. 'Home, home? As in back to the hovel?'

'As in back to see Mum, if she's still there.' She'd once told Zac she felt guilty about never going back, and this was one way to rid herself of at least some of that. More important though, were the words he'd said in reply. *In order to cope with our present, and look ahead to our future, we have to put the past behind us.*

So far, she'd done a pretty crap job of looking ahead. Mandy had been right, if she dared to think of a future with Zac, all she saw was fear and loss. Maybe they didn't have a future. Maybe he was too fancy for her, too neat, too uptight. Maybe she was too messy for him, too mouthy, too much the tomboy instead of the willowy elegant lady. But was she really going to let her fear decide that, for both of them?

Truth was, she'd never met anyone who understood her more, who was as patient, as kind, and damn it, as brave. What he'd done back in the park hadn't been through lack of trust, she could see that now. It had been the opposite – he'd trusted her to have his back, even when he'd knowingly put himself right in the firing line.

Bottom line then, if she could find a way to stop this awful cowardy-custard rubbish, she was going to grab it. She'd faced the horror of believing she'd lost Zac and come through the other side, yet still she'd pushed him away. Maybe she needed to face the other demon from her past. The horror of her parents' relationship.

'If you're going back there, we're going too.' Mandy's voice jolted Kat out of her head. When she turned to face her, Mandy gave her a wide smile. 'Why should you have all the fun?'

He'd only intended staying with William and Helena for a night, but that had drifted into two and before he knew it, he'd spent four days with them. Four days of horse riding with Helena, clay pigeon shooting with William, walks around the estate and gentle runs to get his fitness back. Four days without the presence of Isabelle or Antony to ruin the harmony.

Now it was Saturday, and with an apartment that hadn't been properly lived in for over a month, and filming again on Monday, he regretfully told Helena over breakfast that it was time to head back.

'Oh no you don't. Not yet.' She pierced him with one of her stubborn looks. 'Not until we talk about Kat.'

He wasn't going to do anything as ridiculous as blush. He certainly wasn't going to get choked up. 'What about her?' Calm, measured. He was proud of himself.

'When are you going to tell her that you love her?'

Heat surged up his neck and across his face. 'Sorry?'

'You most certainly will be sorry if you don't let her know how you feel.'

'She knows.' And a lot of good it had done him. Damn, why were his eyes burning again?

'So that's it?' Helena's expression wasn't quite disgust, it was more disappointment. In him. 'You're just going to, what, give up on the only woman I've known you to fall in love with?'

'How is it giving up?' He gave her a brief rundown of his visit to Kat, and the awful conversation they'd had on the doorstep. 'She hates me for what I did, and I can't even blame her.'

'She doesn't hate you, Zac.' Helena's expression softened, her eyes now full of compassion. 'You caught her when everything was too raw. She was trying to support her niece and cope with her own guilt. You've both had a few days to calm down and get the whole thing into a proper perspective.'

Zac gave up trying to eat – his throat had all but closed up now – and pushed his plate away. 'It doesn't matter how long I give it, the facts remain the same. I allowed a killer into their life. I can't forgive myself for that, so there's no hope she'll be able to. And if she can't forgive me, she'll never be able to love me.' Or, to put it another way, she'd not loved him before, so she certainly wouldn't now.

'You won't know any of that for certain if you don't try and make things right.'

He carefully folded the napkin he'd used and placed it on the table. 'I'm not sure it's up to me anymore. She was very clear what she thought when I last spoke to her. To go and see her again could be seen as harassment.'

'Did she tell you to leave her alone?'

'No, not exactly.' *I regret letting you stay in our house.* 'Not in those words.'

'In which case, she's left the door ajar. And I hope, for your sake, you'll at least try and ease it further open.'

Zac pondered Helena's words as he made the drive back to his place. He was perfectly happy to have the door slammed in his face again. When it came to Kat, his ego had long since taken a running jump. What he couldn't live with, was causing Kat – or Debs – any further distress. It tortured him to know that turning up on their doorstep again, might do exactly that.

His apartment felt too impersonal. Too cold. Hell, though it pained him to admit it, the place felt too tidy. Zac had only been back an evening and already he'd taken three of his mum's teapots out of their cabinet and put them on the kitchen worktop. Just to make some clutter.

She'd have smiled, if she'd seen them. She'd been so proud of the blasted things, showing her collection off to anyone who came round. When he'd once asked why she liked teapots so much, she'd told him it wasn't so much what they looked like, as what they represented. A friendly chat, a shoulder to cry on, a pick me up or a soothing word. The beginning of a discussion or the settling of an argument. So much, she'd told him, could be achieved over a pot of tea.

Zac wondered if he should take one round to Kat, or if their relationship was so far estranged even a pot of tea couldn't fix it.

His mobile buzzed in his trouser pocket and he snatched it out without looking who it was. 'Hello?'

'Zac, it's me.' Immediately his heart let out a massive thump. He didn't need the clarification that followed. 'It's Kat.'

'I know who me is.'

'Oh, okay.' A pause, and she sounded a bit breathless. Like she was walking. Or maybe nervous. 'It's not been so long that you've forgotten me then.'

Slowly, because it was all his suddenly weak legs could manage, he made his way over to the sofa. 'I'll never forget you, Kat.'

'Well, that's good. At least I think it is.' She laughed, but it sounded strained. 'Then again, maybe you mean it in a, I'll never forget that bloody woman, kind of way.'

He rubbed at his forehead, trying to order his scrambled thoughts. *Why is she phoning? What does she want? Is this good news or bad?* 'Is there a reason you called?'

'Does there need to be?'

'No, God no.' He expelled a breath, desperate for the conversation not to unravel. 'I'm surprised to hear from you, that's all. Surprised and delighted, though the latter does rather depend on why you're phoning.'

There was another pause, which did nothing to help his wildly beating heart. 'I wanted to find out how you were.'

Was that all this was? He was having a near heart attack over a cursory call? 'Very solicitous of you. I'm well, thank you. And you?' He cringed at the formality, aware that like most of his quirks, as Kat would put it – the way he dressed, his punctuality – it was a defence mechanism.

'I'm well, thank you.' She mimicked his reply, but then blew out an exasperated breath. 'Bollocks to this. You know I can't do polite chit chat. I phoned because I hate how we left things. I was a right cow to you when you came round and I'm sorry, okay? I never meant to take my own guilt out on you.'

His sigh came from somewhere deep inside him. What a godawful mess. 'I'm sorry you feel guilt over something I was responsible for. If I'd been honest about who my father really was—'

'I would still have told you to stay in our house,' she interrupted firmly. 'I've talked to Debs about this until we're both sick to death of it. She reminded me that if I'd not gone with my instinct and instead found you yet another hotel to stay in, and then you'd been shot . . .' He heard her take in a deep, shuddering breath. 'Let's just say she doesn't lay any blame on either of us. In fact she's angry AF – her words – with the pair of us for being so ridiculous about it all.'

'AF?'

'Really? You can't work that out? As fu—'

'Got it.' He hesitated, then went with his heart rather than his head. 'Can I come round?'

A beat of silence, and then a long exhale. 'I'm not at home, none of us are.'

'Oh.' Because he couldn't shake off the thought, he voiced it. 'Is that your way of letting me down gently? Because if it is, if we're over, I'd rather you told me straight.'

'It's my way of telling you Mandy and I, with Debs in tow, are on our way to see our parents. Well, to see if they're still in the same place we grew up.'

'Oh.' He'd geared himself up for rejection, and the relief that she hadn't said the words made him temporarily dizzy. Of course, she hadn't said they weren't over, either, but he'd take the crumb. 'Does that mean Mandy's back home with you now?'

'Yep. She told me to tell you thank you. Her bedroom has never been cleaner or tidier.'

'I rather think it's me who should be thanking her, for the loan of her room.' A wave of acute longing came over him as he thought of that house. Of the evenings spent eating pizza with Kat and Debs. Of the nights spent tangled with Kat in her bed. He cleared his throat. 'Well, have a safe trip. I hope you . . . find whatever it is you're looking for.'

A long pause. 'Thank you. So do I.'

Chapter 36

It had been four days since Kat's visit home, when she'd found out her father had died several years ago, his alcohol sodden liver giving up the ghost. Her mother still lived there though, a woman Kat had found to be surprisingly . . . content.

It had also been four days since she'd phoned Zac.

The visit home hadn't resulted in the dramatic *this is what you should do* vision Kat had secretly hoped for. It had eased some of the guilt she'd felt about abandoning her mum though. And it had made her realise she wasn't, and never would be, like her. So fear of ending up in a relationship like that of her parents, was no longer an excuse she could use to push Zac away.

Now she was just left with a simpler equation. Was she, the human equivalent of a tabby cat, really destined to be with Zac Edwards – the human equivalent of a majestic lion?

'What are you so deep in thought about?' Mandy wandered into the kitchen still in her pyjamas despite it being midday.

'Cats.' Because she didn't want her sister to pry any further, she returned to the topic they'd discussed a lot over the last few days. 'You know I still can't believe Mum thought so little of herself that she was actually perfectly happy in her life with Dad.'

Mandy shrugged. 'We're all different. Mum didn't want a grand love, or passion. She wanted security, and that's what he gave her. Even though it came at a price far higher than we'd ever be prepared to pay.' She slid Kat a sly look. 'What do *you* want?'

The question took her by surprise, but not nearly as shocking as the answer that immediately flashed into her brain, and slid, warm and satisfyingly, into her heart. Zac was what she wanted. Wes had been her first love; a young, naïve love cultivated against the backdrop of army life where she'd viewed everything through a short-term lens. She'd wanted fun, excitement, a challenge. Escape from the drudgery, and the awfulness, of her childhood.

She was a different person now. A woman, not a girl. One who'd known loss and heartache, and was happier focusing on her career than on some fantasy that had no place in real life. Then Zac had turned up. He'd frustrated her, annoyed her . . . and made her rethink everything.

Mandy sighed. 'No need to reply. Your answer is written all over your face. Why don't you go round and see him?'

And that was the million dollar question. Why hadn't she?

Why would a lion want to be saddled with a tabby cat when it could find a lioness?

'If he really is interested, he'll come to me.' She hated that attitude, hated thinking of herself as less when she'd spent a lifetime proving that she was worthy of anyone. It's just she wasn't, absolutely, convinced she was worthy of him.

'That's pretty snotty, considering you told me last time he came to you, you were mean to him.'

It was nothing but the truth, but it nipped at her, mean and sharp. 'Bugger off, Mandy. It's my life, my call.'

Mandy held her hands up. 'Sure. I just don't want to see you making a huge mistake out of some sort of weird ego kick.'

It wasn't ego, it was an embarrassing insecurity, but Kat didn't correct her. Far easier to move the conversation along. 'Did you say Debs was going to a concert tonight?'

'Yep, Ariana Grande at The O2. She's over-the-top excited.'

'I can't believe she got tickets at the last minute. I thought it would have sold out months ago.'

If Mandy hadn't been her sister, if she hadn't lived with her for thirty-one years, she might not have noticed the way she twitched, and her eyes darted, momentarily, away from hers. 'I guess she was lucky. Maybe they were returns.'

'Or maybe there's something else going on that you're not telling me?' Kat narrowed her eyes at her but just then the girl they'd been talking about walked down the stairs. 'Hey Debs. Your mum was about to tell me how you got the tickets for the Ariana Grande concert tonight.'

Debs halted, her gaze flying to her mum. 'I told you not to say anything.'

'Jeez, I haven't said anything. But I've got a feeling you've just let the cat get so close to the opening of the bag, you'll have to let it out, if you get my drift.'

'He said not to tell you,' Debs mumbled.

Kat had a feeling she knew the answer, but she asked anyway. 'Who is he?'

Debs threw her arms in the air. 'God, you know who I'm talking about. He just wanted to do something nice for me, okay? No need to get all funny over it. He's my friend as well as yours.'

Kat paused a moment as her brain joined the dots. 'Zac got these tickets for you?'

'So what if he did? He wanted me to have something to look forward to, after what I'd been through.' Her voice croaked a little. 'He said a bunch of other stuff too, about not being able to make up for it, but I told him to shut up 'cos he was being dumb.'

Kat wasn't prepared for the wave of emotion that hurtled through her. To think he'd been kind enough, considerate enough, to do something special for the girl he'd only known a short time. Yet was it really so surprising? Wasn't that Zac all over? 'But why keep me in the dark?' It was the one thing that she couldn't understand. All that talk about her ending things, telling him it was over – had he decided that's what he wanted now?

'I don't know. He just said not to tell you.' She looked down at the floor, and then at Kat. 'You should make up with him. He's well nice.'

With that, she walked into the living room and turned the TV on.

Mandy burst out laughing. 'See, my daughter knows a good man when she sees one.'

Kat tried to smile, but her brain was working too fast. Was she making too much of their differences, and being stupid, as Debs would say? Sure, Zac had women around the world drooling at the sight of him, but that was the image on the screen. She knew the man behind it, and Debs was absolutely right. That man was well nice.

And if there was a chance that nice man still wanted her after all this, she'd be an utter fool to let him go.

Yet even as she planned in her mind when to go round and see him, a thought still niggled. He'd been in contact with Debs over the last few days, but not her.

Zac drew in a deep breath as he slipped the Aston into the parking space outside Kat's house and turned off the engine.

Taking his phone out of his pocket, he glanced again at the last text he'd received from Debs, an hour ago.

> Yes, she's in. She knows you bought the tickets and doesn't seem too salty about it. Good luck x

He'd learnt that when used by a teenager, *salty* meant angry/upset and not a flavouring liberally applied over chips.

Of course, just because Kat wasn't angry, it didn't mean he wasn't about to have the door shut in his face, though he thought it more likely she'd smile politely and invite him in. Then tell him, maybe over a drink, that they were over. She couldn't forgive him/she didn't like him that much/she'd had her fun and was moving on/she'd decided she wanted Mark, after all.

Zac lunged at the door handle. Whatever she had to say to him had to be easier to hear than all this second guessing he kept doing.

Heart in his mouth, he stepped out of the car and walked up the drive. A few seconds after he'd rung the bell, the door was opened by a slightly older, longer haired version of Kat.

'Wow.' The woman gave him a very obvious up and down

study. 'There's no doubting who you are. You're the man who's been sleeping in my bed.'

'Ah.' He wasn't quite sure what to say to that. Nerves now jangled with discomfort and embarrassment. 'I'm sorry about that. It was extremely generous of you to allow it.'

Mandy – it had to be her – started to laugh. 'Hey, no thanks needed. It's been way too long since I've had any man in that bed, never mind one as hot as you. I'm just bummed I wasn't there to appreciate it.'

He couldn't be sure, but he thought he might actually be blushing now, which only added to his feeling of discomfort. 'I suspect you're happy to be back in it now.'

'I am.' She smiled at him then, and the warmth, the openness, left him in no doubt she was Kat's sister. 'But you don't want to be standing here, talking to me. You want my sister.' She pushed the door wide open and waved for him to go inside. 'Take all the time you need. Debs and I are about to go shopping. I suspect we'll be a very long time.' A beat later, she shouted inside, 'Debs, grab your bag. We're heading out. Now.'

A second later, Debs appeared in the doorway, and Zac felt a rush of affection as she smiled shyly up at him. 'Hey.'

'Good afternoon.'

She giggled and glanced over at her mum. 'See what I mean? He talks so posh.' Then she looked back at him. 'Thanks again for the tickets.'

'My pleasure.' Still feeling unbalanced about being on Kat's doorstep, he slid his hands into his pockets and tried to slow his heart. 'I hope you enjoy it.'

'Me and Anna can't wait. Our mates are all well jealous.'

Zac knew, from the way his heart gave a sudden jump, that Kat had just appeared in the hallway. The moment he met her eyes, everything around him faded away. He wasn't aware of Debs and Mandy saying goodbye, or of walking into the house he'd once lived in. He was only aware of Kat, her incredible dark eyes, that mesmerising face. The trim body dressed in casual jeans and a black T-shirt, yet so much sexier than a tight fitting, plunging neckline dress on another woman.

'You took your time.'

He blinked, slowly coming out of his haze. 'Sorry?'

'I phoned you four days ago.' She huffed. 'Since then you managed to find the time to contact my niece, but not me. I was starting to think you didn't want to see me.'

His jaw dropped. 'Good God, you think I *wanted* to stay away from you?' He so desperately wanted to reach out and touch her, but he couldn't assume he had that right. 'I thought you wouldn't want to see me.'

She shook her head and walked further inside. 'I phoned you, didn't I? I apologised for how I was the last time. I'd hardly have done that if I was still angry with you.' Another sharp exhale. 'Do you want a drink?'

'No, thank you.' He halted as they came to the kitchen. 'And there's a big difference between being angry with me, and actually *wanting* to see me.' He felt his throat close up around his next words. 'Did you want to see me, Kat?'

She walked round the breakfast island and leant against the sink. Zac felt like she was deliberately putting the worktop between them. 'Why wouldn't I?'

He laughed, low and humourless. 'Because you can never

forgive me for what I did? Because you only wanted a fling.' He had to really work on keeping his voice even. 'Because I'm not Wes. Or Mark.'

Chapter 37

Kat couldn't believe what she was hearing. She was the insecure one when it came to wondering if Zac wanted her, wasn't she?

Yet one look at his tortured expression, and she realised she wasn't on her own here. Zac was just as unsure about how she felt. In fact he had to be even more unsure, because she'd been far more squirrely about revealing her feelings.

'I'm in love with you.' His quietly spoken words rocked her back. 'But I need to know if there's any chance one day you'll feel the same way.'

She rarely cried, and never in front of a guy, but she could feel the back of her eyes stinging. 'You utter berk. You want to know the reason I've been dithering about going to see you?' He nodded his impossibly handsome face, those stunning green eyes looking so achingly vulnerable. 'It's absolutely not because I can't forgive you for what happened. It wasn't your flaming fault, so there's nothing to forgive. Now, what else was there? Oh yes, if you were Mark, I wouldn't have slept with you, because as I told you before, I've never fancied Mark. As for Wes, there was only ever one of him, but he was only right for me then, he wouldn't be right for me now.' She paused to drag more air into her lungs. 'The fling, yes, I might have only wanted that at first, but that's because I wasn't sure what else would be possible between us.' Her eyes caught and held his. 'I'm still not entirely sure about that, but I know one thing.' Her heart began to race and she had to cling to the worktop to keep her balance as she said the next words. 'I'm in love with you, too.'

He was an actor, good at mimicking emotion. At hiding his true feelings. Yet there was no way that what she saw on his face, and in his eyes, was anything other than the truth; shock, followed by an almost desperate joy. As if he wanted so much to believe what he was hearing, but was afraid he'd got it wrong. Slowly he wiped a hand down his face, his eyes remaining fixed on hers. 'Would you mind repeating that?'

She rolled her eyes, and just as she started to walk around the island towards him, he pushed off the wall he'd been leaning against and moved to her. They met somewhere in the middle, and immediately he cupped her face in his hands. 'Say it again. Please.'

'I love you.'

His eyes fluttered closed, his expression one of agonised bliss. When he blinked them open again, they glistened like raindrops on moss. 'You've no idea how good that sounds.' Then, before she could say anything – and she still had so much she needed to say – his mouth pressed against hers and he was kissing her as if he'd never get another chance. His hunger, his need, pulsed through her as his hands dropped from her face to clasp her hips, dragging her fully against every hard inch of him. She was drowning in him, her mind floating somewhere up in the clouds, but she knew she couldn't give in, not yet.

Breathlessly she pulled away. 'Wait.'

His sensuous mouth swollen, his eyes ablaze, he gazed down at her. 'What?' A frown appeared and suddenly he looked stricken. 'There's a but coming, isn't there? Damn it.'

Before he could move away, she held his arm. 'It's not a but, it's a question.' Pulse still hammering, she tried to gather her thoughts. 'Can we really work as a couple? You're this,' she waved her hand at him, 'this film star with the flash good looks and legions of women fangirling all over him. Me, I'm a bolshie bodyguard. It didn't work out for Kevin Costner and Whitney Houston in the movies, or Richard Madden and Keeley in the TV series. What chance have we got in real life?'

He let out an incredulous laugh. 'It didn't work out for Keeley because she got blown up. As you're a million times better at your job than Madden, you'd never let that happen to me. As for Kevin and Whitney, they didn't have a tenth of the chemistry we have.' His finger began a gentle trail down her cheek. 'I'm the son of a scumbag, Kat, and you're this gorgeous, smart, fearless, incredible woman. I can see why you're hesitant about being with me, but I have absolutely no hesitation about you. I love you.' His voice caught and he inhaled a deep breath before repeating, 'I love you, Kat, and I want to spend the rest of my life telling you that.'

Her heart bounced so hard she thought it was about to break free. 'The rest of your life?'

'Yes.' He bent to kiss her. 'I don't say that to scare you.

I say it because it's only fair you know that this, you and me, is beyond serious to me. This is it.'

She didn't know what to say, her heart felt too full, her eyes too blurred with tears. 'Will you take me to bed?'

His soft laugh tickled her insides. 'You never have to ask.'

Zac had never known such bone melting contentment. To have Kat back in his arms, his body replete not from sex, but from making love. There was only one niggle, one small, yet ultimately highly significant point that stopped him from feeling deliriously happy.

Kat's reaction to his comment about wanting to be with her for the rest of his life.

It was true she hadn't laughed in his face. Hadn't told him he was delirious if he thought she'd want to be shackled to him forever. Yet she hadn't hinted that, if she wasn't fully on board with the idea, she at least wasn't averse to it.

'Zac?' She raised her head from its resting place on his chest.

'Umm?' His eyes dropped to her naked breasts and he found he couldn't drag them away.

'Hey, I'm talking to you.'

He smirked. 'I can listen and look at your breasts.'

With a strangled noise of frustration, she ruined his pleasure by wrapping the duvet around her. 'This is important.'

Suddenly his contentment started to feel a little shaky. 'What is it?' he asked, gaze firmly now on her. His heart beating that little bit faster.

'Why did you tell Debs not to say anything to me about the tickets you bought her?'

'I didn't want you feeling beholden to me.' Suddenly he found he couldn't look into her eyes. 'I wanted you coming to me because you couldn't live without me. Not because you had to thank me.'

There, he'd done it again. Mentioned a forever future for them.

And it was met by another deafening silence. One which made his heart tighten fiercely in his chest. Could he live with dating her, knowing she didn't want anything more? Knowing she wouldn't ever want to marry him?

'I was on my way to you, you know.'

Her quietly spoken words crashed through his thoughts. 'You were?'

'Just before you turned up, I'd planned to go and knock on your door. Well, to ring your fancy intercom.'

His eyes searched her face, desperate to know if she was telling the truth. 'Really?'

'Really.' She sighed, dropping a brief kiss on his chest. 'You must think what we have has been very one-sided, but I had my reasons for pushing you away, you know. Good reasons, at least I thought they were at the time, though you managed to plough your way right through them.'

He felt the bump of his heart as he asked, 'Those reasons. Are they still valid?'

She snorted. 'I'm in bed with you, naked. They clearly aren't important anymore.'

'They are if they come between us eventually.'

Her eyes flicked to his and for a moment she looked almost shy. Nervous. 'What do you think of tabby cats?'

It wasn't a question he'd been expecting, but there was

something in the stiff set of her shoulders, the tilt of her chin, that told him his answer was very important. 'I've not had many dealings with felines of any description, but if I was to have a cat, I'd choose a tabby over a pedigree any day.'

Her shoulders relaxed a little. 'Why?'

'Because they're strong, smart, independent. They don't sit around all day looking pretty. They get out there and get on with life.'

She nodded, the twitch of her lips hinting that he'd said the right thing. 'And how do you feel about lions?'

'Lions?' He stared at her, wondering what was going on in that amazing mind of hers. 'I think they're beautiful beasts, but the closest I want to get to one is on the television screen.' He raised a hand to her face, tracing his thumb along the smooth skin of her cheek. 'What's going on here, Kat?'

She shook her head. 'No biggie. It turns out I'm not quite as secure in myself as I thought I was, at least not when it comes to thinking I'm right for you.'

'Kat.' He almost barked out her name, so great was his frustration. 'You're perfect for me. It's me who isn't good enough for you, but I'm going to spend the rest of my life trying to be.' He swallowed down his fear and looked her straight in the eyes. 'I want to marry you, Kat.'

He didn't think it was possible for her eyes to get any larger. 'Marriage?'

Ignoring the warning in his head that he might be about to ruin everything, he pushed on. 'I don't mean tomorrow, though if I thought you'd say yes, I'd drop down on bended knee now.' He pressed a kiss to her lips, hoping against hope that her expression was a happy dazed and not a bloody-hell-get-me-out-of-here dazed. 'I plan on dating you first, getting you used to the idea of me being a permanent fixture in your life. Then persuading you to come and live with me in my soulless apartment, filling it with your warmth, your laughter, and your clutter.'

Her face slowly lost its frozen look and hope surged as he watched a wide smile spread across her gorgeous features. 'I like the sound of that.'

Heart in his mouth, he asked the question. 'Which part?'

'All of it. The dating, the living with you.' She bit down on her lip and looked him straight in the eyes. 'The eventual marriage.'

And *now* he felt it. The delirious happiness, his heart so full it almost hurt. 'Thank God for that.' But just as he was about to kiss those bewitching lips, to seal the deal in the most delicious way, she pressed a hand to his chest, holding him back.

'This being with me for the rest of your life. The future marriage.'

He stared down at her hand, and then up at her face, noting the mischievous glint in her eyes. 'Yes?'

'Please tell me you're not expecting to find your slippers by the fire every night?'

Amusement, joy and a fair amount of relief, all came together in an explosion of laughter. 'Good God, Kat. Given your distaste for neatness, I'll be grateful to find my slippers at all.'

Then she was laughing, too, and Zac's last thought, before he swept her into his arms, was that it was a noise he was very much looking forward to getting used to.

Epilogue

Kat stood in front of the mirror, turning first to the left and then to the right.

'You look amazing. Now quit gawping at yourself and do up my zip.' Mandy turned her back towards her. 'This dress had better fit. I never realised giving up alcohol would make me crave sugar instead. It's been hell trying to get rid of all the weight I gained.'

It had been just over a year since Mandy had come back from rehab. Just over a year since Debs had been kidnapped . . . which also meant it had been a year since Kat and Zac had started officially dating.

Kat obediently tugged at the zipper on Mandy's dress, which glided up easily. 'It fits perfectly. All those boot camps are paying off.'

Mandy waggled her eyebrows. 'Yeah, in many ways.'

Her sister had the hots for the guy who ran the boot camps, which explained why she was turning up to them so religiously, but Kat was only too happy to see Mandy's obsession with alcohol turn to an obsession with a personal trainer. Especially as she had a feeling the attraction was in no way one-sided.

'Are you really sure this dress is okay?' Kat asked her as she stared back into the mirror.

Mandy threw her hands up in the air. 'I said so, didn't I? And since when did you care so much about how you look?'

'Err, since I find myself having to walk down a red carpet at a film premiere in front of a barrage of photographers?'

Mandy just grinned. 'Hey, it was your choice to fall for a film star.'

'It wasn't exactly a choice,' Kat muttered, smoothing down the purple silk. It felt so foreign to her. Maybe she should have stuck to black. But she always wore black, and tonight she wanted to look special for Zac. Okay, cut the crap, tonight she wanted to bloody *dazzle* for him. Not that he'd ever given her cause to think she didn't actually dazzle for him every night – it still took her breath away, that look that came into his eyes whenever he saw her. A hungry, possessive look that told her everything she needed to know about how he felt. Tonight was their first public occasion together though, and she might be convinced she was right for him, but damn it, she wanted the world to realise it, too.

Mandy gave her waist a gentle squeeze. 'He'll love it,' she reassured. 'Mostly because it's on you, but then he's apparently blind that way.' Kat gave her a shove and Mandy laughed. 'Okay, okay, you're gorgeous and he's a lucky bloke. Now is Debs still in the blinking bathroom?'

'No.' Debs emerged from the en suite in a cloud of steam, a towel wrapped around her.

Mandy looked at her watch, and then at her daughter. 'Are you planning on going to the premiere dressed like that? If not, you'd better get your skates on.'

'Chill, Mum. There's loads of time.'

The inevitable ensuing argument about how long it took Debs to do her hair – which Kat had to admit was longer than it took for her to make and eat her dinner – was halted by a knock on the door.

'Bet that's lover boy, finally finished with his interviews.'

It always made Kat laugh that Mandy called Zac Edwards, distinguished actor brought up by Lord and Lady Edwards, *lover boy*. Then again, to her and her family, he was simply the guy she'd fallen in love with.

Her hormones sighed when she opened the door. It didn't matter whether it had been a few hours, as today, or a week since she'd last seen him, his stunning looks always took her breath away. And when he wore a tux, like he was now, God help her. 'Well hey there, Mr Edwards. Don't you clean up nicely.'

It was only then she realised Zac wasn't looking at her . . . well, he was, but not at her face. His eyes were skimming up and down her body like they couldn't get enough of her. 'Heavens above, Kat. What are you trying to do to me? It's clinging. There's cleavage. And it's not black.' He raked a hand through his previously neatly combed hair. 'I rather think I'm going to have to drag you back to our room and take it off you.'

His eyes finally made it to hers and her heart skipped a beat as she saw both the desire, and the adoration. To know she was so cherished, and by him. It was beyond her wildest imagination. 'You do, huh?' She gave him a saucy smile. 'Well I look forward to that. After we've sat through this flipping film of yours that everyone seems so excited about.'

'Everyone, including you.' He bent to give her a light, sexy kiss. 'Come on, admit it. You're dying to see me on the big screen.'

'I see enough of you in real life. Tonight is for all those poor women who don't get that dubious honour.' But, she conceded, she was looking forward to seeing the film that had brought him into her life.

Rather than taking offence, he smirked. 'Ah, but you get to see parts of me they don't.' Debs let out a rather loud cough, and looked like she was trying desperately not to laugh. Immediately Zac's focus zeroed in on the other two people in the room. 'My apologies.' Zac gave Mandy and Debs a courtly bow, which should have looked ridiculous, but didn't. 'I forgot there were ladies present.'

'Oh my God, he's such a charmer.' Mandy made a shooing signal with her hands. 'Will you two please bugger off. Me and my daughter need to get ready for this fancy premiere we're going to.'

Kat picked up her clutch bag and walked towards the door. Yes, it was true, she'd actually been persuaded to buy a rectangle of material that was only big enough to carry a stupid lipstick. Like she needed that. What she wanted was a headset so she could listen in to Mark and the team, but apparently she wasn't allowed that tonight. Apparently tonight she was the one being guarded, which, frankly, sucked. 'We'll see you inside.' Apparently – there was that word again – she wasn't allowed to walk quietly into the cinema unobserved like everyone else. No, she had to arrive in a big showy limo and get photographed.

And *apparently*, she was so nervous about the whole stupid walking down a carpet in front of the press thing, she was saying the word apparently far too many flaming times.

Zac glanced sideways at the woman fidgeting beside him. Christ, she was gorgeous. Even sat there looking like she wanted to bolt, in a dress that, while stunning, she clearly didn't feel comfortable in.

He reached for her hand and held it in his. 'We're just walking into the cinema.'

She snorted. 'Yeah, with cameras watching our every move, and reporters ready to pounce the moment they spot you.'

'You could have gone with Mandy and Debs,' he reminded her. He'd given her the opt out, though he'd likely ruined his magnanimous gesture by adding he'd rather she went with him. And then totally dipped into blackmail by telling her he wanted to show the world who he was in love with.

'I could have, but that would have been the coward's way out.' She sat up straighter and gave him a determined look. 'I'm not a coward.'

'Exactly.' It's what he'd been counting on. 'So, to a brave woman like yourself, this is a doddle.'

She had no time to argue with him because the limo glided to a halt, and a doorman, complete with uniform and white gloves, reached out to open it.

'Shit.' The curse was muttered beneath Kat's breath. 'I can't believe you conned me into this.'

Laughter rolled through him as he watched her climb, a tad inelegantly, out of the car.

'Relax.' He held out his arm for her to take. 'And remember, they're far more interested in me, than you.'

She gave him a cool look, which only made him want to laugh harder.

He was accosted straight away, as he knew he would be. Being the star of the film, this was just one of many promotional events he was scheduled to take part in. Usually he disliked this part of his job – he was an actor, skilled at giving lines someone had written down for him, not ad-libbing his own. Tonight though, with Kat on his arm, it didn't feel like a chore. It felt like fun.

Well, it had, until he noticed the way she kept looking around them as they made their way slowly up the red carpet.

'Lift up your left hand.' She gave him a strange look, but for once did as he asked. 'What do you see?'

'A bloody great rock.'

He smiled. 'I was thinking more along the lines of a flawless four-carat emerald-cut diamond, but your version works, too. Why are you wearing it?'

'Err, because you gave it to me?'

He could see another reporter lining up to muscle in, so he knew he had to make this quick. 'You're wearing it because you're my fiancée,' he hissed.

She rolled her eyes. 'Well, thanks for the reminder but I already know that.'

'Then why are you acting like my bodyguard?'

She huffed. 'Because it's easier being that right now.'

Immediately his heart turned to mush. 'Hey, look at me.' When she did, her brown eyes so full of trust, he smiled and kissed her. Then kissed her again. He knew damn well flashing bulbs were going off all around them but he didn't care. 'How about now?' he whispered when he drew away.

Her cheeks were flushed, her breathing quicker. 'I think I prefer being your fiancée.' Ignoring the man with the microphone hovering to the right of them, she tipped her head back up to his. 'But I need a bit longer to decide.'

Laughing, he bent to kiss her again, driving them both mad for a few more pulsing moments. 'Umm, Zac Edwards. Snogging on the red carpet.' She smirked up at him. 'And I thought you were The Good Guy.'

He smiled. 'Haven't you realised it yet? I'm not The Good Guy, I'm Your Guy.'

THE END

Acknowledgements

'So,' my editor said to me, 'how about writing a book about a female bodyguard?'

How could I turn down a challenge like that? So a huge thank you to the fabulous Charlotte Ledger, not only for being the inspiration behind this book, and for guiding me into directions I wouldn't otherwise have considered, but for doing it with such enthusiasm and warm encouragement. I love, love, love writing for you and the One More Chapter team.

My second thank you is to my gorgeous nieces, Gracie and Tiegan, who kindly read through the sections where Debs appeared and helped correct this boomer's language . . . err is that the right word? Or are you cringing again?! A mention too, for my other gorgeous niece, Maddi, just for being herself.

Really I should mention my hubby too, who acted as my beta reader yet again, and gave me the idea of the teapots. And I can't not mention my sons, who might groan and complain when I talk about my writing, but do provide help when I ask for it (give me some cool names, what car should he drive, what should we call his film . . .).

I'd also like to thank members of the writing community, the authors and bloggers, who are always so supportive.

And a shout out to friends and family who, through their unstinting support, have helped with every book I've written. To David and Jayne, Anne and Keith, Shelley, Kath, Karley, Kirsty, Charlotte, Sonia, Gill, Tara and Jane to name but a few.

A big thank you to my lovely mum, too, who has been with me every step of this exciting writing journey, though she does have this confession. 'I do enjoy your books, but I keep falling asleep.' Don't worry, I won't take it personally, Mum. Love you

Most importantly of all, thank *you* for buying *Up Close and Personal*. I hope you enjoy reading Kat and Zac's story as much as I enjoyed writing it.